I0788586

THE BEASTLY TALES

Also by
M.J. Haag

Fairy Tale Retellings
(ALL IN THE SAME WORLD)

BEASTLY TALES

Depravity

Deceit

Devastation

TALES OF CINDER

Disowned (prequel)

Defiant

Disdain

Damnation

RESURRECTION CHRONICLES
(hottie demons!)

Demon Ember	*Demon Escape*	*Demon Dawn*
Demon Flames	*Demon Deception*	*Dmeon Disgrace*
Demon Ash	*Demon Night*	*Demon Fall*

THE BEASTLY TALES

M.J. HAAG

Shattered Glass
— PUBLISHING —

"I'm sorry," I whispered.

Behind me, the beast's growl clicked with his anger. I kept my eyes on the overgrown gravel path at my feet. I didn't try to beg or flee. It hadn't ever ended well for those who'd attempted such methods before me. Better to just accept the punishment quietly.

M.J. HAAG
THE BEASTLY TALES

ISBN 978-1-943051-60-1 (Hardback Edition)
ISBN 978-1-722766-77-1 (Paperback Edition)
ISBN 978-1-943051-70-0 (ebook Edition)
ISBN 978-1-943051-64-9 (Audio Edition)

The characters and events in this book are fictitious. Any similarities to real persons, living or dead, is coincidental and not intended by the author.

Editing by Ulva Eldridge
Cover Art by Covers by Christian
Jacket Design by Shattered Glass Publishing LLC
© Depositphotos.com
© ShutterStock

Version 2020.09.07

FOREWORD

Putting together this special edition was a true labor of love. I wanted the chapter headings to be perfect. Something unique that would accurately represent what I saw in my head for the estate, the gates, and the kitchen door that Benella used so frequently...but my imagination was greater than the photo stock selection. So my oldest son and I did something else. We sketched what was in my head!

Yep, all the drawings were collaboratively hand-drawn by the pair of us.

He wasn't the only one to help with this. I owe a huge thanks to Jessica Wayne for encouraging me to take on this project as well as my team of proofreaders who helped clean up the newly created addition to the scenes from the beast's point of view at the back of the book.

DEPRAVITY

DEPRAVITY

CHAPTER ONE

I wrapped my hands around the cold bars of the massive, black iron gate and glared after the smith's sons, Tennen and Splane Coalre. The pair cast nervous glances back at me as they scurried away from the beast's shadowy garden. They had locked me inside because of misdirected spite. It wasn't my fault I'd seen what I had.

"This is what you get, Benella," Tennen had said as he had pushed me into the beast's lair.

Tennen thought his treatment just. However, the current situation was anything but just.

A strand of my dark hair, loosened from my braid by the encounter, fell across my cheek and partially obstructed my view of my retreating tormentors. I shook the hair away from my eyes and took stock of my situation.

Outside the gate, early morning mist floated around the trunks of the trees, and blue sky shimmered through the gently moving canopy. Inside the gate, neither the light mist nor blue sky penetrated the garden in which I stood. Cast in shadow and eerie silence, the beast's domain welcomed nothing from beyond its walls.

Sides still heaving, I struggled to quiet my breathing. I needed to leave quickly. Tennen and Splane hadn't departed quietly, and it wouldn't be long before the creature came looking for me.

I studied the top of the gate. The iron should have been easy enough to scale, but vines climbed the rock walls and twined with the iron rods. I didn't trust the vines. They tended to move on their own. I didn't much trust the gate, either. It should have been closed and locked.

The birds outside the gate fell eerily silent, and my stomach gave a sickening twist as I realized I'd run out of time. I dropped my head and squeezed my eyes shut.

The beast had come.

A heavy breath gusted across my neck, sending shivers of fear over my skin, and my hands twitched on the gate. In the distance, I heard the mocking laughter of the smith's sons as they raced home.

Taking a slow breath, I forced my fingers from the bars and dropped my hands to my sides. I didn't turn to look at the beast. I didn't need to. Once before, I'd seen his dark shape hidden in mist when strangers, worked into a righteous fit, had come to Konrall and tried to storm the estate.

My breath left me when he clasped my arms, and I suddenly found myself sailing over the wall. I flipped, spun, then floated for a moment before I felt myself drawn back to earth.

I braced myself for the bone-jarring collision. Instead, I bounced slightly on impact. Puzzled, I quickly sat up.

A woven mesh of vines strung between trees had cushioned me from the hard landing I had expected. I scrambled off and turned to stare at the tangled vegetation that had saved me. The vines slithered back from the trees, releasing their hold on each other. Slowly, they withdrew to disappear over the wall from where they'd come.

I stood panting and shaking, looking at the stone wall that

extended beyond sight in each direction. The bars I'd held only a moment ago broke the monotony of the stonescape far to my left. He'd tossed me a good distance. Had it not been for the vines, I would have broken a limb or worse.

My stomach growled hungrily as I bent to inspect my clothes. Father couldn't afford to replace them. Other than dirt and a few small tears, which I could mend, the old worn pants and shirt would last a while longer. I sighed and straightened.

The day hadn't started well. I'd set out to trade for bread using the wild carrots I'd foraged at dawn. Carrots, typically a fall crop, were easy to find in early spring if one knew where to look. The beast's enchanted gardens grew year round. Though he allowed no one inside, a clever girl could still benefit from the estate. On the east side of the property, the plants crept through a section of crumbling wall. Amidst the fallen rocks, I could find any variety of fruit or vegetable. The type changed every day, depending on the mood of the magic.

After the long walk back to town with the crisp roots in my bag, I had waited by the baker's side door, hidden behind one of the discarded barrels littering his yard. Through the gaps in the roughly boarded walls, the heat from the ovens warmed my face as I watched the baker move around his kitchen.

Sweat had already dampened his brown hair and the heat had colored his face. The white apron that covered his girth was well dusted with flour as he worked at the large wooden table, rolling dough and adding ingredients. The smell of yeast and baking bread filled my cramped hiding spot outside.

He lifted something to his mouth and chewed. His jowls jiggled with his jerky bites as he squinted thoughtfully. He sampled everything. When I was younger, I'd asked him why. He'd winked, in a secretive way that made me feel uncomfortable, and said he needed to sample in order to know if the goods were quality.

I didn't care for the baker. That's why I hid in the alley, hoping for a glimpse of his mother. She was kind enough to trade carrots for bread while the baker didn't care how hungry a person was unless they had coin. My father, sisters, and I often went without bread because of it.

As I crouched, waiting for the baker's mother, the smith's wife, Sara, timidly knocked at the baker's door. I saw him smile before moving to answer the door.

"Come in, dear lady," he said, backing up to let Sara enter.

I found it odd that she used the side door. The shop, filled with the goods for sale, ran along the front of the building and had its own entry.

"How's business at the smithy?" he asked in a cordial tone.

"You know it's no better or Patrick wouldn't have sent me," Sara said.

I wondered why Sara's husband had sent her to the baker if their business was slow.

"That's too bad," he said, clearing his dough from the table. "The price has gone up."

"What?" Sara said in a shocked gasp.

"Don't fret. You'll be able to pay, I'm sure. I've looked my fill, you see."

With the table cleared, he moved to Sara and helped her remove her jacket. Though an older woman, she still held her beauty. I'd heard many men in town comment on her pretty features and gentle bearing.

"A taste. That's all I ask. If you don't want to mention the increase to Patrick, I'll not mention it, either, though I don't think he'd mind."

Sara chewed on her lip and struggled with threatening tears. She watched the baker as he laid a cloth on the flour-dusted table.

Then he gave a single, curt nod, backed her up to the table, and helped her sit upon it.

I wondered what they were about. My curiosity held me in place as I continued to peer through a small crack in the wall, so that I might find out.

"As I promised Patrick in the beginning, I'll not lay a hand on you." The baker walked to the door that separated the bakery from the shop and locked it. Then he locked the side door.

"Flip back your skirts."

Sara lay back on the table and did as she was told. I was shocked to see bare legs and no underthings, but I began to understand the baker's price. At sixteen, though still innocent, I was far from naive. I'd spied my sister, Bryn, kissing Tennen on occasion. A loose blouse and a hand on her breast usually accompanied the kiss.

"Draw your heels up to the table, and drop your knees to the side so I can see you better," the baker said in a husky voice. I could see a bulge under his apron as he watched Sara do what she'd been told.

He dropped to his knees, kneeling between her splayed legs. My view became slightly obstructed by her foot, but I saw and heard enough to know he licked her. Repeatedly. Sara started making little gasping noises, and I wondered if it hurt.

True to his word, the baker didn't lay a hand on her, but he did on himself. He reached under his apron and began tugging on himself. His grunts mingled with her gasps. The sounds they made remained muffled until the end when they both increased in volume for just a moment. Then, silence fell. The baker gave Sara one final slurp and rose to wash his hands.

My cheeks flamed from what I'd just witnessed, and I felt sick.

Sara sat up, equally flushed. She refused to look at the baker as she straightened her skirts and stood on shaky legs. The baker wrapped a large loaf of bread, fresh out of the oven, and handed it to her.

I didn't want to stay and hear anymore. Silently, I rose and crept from my hiding spot, willing to wait for another day to catch the baker's mother. My list of reasons to avoid the baker had just grown.

That was when I turned the corner and ran into Tennen and Splane. They had both been leaning against the neighboring building, waiting for their mother. Neither had noticed me at first, until Tennen ran his hand through his dark hair. Splane's golden head was turned to study his brother, until Tennen froze.

The pair had taken one look at my face, somehow sensed I had seen their mother with the baker, and had started toward me. Forgetting about the carrots in the pouch slung across my shoulders, I'd run, and they'd given chase.

A chase that could have ended much worse, I thought.

Sighing, I checked that the carrots were undamaged from my fall, grabbed one out, and started munching on it as I walked. There'd be no going back to the baker's today. I hoped Bryn would be able to make something of the carrots.

Birds chattered around me, and the mist dissipated the closer I came to home. The trees thinned, and I spotted the curling wisps of smoke from Konrall's chimneys ahead. At our cottage on the outskirts of the village, I wiped my feet on the rug before letting myself inside.

The smell of breakfast surrounded me and, despite the carrot I had eaten, my stomach growled again. Bryn stood before the stove, stirring something. Everything else was quiet. I glanced around. Two cups sat near the edge of the sink. Father and Blye had already left for work.

"Any luck this morning?" Bryn asked as she plated an egg and some greens for me.

"No bread. But I do have a lovely bunch of carrots." I set the carrots on the table and sat at one of the four chairs.

I lived at home with my father, Benard, and my two sisters, Bryn and Blye. Father taught the local children for a modest fee, and Blye helped the seamstress. What little money Blye brought home, she gave to Father. Mostly, Blye received scraps of lace and ribbon as payment, which she kept in a box in our room. She was clever with a needle and thread. So much so, that no one could tell I wore hand off clothes from my sisters.

"Mr. Medunge wasn't cooperating again?" Bryn asked.

She knew the baker didn't often trade. He required coin. Except this morning. I stirred the eggs on my plate, wondering if I should mention what I'd witnessed. I wasn't even sure if I could talk about it, but shouldn't someone know that Mr. Medunge had gone too far? I recalled Sara's face, flushed and uncomfortable with a trace of disgust when she had stood. She wouldn't like anyone knowing what she'd done for bread, so I kept the tale to myself.

"I didn't bother with him. It's easier if I wait for Mrs. Medunge."

Bryn cleaned up breakfast from the stove then turned toward me.

"If you have no plans for today, would you circle the estate? We're running low on just about everything."

I glanced at the shelves near the stove. Crocks and cloth sacks lined the aged wood planks. Granted, a few of the sacks drooped loosely at the tops, but they weren't empty. It took a moment for me to realize it wasn't supplies she wanted but my absence.

Bryn had it in her head that Tennen, the same Tennen who'd locked me in the beast's garden, would make her a fine husband. She thought the Coalre family was wealthy and wanted a comfortable life. Little did she know. However, I needed no further motivation to eat quickly and bring my plate to the sink. I didn't want another run-in with Tennen or Splane so soon.

Because of Bryn's unshakeable infatuation with Tennen, I didn't bother telling her what he'd done. Any remotely negative remark toward the Coalre family would result in retribution from Bryn, usually in the form of inedible food.

Taking the fresh carrots from the bag, I searched the sacks on the shelf for any aging vegetables. Wilted greens caught my eye, and I swapped them for the carrots. Calling out a farewell to my sister, I left her to her affairs and once again trekked toward the beast's estate.

I didn't mind the time I spent outdoors. It was a vastly acceptable pastime compared to my sisters' chosen occupations. Sewing for an extended period numbed my mind, as did cleaning and cooking. Amongst the trees, however, opportunity for adventure abounded.

In the woods, just before entering the thicker mists, I set several snares with the wilted greens. I'd learned long ago not to set my traps any closer to the estate. Odd things happened to them if I did. I often found the ropes chewed to pieces and, once, animal feces in place of the bait in the exact center of the unsprung trap. It didn't take long for me to determine the vegetation wasn't the only thing enchanted around the estate.

With the snares set and nothing else to do, I went to the nearby stream that ran perpendicular to the estate, flowing south near Konrall. Since most people didn't venture this close to the estate, I enjoyed enough privacy for a swim. Clothed, of course, since the waters still ran cold; and I didn't trust Splane to stay home while Bryn entertained Tennen. I didn't linger long.

Chilled and wet from my time in the water, I shivered as I walked my way around the estate, heading east. It typically took me most of the day to complete the circuit, but I didn't mind. Gradually, the wall curved north, and I passed the place where things usually grew. I was not surprised to see barren ground, even though I had picked only a third of what the estate had offered that morning. A third seemed more than a fair share to me, and the estate seemed to agree for, if I returned later in the day, as I did now, it never offered more.

At the northernmost point of the walled property, I spotted a unique flower growing from the mortar. Its roots barely clung to the hardened surface, but I didn't puzzle over it. I knew that anything was possible at the estate or near its wall. I plucked the flower, placed it in my bag, and continued on my way.

Several hours later, I came back to my traps and found I was lucky to have caught a fat rabbit. Its dull eyes let me know it'd been waiting for me awhile.

With the rabbit slung over my shoulder, I started home. Bryn could make a wonderful rabbit stew, and I knew to look forward to it for breakfast.

At home, Bryn had already cleaned up dinner but had left a plate for me near the stove to keep it warm. She thanked me when I showed her the rabbit, but insisted I clean it before I ate. She didn't want it staring at her any longer than necessary.

Tired, hungry, and wanting to change out of my stiff clothes, I went to the back and cleaned the rabbit, keeping the skin for the butcher. The butcher, a kind man, took many different things in trade for meat. My luck with snares didn't often require me to visit the butcher, but it didn't stop me from helping him when I could. I had no use for the skins, but he cured them and sold them to traveling merchants or anyone else looking for leather or fur. It didn't amount to much money for him, but it did make it possible for him to be charitable to my family when the need arose.

With the carcass clean and the skin set to dry, I brought Bryn what she needed for the stew and sat down for my own rushed dinner. I hadn't forgotten the flower and wanted to ask my father about it.

My father, a brilliant man, often fell under the thrall of the books that lined his study walls and didn't hear me when I first knocked. I knocked a second time to get his attention. He looked up with a smile and motioned me in, setting his book to the side.

"What do you have there, Bini?" he asked.

I grinned at him, liking that he had used his pet name for me. It meant I had his full attention.

"I found this near the wall. Do you know what it is?" I handed the delicate flower to him.

"It's a primrose, dear. We don't see them here." He set the flower on his desk and stood, eyeing his shelves. "Let's see..." He moved to a section and took a book from its place. Flipping it open, he read for several moments, occasionally turning several pages at a time. "Here," he said, handing me the book.

In it, an artist had sketched a likeness of my flower. Once common to many places around the world, its numbers had dwindled as ladies, enraptured by its sweet smell, tore it from the ground in vast quantities to make perfume. I frowned at the book then at the flower. I shouldn't have picked it.

"I would think your sister, Bryn, would like the flower if you have no use for it. She could make a light scent from it. Very small, of course. Fun for her to try, no doubt," he said as he went back to his book.

I scooped up the wilted flower, replaced the book, and did as he suggested, feeling guilty.

WITH RELIEF, I tucked the warm loaf of bread into the bag hanging from my shoulder. The crust crackled as I handled it, sending the yeasty smell into the air to tickle my nose; and I couldn't wait to get back to the cottage to show Bryn.

After two days of patiently waiting, I'd finally had a bit of luck. In need of a visit to the outhouse, the baker had called for his mother and asked her to watch the browning bread.

Mrs. Medunge called another thanks for the carrots and wild onions and waved a farewell from the side door. I spared her a brief wave in return and hurried from the cramped alley between the bakery and the baker's storage shed.

Konrall consisted of one main dirt road that divided the village north to south. To the north, it led to the next village, Water-On-The-Bridge, some twelve miles away. To the south, it led to farmlands and little else. But here, in the middle of the village, its stone filled ruts lent a clean look, as did the trim grass growing between the line of buildings on each side of the road.

It was a pleasant enough way to walk if it wouldn't have brought me too uncomfortably close to the blacksmith. I'd successfully avoided Tennen and Splane since our last run-in.

As I neared the butcher, Sara, flanked by Tennen and Splane, left the smithy and headed in my direction. Panicking, I stepped through the butcher's open door, startling him.

"Ho, there, Bini!" cried Mr. Flune with a laugh. "Are you so hungry to come running through my door?"

"I'm sorry for startling you, Mr. Flune," I said. "I wanted to see if you found the hide I left at your door yesterday."

"I did indeed," he said with a kind smile. "It's a beauty. We don't see white fur often, so it will fetch a fine price." He stepped back from his butcher's block, away from the meat laid out for slicing, and reached for a small wrapped package. "This is for you, a trifling token of thanks for such a prize."

Smiling widely, I took the package, liking the mystery of it. He often gave me small things to take home, and I never knew what they might be. I thanked him and, after checking the road, went on my merry way, happy with the day's trades.

When I walked through the cottage door, Bryn was consoling a sobbing Blye.

"What's happened?" I asked. Blye should have been at work; the day had just started.

"The seamstress can't afford to pay me this month. There are too few orders."

Though Blye didn't earn much, what she did earn, helped. With that disheartening news, I pulled the bread from my bag and set it on the table.

"It's still warm," I said quietly to Bryn. I handed her the package, too, having already peeked at its contents. A dollop of pig fat glistened within.

Meanwhile, Blye continued to sniffle and sob. Though I considered the loss of her coin sad news, I didn't understand why Blye would choose to wail in self-pity rather than look for a solution. It was a waste of time to carry on as she was. At the very least, she should have faith our father would not let us fall into destitution.

"Blye, we'll pull through," I said. "We always do. Please stop crying. You don't want Father to come home and see you like this." Her gaze flashed with displeasure, but she wiped at her eyes. I took that as a good sign and continued trying to cheer her.

"You are clever with a needle and thread. And, you still have bits of the materials she's given you. You'll find something clever to do with those. I know you will. I'll probably see someone wearing a bit of it in their hair or on their breast next week."

Her eyes widened, and for a moment, I thought I'd offended her. But, she popped from her chair, a slow smile creeping onto her tear-stained face.

"You are the brilliant one, Benella. Their hair," she said excitedly. "I can make pieces to exactly match the existing dresses."

I had no idea what she meant but nodded my agreement. She

dashed back to our room, saying she needed to start right away and that I should bring her anything pretty I found on my wanderings, like feathers and such.

"You always seem to find the right side and turn it up." Bryn shook her head then cut me a slice of the bread and spread a thin layer of our fresh butter on it. "Here. Take this with you. I know you'll want to walk around and find something for Blye right away."

I reached for the bread as she expected, even though I didn't really want to walk the estate so soon. Blye would appreciate anything I found, especially if I found it quickly. If I stayed, she would probably start crying again. Taking a bite of the bread, I grabbed my bag and left.

The dark woods surrounded me with a sense of peace. Many of the village folk didn't like foraging so close to the estate, and that made my foraging much quieter and easier. Before I reached the shadowy mists, I heard the cry of a large bird above me. I followed it with my eyes and watched it land on a forked branch of the largest tree in the area. Not far from its perch, I spotted a twig nest that was wedged in the crotch of the two branches. The bird ruffled its white and grey feathers and hopped forward to begin feeding its squawking young.

Wrinkling my nose, I eyed the bird's feathers then adjusted my bag and set to climbing the enormous tree. The bark bit into my hands and scraped the skin of my legs through my woolen trousers as I scrambled from branch to branch. The bird noticed my ascent and shrieked at me before taking flight.

Minutes later, I pulled myself onto the branch that held the nest and glanced at the tangle of twigs. Slowly, I inched forward, clinging to the branch so the wind didn't catch me unaware. The large chicks, blind to what approached them, chirped at me hopefully and opened their mouths wide. Soft down feathers the size of my hand lined the nest and cushioned the chicks. Those beautiful white feathers would be a prize in any lady's hair.

I removed several from the nest, careful not to touch anything else. I didn't want to scare the mother off or rob the babies of their warmth.

The climb down took much longer than the climb up, and my legs began to shake with the strain before I reached the ground. In the distance, I heard voices and worried they might be Tennen and Splane's. Despite the tiredness I felt, I hurriedly dropped the last few feet, managed to land softly, and quickly disappeared into the mists.

I traversed around the wall, finding more treasures. The place where the primrose had grown now had several more delicate flowers. Carefully, I plucked the buds, leaving the roots to grow. Bryn hadn't been able to make anything with the single flower, and I doubted she'd be able to do much with the six I'd just found, but the candle maker might.

Not far from the primrose, I discovered a large spider spinning a silvery web. It noted my attention and spat web at me. I jumped back in surprise, and the web missed me and landed on the grass. It shimmered in the mist. Keeping an eye on the spider, I bent to touch the web. It didn't stick to my fingers. Instead, its strong silk slithered over them softly. It would make a fine thread. The spider didn't seem to notice me pulling the mass of web from the grass.

Hungry and tired, I returned home well after dinner. A covered plate waited for me in the quiet kitchen. Sitting to eat, I heard Bryn and Blye talking softly in our room and knew our father read in his study, as he did every night after dinner.

It didn't take my sisters long to come from the room and inquire after what I'd found. I set my food aside and pulled the thread and feathers from the bag. Blye exclaimed over the thread, asking where I'd found it. When I explained about the spider, she begged me to return the next day to try to get more. I nodded my agreement, and she left with her prizes to go sew.

THE CANDLE MAKER eagerly accepted the flowers, saying a scented candle was worth its weight in silver. Then, he sadly admitted he had nothing to give me in payment until it sold. Though disappointed, the lack of payment didn't stop me from looking for more flowers as I walked around the wall to find the spider. But the day didn't gift me with either of them. The primrose plants that I'd plucked free of any flowers the day before were completely gone. The spider, too, had vanished along with his pretty web. Even the patch that usually yielded some type of food had nothing. I eyed the wall sadly, wondering why it was being so uncooperative.

As I neared the gate to complete my journey around the estate, it swung open of its own accord. Heart thumping wildly in my chest, I froze and stared at the black iron, listening for the telltale sounds of the beast's approach. Nothing sounded but the wind. It puzzled me why the gate would open as it had. I didn't think it was an invitation. Especially when the wall hadn't been very bountiful like it usually was. Guilt struck at how much I'd taken over the last few days without giving anything in return. Usually, I only took carrots, onions, and the like. What if the estate expected compensation for the other things I'd taken? Worried that might be the case, I checked my bag for an offering but found nothing. With unease, I walked away.

The day grew pleasantly warm as I made my way home. When I neared, I went around back to check my own garden's progress. The onions were just sprouting little green tops, and the peas were an inch high. I hoped the warm weather would hold.

"Well, how much did you get?" Bryn's voice carried through an open window.

I looked up in surprise. The voice had come from our shared bedroom window.

"A silver!" Blye said. I smiled, knowing they were talking about Blye's first hairpiece.

"And I'm hiding it in the usual spot," Blye continued. "I wish Benella didn't even know I'd been working on it. What if she mentions something to Father?"

My smile faded as I listened.

"We'll keep her busy searching for more things to use. It should be fine," Bryn said.

"I'll give the coin of every third sale to Father just like I did when that fat cow paid me. I still can't believe she said she couldn't afford to keep me on. I sew better than she does. She'll lose business fast now, I swear. I hate this town and refuse to be stuck here for the rest of my life."

"At least you can save decent coin to leave. What I've put aside in change from Father's food allowance is nothing in comparison," Bryn complained.

How could they withhold any coin from Father? He provided us with food and shelter and love. I didn't understand them.

"I told you, if you marry Tennen, you won't have to worry anyway. Their mother is one of Mrs. Stinich's best customers. They obviously have money."

Although the news that they were hiding coin away annoyed me, I refused to act on my emotions as impetuously as they did. Turning away from the window, I quietly walked around the house and entered through the front, making plenty of noise. Both came out with smiles and asked what I'd found. I didn't feel too badly when I admitted there was nothing.

"What about the web? Surely you could have taken that if the spider was gone," said Blye with a hint of reprimand.

"The spider took the web with him. There was nothing left."

She glowered at me for a moment before smoothing her face into a sympathetic expression. "Thank you for trying. The estate is fickle. Perhaps tomorrow will be better."

"Could you take some of the carrots to the bakery and see if you can trade for bread again?" Bryn asked, changing the subject.

"I'd rather not. It's hard to catch Mrs. Medunge, and the baker refuses to trade."

"I heard from Tennen that the baker looks kindly on you. I think you just need to ask again," Bryn said.

I really didn't want to approach the baker again.

"Is there nothing left of the coin we set aside for food?" I asked without a hint of recrimination.

"No," Bryn said, turning away. "I'll make do with a soup tonight, but meat and bread would be appreciated tomorrow."

CHAPTER TWO

I FORCED MYSELF TO APPROACH THE BAKER AFTER THREE DAYS OF little game or harvest from the estate. Taking my time, I walked to town with my bag slung across my chest. The wilting carrots thumped against my hip with each stone-kicking stride. Because of my musings and lack of concentration, I didn't see Tennen and Splane idling against the tinker's building until they spoke to me as I passed.

"Well, hello, Benella," Tennen said.

Startled, I turned to face him instead of ignoring him. His eyes narrowed on me. I looked around at the light foot traffic and saw no one near enough to help me. The baker's side door opened and Sara, looking flushed, stepped out with a loaf of bread.

My eyes darted from her to Tennen. He shook his head slowly.

"Bad timing," he said harshly.

My first instinct was to run, but I knew they would catch me before we cleared town. While trying to think of a way to avoid a beating, I gained the baker's attention, and he called to us.

"You boys walk your mother home. Benella, come inside and let's see what goods you have to sell."

Run and risk a beating or face the baker?

"Not so much better than the rest of us, now, are you?" Splane said softly.

His statement confused me. How had I ever given them the impression I thought of myself as better? I had crouched, hiding behind the crates by the baker's shop for hours, cold and hungry, waiting for Mrs. Medunge to appear. The whole village was poor with the exception of the baker. Shaking my head, I turned and walked toward the horrid man.

Sara didn't meet my eyes as I passed her, not that I blamed her. I hoped for her sake, the baker's price wouldn't climb any higher.

The baker grinned at me in welcome and held the door open, but I stopped a few feet away, reached into my bag, and offered him a carrot for inspection. From the corner of my eye, I watched the Coalre family walk away.

"Come now, Benella. There's no reason to do this outside. Come in."

"I'd rather not. Are you interested in trading carrots for bread, today?" I asked bluntly.

"We've enough carrots. Perhaps we can come to some other arrangement."

Swallowing a gag, I took a moment before answering.

"I think not." I placed the carrot back into the bag and turned to leave with the hope that both Tennen and Splane would be well away already.

"Benella," the baker said. "I've always thought you a pretty thing. My mother commented the other day on how pleasant you are to talk to and reminded me of my very unwed status. Perhaps, it's time to change that."

I ran and didn't look back.

I caught up with Father on the path to our cottage. At the sound of my thumping feet, he turned with a smile on his face.

"Anything interesting from the estate today?"

I slowed to walk beside him, heart hammering and stomach heavy. How could the baker even hint at marriage? The thought of his heavy body pressed against mine sickened me.

"Bini, what's wrong?" Father asked, stopping. His blue, watery eyes studied me with concern, really seeing me for a change.

"The baker hinted at marriage."

"Ah..." he said enigmatically. "And that upset you?"

"Yes. I know I won't be able to live with you forever, but I would choose a man I could care for. One that wouldn't smother me in my sleep with his girth."

"Bini," he chided.

"He's not a good man, Father," I said firmly, hoping he would understand.

"Then, don't take his hint seriously."

Having his support calmed me. We walked the rest of the way home in silence. Bryn had no supper waiting when we returned home.

"No bread?" she asked. I shook my head and handed her the carrots.

"No worries, dears," Father assured us. "I wasn't hungry, anyway." He drifted to his study, leaving me to face Bryn's frown.

"Did you even ask?"

"Yes. He was quite clear that he wasn't interested in trading for carrots. I told you, I only have luck with his mother." I didn't like her tone, especially when I knew she had coin hidden aside that could have bought the bread.

She sighed.

"Can you try to set traps yet today? Perhaps we could have something fresh for Father at breakfast, then."

For Father, I nodded and headed back out toward the mist-filled woods. The sun hung low in the sky, sending the already dusky woods into further shadow. The dark didn't bother me. I set a few traps and walked toward the break in the estate's wall, hoping for some type of bounty. The ground sat barren, the same as it had for the last several days.

While staring dejectedly at the brown patch of dirt, I heard a faint scuffing sound behind me and turned in time to see Tennen step out from behind a tree. He held a thick segment of a broken branch. The determination in his gaze told me I wouldn't go home without injury this time.

Pivoting, I thought to run away, but Splane stepped out from behind another tree, effectively blocking the route. The hole in the wall mocked me. It was the only open path, but I knew what waited if I dared take it. No matter what I chose, I'd return home with bruises and most likely something broken.

"What did I ever do to you?" I asked Tennen, who I viewed as the bigger threat.

Instead of answering, he rushed toward me with the branch raised. I waited on the balls of my feet until the last second, then ducked under his swing in an attempt to get behind him so I could run. The movement hadn't been deep enough though because the branch raked my back. I hissed in pain, but kept moving. The gate loomed ahead, but I knew I dared not enter. I tried veering to the left toward the village, but Splane threw his rock and hit my left shoulder, effectively driving me toward the entrance. Defeated, I acknowledged they meant to corral me into the estate and darted toward the gaping black iron gate.

They chased after me, panting heavily in their exertion to catch up. As soon as I cleared the opening, the gate slammed shut of its own accord, the clang of the metal sounding my doom.

Skidding to a stop, I spun to stare at their disdainful faces a distance from the iron bars. They weren't stupid. The bars didn't guarantee their safety. The beast had been known to venture out on occasion.

Splane saluted me in farewell and took off running. Tennen waited, watching me. When his eyes widened and the color drained from his face, I knew the beast had arrived. I watched Tennen spin and sprint away then hung my head in defeat. My back burned and shoulder ached. Had I a choice, I wouldn't have run through the gate. I had known it would only add to my hurts.

"I'm sorry," I whispered.

Behind me, the beast's growl clicked with his anger. I kept my eyes on the overgrown gravel path at my feet. I didn't try to beg or flee. It hadn't ever ended well for those who'd attempted such methods before me. Better to just accept the punishment quietly.

His growl grew louder as he crept closer, and his breath skimmed my back. Tennen, the bastard, had ripped my shirt with his vicious swing.

Something warm and wet touched my abraded skin, eliciting an involuntary hiss from my lips and a quick step forward. The growl intensified, and I froze. Had the beast just licked me?

In all of the stories told of the estate, I'd never heard any where the beast devoured trespassers. Fear of just that locked me in place, and he stepped forward and repeated his stroke. The slow drag of his tongue hurt as much as it soothed.

Several times, he covered the area from mid-back to left shoulder. The fabric of my shirt ripped further as he forced it aside with his face. I didn't move or make any further sound. With each stroke of his tongue, the pain of the scratch faded as did the throb in my shoulder where the stone had hit.

One moment he licked my skin and the next I sailed through the air, somersaulting only to land gently in a pile of hay. Coughing at the plume of dust my landing had stirred, I waved my hand in front of my face and looked at the empty place just inside the gate.

For whatever reason, the beast had spared me.

Bryn gasped when I walked through the door. I knew I looked a mess but thought the gasp a bit of an overreaction. She hadn't even seen the back of me, yet. Blye, hearing our sister, stepped out from our room just as Bryn asked what had happened to me. Knowing Bryn wouldn't want to hear of Tennen's attack, I opened my mouth, ready to tell her that I had run into a branch. But, Father stepped out of his study. I snapped my mouth closed.

At that moment, I loved and hated my family because of the tangled web of lies that held my tongue. Bryn hoarded Father's coin in hopes of attracting Tennen's "wealthy" hand, Blye hoarded coin to run away to a town with more prospects, and I had no doubt our intelligent Father knew of both their activities but said nothing because he was content in this poor village. All of which put pressure on me to scrounge the countryside for food and trade with that pig of a baker.

I refused to add to the lies. My anger couldn't last, though, as I watched my father's eyes soften. They were my family, all that I had.

"Well, Bini?" Father asked. "What happened to you, dear?"

"I'd rather not talk about it," I said sullenly.

"Come into my study."

Without a choice, I followed him and listened to another gasp as my sisters saw the damage to my coarse cotton shirt. I'd be forced to wear my dress tomorrow, and that annoyed me.

Father held the door for me and shut it with a soft click after I entered. I stood facing his desk while he circled around me, clucking his tongue. Behind me, he lightly touched my back where Tennen's branch had ripped into my skin.

"Looks like something scraped you, hard. Luckily, it didn't break the skin. A branch, perhaps?"

He circled around me once more to sit in his chair, studying me as he moved. I kept my face relaxed, even though I fought a growing tension. The branch had cut me, I knew it had, but somehow father only saw a scrape. The only explanation I could form was the beast's tongue. Had he really healed me? If so, to what purpose? And why throw me into the hay on my second trespass? Everyone knew that being caught a second time meant some kind of injury.

"Tennen swung a branch at me, and Splane threw a rock while I was setting traps near the estate," I said, speaking the truth.

"Why would Tennen do such a thing? I thought he liked your sister."

I snorted softly before I could stop myself and glanced at the door. Father rose quietly and peered out the door. I caught a glimpse of Blye's skirt as she turned the corner to our room.

He shut the door and raised a brow at me, encouraging me to speak.

"I saw something I wish I wouldn't have. The baker is trading for bread, but has no interest in produce. He...wanted something from Sara." A flush crept into my cheeks, and I couldn't say more.

"I see," my father murmured in surprise. "And Tennen?"

"When I fled from the baker's alley, Tennen and Splane were there, waiting for Sara. They knew I saw something I shouldn't have, and they have been making my life difficult since. They said I think I'm better than them." I met my father's eyes earnestly. "I've never knowingly given them cause to think that. We're just as poor as the rest thanks to Bryn's stealing and Blye's hoarding."

He didn't act surprised by what I said. Instead, he seemed saddened, and I knew then that I had been right. Father was aware of both my sisters' activities.

"I'm sorry you are the one to suffer for our failings. I can begrudge neither Blye keeping the coin that she works so hard to earn, nor Bryn the coin she sets aside since she keeps my house. I only regret there is nothing I can give you for your care of us."

He looked away to stare out the window for several long moments while I squirmed under my guilt for thinking poorly of him. Of course, he knew what went on in his house. I should have trusted he had a reason to allow it.

"Perhaps there is something I can do for you, now," he said. "Blye. Bryn," he called loudly, startling me. He never raised his voice.

The door opened moments later, and they crowded into the study with us. I wondered how much my sisters had heard.

"Bryn, your sister has suffered some injuries that require a hot soak. I know it is an effort, but—"

Bryn waved away the rest of what he would say.

"I'll ready a bath for her." She turned and left.

"Blye, your sister has so little in the way of clothes and cannot afford to lose a shirt. Can you mend it?"

Blye stepped behind me, tisking. "I could, but she'll look like a beggar. Better to take the shirt apart and use some of my spare cloth for a new back panel."

"How long will that take?" Father asked.

"I should have it done tomorrow evening."

He thanked her and waved her away before turning back to me.

"Go clean up and let your sister have your shirt. Tomorrow you'll have to suffer your dress." He gave me a small grin, knowing I preferred my trousers. "The day after, I will have an errand for you, so do not make any plans for that day." He stood and planted a kiss atop my head.

Knowing I was dismissed, I stood and left his study to find a waiting Blye. She didn't look angry, so I didn't think she'd heard the part about her hoarding her coin.

"Bryn's heating water in the kitchen. Could I have your shirt? I'd like to wash it before working with it."

I didn't blame her for wanting it clean. Tracked with dirt and beast spit, it didn't look pleasant. Since Father stayed in his study to assure privacy our small cottage lacked when any of us bathed, I quickly shrugged out of the shirt and torn bindings and handed everything over to her. She walked through the kitchen and out the back door to the well. Naked from the waist up, I covered myself with my arms and went to the kitchen.

The skin of my back felt tight, and my shoulder still ached a bit when I stretched it forward. The beast had healed me but not completely. As I sat on a chair and waited, I wondered again the reason behind his mercy. Thinking of the puzzling beast was much more pleasant than the baker's depravity or my sisters' deceit. Yet, my thoughts tended to wander in their direction.

Bryn had the fire stoked to heat the water, so I was comfortable while she sweated. A while later, she pronounced the tub ready and moved the bathing screen in front of it before stepping outside to cool herself.

I stripped down and slid into the water with a contented sigh, putting thoughts of the baker, the beast, village boys, and family lies from my head.

CHAPTER THREE

In the morning, I was last from bed, not wanting my sisters around when I dressed. Blye had thoughtfully hung my dress the night before so the wrinkles from storage would fall out on their own.

The dress was a gift from Blye and my father for my birthday more than six months ago. Father had supplied the material, and Blye had worked on it for weeks, making me stand for several painfully boring fittings. I typically only wore it on washdays and then hid in the cottage with it. Blye usually laughed at me.

Light blue with a full skirt edged with a white ruffle, topped with a square-necked, long-sleeved bodice, it truly was a thing of beauty, but I looked so different in it. I didn't think it made me look awful, just overly feminine. Secretly, I was concerned with the responsibilities wearing such a dress might bring. With my britches, most people let me go my way. Sighing, I stood and slipped the pretty dress over my head, not bothering with any bindings.

Medium height with my mother's dark sable hair and hazel eyes and my father's slim build, I looked a gangly youth in my britches and shirt. Now, the dress removed the gangle and turned me into a slender young woman. I knew that was what I was, but I didn't like it. The dress also shoved my small breasts high as if I wanted to put them on display, like produce at a market. The errant thought of selling them led to thoughts of Sara and the baker, and I decided that hiding in my room all day really was the best option.

A knock sounded on my bedroom door as I nervously smoothed my hands over the skirt. Only Father knocked, so I called for him to enter.

"You look lovely, Bini," he said with a caring smile. "I know you would prefer to stay inside, but would you walk with Bryn to the candle maker? I need another candle."

Father read by the light of the fire in his study most nights, but needed the candle for any writing he might do at his desk.

I nodded my assent and accepted the copper he handed me.

"Get the best you can with that." We both knew it wouldn't be much, but neither of us spoke it, just as I didn't question why Bryn couldn't go alone.

The candle maker had taken a dislike to Bryn a few years before. She'd gone to purchase candles from him, and the encounter had gone badly. He'd set his price and wouldn't come down from it. She'd called him a miserly old man, which he was, but he was also nice and didn't like being called names. Regardless, she'd only gotten angry because she was a miserly young woman trying to pinch a copper whenever she could for her own selfish purpose. I didn't see how she could fault the candle maker for doing the same.

At least, by having Bryn accompany me, Father had given me the safety I needed to go about in my confounded dress. If I met up with Tennen and Splane alone while wearing it, I'd never stand a chance at outrunning them.

After lacing up my sturdy boots hidden beneath my skirts, I

straightened my shoulders and headed to the kitchen. Bryn waited by the door and wore her best dress. She'd been blessed with Father's fair hair and pale eyes and our mother's curvy figure. Seeing her, I shored my resolve to ignore the stares the pair of us would receive. I knew everyone would compare us and didn't want to contemplate who would come ahead in the comparison.

"I think you've grown, Benella," Bryn commented, eyeing me dispassionately.

I quickly looked down at my skirts, which still hovered an inch above the floor.

"Not in height," she laughed as she turned away to open the door.

Refusing to think on her comment, I followed her out into the sunlight, feeling awkward as the skirts brushed against my bare legs. I didn't own any stockings, just socks and boots fit for a young boy.

"I hope Father gave you coin. I have none to spare for the candle maker," she said as I closed the door and rushed to catch up with her.

"Not enough, but the candle maker is nice, so I'm sure we can come to an agreement."

Bryn had no reply.

We walked the rest of the way to town, each lost in our own thoughts, mine mostly fervent wishes not to run into Tennen with Bryn at my side. My wishes didn't go unheard. The anvil laid quiet and the billows lax when we left the path for the main road. Relieved, I crossed the street and entered the candle maker's home. The soft chime of the bell attached to the door greeted me.

"Benella!" the candle maker exclaimed, welcoming me with a smile.

Sitting at a table near his hearth, he removed a line of strings from a pot of melted wax and set it on the holder to the side. He had once explained that his candles were the best around because he took care to ensure the candles stood straight the entire time, thus burned their wax evenly.

"What brings you in today?" he asked, standing. His bones creaked and cracked with the effort, but I didn't try to insist that he sit for our discussion. He held a firm belief that he honored his customers by standing to wait on them. His gnarled hand patted down his wispy white hair as he slowly straightened his frame.

I held out the copper.

"Father sent me for a candle. I know you offer nothing but the finest, but he'd like something modest if possible."

"Benella, your honeyed words are a trap for an unwary man, to be sure." He grinned at me, laughing and mumbling "nothing but the finest" under his breath. He didn't take the proffered coin, rather he walked to the shelves and rummaged through the pale candles for a moment before pulling out a thick one with a satisfied sigh. A blackened wick poked from one melted end.

"This is one I made for myself," he said, handing it to me. "A gift for the flowers, until I can pay you properly. Tell your father it will burn at least ten hours if he trims it."

I nodded my thanks, accepted the candle, and curled my fingers around the copper.

As I left, I debated about the coin. If I gave it to Father, he'd most likely give it to Bryn for supplies, which we wouldn't see. But, with Bryn at my side and a copper in hand, I could go to the bakery, avoid the baker, and buy some flour. After all, a copper wasn't enough to buy a loaf of bread these days.

Bryn waited for me outside. I handed her the candle, and she placed it in her bag without comment.

"I'd like to go to the bakery and see how much flour I can purchase," I said, stopping her when she would have turned home. She raised her brows at me, no doubt surprised by my willingness to linger in town when wearing a dress, and followed me without comment.

The door to the bakery stood propped open and waves of heat rolled out. No one lingered within to trade gossip today. I stepped onto the porch and quickly ducked inside the store. Miss Medunge sat on a stool behind a counter lined with a narrow variety of fresh bread. She smiled at me and waved me in.

"The bread's been picked over already. This is what's left until dinner," she said, pointing to the loaves.

"I'm interested in purchasing flour, however much a copper will get me," I said, setting the coin on the counter. I could almost taste the biscuits I imagined Bryn would make.

She pursed her lips in thought. "Just under two handfuls, I think. Do you have a bit of cloth for it?"

I cringed. "I hadn't thought of that."

"Don't worry. I can loan that if you promise to bring it back."

Nodding my promise, I watched her go through the door to the bakery. The aroma of fresh bread made my mouth water as I waited. When the door swung open, I looked up expecting her smiling face but, instead, met the eyes of the baker. In his hand, he held a small bundle of cloth tied with a bit of string.

"Benella, I couldn't believe it when my sister told me you were here to buy flour," he said while his eyes wandered over me, mostly lingering on the exposed skin of my neck and chest. "And so prettily attired. I didn't know you owned a dress."

I didn't care for his tone.

"Here is the copper," I said, scooting it across the counter with one finger.

He smirked at me and held out the flour, waiting until I reached for it to grab my fingers with his other hand. He petted them with his own sweaty digits.

"Perhaps, I will see you later," he whispered, setting the flour bag in my palm.

I said nothing, staring at him while maintaining a straight face. Eventually, he released my hand, and I turned and slowly made my exit. Sweat beaded on my upper lip when I stepped out into the cool air, but my fate didn't turn any better. Tennen stood near Bryn, and they spoke quietly. When he heard me, he looked up with a gleam in his eyes.

"Needed to see the baker?" he asked with a laugh.

Bryn, not liking that I'd immediately stolen his attention, pouted prettily, but he ignored her.

"Yes. We had a spare copper and needed flour."

A blaze of anger lit in his eyes, and he took a step toward me. Bryn stopped him with a simpering hand on his arm.

"Tennen, our walk?"

He looked down at her, and for a moment, I saw his disdain. Then, his face cleared, and a smile curved his lips.

"Of course." He took her by the arm and led her up the road toward our house. I followed with my flour protected in my hands.

When we reached the cottage, Tennen bowed his farewell and left without looking at me again. Bryn walked inside as if nothing had happened. I handed her the flour and fled to Father's study, content to read until he returned home.

Hours melted away while I devoured the words on the pages. I'd stopped attending school years ago when I'd quietly corrected Father after class, regarding one of the mathematical concepts he'd been teaching. Since then, he let me use his study whenever he wasn't home. I remembered most everything I read that interested me, and many things did. The botany book he'd used to identify the primrose captivated me until he strode through his study door.

"What a lovely sight. A pretty girl reading a book," he said.

Neither of my sisters showed much interest in books, but he didn't fault them for it.

I placed a marker in the book and set it to the side. "I've warmed your chair for you," I said cheekily.

He laughed and shooed me from the room, settling comfortably into his chair. I passed the room I shared with my sisters and saw Blye sitting on the bed, placing careful stitches into my shirt. The back panel didn't look new, just smaller. I didn't pause, not wanting to know what she had to do to fix it, and made my way to the kitchen. Bryn had the biscuits in the oven with the door slightly ajar so she could watch them brown. A knock sounded at the front door, and we stared at each other for a moment before she waved for me to answer it. I wished for my trousers as I pulled open the door.

"Benella," said the baker. "Still lovely in your dress. Is your father home? I would like to speak with him."

My legs shook. I knew the topic of conversation he wanted to have with my father but assured myself that Father understood my distaste of the man.

"Come in," I managed without a quaver. I stepped aside and let him into the kitchen.

"Wait here, please."

Leaving him to criticize Bryn's biscuits, I tapped on Father's door. Without waiting for his call to enter, I stepped in, quickly closing the door behind me.

Father looked up from his book in surprise. He still wore his jacket and simple neckcloth. Papers from his few students lay spread out on his desk.

"What is the matter, dearest?"

"He's here," I whispered in a panic. "The baker. He saw me in this senseless dress today." I gave the skirt an agitated shake. "Now, he wants to speak with you."

"Ah," Father murmured distractedly. "Perhaps, once he's in the study with me, you'd like to go for a long stroll and forego dinner?" I nodded emphatically, liking the way Father thought. The baker, now that he had come to state his intentions, would not leave easily.

I opened the door and called to the baker. Given the size of our small cottage, he had no trouble finding me. Despite stepping aside, he still brushed against me as he passed; and this time, I couldn't suppress my shiver of revulsion. His low throaty chuckle drifted to me as I closed the door.

With a quick step, I checked on Blye's progress, hoping to change before I left, but she still sat in the room placing careful stitches. In the kitchen, Bryn removed the biscuits from the oven.

"May I have one?" I asked, grabbing my bag from the hook.

She made no comment about my leaving, just wrapped a biscuit in a cloth and handed it over. I fled the cottage quietly, hoping the baker wouldn't hear my escape.

The woods didn't feel the same as I wandered beneath their swaying limbs. The skirts encircling my legs made passage difficult. I had to avoid stretching bramble and muddied paths and made far too much noise as I moved.

When I finally reached the spot in the estate wall where the rocks had fallen, I saw nothing to harvest. Though the walk had felt torturously long, I doubted enough time had passed to see the baker gone from the cottage. Deciding a walk in the dark didn't bother me, I turned east to make a full circuit around the wall, but a sound to the west stopped me.

A creak of wood and the crush of gravel under iron drew me toward the gate where a cart fixed with a long pole like a mast waited. The gate stood open and the cart sat just outside of it. Had someone from the estate pushed it out? What a peculiar cart. I caught sight of a tangle of freshly shorn vines laying loose at the base of the pole and felt my stomach twist. The pole, the cart, the vines...I'd seen it all before when the men had attempted to sack the estate. They'd meant to tie the beast to it and burn him. Instead, they'd been run or thrown from the estate and had abandoned the wagon, which had been later retrieved by the smith.

Turning to flee, I crashed into something solid.

"Just the person we wanted to see," Tennen murmured, clamping his hands down on my upper arms. "I thought you might run when the baker came calling."

I lifted my knee to hit his groin, but my skirts hampered the move, and I only grazed him. Still, he bent slightly, bringing his head close to mine. I jerked forward, hitting his head with my own. His hands left my arms, and I tried to run. However, the knock I'd given myself against his hard head turned me around, and I stumbled straight into Splane's waiting arms. After witnessing his brother's abuse, he quickly spun me so I faced away from him.

"Bitch!" panted Tennen, holding his nose with one hand while reaching for the vines with the other. "I hope the beast rips you open."

His sudden punch to my stomach caught me off guard. I barely noticed Splane's abandonment of his hold as the need to draw in a breath occupied me. Tennen roughly grabbed my wrists, pulled them behind my back, and tied them as I remained bent over in pain. Together the brothers hauled me onto the cart. I caught my breath enough to struggle, but it did no good. They lifted me over their heads and struggled to thread the pole through my bound arms.

"Idiots," I said when they finally stepped back, sweating and red-faced from their efforts. "You should have tied my wrists together after you had me in front of the pole."

They ignored me and jumped from the wagon. I listened to

them grunt as they began to push the cart through the gates. Not again, I thought, eyeing the beast's domain.

Desperate, I leaned forward so my wrists pulled against the wood, then tried to place a foot on the pole, hoping to boost myself up and perhaps climb to the top. My heel slipped on my skirts.

"I hope the beast catches you!" I screamed at them, no longer caring if he heard the noise we were making. Oh, I still feared him but preferred he catch all of us and not just me. Perhaps I would then have a chance.

They laughed as the cart stopped moving. Facing the estate, I saw nothing but overgrown vegetation and trees. I twisted, trying to see Tennen and Splane. Instead, I heard the creak of the gate as they pulled it closed.

"We're not afraid of that thing," Tennen said, a distance behind me.

"Bold words for little men standing outside the gate," I said. "Come inside and see if you fare so well. Do your own dirty work instead of waiting for someone else to do it for you!"

"Someone? You mean something. This is the third time for you, isn't it, Benella? You won't bother us again."

Tennen spoke the truth, and I struggled against the thin vines binding my wrists. The beast would not forgive a third trespass. I wriggled and writhed and panted as I fought against my binding. Pain bit into my wrists with each frantic tug and twist, and my fingers grew slick. My hair came loose from its long braid and tangled in front of my face, obscuring my vision.

Tennen's laughter taunted me and my pathetic struggles until the sound abruptly stopped. I stilled and tried blowing the hair from my eyes. For a fraction of a moment, I caught a glimpse of black eyes and brown fur before my hair once again blocked my view. I froze. The beast. He was here, mere feet away.

The dark trees around us had gone eerily quiet as if holding their breath. The silence allowed the low rumble of the beast's growl to echo, surrounding me with his menace.

A scrape against the ground and a faint creak of the wood was all the warning I had before the beast pushed the cart and sent it flying to crash upon the gate. The bone-jarring stop rattled my teeth as my head smacked back against the pole. The momentum sent me forward again, a sudden jerk stopped by my tied wrists. The vines bit deep, and I grunted in pain.

Behind me, Splane squealed like a girl a moment before I heard their hurried retreat. I laughed groggily as my ears rang and the world spun from the thump to my head.

"Two little girls, that's what they are. They should be wearing a dress," I mumbled, wincing at the pain at the base of my skull.

"Why have you returned?" asked an angry voice in a deep scraping growl.

He could speak? With a curtain of hair in the way and my vision not cooperating, I closed my eyes in defeat.

"That should be apparent, I'd think. To die."

"Why do you wish for death so badly?" the voice asked. Some of the anger had faded from it and was replaced by curiosity.

"Does it look to you like I came here by choice?" A harsh laugh escaped me. "It's not my wish, but theirs, that I die."

The longer I stood there, the more my injuries started calling attention to themselves. My shoulders ached from their position and the recent collision with the gate. My wrist oozed blood and my stomach twisted with nausea. His silence along with everything else made my next words dangerously impudent.

"Recent events having left me in a poor mood, I'd rather not waste any more time on idle conversation. I hurt everywhere and think I may vomit soon so, please, just be done with it."

The vines around my wrists loosened, and I fell forward onto something hard, furry, and warm. Draped over the beast, I realized, a moment before we were moving.

Sadly, I vomited before fainting.

"…SHOULD I?"

The shrill voice cut through the fog clouding my mind, and I blinked my eyes open to stare at the rough shingled roof blurring above me. A growl filled the air, and my stomach lurched, not from the growl, but from the sour taste lingering in my mouth. I gagged.

"Leave us," the feminine voice commanded.

A door slammed, and I turned on my side to dry heave. A gentle hand ran over my hair, lingering on the spot at the back of my head where I'd smacked against the pole.

"There's the problem. Let's sit you up."

She leveraged a thin, wiry arm behind my shoulders and helped me sit. Slowly, my vision cleared and an aged, haggard face filled the space before me. White hair twisted tightly behind her head and pulled the skin of her face, smoothing a few of the deeper creases. Her brilliant green eyes glinted at me with cold humor.

"Got in the way of something, I'd say," she murmured, leaning in close, her gaze shifting back and forth to study mine. "Best to stay awake tonight. You'll feel sick, which is normal. Drink lightly. Don't eat until your stomach stops twisting."

Without mercy, she tugged me to my feet. The ground tilted and heaved, and I spread my stance wide to keep from falling.

"Smart girl," she said with a laugh. "Too bad he brought you to me. You can't stay here. Out you go." She nudged me toward the door.

The stomach I'd thought empty heaved again, and I left a gift on her floor before I managed to clear the threshold. Her insulting laughter rang out behind me before the door closed and silence enveloped me.

Reaching out, I braced myself on the door. Night had claimed the sky and the half-moon weakly highlighted the area, not that it did me any good. The pain in my head clouded my vision. How would I manage a walk home, especially when I didn't know where I was? I recalled the beast's growl and knew I had to be somewhere within the estate. South, then, was the way to go. I lifted my head to the moon, trying to focus enough to get my bearings.

I took a lurching step away from the door, my skirt swishing through the grass. Within seven steps, I heaved again, and my eyes watered. The muscles in my stomach protested, and I wished for a cool drink to rinse my mouth. Instead, I received a growl.

"Vomit on me again, and you will suffer," he said before he swung me over his shoulder. The grass flew past us, and I clenched my teeth as blood rushed to my head and pulsed in my ears. My vision clouded, and I knew I'd faint again and wondered if that counted as sleeping. The beast sensed something, though, because he stopped his run, and I found myself standing before him in the shadowy light beneath a tree.

"What did she say?" he demanded.

When the world tilted, I didn't try widening my stance. Instead, I let my weak knees fold and sat heavily on the ground.

"Don't sleep or eat until my stomach stops twisting. Drink lightly and get out." I partially groaned as I struggled to my knees and heaved again, aggravating my stomach muscles and the lump on the back of my head. I spit weakly and let my head hang.

"Running upside down made it worse," I said, swiping at my lips.

"You blame this on me?" His low growl increased in volume and clicked with menace as he crept close to me.

"Well, it was your fault that I hit the back of my head against the pole. Before that, only my wrists bled."

He roared in response, which brought back the ringing in my ears. I paid his anger little mind as I sought refuge from my pain in the cool grass and closed my eyes.

"What are you doing?"

"Going to sleep."

"The witch said not to."

"And you just roared at me. So what? If I die, I die. I'm tired of being bullied by you and the idiots in the village. If I live, so be it. At least, I'll have had a few moments of peace."

His feet padded softly, rustling the grass and scraping the dirt until he stopped behind me. Lying on my side with my face cushioned by my arm, I'd saved the back of my head from touching the ground, but also left it open to the beast's inspection. He huffed a great breath, blowing my hair over my face. Then he began to lick the lump he'd made.

I couldn't help the sigh that escaped me as the ache eased and the twisting in my stomach faded.

"Thank you," I whispered.

He grunted and kept licking for several more minutes. Without the nausea, it lulled me to sleep.

CHAPTER
FOUR

"CAW!"

I bolted upright at the loud cry in my ear. My stomach muscles protested at their overuse, and I suffered a brief period of disorientation. I recalled the night before and studied my surroundings. The shaded glade only sported a few tufts of low growing grass on the outskirts. A soft patch grew in the center where the sun struck at midday, the very patch on which I'd previously reclined until the crow, hopping on the ground a few feet away, had rudely woken me.

The crow cawed at me again, but I ignored it as I struggled to my feet. The aches of the night before lingered in my shoulders and stomach but remained absent elsewhere, drawing my attention to the smooth and unblemished skin of each wrist. The memory rose of how the beast had eased the ache in my head. I glanced around the glade but felt certain only the crow and I entertained it now.

Given the dangerously unpredictable nature of the beast, I thought it best to keep my company to myself, and I began to carefully pick my way through the trees, heading toward the general area of the gate. As soon as I started walking, the crow took flight only to land on a branch ahead of me. I ignored the bird for the most part since it kept quiet when it flew but listened closely to the surrounding wood as I made slow progress through the estate lands.

It didn't surprise me when I spotted the gate ahead and it grated open on its own, the estate obviously ready to be rid of me. Of the beast, there was no sign. Muddied and disheveled, I made my way home in dawn's first light.

A FAMILIAR GASP greeted me when I opened the kitchen door. Behind me, a furious flutter of wings sounded, prompting me to ignore Bryn's incredulous stare and quickly close the door before the annoying crow decided to let itself in. It cawed at me through the wood.

"Benella," Bryn finally managed to cry. "Father's been so worried." She stood by the stove with an apron wrapped around her dress. Eggs fried in a pan, and a small crock of fresh goat's milk already rested on the table, waiting for Father.

The study door opened, and Father hurried out fully dressed for the day, his expression putting truth to Bryn's statement. His eyes swept me and relief erased the worry.

"When I mentioned a walk, I didn't think you'd stay out all night, child," he said mildly, seeing me whole and healthy.

"An unplanned event to be sure," I said. "I ran into a bit of dirt and will need another bath."

Bryn gave a small, exasperated huff.

"I can't haul water for you again, Benella. I'm supposed to go with Tennen to—"

"Bryn," Father said softly. "I'm sure it wouldn't over trouble you to help with two small buckets, just enough to rinse the dirt from your sister's hair." As he spoke, he circled me and lifted the hair on the back of my head.

"Surely this unplanned event had a few interesting turns," he murmured for my ears only.

I gave the barest of nods, and he stepped back from me. I appreciated that he didn't question me further.

"At least the dress survived unscathed," he said.

Blye harrumphed from the doorway of our room. She'd joined us so quietly I hadn't noticed her.

"Its hem is stained with mud. I wouldn't call that unscathed."

"Better than ripped," Father said in a tone that didn't allow for argument. "Benella, I would speak with you before I leave about an errand I need you to run. Would you mind stepping into my study before you wash?"

"Of course, Father," I said, more than willing to escape my sisters' pique.

He surprised me by not asking of my night once he closed the door behind us.

"I apologize for asking this of you, but I need a message delivered to the Head in Water-On-The-Bridge as soon as possible."

The request disheartened me. The walk would take me most of the day there and back, and sleeping on the ground the prior night had done little to leave me feeling rested. But, I reasoned with myself, a whole day with no other obligations might be nice. I rolled my shoulders, feeling the ache in the joints, and tested my stomach. Nothing I couldn't handle. So, I nodded my agreement. Outside the window, a crow squawked.

"Fetch your mended shirt from Blye. I'm sure you'll be more comfortable in it," he said. "See me when you're ready to leave."

I nodded and quietly crept to my room. After carefully closing the door, I looked around the room. My shirt lay neatly on the thin comforter of my narrow bed. Something about it looked odd, but I couldn't determine what when I lifted it up. As usual, Blye's stitches ran small and straight, making it impossible to see where she'd made any change. I slipped out of the dress and pulled on my trousers then bindings.

Outside, I heard a flutter of wings; and as I looked up at the partially shuttered window, the crow used his beak to make room for himself on the ledge. Blye opened the door behind me before I could shoo the crow away.

"Did you try it on?" she asked impatiently.

I turned away from the voyeuristic crow and shrugged my arms into the shirt. It fit, but it pulled snugly from shoulder to shoulder across the back. Frowning, I closed the front and began to button it up, seeing the problem immediately. The shirt buttons strained to close the gap between the front two panels and created small spaces where anyone could see my bindings or stomach for that matter.

Disappointment clearly on my face, I looked up at her. Her expression remained impassive.

"Well, I tried. The cloth I had didn't match, and you would have looked like a patchwork. Perhaps Father can save for a new one. Until then, you do have the dress."

I stared after her as she glided from the room and closed the door. The dress? In a disbelieving trance, I walked across the room to one of the compact chests sitting on the floor at the foot of the larger bed that Blye and Bryn shared. There was one chest for each of my sisters, gifts from our mother, who'd died before giving one to me. She'd meant them as a place for us to store the things we would collect for our own homes.

Carefully lifting the lid of Blye's chest, I gazed at the yards of folded fabrics stacked neatly on top of each other and the various lengths of ribbon lying on top of them. Threads of several colors twined around a thin spindle. Under the spindle, a simple bolt of roughly woven cream cotton material rested all but forgotten beside the prettily colored fine weaves. I would have liked to think Blye had overlooked the material; but wrapped in a bit of coarse thread, the section on my shirt she'd taken away sat beside it. She was right. The colors didn't quite match, but she had enough of the other material to make me a whole new shirt if she chose to. It hurt knowing she couldn't spare anything for me when I'd given so much to her.

A clicking at the window distracted me; and I let the lid close softly, leaving the contents undisturbed. The crow opened and closed its beak several times without making any other sound and then took off from the sill, leaving me in peace.

Shaking out the dress and brushing as much of the dirt from it as I could, I spread it on the bed and went to the kitchen to wash up. Two kettles rested on the stove in the vacant kitchen. I fetched a cloth and tested the water. Still cool. Frowning, I checked the stove. Bryn hadn't even added wood to it to heat the water. Sighing, I set to washing in the cold water, wiping my skin, but foregoing rinsing my hair. Instead, after I finished and changed back into the dress, I ran a brush through it then braided it again.

Tossing the water into the garden out back, I noticed the crow watching from the top of our tiny outbuilding that housed the goat and a few garden tools. It watched me closely, its quiet more disturbing than its previous cawing. I thoughtfully narrowed my eyes at it before going inside.

Finally ready, I knocked on Father's study door. He stood before the window, staring out at nothing when I entered, but quickly turned to hand me a sealed letter.

"Try to be home before dark and save me from another night's worry, Bini," he said softly, kissing my cheek.

I nodded and moved aside to let him pass. He'd obviously been waiting for me so he could leave for the school and ring the bell to call his pupils.

THE CROW FOLLOWED me as I walked away from the cottage, heading northwest toward the road. I wanted to angle north enough to miss any possibility of running into Tennen or Splane. I imagined by now, Tennen knew I'd returned home, thanks to Bryn, and wondered at his reaction.

Lost in thought, I continued my journey until the crow flew at me from the left, making a racket and flapping in my face. Raising my arms for protection, I turned away, instinctively taking several large steps to put distance between us. So far, the crow had just followed me; the violence of its sudden attack left me with a racing heart and confused. I had no food with me to give it cause to chase me, even though the journey promised to be long and tiring.

It retreated, and I tentatively lowered my arms to look for it. It had perched on a branch not far to my left. It cocked its head, studying me intensely. Warily, I gave it wide berth and tried striking out northwest again. Every time I veered even the slightest bit in a westerly direction, it flew at me.

Scowling, I headed north to the estate. It followed me closely, herding me to the gate, which swung open at my approach. I stopped to look at the crow.

"I truly feel I've tempted fate enough. I don't suppose you'd leave me in peace if I went no further."

It cawed angrily, and I sighed, eyeing its sharp beak. Hoping the beast's benevolent mood remained intact in the light of day, I stepped through the gate. As soon as it slammed closed behind me, the crow flew off north toward the center of the estate.

Nervously, I lingered by the gate, unwilling to risk increasing the beast's ire by going any further.

After several long minutes the small, unidentifiable noises made by the wildlife in the surrounding area quieted. The typically blurred air grew murkier, making it hard to see more than a few feet beyond where I stood. A caw sounded nearby, the sharp ring of it dampened by the mist.

"You returned." The beast's disembodied growl floated to me.

Standing my ground, I slowly scanned the darkest areas in front of me.

"Not by choice. I think your crow would have eagerly pecked out my eyes had I not abided by its direction."

Silence answered me. Had I misunderstood? Was the crow not his messenger? My stomach churned, and my gaze darted from one shadowy object to the next as I tried to discern which might be the beast. After a few moments of straining to see or hear any indication I wasn't alone, I bravely spoke.

"I'm very willing to leave you to your peace if you would kindly convince the gate to open."

"Before you leave, you may ask of me one thing you need that I can find within the walls of my estate," he said with a low rumble.

My mouth popped open. Generosity from the beast was the last thing I'd expected.

"I...thank you for your offer," I said slowly, "but I've taken so much from the estate already."

"You scorn my offer?"

The roar of his rage momentarily deafened me and startled nearby birds from their roosts. Rubbing my ears, I hastily tried to assure him.

"Never scorn. To the east, a portion of your wall has crumbled and often the area beyond offers a small harvest of edible roots no matter what time of year. Many times it's helped feed me. And just the other day, a spider threw its fine webbing at me, strong enough to use as thread. To my shame, I've never scorned the bounty of your estate. I've repeatedly taken without asking until finally it stopped offering. So you see, I can't possibly accept more."

An annoyed grunt sounded to my right, but when I turned in that direction, I saw nothing.

"Regardless, ask of me one thing you need. Only then will the gate open."

I frowned at his stubborn insistence. Why did I need to ask for something? Perhaps it was a trick, and if I asked for the wrong thing I'd be trapped in the estate forever. He'd said something in the estate that I needed. Need must be the key. If Blye stood before him, she would say she needed something silly like thread or material, but I knew neither could be a need.

"I can think of nothing I need. We always have enough food to keep from starving and a roof to keep us warm and dry."

"I don't care about your family," he said sharply. "Whatever you choose must be for you and you alone. You waste my time. This is no riddle to debate and stew. Just choose," he bellowed, causing me to jump.

Thoughtfully quiet, I nibbled at my lip. It was on the tip of my tongue to ask for a man's shirt. I even opened my mouth and made a small noise before snapping it shut as a surprising thought stopped me. I could hear his growing agitation in the increased volume of his growl.

"Refuge," I whispered.

The growling stopped.

"What do you mean?"

"You want me to ask for one thing I need from within the estate. I'm asking for refuge when I need it."

Behind me, the gate creaked open. I spun and raced for the breach, not waiting for his answer. The crow's cackling caw followed me through the trees until I reached the point where the mists faded.

Near the road, I paused to bend and catch my breath. Four times I'd stood within the walls of the estate and escaped with my life; and now, with his offer, I'd ensured my safety if I should ever find myself within those walls again.

After a few moments, I wiped away the sweat that had accumulated on my brow and started my journey. The letter from my father rested within the bag that lay limp against my hip. I wished I had something with which to carry water, for I sorely needed a drink and my journey had just begun.

Recalling Father's request to return before dark, I lengthened my stride and followed the road from the estate northwest.

THE ROAR of rushing water announced the Deliichan River, which bordered the hilltop village of Water-On-The-Bridge. Eager to deliver the message, I strode forward around the last bend in the road and caught my first glimpse of the water-slicked bridge. In winter, the spray from the water that crashed upon the rocks below froze on the thick, wood planks to create a treacherous trek across.

For as long as anyone could remember, there had always been water on the bridge, the reason for the village's name. They'd tried moving the bridge, but the river didn't tolerate additional bridges well, and they usually fell to ruin shortly after their completion. Only this one remained steadfast with very little repair needed.

Because of the precariousness of the bridge, many merchants ended their routes at Water-On-The-Bridge, not bothering to trade with Konrall. The baker made the journey once a month for his flour from the mill while the tinker only rode this way when his supplies ran low. The seamstress and the candle maker dealt with the single traveling merchant who still traversed the bridge.

My footsteps echoed hollowly on the planks and fine droplets settled on my cheeks as I crossed. The mill stood as a tall sentinel on the opposite side of the river, its elevated floors hovering a few feet above the water, steady on the thick stilts sunk deep into the riverbed. The waterwheel that turned the stone grinder spun slowly in the swift current, but I knew its power and the fine powder it turned out.

The road on the other side of the river suffered deep ruts due to the constant traffic from the town to the mill. I took care to traverse the shoulder so I could view the bustling trade without fear of being run down by horse or wagon. There was much to observe.

Water-On-The-Bridge presented a larger variety of trade than Konrall, including things a proper lady shouldn't stare at. However, without my father accompanying me, I took the opportunity to watch the alehouse women, whom I knew if asked, would serve more than a drink.

A tall brunette laughed loudly, throwing her head back to expose her neck. It made her look pretty, smoothing the lines of her loose skin and bringing a natural flush to her mottled complexion. Her customer, a man at ease while he sipped ale at a table, watched her chest with interest. Her dress pushed the tops of her pale breasts up on display much as my dress did. The man reached forward and pulled her close with a tug on her skirt. She leaned down to hear what he said, and he buried his face in her cleavage. She laughed harder as I passed from their view.

The scene made me distinctly uncomfortable with my own display, but I persisted forward, knowing the house I sought was highly respectable. Mr. Jolen Pactel, the current Head, lived past the House of Whispering Sisters, which I found entertaining since his purpose was to maintain the peace and theirs was to bring peace, but in completely different ways. As Head, Mr. Pactel settled disputes and set down judgments in place of the Liege Lord, an absent fellow for near fifty years. The title of Head wasn't an elected one, but an inherited one; and the Pactel family had held the position of Head for the last forty years with fair rulings. The House of Whispering Sisters brought peace, one client at a time, with their sweet smelling smoke, veiled faces, and unveiled bodies.

With nothing to trade and no coin, I suffered the delicious aromas of simmering stews and baking pastries as I walked through the market district. The cloying smoke from the Whispering Sisters house fogged my head briefly as I caught a glimpse of a pale, slim torso and a grey veiled face through an open window.

Away from the noise of commerce, I stepped under the arched stone wall that bordered the two-story house of the Head. After a single knock, the dense oak door swung open, and a thick-armed man greeted me with an impassive look.

"Good day. I have a message for the Head from Mr. Benard Hovtel of Konrall."

The man stepped aside and bid me to enter. I willingly stepped into the spacious entry and admired the smooth sanded plank floor covered with a pretty, woven rug. Spring flowers adorned the side table, scenting the air sweetly.

"This way," the man murmured, leading me toward a small room near the back of the house.

A smaller man sat behind a desk there. Sitting in a chair in the corner near the door through which we walked was another thick-armed man. I understood the business of the Head and knew men strong enough to help keep the peace were needed.

"She has a message for the Head," the man announced behind

me once I entered the room. Without waiting for a response from the man behind the desk, my escort left.

The short, thin man at the desk looked up from his papers, and with a pleasant smile, he stood when he saw me.

"Good day, dear lady," he greeted me. "Mr. Pactel is currently occupied elsewhere in the Water. May I be of assistance?"

"I'm not certain," I said hesitantly. "My father sent me here to deliver this message to Mr. Pactel." I reached into my bag, heard the man in the corner shift behind me, and quickly withdrew the sealed letter. When I glanced over my shoulder, the man was just settling back into his chair, eyeing me critically.

"And you are?"

"Sorry," I said, remembering myself. "Benella."

"I am Tibit. Would you mind if I read the letter?" He didn't reach for the letter I held out, letting me decide first. Since I had no idea what it contained, I didn't know what to say. Though my father trusted me, at least I thought he did, he knew to what extent I could protect his letter and surely wouldn't write anything of significant importance.

"I think that would be fine, Mr. Tibit."

"Just Tibit will do," he said politely, reaching for the letter. He broke the seal and scanned the contents. "Ah, yes. The school master."

"My father," I clarified.

Tibit looked up at me with a half-smile.

"Tell your father the offer still stands, and we are pleased to hear he is finally considering it."

With that, he moved back to his desk, effectively dismissing me with not one offer of refreshment or further explanation. I kept my disappointment from my face and thanked him for his time before taking my leave. A hint about the offer after which my father had inquired would have been nice, but a drink much more welcomed.

AFTER SOME TIME on the road, the rattle and clink of a wagon sounded ahead. Cautiously, I moved aside. Traffic from Konrall was rare, and I wasn't sure what to expect. Perhaps the baker was heading toward the mill for his flour. I quickly fled the road. The mist welcomed me as I slipped through the trees in the direction of the wall. The rattle of the wagon grew louder as it neared.

Peeking through the trees, I sighed in relief when I spotted the traveling merchant's wagon but didn't step out to greet him. I didn't want to startle the horses. Exhausted, I trudged the rest of the way home to arrive before dinner and Father's return.

"Where did Father send you?" Bryn asked, opening the cottage door before I could knock.

"Please, sister," I said. "I'm tired, thirsty, and hungry. Let me in so I can sit."

She scowled at me but moved aside so I could shuffle into the dim cottage. The sky had grown increasingly dark during my journey home, and now a thick, light grey blanket of clouds covered the sun. With no candles to spare, Bryn had lit a fire in the hearth to try to brighten the kitchen. I sat in a chair and sighed when she sat across from me.

"Well?"

It wasn't that I expected my sister to wait on me. I'd just thought she would have the courtesy to offer to get me a drink after knowing I'd been gone all day. Tiredly, I stood and fetched myself a cup of water.

"Benella. Really, where are your manners? I'm asking you a question," she said.

"Water-On-The-Bridge," I managed to say between gulps.

"How unfair," Bryn cried.

Blye stepped into the room from our bedroom, two panels of

fabric in her hands and pins in her mouth. Bryn spotted the question in her eyes and explained.

"Father sent Benella to Water-On-The-Bridge." Bryn turned back to me. "We're both older. We should have been allowed to go."

I set down the cup with a laugh.

"You would have walked twelve miles and back in a single day without any food or water? I doubt not."

Bryn had the decency to look slightly embarrassed. "I thought Father sent you in a wagon."

"With what coin?" I said, exasperated. Her face took on a flushed hue, and Blye's eyes rounded. "I'm tired," I said quickly before she could respond. I turned to head to our room.

Blye spit the pins out into one of her hands.

"You can't go in there. I'm using your bed to lay out my dress pattern." I stared at her. Using my bed to make another new dress for herself? Perhaps, if I hadn't been so tired, my temper would have sparked, but I couldn't find the energy.

Instead of answering, I turned and let myself into Father's study, closing the door behind me. His chair wasn't very comfortable to sleep in, but the rug before his hearth would suit me fine. I lay down on the floor and closed my eyes.

CHAPTER FIVE

The shoulder pressing into the rug ached with cold, and my eyes felt hot and gritty as I blinked them open. Outside, the wind blew, rattling the branches, and a slight breeze came down the unlit chimney in Father's study.

"Come eat some warm soup," he encouraged, helping me to my feet.

In the kitchen, Bryn and Blye waited at the table. The unusual sight gave me pause. They never held dinner for me. As soon as I sat, Bryn started serving a thick vegetable soup.

"I assume everything went well at the Water, Bini?" Father asked while we waited.

"The Head was absent, but Tibit said they were pleased you were considering their offer."

"What offer?" Blye inquired.

"A private teaching position."

Bryn paused in her ladling.

"That's the one you considered before we moved here, isn't it? Four years is a long time for a position to remain open. What's wrong with it?"

"The position is fine. The pay is slightly more than I make now," he assured us.

I watched my sisters' eyes glimmer with excitement, but I felt wary.

"Why didn't you take it four years ago, then?" I asked.

Bryn passed the soup around. It filled the void in my stomach and warmed my blood.

He gave me a slight, sad smile.

"The cottage is not fit for a family of four." Before my sisters could ask how he meant for us to live there if there wasn't enough room for all of us, he added, "But now you are of an age to marry."

Blye clapped her hands with a huge smile.

"You've accepted the baker's request for Benella, then?"

My stomach dropped, and the soup I'd recently eaten soured in it. Surely, he wouldn't force me to wed the Baker after what I'd told him.

"Benella is still too young to wed, just as you were too young in my mind four years ago."

Blye's face turned to stone. "Surely, you don't expect one of us to wed the baker."

"I will not force a groom onto you if you have no care for him. That said, are there any you care for?"

"I'd accept Tennen if he asked," Bryn said demurely.

"I'm afraid that match wouldn't suit you, dearest. The Coalre family is as out of coin as the rest of us, and I would not have you going into a marriage with false ideas or hopes," he said calmly between sips of broth.

I stayed focused on my own meal, but from the corner of my eye saw my sister's face flush at Father's blunt words. Part of me wanted to cheer him in his softly worded criticism of her shallow nature, but I squelched that part, knowing it unkind to Bryn. As Father stated, she did work hard, most of the time, to keep the cottage a home. What would happen when she and Blye both wed? Who would mend for Father and cook for him? I could do a fair job at a meal if a person didn't mind a lack of variety. Mending bored me to tears, but I could sew a straight line. I'd never have the skill of either Bryn or Blye, though. Unless my future husband was a tailor, I didn't see that my lack of skill would matter.

"If you have no preferences, I'd like to announce your intent to marry and see what offers we receive," Father said into the silence.

"How soon?" Bryn whispered.

"In the morning, I'll talk to the baker. By evening, the rest of the village should know."

A FLAT-FACED SHEEP farmer from the south came to offer for Blye after Father returned home. The short, muscled man spoke plainly of his need for someone who could weave and sew well and promised himself to be a soft-spoken, gentle man. Given his propensity to gaze at the ground when speaking to Blye instead of meeting her gaze, I agreed with his self-assessment. After listening to his offer, Blye kindly declined.

Bryn consoled Blye after the man left, saying at least someone had come for her. Though Father had discounted Tennen, I felt sure Bryn still held out some small hope that he would appear and offer for her nonetheless. She quietly served another dinner of vegetable soup; and I knew, dress or no, I needed to attempt to set traps the following day.

I CREPT from bed during the twilight hour when the birds sang gustily before the dawn. Shaking out my dress, I frowned at its dingy, pale blue color. It needed a washing desperately, but I put it on anyway and hustled out the door before Father rose from bed. The cool air prickled my skin; and I set out toward the estate, carefully placing traps on my way, to check the enchanted dirt that spilled from the wall.

When I reached the rough patch of soil, I wasn't disappointed by barren earth. A single line of turnips thinly dotted the expanse, starting from the edge to lead toward the tumbled rock. The row didn't stop there but continued with uprooted turnips lying on their sides over the rocks and into the darkened woods within, a blatant invitation that struck me as very wrong. I stared at the roots while biting on my lower lip. My stomach growled. I wanted the food, no doubt about it, but I wasn't willing to fall into some sort of trap, which was how it appeared to me. I recalled all of the other times I'd harvested there and walked the boundary, looking to pluck any bounty I could find.

Rifling through my bag, my hand clasped around a spare ribbon I used to tie back my hair. The color had faded and the ends were frayed, but I laid it down on the ground anyway.

"It's not much, but all I have," I whispered, "for the things I've taken in the past. Thank you."

Before I changed my mind, or my hunger changed it for me, I darted away. Behind me, I heard the vines moving and ran faster, hoping the estate wouldn't hold a grudge over everything I'd taken. It was the only explanation I had for its odd behavior.

I should have known I couldn't outrun magic. The vines flew along the ground and caught me by the ankles while others stretched down from lofty heights within the canopy to curl around my upper arms and lift me high.

"Please," I whispered as they shuffled me back toward the wall. "I meant no offense."

Ahead I saw the turnip filled dirt and crumbling wall. The

vines didn't set me down there. They kept shuffling me forward over the wall and through the dark misty trees as the sky began to lighten. Finally, before a large gnarled oak growing at the edge of a pond, they released me. I landed with a splash in the waist-deep waters and scowled. Dripping wet, I stood weighed down by my heavy skirts.

"Confounded dress," I muttered, struggling toward the shore.

The tree groaned, a low noise of wood rubbing on wood, then gave several small splintering cracks as the surface of the trunk began to shift. I stopped my approach and stood still in the knee-deep water to watch with wide eyes as a face formed within the wood. Rough, slashed bark eyes squinted at me, and a great long nose twitched as if the eyes couldn't believe what they saw. Below the nose a wide mouth opened slowly, looking as if the tree was breaking and about to topple. Instead, it spoke.

"Teach him," it said in a series of cracks and groans. The leaves above trembled with its effort.

"Who?" I whispered, fear and awe having stolen the volume from my voice.

"Free us," it continued as if it didn't hear me. The trunk tilted forward again as the mouth closed and the nose sank back into the bark, leaving only the slitted eyes until they too winked out of existence.

Looking around at the woods, I waited for more, but nothing else happened for several long minutes. Shivering, I climbed out of the water and walked back toward the wall. This time, I took the turnips, every one of them.

From the traps, I managed to gather two rabbits, which pleased me until I wondered how to skin them without dirtying my dress. After my dunking, it was clean once again. While I contemplated my dilemma, I continued home, glad to see a faint glow in the kitchen window. Bryn willingly surrendered her apron, only raising a brow at my damp state, and I set to work, eager to eat rabbit for breakfast.

Father stepped from his study as I handed over the dressed game to Bryn along with her now dirty apron.

"Father, do you know of the estate's history?" I asked, ignoring Bryn's peevish glance.

He shook his head.

"Only what we know from the villagers, that the beast guards the estate for the Liege Lord to prevent theft and whatnot," he said absently, looking in our food storage for something to eat.

He was right. The information he knew was nothing I hadn't already heard. When we'd moved here, I'd been young enough that I hadn't cared about the beast or the estate beyond the need to stay away from them. However, since both the estate and the beast seemed to have taken an interest in me, I needed to learn more.

"I'll bring some of the rabbit to the school when it's ready if you'd like," I said to him.

He nodded his thanks and left as I moved closer to the stove to dry and enjoy the scent of cooking meat. Bryn left to milk the goat and check for an egg from our single hen. In the warm silence, I contemplated which of the villagers might know more regarding either the estate or the beast. Miss Medunge, the baker's sister, loved gossiping and probably knew everything about everyone, but I didn't want to chance meeting up with the baker. The butcher hadn't lived here as long as we had, and the seamstress didn't have any interest in anything other than her cloth and customers. The Coalres were out of the question for obvious reasons. That left the candle maker.

AFTER TAKING a covered plate to Father, I cautiously hurried to the candle maker. I'd yet to face Tennen or Splane after their last attempt to have the beast kill me and wanted to keep it that way.

The candle maker's bell above the door rang as I let myself in after a brief knock. He looked up from his work with a smile.

"I hadn't thought to see you so soon," he said. "But I'm glad you're here, nonetheless. I have something for you." He stood with a grunt and shuffled to a low shelf near the back of the room. Lying on the rough board, a blunt silver glimmered in the daylight. He plucked it from the wood between two time-twisted fingers and shuffled toward me, wearing an excited grin.

"Timmy couldn't believe the primrose candle," he said, handing me the coin, which I took reluctantly. "If you find more flowers, bring them to me and there will be more silver for you," he promised.

I fisted the silver but didn't turn to go.

"I was wondering if you could tell me a little about the history of the estate. Or perhaps, something of the beast."

"It would brighten the rest of my morning to spend it telling you stories from my youth. But, come, sit. I can't forget my work while we talk."

He nudged another chair close to his worktable, and I willingly sat with him. The candle maker's cottage was always pleasantly warm. He checked his strings and started his tale.

"I was about your age when the Liege Lord disappeared, but I remember the years before that well enough to be glad of his absence. He was a man far too concerned with his own pleasures than that of the people who looked to him for protection and justice. Justice," the candle maker scoffed. "Back then it was a mockery. The Head at the Water used the position to swindle the businesses and bully the people he didn't like. The Liege Lord did nothing. He couldn't. He was too busy strutting from bed to bed, not caring what women occupied it with him."

I kept quiet, afraid he'd recall his audience and stop his open retelling.

"I shouldn't say that," he said. "He did care. Only the pretty ones. Young. Old. Single. Married. He made no distinction." He snorted disgustedly. "I'm ahead of myself. The estate has been there over three hundred years and has passed from father to son. While the last Liege Lord's father had lived, things were peaceful and prosperous. After his father died, the Liege Lord started his whoring. His mother, too ashamed of her son, retired to the South and died there not long after. The young Lord just sank deeper into his depravity. Things were getting to the point where I was thinking of heading south, too—the southern liege lords are good to their tenants—but then he disappeared. He just stopped going to the villages. Stopped his whoring. The Head went to the estate but found it empty. He thought to make himself a little coin and take a few things, and that was the first time the beast made himself known. Oh, that Head ran down the road, here, screaming something fierce. Took several men to hold him down and pour ale down his throat before he calmed enough to tell what happened. 'Course no one believed him, and a group went to the estate to see for themselves."

He cackled at the memory.

"That's when the legend of the beast really started. The Head went back to the Water, but soon came with all sorts of people interested in trying to kill the beast to get to the Liege Lord's treasure. But that beast protected it something fierce. Many men died trying to get past the gate. As time passed and the flow of would-be pillagers slowed, some folks managed to get in the gate, but never very far. I think the beast knew they were just curious for the most part and didn't harm them. But those that return for a second visit, well, he doesn't treat them as well."

"What about the Liege Lord? Where did he go?"

"Some say he went south to mourn his mother, but fifty years is a long time to mourn. No, I think he's at the estate," he said softly. "I think he never left. That beast keeps him as cornered in the estate as he does keeping folks out. I just can't figure out why."

I thanked him for his time, and at the last moment, remembering the coin curled in my fist, thanked him for that as well. He certainly had given me plenty to think on.

Leaving the candle maker, I collided with Sara, the smith's wife. I didn't pay her as much attention as I did Splane, who trailed behind her. He glared at me as I smoothed my skirt with both hands while absently apologizing to Sara. The feel of fabric against the sweaty palm that used to hold a coin froze me in place. I'd dropped it.

"Excuse me, Benella," Sara said stiffly, a deep hue of crimson flooding her face.

Did she too know what I'd witnessed? I felt horrible.

A glint in the dust at our feet caught my eyes. I looked down at it, making my notice obvious.

"I think you dropped something."

Sara's eyes followed mine and rounded. She didn't hesitate, but snatched up the blunt silver.

"We don't need your charity," Splane said mulishly.

His mother's fingers curled tightly around the coin. Easy words for him when he didn't need to spread his legs for the baker.

"Charity?" I asked, feigning puzzlement. "How would I come by a blunt silver?" I let the doubt in my voice speak for itself.

"Don't be ridiculous, Splane," his mother scolded. She didn't look at me or thank me, simply changed directions and went to the baker, through the front door. Splane hurried to follow her.

I hoped that would help end some of the animosity they had toward me. Walking back to the cottage, I pondered the candle maker's tale, unsure who in that story I needed to free or teach. Part of me was inclined to believe it was the Liege Lord trapped in the estate like the candle maker suggested, but why would I want to free such a bane? Perhaps that's what he needed to be taught...proper behavior.

As I neared the cottage, the goat bleated pathetically in the back, so I walked around to investigate. There, within sight of the open doors, Tennen had Bryn pinned to a mound of fresh hay. Her skirts were hiked up to her waist and her legs wrapped around Tennen's rapidly pumping, naked backside. Neither noticed me.

I pivoted back around the corner and pressed myself against the wall, out of sight and in shock. The goat's bleat drowned out most of their mingled moans. After a few moments it quieted, their moans and the goat's protests over their use of her bedding.

"Tennen," I heard Bryn say softly. "My father wants me to marry soon."

"You are of an age."

I cringed for my sister loving such a fool.

"As are you," she said.

In the silence, I heard the soft rustle of clothes being righted.

"I would be a good wife," Bryn said.

"Why would I want to marry you when I've already fucked you? It's nothing special anymore."

Hearing her soft gasp, I quickly moved to the front of the cottage and let myself in. Not trusting either of them, I hid in Father's study. How could Bryn give him so much of herself? Hadn't she seen the type of man he was? He reminded me of the Liege Lord in the candle maker's story. How many Bryns had he left behind? Poor Bryn. I wanted to go out and comfort her, but she would not react kindly to my knowing her shame. She'd given herself and been rejected for it.

So, I waited quietly in the office. When the cloud-covered sky dimmed enough to indicate Father's impending return, I slipped out the window. The dress hampered me—it was more of an inelegant tangle and fall out of the window—but I managed to leave the house without being detected. I circled the woods in front of the cottage to step out onto the path and reapproached our home from a distance.

Bryn didn't look up from whatever it was she stirred on the stove, but it didn't matter. The desolation on her face was plain to see.

"Is Blye home?" I asked, truly wondering where she'd been through Tennen's visit.

"No. She took a few of her creations to the seamstress this morning and hasn't been back." She barely whispered the words, and as soon as she finished speaking, she went out the back door without a word.

I didn't stay to listen to her soft sobs but fled once again to Father's study to read about plants.

AT DINNER, Father announced his plans to travel to Water-On-The-Bridge the next day. He had many books in his library and knew he couldn't leave them all to move in one trip, so he hired a wagon and asked if either of my sisters would like to join him. Both promptly said yes, though for very different reasons. Blye explained she wanted to speak with the seamstresses there to see if she could apprentice for room and board, a sure way to lengthen the time limit of remaining unwed so she could seek a suitable contender. Bryn stated plainly that no one in Konrall would ask for her, and she would like the chance to meet the eligible men the Water had to offer.

Father agreed to take them both and asked that I stay to teach his class. With a feeling of dread, I agreed.

THE NEXT MORNING, we worked together to load the wagon, which Splane had driven over at dawn. Bryn made no comment about Tennen's whereabouts. With the back loaded with books carefully packed in crates and covered with oiled cloth, Father eyed the dark skies.

"We'd best be off," he said to my sisters. He handed me his lesson plan for the day, hugged me farewell, and climbed aboard to take the reins. They left me standing by the cottage door, and only Father gave a backward glance.

"Watch for us near dinner," he called before they disappeared into the trees.

I walked the path to the schoolhouse, warily watching for Tennen and Splane, unsure if the blunt silver had helped our relationship or not. When Splane dropped off the wagon, he'd spent so much time gaping at Bryn, he hadn't spared me a glance. The Coalre boys couldn't keep a secret, it would seem.

The butcher's daughter, Magdaline, stood at the school doors waiting for me. Twelve and shy, she chirped a surprised greeting at me, her eyes wide.

"I'm teaching in my father's place today," I said with an amused smile. "I hope that's okay."

She nodded enthusiastically.

The day went quickly with only a handful of students in attendance. I followed my father's lesson plan and enjoyed the children's wit. It felt odd thinking of them as children when only a few years separated us.

Finally, I dismissed them and closed the schoolhouse doors. A steady rain fell outside. Walking the path in the evening light didn't bother me as much as the rain did. I jogged along the path, reaching the cottage quickly. The kitchen felt cool and damp since the stove had gone out. I relit the fire and warmed my fingers before searching for something to eat.

A slight scrape on the floor alerted me that I wasn't alone. Spinning, I watched Tennen take another step closer to me, having just come from Father's study. His dry hair and cruel leer told me enough of his intentions that I knew I needed to run. Again. The door leading to the backyard waited to my left and the door to the front of the cottage to my right.

Frozen, we eyed each other. One chance. I cursed my dress, steeled myself, and feinted to the right. Tennen bolted into action, moving toward the front door as I shifted my weight and sprinted for the back.

Behind me, I heard him slip and curse, but I didn't stop. The back door banged loudly against the outside wall as I shoved it open and flew into the rain. I hiked my skirts high to free my legs. North. Refuge. The rain-slicked ground slid easily underfoot as I tried to run. The sound of Tennen's close pursuit set my heart racing. I'd never make it. I danced around the sparse trees and ducked under the occasional branch, panting and struggling to keep my footing while hoping Tennen wouldn't.

A wall of mist stood before me, and I shouldered into it, losing myself for a moment.

The skirts grew heavier as they soaked up the falling rain, and my arms burned with their weight. I slid and fell forward, too late dropping the skirts as the ground rose to meet me. I landed hard on my stomach and my face hit the ground with enough force that it bounced. Thankfully, hitting the spongey ground didn't hurt much.

Tennen, who'd been on my heels, tripped on my skirts before I could scramble to my feet and landed heavily atop me. The impact drove the air from my lungs in a great oof. We lay like an X on the ground, his torso crossed over mine, effectively pinning me.

He laughed above me.

"You never had a chance."

I couldn't answer. I could barely breathe with his weight on me. I tried struggling, but the mud that cushioned my fall made it impossible to do anything more than flail.

"Ho, ho! What's this?" he said, touching one of my bared legs.

I struggled harder, but his hand just slid over my mud-coated skin, inching its way upward.

He put his free hand in my hair and pulled back hard, forcing me to arch off the ground. He leaned in toward my ear, never stopping his exploration. "No stockings? Naughty, Benella. Maybe I had the wrong sister."

His hot breath fanned my cheek, and my anger boiled. I arched further back, trying to hit his head with my own as I'd done before. He laughed.

"Not this time."

His fingers found the edge of my covering and slid underneath to stroke my buttocks. I screamed in fury, twisting sharply. The move pulled out some of my hair. He tried to hold me tight, but the mud and the rain made me too slippery to grip. I struggled further, clawing a handful of mud and decaying vegetation. Twisting, I slapped my handful of glop across his face, effectively blinding him. He grunted and pushed my head away, releasing my hair.

As he shifted to the side to wipe at his eyes, I took the opportunity and scrambled out from under him. Full of mud, I struggled to gain my feet and when I did, I slid more than I walked.

"You think you're any different from the rest of us?" he cried.

"No," I yelled back at him while looking for something I could use to bash him over the head. "How can I possibly be any different? Look at me." The frustration over his blind, illogical hatred pooled in my blood.

"We all look at you," he said. "You're too good to look back. And when you do, it's to look down your nose at us."

He climbed to his feet, towering over me, hate plain on his face. His statement stunned me, and I stared at him with a frown. I'd never looked down on anyone. Had I? I gave what I could to the butcher to help those less fortunate. I'd even helped Tennen's mother. How could that be looking down on anyone? I opened my mouth to protest but stopped when I felt something circle my waist. Tennen laughed as I looked down. Vines looped around me and began tugging me backward. Were they here to protect me and give me refuge? With the estate, I never knew what to expect.

My gaze flew to Tennen, and his eyes narrowed on me.

"How many times have you gone to the estate and walked away uninjured?"

"Never uninjured," I said with a snort. I didn't clarify that the injuries were due to him and his brother or self-inflicted.

The vines pulled, and I slid several inches along the ground. Another vine crept along the ground beside me, extending toward Tennen. He saw the vine and eyed me dispassionately.

"I hope you're hurt even worse this time."

Then he turned and walked away, leaving me behind.

I tried standing, but the vines didn't loosen. The one that had crept toward Tennen curved and wrapped around me instead. The single vines twisted together to create a thick rope that hefted me into the air and once again moved me toward the estate in a slow shuffle.

CHAPTER
SIX

The vines deposited me just inside the firmly closed gate. Muddy rivulets ran from my clothes, and I tilted my face toward the falling rain to wash away the mud still clinging to my skin.

A voice from the gloom startled me.

"What would you have of me this time?" the beast asked.

I spotted a large, dark shape to my right and tried to focus on it through the rain as I began to shiver. The warmth I'd worked up from the run had left during the slow passage here.

"Refuge," I said, stammering with cold. "I can't return home until my father does."

The beast grunted, and the shape to my right moved, growing larger as it rose from its crouched position.

"Follow me," he said, moving into the falling darkness.

Hesitantly, I followed, wrapping my arms around myself as my wet skirts clung to my legs. His shape always remained far enough in front of me that I could never quite see him clearly. Eventually, a large structure loomed before us, its details hidden in the enchanted mist that filled the estate at its whim.

Ahead, something made a soft creak of protest. I followed the noise and found an open door leading to a vast, dark, cold room. I stepped inside, glad to be free of the rain.

"Light the fire and warm yourself," his disembodied voice said from the darkness. "Walk straight ahead. You will find what you need."

Arms extended, I shuffled forward in the dark until I touched stone. Running my fingers lightly along the porous surface, I discovered I stood before an enormous hearth. Head level, a stone mantel held what I needed to light the fire. I blew on my fingers to dry them before attempting a spark. It took several tries to start the waiting tinder; but when I did, I felt an overwhelming surge of relief. The tiny bit of light the small flame threw into the room helped dispel some of the gloom. I looked out into the wall of black surrounding me and wondered where he waited. The faint outline of the still open door was the only other object I could see outside the circle of light.

For the next several minutes, I fed the hungry flame. Soon, it cast enough heat that I could sit back on my heels and warm my hands.

"I will check for word on your father's return. Stay here in your refuge," he growled in a curiously angry tone. The door slammed closed.

Why had he gotten angry? Looking around, I saw nothing that might suggest an answer. Standing, I moved to the woodbin set back from the fire and took some larger pieces to place on the established flames. In a few minutes, only a few black shadows remained in the furthest corners of the room, and I clearly saw my surroundings.

I stood in a large kitchen, and it appeared as if it had been ransacked. Pots lay on their sides on the floor, a table near one wall had been splintered in two, and claw marks savaged just about every surface. My stomach dipped a little at the evidence not to trust the beast's precarious kindnesses.

With the new light, I saw how caked with mud I remained. My dress was heavy with it, and it clung to my legs. The muck would itch when it dried. Walking around the kitchen, I found a hand pump for water and a large kettle with a handle. Doggedly, I worked to fill the kettle then struggled with its weight as I crossed the room and set it on the metal arm above the fire. Using a rod to nudge the arm, I swung the pot toward the back of the hearth so it dangled just above the dancing flames.

Searching again, I found a few cloths that appeared relatively clean and a very large wooden tub. I stared at the tub for a long while, debating. He'd promised refuge, but could I trust it enough to wash? No. I left the tub where it lay upside down in a corner of the room and fetched another pot of water.

I tried washing with the first tepid pot, but my dress was too coated with mud. Every time it touched a newly cleaned spot of skin, it left a mud streak. Sighing, I dragged the tub over to the fire. I filled it a quarter of the way with cold water and then dumped in a pot of boiling water. With patience, I slowly filled the tub halfway with water, then I stood staring at it. The mud on my scalp had dried, pulling my skin tight. I wanted to be clean but didn't know when the beast would return. Eyeing the door, I went to the broken table and dragged half of it over to the tub. Standing on its short edge, it made a modest privacy screen. I could use it to dry my dress, too.

The water began to cool as I debated. I knew I shouldn't. I would regret it without a doubt. Something bad would happen. Surely only an idiot would undress in a strange house with an angry beast lurking about. But he'd promised refuge. My scalp ached where Tennen had pulled out the hair, and the mud on my legs was making me itchy. Even with the fire blazing, it didn't warm the room or dry me fast enough to drive away the chill.

The curling steam from the filled tub had me hurriedly undressing.

"Idiot," I mumbled to myself.

A sigh escaped me as I sank naked into the water. With the hearth on one side and the table on the other to reflect back the heat, I relaxed a little. The tub was easily twice the size of the one we had at the cottage. I quickly ducked under the surface to rinse my hair. When I popped back up, I eyed the slightly dingy water. Rubbing my skin, I washed as best I could.

I was about to stand when the beast spoke from the darkness.

"How many times have I spared you?"

Like a startled hare, I froze, heart hammering. Blood rushed loudly in my ears, but still I strained to listen.

"Well?" he said in a growl.

"F-four," I whispered.

"Four," he agreed. "And I offered you any one thing you would have from the estate."

Shifting to my hip, I cautiously looked around but couldn't see him in either direction open to me. I looked at the table and could envision him crouched just behind it.

"What can you offer me in payment?"

"Payment?" I said, suddenly very afraid and wishing I hadn't given the blunt silver away.

"Yes," he said, growing annoyed. "Payment. What do you have?"

"Nothing," I whispered in horror. Surely he couldn't offer me refuge then fling me over the wall to my death because I hadn't been aware it required payment.

A clicking growl echoed in the kitchen.

"Come now. Not nothing."

My heart sank as I realized what he wanted.

"*I* am not payment."

"And why not? Did I not care for you? Heal you?"

"Yes," I said slowly.

"Stand, so I can see you."

"No," I said, sinking lower in the water.

His angry roar filled the kitchen.

"You would deny me after all I've given you?"

"You mean what you gave me freely," I said bravely. "You never asked me if I wanted to be healed. You gave that freely. I never asked you to spare me."

"But I did offer you one thing," he said.

"And forced me to accept it in order for my release. You cannot demand a price for things freely given."

Smothering silence claimed the room for several awful, long minutes. The water began to cool. I continued to watch for the beast, but he made no sound. My fingers wrinkled.

"Are you still here?" I asked as my bravery began to fade.

"Yes," he said with an angry growl.

"You offered me refuge. Please leave so I can dress."

"No," he said smugly. "I will not freely give you my absence. I will need payment to leave."

I snorted before I could stop myself.

"Payment. To leave."

"Yes. Stand so I can look at you."

"I am not a whore."

"How does rising from the water make you a whore?" He laughed.

Glaring at the table, I had no answer. It didn't make me a whore, but I would feel used and cheap. I thought of my sister and cringed. I didn't want to let anyone take advantage of me like that. The fire started to die down, the flames licking the wood receded until just a few remained to dance on top the red hot coals.

"You ask too much for too little in return," I said.

"What would you have of me?"

His willingness to bargain gave me hope.

"A dry shirt to cover me. Something to eat if you have it."

"Done," he agreed too quickly. "Now stand."

His impatience worried me.

"Not yet. I want to see the shirt you have to offer me."

He roared this time.

"Do you think me a fool? When I leave to fetch it, you will rise from the water and dress."

"Had I thought of that, I probably would have," I admitted. I'd been too worried to think that far, but as soon as he would have left the room, I was sure I would have done just that. Given his anger, I was glad he didn't leave and give me the chance.

"I will remain in this water until you return as long as it doesn't take so long that the fire dies."

Silence greeted me again. I waited a few moments and asked, "Are you there?"

No answer. Despite my promise, I considered rising from the water and dressing.

The sudden appearance of a shirt tossed over the jagged edge of the table startled me. The white material of the fine shirt seemed out of place against the wood. I quickly reached for it, but it disappeared over the edge again.

"Stand up. Now." His angry growl sounded nearby.

I really had no choice. I could sit in the water until I rotted or his anger got the better of him and he pulled me from the water regardless of his promise of refuge, or I could stand on my own and hope for the shirt.

"I'll stand," I said quietly, gripping the sides of the tub. "And when you feel you've shamed me enough, feel free to reward me with a shirt."

I stood facing the table, hoping it would offer me a bit of modesty since it came to my waist. And it did until he flung it to the side. The dying fire and the long shadow I cast hid him again, and I hoped the lack of light hid me as well. I wanted to close my eyes but dared not. Instead, I looked down and stepped over the edge of the tub.

"Shame," he whispered. "There is no shame in this. Only desperation." He sounded slightly sad.

I didn't have time to reflect on it because the shirt sailed out of the darkness and landed on my head, blinding me. The door opened and closed before I could pull it from my face. Quickly putting my arms through the sleeves, I threaded the buttons through their holes before turning to add more wood to the fire. As I guessed, I stood in the kitchen, alone once again.

My dress lay in a heap on the floor. I thought of putting it back on, but then wondered what I'd do. Unless my father had returned, there was as little safety for me outside the estate as there was inside. Sighing, I tossed my dress into the bath water. After rinsing it as best I could, I wrung it out and hung it over the edge of the table, which I again pushed close to the fire.

It took me a while to empty the tub with the bucket, but eventually I had all the water outside, and I turned the tub upside down and used it as a chair. The long shirt fell to the tops of my knees when I stood. When I sat, it rode a bit higher in back, but protected me enough that I didn't have to sit bare bottomed.

My eyes grew heavy as I waited for the dress to dry, and the stack of wood beside the hearth grew smaller. My stomach growled, and I recalled my request for food. Standing, I searched for something on the kitchen shelves and found a surprising bounty of hard cheese and dried fruit. I took a small portion of each and sat back by the fire.

After about an hour passed, the door flew open again. My heart pounded within its boney cage, and I moved to turn around, but his words stopped me.

"Do not turn. Stay as you are." He sounded angry. Beyond angry, actually. His growl was so severe it was hard to understand him.

I stayed still, staring at the flames while I strained to hear him move. Suddenly he spoke from right behind me as he gently touched my hair, his tone conflicting with his touch.

"Your payment went to waste."

Unsure what he meant, I remained quiet. He touched a tender spot near the crown of my head, and I flinched.

"Hurt again, girl?"

"Benella," I murmured, very uncomfortable with him standing so close behind me.

"Not a pretty name," he said with less of a growl.

"It's after my father and mother," I said slowly as his touch feathered over my head as if trying to find where I was hurt. "My mother had hoped after two daughters, the third would be a boy and planned to name him after my father, Benard. When I arrived, she'd been so upset that my father had suggested I still carry part of his name and hers as well, Nadelle. Benella is better than Nadard."

The beast gave a surprised grunt, and he parted my hair. I knew what he intended and leaned forward out of his way.

"I cannot accept any more from you without knowing the price."

He snorted.

"I give this freely." He tugged me back and touched his tongue to my head for a second time. I wondered what he'd do if he got a strand of hair in his mouth, but then supposed licking my head wasn't so different from licking his own furry hide.

It soothed the bare patches so much that I began to doze and leaned back against him. His warmth cradled me, and I fell asleep.

AT SOME POINT during the night, strangely muffled sounds of cawing roused me from a deep sleep. Curled on my side, I snuggled deeper into the pile of furs lying under me. From the darkness, something growled softly and silenced the bird as a large, warm hand soothed my hair. I sank back into my slumber.

In the morning, I stretched with a yawn and groaned. The cold cobble floor made me ache, and I sat up with a shiver and a frown. Hadn't there been a pile of furs last night? Studying the kitchen, lit now by the sun that shone through several windows set high on the walls, I saw only my dress, boots, and underthings. No furs.

Recalling the hand on my head, my mouth popped open. The beast. I sprang to my feet and looked around, the shirt brushing my legs. Everything clicked back into place, and I hurried to dress as I worried what Father might be thinking.

I hesitated to take the shirt as I couldn't remember how I'd asked for it. Unsure if it really belonged to me now or not, I folded it neatly and set it on the broken table with a look of regret.

WHEN I WALKED into the cottage looking disheveled, Bryn only spared me a censuring glance; and I knew I'd arrived in an untidy state too often in recent days. She washed dishes in a small tub on a plank counter near the stove. The table was empty and only the lingering hint of cooked food perfumed the air.

"Go borrow one of Father's shirts. You'll need to wash your dress before you can wear it anywhere. Father wants us looking presentable tonight. We're to dine with the Kinlyn family." Her flat tone told me what she thought of the idea, so I didn't ask any questions about why we were going. At least I would get to eat.

Father's bedroom door stood open, the trunk for his clothes at the foot of his bed clearly visible. Feeling intrusive, I knelt before the trunk and tipped the lid back. I hadn't ever looked in Father's trunk, as I never did the laundry. Bryn washed everything, folded it, and tucked it neatly away.

Inside the trunk, two distinct piles of clothes defined my father's sad wardrobe. On the right, his two neatly folded white shirts and spare pair of trousers waited for their next use. The left pile doubled what the right had to offer with the addition of two neckcloths, worn and frayed, lying on top. Everything in the left pile had been patched or mended in some way. Loose threads dangled from frayed sleeve cuffs and patches adorned knees.

Carefully moving aside the neckcloths, I took the top shirt from the mended pile and shook it out. It would service for wearing on my treks in the woods and for around the cottage. I placed the neckcloths neatly back into the trunk and closed the lid.

In my room, I glanced once at Blye's trunk of cloth and pushed back my resentment. I knew she mended his clothes and did a good job of it too, but she could easily make Father a new shirt. Was it fair to resent her when I'd ignored my own opportunity to help Father? After all, I'd slept in a very fine shirt Father could have used. Granted, it would have been a bit large, but Blye could make a shirt smaller. She'd proven that already.

Dressed in my familiar trousers and a borrowed, threadbare shirt, I bunched up my dress and took it outside where Bryn usually did the washing in good weather. Then, I began the long process of hauling water and soaping, scrubbing, twisting, and rinsing the dress. The process had to be repeated several times until the cloth began to look blue again. Giving it a final wring, I tossed it over a line Bryn had tied outside and wiped my hands on my pants.

My stomach growled, and I eyed the sky. Inside, the cottage remained quiet, and I wondered where Blye had gone. Wrinkling my nose at the thought of going inside, I set off walking east away from the village and the estate to see what the woods might offer me to eat. Though my intentions to stay away from the estate were pure, my mind kept going back to the shirt and the cheese; and soon, my feet were taking me north.

First, I checked the ground by the tumbled rock and found peas growing so thick that the plants twined together into a solid blanket. I stopped to pick a few, nibbling them to take the edge off my hunger, then stuffed a handful into each pocket, regretting my lack of a bag.

Continuing on, I walked the perimeter of the wall until I reached the gate, which swung open in a slow, loud arc to announce my presence. Assuming nothing, I stayed standing outside of the estate and looked over my shoulder, eyeing the peaceful trees behind me. Shadows claimed those nearest the estate, but in the distance I could make out some sun dappled branches.

Swallowing hard and hoping no one stood near enough to hear, I looked back into the shadowy estate and called out, "Are you there?"

Silence answered me.

"The shirt...I left it because I wasn't sure if you meant for me to keep it or not. If you did..." Nothing inside the estate stirred. My stomach growled, and I reached into my pocket for another peapod. I chewed thoughtfully, enjoying the crisp sweetness while wondering if he waited somewhere inside, listening to me.

After several long moments, I gave up and turned back the way I'd come. I harvested more peas and carried home what I'd picked in the loose ends of my shirt.

Leaving all but a handful of my harvest on the kitchen table for Bryn to do with as she would, I secluded myself in Father's study, picking a book at random to entertain myself until dinner. Occasionally, Bryn or Blye's quiet voices would break through my concentration, but never long enough to listen to what they said.

Father arrived home and, with a twinkle in his eyes, complimented me on my new shirt. I met his smile with a grin of my own as I replaced the book I'd just finished and went to check on my dress. The damp air hadn't helped the cloth dry through, so I was forced to wear a slightly soggy dress to the Kinlyn's.

They lived close to two miles outside of town to the south, a long walk for Bryn and Blye, who never ventured further than the village on foot. Both walked side-by-side quietly matching steps as if on a march. Father and I walked behind them. Other than his cheery greeting to me when I'd returned home, he'd said little. Unlike their subdued moods, I happily looked forward to dinner. Anticipation of a good meal was only part of it. This would be my first official dinner at someone else's home.

Mrs. Kinlyn, who I'd never met directly but had seen in the village on a few occasions, stood in the doorway of their modest home, watching for us. The trees had been cleared from around the house for quite a distance to allow for an animal shed and several fields. Uprooted trees at the edge of the fields, bordering the woods beyond, foretold of bigger fields for next year's crops.

"Welcome," Mrs. Kinlyn said with a smile as she motioned for us to enter. She looked close to Father's age, perhaps a bit older, with windburned, brown skin. Tiny white lines fanned from the corners of her eyes from squinting in the sun. I found her happy smile infectious and smiled in return. My sisters murmured polite greetings.

Inside the square home, a single wall divided the room in half. At one end of the room, a long table with several chairs around it took up most of the space along with the hearth. The other side of the room held the kitchen with a modern iron oven. Two closed doors interrupted the plain wall, and I guessed they led to bedrooms.

At the table, six men sat waiting. Well, almost men since the youngest looked about nine. They all appeared freshly washed, and I bet they wore their best clothes like we did. The Kinlyn children had all inherited their mother's smile.

"Please, sit. Everything's ready. Henick, help me with the roast, please," Mrs. Kinlyn said.

One of the older boys stood to help his mother while Mr. Kinlyn rose to greet Father and shake his hand. Introductions were made. Henick, the oldest at twenty, smiled when his father said his name. Renald, the next at eighteen, nodded politely, his smile never wavering. Kennen, close to my own age, winked at me when his father said his name. I wanted to wink back, but all eyes were on me so I just smiled in return. The introductions ended with Bolen and, finally, Parlen.

Mr. Kinlyn directed us to our seats with Father and me sitting near Mr. and Mrs. Kinlyn, and Bryn and Blye sitting at the other end of the table with Henick and Renald. Seeing the arrangement, I knew I had been correct in the purpose behind the dinner. The youngest, Parlen, sat to my right with Kennen across from me.

I listened with half an ear to Henick and Renald's attempts to converse with my sisters. They politely asked after the interests of my sisters, but neither answered in enough detail to inspire an intelligent response. So the brothers started explaining about their father's plans for their crops. I couldn't understand Bryn and Blye.

All of the Kinlyn men were handsome enough and had pleasant natures. Why weren't they giving them a chance?

"What do you do here, Parlen?" I asked the sandy blonde boy sitting beside me.

He politely wiped his mouth before answering. "When we need to dig around a tree before pulling it, I help with the digging. Otherwise, it's care for the animals and hunt for game."

"Really? What do you hunt?" interest spurred me to ask.

"Mostly rabbit and wild hen," he said. "But once I came this close to bagging a wild pig." He held his thumb and forefinger up with an inch of space between.

Kennen laughed and picked up the story.

"He's lucky the pig escaped the trap before he tried to wrestle him down. It had tusks enough to bleed him."

"Kennen," Mrs. Kinlyn said in quiet warning.

The only good conversation to be heard and it wasn't fit for the dinner table. I suppressed a sigh and tried again.

"I trap rabbit, mostly. We don't have anything else wild so near the village. If I cross the river to the east, I can usually find some type of bird."

"River?" Parlen perked up.

"It runs south, just east of the village," I said slowly, trying to visualize how far it might be from the Kinlyn farm. "I'd think you'd run into it less than an hour's walk east."

"S'True," Mr. Kinlyn said in his quiet way. "Runs slow and deep for a bit."

"Good fishing?" Renald asked with interest. All of the Kinlyn boys watched their father closely.

Mr. Kinlyn laughed slowly.

"Looks like we should rest the trees tomorrow and try for some fish."

The boys agreed with a laugh. Liking the happy calm

atmosphere of their home, I listened to their plans and ate until my stomach ached.

THE WALK home seemed to take longer, but at least we didn't walk in silence. Father asked Blye what she thought of Renald.

"He seems nice enough, but I'd still like to try to apprentice at a seamstress in Water-On-The-Bridge. The one we visited yesterday wanted to see an example of my work and said she would consider me if it was well done."

Father nodded without comment and then asked Bryn what she thought of Henick.

"If I marry him, I will die before my time," Bryn ominously predicted.

I wanted to ask her how she could possibly know when her *time* was but kept silent.

Father made no comment either.

CHAPTER
SEVEN

THE SUN SET AS WE FOLLOWED THE MAIN ROAD TO THE VILLAGE. In the distance, the baying cry of a lonely dog broke the evening's quiet. The scuff of our footfalls on the packed earth kept us company.

When we returned home, a large chest rested on the ground in front of our door. Attached to the clasp, a single piece of crisp parchment fluttered in the slight breeze. Father plucked up the paper before any of us could move close enough to read it and brought it inside, heading for his study. Bryn and Blye stared at the chest for a moment, neither moving to touch it. Skirting around it as Father had, I followed him to the study. After a brief delay, I heard Bryn and Blye follow.

"It would appear news of your need to marry has spread," he mumbled looking troubled. "This note worries me."

He handed the sheet over for us to read.

Sir,

This trunk is but an example of what I can offer for your daughter should you willingly part with her this very night.

Be warned, once you part, you will never meet again. If you consent, have her await me alone outside your front door in place of the trunk. If I find the trunk as I left it, I will know you have declined.

I COULDN'T MAKE sense of the scrawled signature that decorated the bottom of the page.

Neither Bryn nor Blye spoke as they both left to see what the trunk held. Father followed them while I narrowed my eyes on the writing. Who would mysteriously want to take one of them after the sun fell? And the request hinted that he had no desire to meet Father in person.

Setting the letter on Father's cluttered desk, I slowly followed the sound of an excited squeal.

"Look at this!" Blye cried, pulling out a long length of smooth material that rippled in a cascade when she draped it over her arm.

Leaning close, I eyed the contents of the trunk. Obviously, the mysterious suitor meant for Blye to join him. Neither Bryn nor I had much care for material, though watching Bryn's appraising gaze, I guessed she might be gaining an appreciation for it.

"I've never felt anything so fine," Blye whispered, gently stroking the fabric. "To wear this...I would feel like a princess."

"So you'd accept some unknown man?" Bryn asked.

"Wouldn't you for this kind of wealth?" Blye said with a laugh.

Neither looked at Father, but I watched them all as they spoke. Father studied the contents warily. Blye saw nothing more than the wealth, not even the jealousy in Bryn's gaze.

"I cannot allow it," Father said finally.

Blye's head whipped toward him; her disbelief plain. He held up a hand before she could protest.

"The wealth is alluring, but what if the man or your place in his life is not. I recall Bryn's words about the Kinlyn's hard life.

They are a happy family with wealth enough of their own, but Bryn knew it wasn't enough. You know nothing about him, and I fear sending you off into an unknown life without the assurance that I might check on you occasionally."

Blye said nothing as tears spilled over from her eyes and slowly rolled down her cheeks.

"We will not reject the offer outright, however," he said. "I will write a reply to leave with the trunk explaining a father's need for assurances of wellbeing and happiness."

Blye nodded and began folding the material with Bryn's help as Father turned to retreat into his study once more. Blye could cry her pretty tears, but she was foolish to think wealth enough of a basis to marry a man. Look at the baker. He had plenty of wealth, but would that be enough to lie still each night as he lay beside me? I shivered at the thought. No amount of wealth would make that image pleasant enough to endure.

Leaving them to their cloth, I crept to our room to change from my dress. Having worn it as it finished drying, my skin felt itchy; and I couldn't wait to put on my loose nightgown and scratch my stomach.

In the dim light of the room, something white stood out on my coverlet. Lighting the single candle stub we reserved for emergencies, I found the shirt I'd worn the night before laid out neatly on my bed. My stomach dipped. The beast had heard me at the gate. But why hadn't he answered then? Why bring it to the cottage?

Hearing someone approach, I quickly blew out the candle and plucked the shirt from the bed. Blye shuffled into the room and mumbled that she was tired. I left the room, hiding the shirt from her view and knocked on Father's study.

He called for me to enter in a slightly harassed tone. Feeling guilty for interrupting him, but not wanting either of my sisters to see the shirt before he did, I opened the door and slipped inside.

"I'm sorry for interrupting, but I wanted to give this to you." I held out the shirt.

When he looked up from his writing and his eyes focused on what I held, he set his ink aside. "Not from the chest, but just as fine," he deduced. "Where did it come from?"

"The estate," I said without reservation. I'd gathered so many odd things from the enchanted estate it rarely drew any notice when I came home with something new. Though, everything in the past had been something to eat.

"This is a surprise. Tell me how you came by it exactly," he said, standing and taking it from me. He studied it closely, missing my blush.

I couldn't retell all of the details, just enough to appease his curiosity.

"Tennen was in the cottage when I returned from the school. There was no doubting his intentions. I ran out the back door straight toward the estate, hoping to lose him in the mist." I decided to skip the part where Tennen had almost caught me, too. "The estate let me enter, giving me refuge and that shirt because I was soaked from the rain."

He listened intently and looked up from the shirt when I finished.

"The rain kept us on the road longer than I'd planned," he said. "I had anticipated returning before you returned from the schoolhouse. When we didn't, I worried about you. Then, arriving home late and finding your bed empty..." He sighed. "I'm very relieved you weren't forced into..." He shook his head unable to finish.

"Staying at the estate wasn't so bad," I admitted.

"I advise you to avoid going near it for a while. The beast

neither forgets nor forgives trespassers. You're very fortunate to have walked away as many times as you have."

Watching him walk to his chair behind the desk, I realized he wasn't referring to my jaunts to search for food, but that he knew about my other trespasses. I didn't wonder how. As the schoolteacher, he heard all the whispered rumors from the village children. No doubt someone had witnessed or heard something.

"At the time of each trespass, I feel I made the best choice of those given me."

"You usually do," he said with a half-smile. "Now excuse me while I compose a hopefully polite refusal to an unknown person. Tomorrow, I'll ask the baker if he noted anyone of interest passing through."

My stomach sank, but not with mention of the baker. The arrival of the shirt on my bed and the trunk at the door could not be coincidence.

"Father, it bothers me that this suitor mentioned no name, just wrote daughter. Perhaps when you word your reply, you could mention Blye's name so there is no mistake about which daughter this person would expect if you come to an agreement."

Father made a thoughtful noise and nodded. Already his eyes drifted to the window as he sank into thought. I left him quietly with his new shirt and crept to my own bed.

I woke late after having trouble sleeping the night before. The sun already rose above the treetops when I stepped outside dressed in trousers and Father's old shirt. I finished braiding back my hair as I walked east toward the river. My bag bounced gently against my hip with nothing but a bit of string and a hook in it. Today, I'd fish.

At the stream, I peeled off my boots and socks. The chill from the spring ground penetrated my feet, but I ignored it as I rolled up my pant legs. I'd fished before and knew the risks. Hooks were precious, and if the line pulled too taut, I would be forced to step into the water. Walking home with cold wet feet would make for a miserable journey.

Finding a long, straight branch thin enough to hold over the water proved to be a bit of a challenge. It took me a good hour, and I wished I hadn't been so careless with my old rod last summer. I'd accidentally stepped on it while pitching hay into the shed for the goat. Since I typically stored it in the rafters, I had no idea why it'd been on the ground in the first place. I'd been especially careful with it because I'd had such luck—we had fish for almost three weeks straight—before the fatal break.

After peeling offshoots from the branch, I tied the string on the end, baited my hook, and set to work enjoying a quiet afternoon while nibbling on day-old peapods. Too soon, I had enough fish to fill my string. While sitting on the bank to put on my socks, a loud caw from across the stream slowed my progress as I looked up. Perched on a thick branch of a tree on the other side of the stream, a crow watched me with one eye while its head turned toward the north.

"Mr. Crow, are you following me?" I asked with amusement. It blinked an eye at me but remained quiet.

As long as it only watched, I didn't mind its presence. I didn't, however, want it driving me back to the estate. After tugging on the last boot and tying the lacing, I pulled the smallest fish from my line and set it on the ground.

"Here you go."

I stood and casually walked away. When I heard a rapid flap of wings, I casually looked over my shoulder and watched the crow land and feast on the fish. Smiling, I journeyed home, lengthening my strides so the fish didn't turn bad before I got there.

Bryn didn't look too pleased when I presented her with a dozen fillets.

"I hope I marry soon," she muttered. "I won't tolerate another three weeks of fish."

Realization about what had actually happened to my old fishing pole hit me, and I took care to hide the current pole well before returning to clean up the fish remains. It was smelly business, but the garden did well when I buried the remains.

Washing up outside with a harsh lye soap to rid myself of the smell, I wasn't surprised to hear the flap of wings and a caw nearby. The crow sat perched on the shed roof.

"Sorry," I said, watching the creature while I dried my hands. "I buried the remains of the others in the garden."

"I need you to buy some flour," Bryn called from inside.

I made a face. I had avoided the baker since he'd stopped by to speak with Father. Why would I march right into his store?

"Please ask Blye."

"I can't go!" Blye cried from the open window of our bedroom. "I'm working on the dress to show the seamstress in the Water, and Father's asked me to take in a shirt he somehow acquired."

It pleased me to know he didn't tell Blye the shirt came from me or, rather, the estate through me. She would insist I go back and try to procure more clothes. But I didn't like that she refused to fetch the flour.

"Bryn, can't you go?"

"I'd rather not face..."

I sighed. Her need to avoid Tennen was due to wounded pride over her own stupidity. My reason to avoid the baker was self-preservation. Still, I knew I'd go.

"Fine. I'll need to change." I wouldn't walk into the village wearing a threadbare shirt that easily displayed the outline of my bindings.

"Just hurry," Bryn said impatiently. Holding in the urge to make a face at her, I marched to our room, where Blye sat on the bed concentrating on her stitching, and quickly changed into the dress.

When I went to the kitchen to ask Bryn for the coin I needed for the flour, she handed me peas. I wanted to scream. Instead, I stomped my way into the village, marched through the front door of the bakery and asked to speak with Mrs. Medunge. Of course, the baker's sister went to fetch him instead.

"Benella," he said when he walked through the door from the back. "So lovely today. What can I do for you?"

"I'd like to trade these peas for flour," I spoke woodenly, setting the cloth wrapped bundle on the counter. It was the same cloth they'd loaned for the flour the first time.

"I'm sorry, my dear—"

I would never be his dear.

"—but I can't trade. It's coin only. If others heard I accepted produce for flour, no one would want to pay me coin again, and I'd be overrun with produce."

"I understand." I scooped up the peas with two hands and left the cloth on the counter. "The cloth is yours. Good day." I turned to leave.

"Wait. I hate seeing you leave upset. Come in back, and we'll talk."

I kept walking, and he called after me again. Next, I went to the butcher and asked if he would trade a copper for the peas. He apologized and explained that he'd taken trade in payment for the last several days and had no coin, affirmation that the baker's assessment of trade had a grain of truth. When I stepped out, the baker stood in the door and silently waved me back across the street; but I had another option left to me. Cutting diagonally across the road, I used the toe of my boot to knock at the candle maker's door.

The candle maker opened the door for me after several long minutes, during which I endured the baker's constant stare.

"Benella, come in," he said with a small smile. "What do you have there?"

"Peapods. Would you be willing to trade? I need a copper to buy flour."

"Ah." He nodded in understanding, holding out his hands. My shoulders sagged in relief.

"What happened to the blunt silver?"

Groaning before I stopped myself, I admitted, "I gave it to someone who needed it more."

"Interesting that Mrs. Coalre came in just yesterday to buy a candle. I thought they were out of coin, too."

I remained quiet and watched him set the peas on his table so he could shuffle over to a shelf.

"I'm not one for peas, but you allowed me to hold the flowers without asking for payment, so I can hardly deny you such a small request." He plucked a coin from a very tiny pile and brought it to me.

"Thank you," I whispered, grateful for his kindness.

"Go buy your flour, dear," he said with a small wave as he settled back at his chair.

I promised myself that I would venture to the estate soon and circle it as many times as needed until it surrendered some more of those rare blooms.

The baker brightened when he saw me step from the candle maker's but frowned at my empty hands. I marched up to him, pulled a cloth from my bag—one of Father's old neckcloths—and handed him the coin without trying to step inside.

"However much flour that will buy me, please," I spoke softly, trying to keep the anger from my tone.

He turned and handed both to his sister.

"A handful, no more," he cautioned her before turning back to me with a slight scowl.

We stood several feet apart, but I felt like I faced him toe to toe. I kept my face impassive until he heaved a sigh and let his eyes drift to my chest. Thankfully, his sister didn't leave him much time to stare.

Accepting the bag, I quickly retreated, meeting up with Father as he left the school.

"What have you been up to?" he asked, eyeing the street behind me.

"Bryn sent me for flour." I'd kept my tone pleasant, but he paused to study me.

"Very unkind," he said before walking again.

"It wasn't intentionally so," I said, defending her. "She's upset that Tennen hasn't tried to offer for her even though she knows you wouldn't agree to the match. She thought he had affection for her and isn't seeing anything beyond her wounded pride."

He said nothing. When we arrived home, I handed the flour to a mildly surprised Bryn and went to change back into my trousers. To occupy myself, I weeded the small garden while dinner cooked. In the quiet, I remembered the crow and looked to the roof of the shed.

The crow was gone.

I BELIEVED the breaded fish tasted delightful but kept that thought to myself, fearing for my new pole. Everyone ate in silence, and I wondered why. They didn't leave me wondering long.

"Do you think we'll hear anything tonight?" Blye asked.

Father set his fork aside and steepled his fingers. "I wouldn't presume to guess. The note was notoriously brief, and we have no idea if the man in question lingered in the area. Travel may have been the reason for his request to take you with him last night. We can only wait and see."

She went back to eating in silence, but the conversation had me straining to hear outside the cottage. Would we walk out in the morning to find another note on the door?

THE NEXT MORNING, nothing waited outside. Bryn started packing in earnest while Blye went back to her quiet sewing. Father, having no students to teach that day, insisted on walking with me as I foraged. Typically on the days he didn't need to teach, he used the time in his study to research. Having moved many of his books already, no doubt his reduced selection had something to do with his wish to accompany me.

The sun shone brightly as we walked toward the estate.

"Nothing from the mysterious suitor last night?" I asked, already knowing the answer.

"To your sisters' disappointment, no." He kept pace with me, watching the trees around us. Soon we came to the part where the mist crept along the bases of the trees.

"Peculiar," he said, looking up.

"What is?" I looked up but only saw the same wild, tangled vegetation I always did.

"The vines in the trees appear to be moving," he murmured, tilting his head to watch. "I heard the ones near the wall move as if alive, but this far from it? I wonder..."

I knew they moved, but said nothing, not wanting to explain how I knew. The night that Tennen had almost caught me still filled my dreams with running through the darkness.

"The place I usually visit is just ahead. The last time it offered peapods in such abundance I almost cried for not having my bag with me."

"Odd of you to leave without it," he said, focusing on me again.

Inwardly cursing my slip, I smiled sheepishly and shrugged. The mists thickened the further we went toward the estate until we only saw the immediate area around us. I wondered at the unusually menacing feel of it.

"Perhaps we should head back," I whispered, stopping abruptly to study the mist around us.

"I'm glad you think so," he returned just as softly. "I kept quiet, trusting your expert guidance, but the feel of this place—"

I spun toward him and saw vines wrapping around his waist. His eyes were wide with shock.

"Father!" I flew toward him, tugging at the vines, but they didn't budge. More crept toward him, starting a slow familiar shuffle I knew would pull him into the estate. He read the fear on my face and tried to reassure me.

"Stay here, Benella. I'll return soon. This is only my first offense."

I kept pace with him, but the vines tugged him up into the treetops and out of my sight.

"Don't follow me," he called in warning. "You've trespassed too many times already."

Ignoring his warning, I spun and ran blindly toward the gate. Panting, I arrived to hear it creak open, barely able to make out the mist shrouded bars before me.

"Please," I begged. "My father didn't mean to trespass; he was only following me."

A growl started in the dark mist to my right, and I knew the beast waited for me.

"You refused me?"

Concerned about my father, I frowned in confusion before I

realized what he meant. The trunk. I played as if I didn't understand. If the beast continued talking to me, he wouldn't be able to toss my father over the wall.

"If I recall, I did not refuse your last request of me. I still have the shirt to prove it," I answered, still slightly out of breath.

"The trunk," he said.

"The trunk someone left for my sister, Blye? What of it?"

"The offer was meant for you," he said in a deceptively soft growl that unnerved me.

His direct answer surprised me.

"Me? Why would I need all that cloth? I don't sew. Blye does."

"You wanted a shirt. I offered the means to own several shirts."

I didn't know what to say except, "Why? Why did you offer for me?"

"You need not concern yourself with that," he growled his frustration. "Will you assent?"

"I cannot."

Birds in nearby trees screamed in protest at his rage filled roar and took flight in a rush of a dozen flapping wings.

"Only a few days ago you lay on the ground, telling me you cared not whether you lived or died. Holding so little value to your life, why not agree to my offer?"

With effort, I kept my voice soft and even to hide my fear.

"Value is an odd thing, subject to whim. What one might find value in, another might not; what has value today might not have value tomorrow, depending on the wants and needs of the evaluating individual. You prove this yourself with the same example you just provided. Several days ago when I lay on the ground indifferent to what fate might decide, you were not so interested in me. The issue is that neither of us understands the reason why we changed our minds."

He remained silent, perhaps thinking I had more to say on the matter. I didn't want to push him any further though, so I let what I said linger in the quiet for a while before speaking again.

"My father?"

"Is unharmed," he spoke softly just behind me. My stomach twitched in surprise, but I managed to quell any other reaction to his unexpected nearness.

"May I have him back, please?"

Gently, he touched the back of my head, a single stroke of my hair from crown to the tip of my braid, which ended mid-back. He lifted the braid and tugged on it slightly. I held still before him, listening to my great gusting breaths as I remembered the last time he'd touched me when I'd thought him a pile of furs.

"I will return him to you whole and healthy in hopes that you may yet change your answer, Benella," he said as his fingers threaded through my hair, loosening the braid.

As soon as my hair fell free, he disappeared.

After a few moments, I heard the rustling of leaves above, and the mists lifted enough that I spotted Father trussed up in the vines high above. As soon as he spotted me, he went from looking intrigued to looking worried.

"Go, child!" he called in an urgent hush. The vines began their stretching descent to bring him to the ground. "I just heard the beast's roar and know he must be near waiting for me. You shouldn't have come inside the wall."

I remained despite his urging to flee. When his feet touched the ground, the vines loosened and then shrank away.

"What an amazing journey," he said, watching them for a moment before remembering where we were and the imminent threat of the beast.

"This way," I motioned him to follow before he could say anything. We walked through the gate, which slammed closed behind us with a metallic clang.

FOR THE NEXT SEVERAL DAYS, I stayed away from the estate, not out of fear, but because Father forbade me to return. I struggled to find anything in the area outside of the estate's boundaries. Though the fish were plentiful, I knew Bryn and Blye grew tired of them. Bryn tried cajoling me into another trip to the baker; but with nothing to trade and her unwillingness to part with a coin, I left her angry while I went to fish.

During this time, we entertained several more suitors, which both of my sisters rejected out of hand. Father nodded each time, accepting their answer; but I read the concern etched in his expression. Then one day, with solemn acceptance, he said we should begin packing our belongings to leave the next morning. None of us questioned him, but we all wondered how we would live in the tiny two-room house.

IN THE MORNING, Father walked to the smith to borrow the wagon he'd used last time. Into it, we packed the rest of the books, Father's bed and my sisters' bed, our trunks, cookware, and the last of our food. The desk, table, and remaining bed stayed with the house to entice the next schoolmaster. While we worked, a crow cawed at us incessantly.

When we had everything loaded, Bryn and Blye climbed onto the bench seat with Father while I sat on the backend of the wagon. The crow quieted as Father clucked the team forward, and I wondered what he would tell the beast.

We pulled onto the main road of town, and I noticed the butcher outside his door and gave a wave of farewell. The baker watched from the shadows of his porch, but I pretended not to notice. Sara stood near the quiet anvil at the smithy, looking down at the ground. I wondered what would become of her husband's dealings with the baker, knowing the blunt silver had already run out for her.

Clearing the village, the wagon jostled ponderously north until the road curved near the estate. There the woods remained eerily dark and quiet until it too passed from sight. Riding in a wagon, even if it was a butt-bruising ride, ensured a more pleasant second trip to Water-On-The-Bridge.

Arriving well before lunch, Father took a circumspect route to our new home, avoiding the main thoroughfare with its questionable businesses. We worked together to unload our belongings, cramming them into the main room of the very small house. Then Father drove the wagon back to the smith. While he was gone, Blye packed her precious dress and walked to the dressmaker, who agreed to hire her but could not offer her lodging.

Bryn and I put together Father's bed in the main room and set up their bed in the single, private room. With effort, we also managed to wedge in the three trunks. When we finished, I eyed our house with dismay.

The kitchen came equipped with a stove and dry sink like our prior cottage. Near the stove sat a table for two with two chairs. Not three feet from that, Father's bed sat against the back wall between the door to the backyard and the door to our room. A fireplace, cleverly set on an interior wall, worked to heat the main room and the room beyond. Before the fire, a worn stuffed chair would welcome a weary scholar. To the right of the fireplace, just before a window set into the front of the house, sat a desk and several shelves that already brimmed with Father's books. To the right of that was the front door, bringing my slow turning tour to an end.

In all honesty, this house was meant for a single man or a married couple. Father had no room for any of us.

Excusing myself, I went for a walk to check the market district. Better to learn costs and who would be willing to trade right away. By dusk, I'd determined the only thing we'd changed was the size of our house. But, at least, I didn't have to worry about the baker or the smith's sons.

Sighing, I returned to our new home empty-handed. Father already pored over his books, and a very watery version of stew waited for me.

WE CELEBRATED Father's first week of pay by purchasing meat and flour. After not eating anything the prior day, all of us looked forward to the meat pie Bryn fixed. As I bit into my portion of the meat pie and gravy dripped down my chin, I thought nothing could have tasted better. However, too soon those supplies ran out, and we were back to going hungry. I noticed Father's neckcloth seemed a bit longer and the shirt that Blye had just tailored for him a little looser. My own dress gaped a bit from my waist now.

What really bothered me was Blye's success at the dress shop. She would come home talking excitedly about her customers, but never about her pay. After two weeks of living in the Water, she came home with a new dress, saying she needed to look the part to work at such an upscale shop. She gave her old dress to Bryn, who accepted it with a smile of thanks and a comment that a second dress would be handy.

That day, I put on my bag and left the village to forage. The nearby country had been picked fairly clean, so I headed in the direction I knew. Not far after passing over the bridge, I stopped until a curious wave of dizziness passed.

I trudged east, watching for signs of the estate. As soon as I saw the mist creeping around the bases of trees, I sighed with relief and turned north into the mists. The skirt of my dress still wasn't ideal for setting traps, but it was the only thing I owned that I could wear in the Water. Father's old shirt would give too many people lewd ideas.

Too soon, I reached the wall and turned to follow it east—ignoring the gate that swung open in invitation. Finally, I reached the patch of ground that usually held some sort of bounty. The sight of withered brown tops of potato plants greeted me. Using my hands, I clawed at the ground until my bag brimmed with the brown globes. When I stood, the weight made me cringe. Carrying ten extra pounds from here to Konrall wouldn't have been a problem, but to the Water? It would be a trying journey. Still, I hoped for something in my traps as well.

Retracing my steps, I approached the gate and nearly screamed when I was pulled from behind into the maw of darkness. Two strong hands gripped my upper arms and held me against a very large, furry frame.

I didn't turn to look. I knew who had me, but I still remained unsure of his mood.

"Will you assent and stay, Benella?" he said softly.

CHAPTER EIGHT

"I cannot—"

"Then why have you returned?" he roared, hurting my ears and thrusting me away with enough force that I stumbled and lost a few precious potatoes.

"Because I'm hungry!" Angry, I picked one up, spun, and threw it into the dark. The muffled thud of the potato finding a target in the dense dark fog had me quickly regretting my loss of temper.

"I'm sorry," I whispered.

"If you had stayed, you would not be hungry."

Such an open, foolish statement. Perhaps I wouldn't be hungry because I would be dead. I kept my thoughts to myself and waited.

"So you walked from the Water just for food?"

He sounded very calm, and it worried me.

"Yes," I said.

"From my estate?"

I nodded, my throat suddenly tight.

"Then I think it fair to ask for something in return."

I remembered his last price and started to lower the bag of potatoes to the ground. I would not do that again. I wasn't in a desperate enough situation.

"Wait. Before you give up your prize and have to return home with nothing but dirt-caked nails, listen."

I paused with the bag almost touching the soil.

"I will generously give you as much food as you can carry in return for an hour of your time."

Shaking my head, I set the bag down and barely saw the potatoes spill out.

"Stubborn," he yelled in an almost inarticulate roar. "Why not?"

"I've told you once; I'm not a whore."

He growled long and loud, the sound moving around me as he circled. I wished I could see through the mist.

"Who said anything about whoring?" he said finally. "I need someone to clean the estate."

I couldn't hide my surprise.

"Just clean?"

"Yes," he ground out.

"Then, I can accept," I said, quickly bending to pick up the potatoes. Before the last one fell into the bag, he bade me to follow.

Only the sound of his footfalls led me because as we walked, the heavy mist seemed to trail us, or at least me. It was disorienting to walk blindly ahead. Well, not blindly, but seeing less than two feet before me was hardly reassuring at the fast pace he assumed. We walked a far distance when, suddenly, the same door from my prior visit loomed ahead.

I opened the door and went inside. For a moment, I saw little; then light streamed into the room from the high windows. For a moment, I wondered about the mist that had accompanied me then apparently vanished. But, the state of the kitchen distracted me. It was just as I'd left it, the large tub upside down near the cold hearth and the table turned on its end as a privacy screen.

"What would you have me clean?" I asked. Silence answered me.

Shaking my head, I set to work righting as much of the enormous kitchen as I could. I set shelves back onto their mountings, then lined them with the various cooking pots and stirring spoons that littered the floor. I pried apart one of the table halves and set the wood near the hearth for burning. Several chairs, broken beyond repair, joined the growing pile. The remaining chairs, which had a hope of being repaired, I sat near one wall. Nothing but dust and debris carried in by the seasons remained on the floor when I finished.

Though I knew I'd spent longer than the bargained hour cleaning, I went outside in search of grass and twigs to make a rough broom. When I finished, I spent a good while longer sweeping. Satisfied with my work, I swept the last bit outside the door and went to the counter to shoulder my prize, the bag of potatoes.

When I turned back to the open door, I saw the dark mists swirling toward it and knew the beast approached. It snuffed out the sun shining through the windows and cast the room into premature evening gloom. My eyes didn't adjust quickly enough to see him move into the room, but my ears picked up his feet brushing against the cobbled floor as he strode toward me.

"You've met your end of the bargain and more. Will you return tomorrow?"

"I won't abuse your generosity," I declined carefully. "I have enough to feed us for a week if we're careful."

"A week?" He scoffed. "Come back tomorrow, and I will have sun-ripened tomatoes for you."

My mouth watered.

"And the price?"

"The same. An hour of cleaning."

I frowned as I considered the offer. He'd left me alone to clean this time, but would he do so the next time? And why did he suddenly want someone to clean for him? Food and answers were only likely if I returned.

"I'll see you tomorrow," I said.

He grunted and made another slight noise so soft and so brief I couldn't be sure what is was or what it meant.

He led me to the gate, then disappeared. The walk home wasn't as terrible as I'd anticipated. I had a rabbit to carry in addition to the potatoes, but it was the promise of tomatoes the next day that lightened my step. Before returning to the house, I traded half the potatoes for coin, hoping I wasn't making a mistake, and purchased some oats and milk for breakfast. Living in the Water, we hadn't had room for the goat; and Bryn had sold her to the butcher. I wondered where that coin had gone.

When I walked through the door with potatoes, milk, oats, and rabbit I was surprised that Bryn wasn't inside. I placed the items in the kitchen storage and went to clean up before anyone returned. Dirt smudged my dress from cleaning, so I changed into my trousers and shirt to take the dress outside and air it, which meant hanging it on the line of rope strung between trees and beating the dirt from it. After I finished, I hauled water from our private well to wash my hands and face.

By the time Bryn returned, I once again wore my dress and was reading a book while sitting comfortably in the stuffed chair before the cold hearth. She asked where I'd obtained the food, and I asked where she'd been. She didn't answer so neither did I. She lit the stove, and I listened to her start preparations for dinner. I tried not to let my mouth water.

Father said nothing when we sat down to a dinner of rabbit and baked potatoes, though he did glance at me. Just as Blye and now Bryn had their secrets, so did he. None of us knew where he taught; and when asked, he evaded the question.

THE NEXT MORNING, after a hearty meal of milk soaked hot oats, I set out for the estate better prepared.

As I had the day before, I set traps at the edge of the mist before turning north toward the gate. The dense fog of the day before didn't reappear as the gate swung open with a high-pitched screech. Instead of ignoring the invitation to enter and continuing to the dirt patch, I stepped through the gate. I wanted to leave the tomatoes on the vine until the last minute.

Within the beast's domain, only the barest hint of white mist clung to the air.

Walking north, where I thought the house should be, I gasped when an immense structure came into view. I counted two stories of windows on the wing with the kitchen and four on the main building, which extended far into the surrounding trees. I could easily clean one hour each day for the next year.

Inside, I viewed my work from the day before with satisfaction. On the butcher's block in the middle of the kitchen a note lay waiting next to a plate with cheese, bread, and a cup of cold spring water.

Eat and rest before you continue your work on the kitchen.

I set my bag beside the plate and drank deeply. Then I looked around the kitchen, wondering what else he would have me clean, until I spotted the four doors in the kitchen which had been locked the day before. All now stood ajar. The first led to a long room lined with three beds. Dust coated everything. The next door led to a hall. Walking the hall, I came to a set of steps set in the left wall. They led down into pitch black, and a cold draft drifted up to swirl around my ankles. I kept walking and found a door to the right that led to a linen closet. Everything in that room looked white and new, except again, for a fine dusting. The door at the end of the hall remained locked though I saw no keyhole.

Turning back, I retraced my steps to the kitchen. There, I took my bag to the servant's quarters and quickly changed before exploring the other doors off of the kitchen. One long room held a variety of foods, all looking surprisingly fresh. The next led to a small study filled with shelves of books. Curious, I plucked a book from its perch and opened it to find a page detailing how to dress and stuff a quail. Books on how to cook. What a splendid idea. Reluctantly, I replaced the book and returned to the main kitchen.

Though, I'd done a fair job, the hearth still needed attention. Squaring my shoulders, I set to work.

An hour later, I had removed the ash and brushed the stone clean. It hadn't been as dirty as I'd thought. I set new kindling down, ready to light should anyone have a need, and picked up the final bucket of ash. Outside, as I dumped it a few steps from the door in the overgrown weeds, I noted a swirling mass of dark fog rolling my way.

I hurried back inside and moved to the water I'd pumped after emptying the first bucket of ash. The wind had taken the dark powder and dusted me generously. By letting the water sit for an hour, I could use it without shivering. I quickly washed my hands and face. The door opened when I had a towel pressed to my face for drying.

When I opened my eyes, I could only see faint outlines of the objects in the now familiar kitchen. The shadow of the beast paced on four legs just inside the door. His back easily stood as high as my shoulders. I could make out little else about him. Yet, what little I saw was enough to make my knees weak. I rather liked the mist.

"You made better progress yesterday," he said with a low rumble.

I frowned at him.

"The work yesterday was easier." He grunted in response. "I'll just go pick my tomatoes and be on my way."

"Will you stay, Benella?" he asked quietly, confusing me.

Hadn't he just complained about my work? I was reluctant to keep giving him the same answer he'd received so poorly in the past yet had no reason to answer differently.

"I cannot," I said.

He whirled about and left with a roar. Gradually, sun began to filter back into the room. Near the door lay just enough tomatoes to fill my bag. I rushed to change and used my dirty clothes to cushion between the layers of the soft red orbs.

When I reached the gate, the beast's mist surrounded me again, forcing me to stop walking.

"Tomorrow, there will be meat if you return. As much as you can carry home in return for an hour of cleaning."

I knew I would sell the majority of the tomatoes since they didn't last long. The coin could buy meat, or it could be used to buy more milk and oats. I nodded in agreement, and the mists lifted enough that I set off for home.

As I had the day before, I arrived before anyone else. When Bryn returned she exclaimed over the tomatoes but didn't question how I'd obtained them; and I, in return, didn't ask her where she'd been.

Since moving, I slept in Father's bed and he in his chair, as there was no room for me in with my sisters. He made very little noise when he rose and hadn't yet woken me. However, exhausted from my day's work, I'd fallen asleep early. Even the slightest noise would have woken me the following morning.

Laying in the dark, I listened to him dress then walk out the back door. When I heard the scrape of the bucket as he lowered it for water, I quickly rose from bed, dressed, then once again crawled under the covers. I wanted to respect Father's unspoken wish to keep where he taught private, yet his secrecy worried me. Bryn and Blye's secrecy I could accept. It was part of who they were. But, Father had never kept secrets before.

He quietly reentered the cottage but didn't eat. He only washed and grabbed his materials for the day before leaving via the front door.

Flipping back the covers, I quickly eased the front door open and set to following him.

He headed toward the center of town, passed the Head's house, then slowed before the house of the Whispering Sisters. There, he went to the back door and nodded to the guard standing there. The guard started to nod in return, but then caught sight of me. Father turned and saw me standing half hidden behind a tree.

Even from this great distance, I saw his shoulders slump. I stepped out from my hiding place but remained near the tree as he turned to walk toward me. My heart went out to him. He was a moral man and didn't understand how a woman could go into such a trade. We'd talked about it at length on several occasions during a family dinner. I knew the lectures were to help us, his daughters, stay innocent for our future husbands.

That he'd taken a position in the house of the Whispering Sisters to educate the women there must bother him a great deal. And I knew why he'd done it. To remove me from Konrall. To keep me safe.

When he stood before me, his guilty eyes met mine.

"Benella, I—"

"Didn't eat breakfast. You can't keep doing that. I see the weight you are losing. Without you, I have no one, Father." His eyes widened in surprise. "Do they offer you food?"

He slowly shook his head, and I knew I'd puzzled him by not asking why he went there.

"Then tell the man at the door I'll be back with food for you." He opened his mouth to protest. "I won't go in. I'll just hand it to him. Eat it all."

Before he could object, I spun away toward the market district. There, I bought three pastries with the coin I had left from the prior day. I ate one pastry myself and handed two to the very stoic looking guard at the back door.

"The second one's for you if you'll ensure my father eats his portion," I said.

The man's lips twitched slightly, and I hoped that meant he agreed. I thanked him then went on my way.

The walk through the market street was peaceful so early in the morning with only the scents of baking bread to keep me company. The mill lay silent as I passed it and started my trek over the bridge.

When I reached the edge of the estate, I checked the traps I'd left overnight and was disheartened to see they remained empty. The bait I'd placed was gone. I took them down and headed into the estate.

Instead of a note, a large stag waited on the butcher block, along with an empty barrel and a burlap bag of salt. I frowned at it all. I'd watched Bryn put up salted meat when I was younger but had no idea about the particulars.

Going to the office, I paged through the books for over an hour before I found one talking about salted pork. Shrugging, I used that as a guide to butcher as best I could. I was used to skinning and cleaning small animals. A larger one proved more time consuming and messy. Blood dotted my clothes and smeared my forearms. Before I was halfway through, I lit the fire to start water heating. I would need to wash out my shirt.

Soon the barrel was full of meat, salt, and brine. I tapped the lid in place and strained to move it to the food pantry. There I found waxed cloth which I used to package the remaining meat I meant to carry home. The large carcass glistening on the butcher's block daunted me. I had no idea what to do with it. I couldn't just dump it outside the door as I had with the ash and debris.

"Sir," I called politely, thinking the title better than beast. "What am I to do with the remains?"

A dark mist swirled into the kitchen almost immediately, and I listened to the scrape of his feet on the floor. I wondered if he'd been so close all along. A few rustles of movement and then silence. The mist only lasted a moment and when it cleared, the carcass was gone, leaving only the bloodstained block.

I scrubbed the surface with a brush I found then rinsed the top thoroughly. My arms grew tired from all of the water I needed to pump. Finally, I moved to the heated water and poured it into the large tub along with some cold water. Having been foolish once, I wasn't about to bathe again. Instead, I stripped from my shirt, knowing my bindings hid the important bits, and washed my arms and face. My shirt went into the dirty water. As I was rinsing it, the mists returned. I wasn't surprised.

"Tell me you'll stay," the beast said softly. I could feel his eyes on me as I rose and set my shirt over the back of a chair near the fire.

"Tell me why you want me to," I said, bending to scoop the used water from the tub with a smaller bucket. He remained silent as I moved from the tub to the door several times. I rinsed the tub and turned it over to sit on. He moved up behind me and touched my hair.

"Will you return tomorrow?" he asked instead of answering my question.

"I don't know," I answered honestly, thinking of my father. I needed to speak with him about why he went to the Whispering Sisters. I felt certain it was in a teaching capacity, but why hide it?

The beast growled behind me.

"The next day, then."

I nodded, knowing we needed the food, and I would not be able to stay away for long.

WHEN FATHER LEFT the next morning, I didn't pretend to sleep. Instead, I rose with him. There were no oats left. I'd only been able to purchase a small amount, and Bryn had salted the meat to put in storage for hard times. I wondered how much harder our time needed to be before we could eat the meat but didn't protest her decision. However, the storage left Father and me with nothing to eat. He didn't say anything, and neither did I.

We left together, and I walked with him all the way to the Whispering Sisters then told him I would return with a pastry. He nodded and went inside.

Using my last copper, I bought him the pastry fresh from the nearest baker's oven. The glaze ran on my hands, and I quickly licked it off as I walked back to my father's place of employment. The guard didn't offer to take the pastry. Instead, he opened the door and nodded for me to enter.

My stomach dipped with excitement. To see inside the house was something I'd never imagined. They catered only to male guests, and the only females allowed were those employed there. I kept my enthusiasm from my face as I stepped inside.

Soft music drifted down the halls along with the cloying

smoke. My head began to spin as I walked down the dimly lit hall. A woman walked toward me. She wore only her grey facial veil, her heavy breasts with their dark nipples and thatch of hair between her legs visible for anyone who cared to look. I tried not to look but couldn't help myself. Even changing at home, my sisters and I gave each other privacy.

As my eyes swept her from head to toe, I noted she carried a cup. I moved aside as we neared, but she stopped and held out the cup to me. I hesitated to take it.

"Thank you, but I'm just here to bring my father, Mr. Hovtel, something to eat."

The woman laughed softly.

"I know, child. Drink the tea so the smoke doesn't bother you." She held out the cup again, but I didn't notice. The sound of her voice mesmerized me. It was so soft I had to strain to hear, and it had a sighing quality that hinted at a hidden yearning.

"How do you speak like that?" I asked, slipping into my father's world of observation and study. I was his daughter, after all.

She laughed again.

"After you feed your father, I will teach you if you'd like."

I nodded, accepted the cup, and drained it. Almost immediately, some of the spinning stopped. As it did, I realized I still stared at her breasts; and I quickly looked up to meet her eyes through her veil. I saw amusement there.

She took the cup back and led me down the hall. I couldn't help but watch her butt as she walked. Every move seemed slow and rolling, a smooth dance to call attention to different areas of her body. I felt no attraction, but curiosity bit into me deeply. No shame entered a single movement, even when she bent to stroke a cat that ambled down the hall, giving me a clear view of her...well, everything.

She surprised me by stopping suddenly in front of a door. She tapped on its surface instead of knocking, then opened it. She motioned me inside and followed me. Father sat at a desk, looking decidedly uncomfortable as he lectured on mathematics to four very naked and veiled students.

His voice seemed overly loud after the way my guide had spoken to me.

When he caught sight of me, his eyes widened in surprise, and I apologetically held out the pastry. He obviously didn't want me associating with his students for very visible reasons.

One of his students, who reclined before his desk, rose gracefully and took the pastry from me.

"I'll see you this evening," Father said, sounding strained.

I nodded and left without a word, my guide closing the door for me.

"Would you still like to learn, daughter of our teacher?" she whispered softly beside me.

I couldn't think of anything I wanted more at the moment, but I knew what my father would think. Or did I? As she pointed out, my father was a scholar. He, more than anyone I knew, understood what it meant to have a burning curiosity. Often he commended me on my tenacious pursuit of knowledge. Would he this time?

With resolve, I nodded. She led me to a set of stairs at the end of the current hallway. One led down, where I could hear gentle splashing sounds, and the other led up. Bright light and laughter spilled from the upstairs.

She hesitated at the landing.

"Perhaps it would be less shocking to go to the bathing room. It sounds as if most of my sisters are upstairs."

Without waiting for my answer, she glided down the candlelit steps which opened to a large underground room. Red dyed fabrics covered the rock walls, and large tubs filled with steaming water were placed throughout the room. An arched opening covered by another piece of red fabric led from the room.

A single woman, wearing the same style veil as my guide, occupied one of the many tubs.

"Good morning, sister," my guide whispered. "Are we disturbing you?"

"Not at all. Who is your friend? A new sister?"

My guide giggled, a tinkling sound that made me smile.

"Our scholar's curious daughter. She would like to know how we learned to speak like this."

"Come, sit near me. I would like to listen," the woman bade, standing to motion to the cushions set on the floor near the tub. Other than my father's chair, I hadn't noticed anything more than a cushion on which to sit. I sat next to my guide. The woman in the tub didn't sit until we sat, making it impossible to avoid seeing everything above the water that lapped at her knees. Her small nipples, rosy from the warm water, stood out from large breasts. No thatch of hair covered her lower parts or limbs.

"What is your name, child?" she asked, a smile curving her mouth. The veil fell to the top of her upper lip.

"Benella," I whispered back. I hadn't meant to whisper, at least not consciously. It just seemed too quiet and peaceful to speak regularly.

They both laughed lightly. The one in the tub introduced herself as Aryana and my guide as Ila.

"Why did you speak in a whisper?" Aryana asked.

"It feels wrong not to. Everything here is quiet and peaceful. I didn't want to disturb that."

Ila reached over and patted my arm with a smile.

"That is the heart of why we speak as we do. To bring peace to others, we must keep peace in ourselves at all times. We struggle; but when we do, we surround ourselves with our fellow sisters until peace returns. Speaking as we do comes with practice, but also deep peace."

"Drinking the tea every day doesn't hurt either," Aryana wryly interjected. "After prolonged drinking, the tea roughens our voices, making it uncomfortable to speak above a whisper. It also adds the husky quality that most find appealing."

"Ah," I said, feeling enlightened. Now that I had a little knowledge, I wanted more. "Why so many bathing tubs?"

They both laughed again.

"Definitely curious, this one," Aryana whispered with a wide smile. "Benella, the knowledge of this house is kept within the sisters and the clients we serve."

She didn't say it harshly, but I still felt embarrassed for assuming too much.

"I'm truly sorry. I meant no offense."

"Such a sweet girl," she said thoughtfully. "I can see you ask out of innocent curiosity, and I am willing to answer any questions you may have on one condition."

I nodded eagerly.

"You must never speak of what you learn here to another person. If you can swear to that, I will tell you anything you like about our sisterhood."

Quickly swearing to her that I wouldn't dare speak of it—she laughed at that—she willingly explained about the tubs.

"We open our doors to our clients after ten in the morning. Many seek our comforts later in the evening. No matter when they seek us, we strive to have everything ready for them. Men are, by nature, aggressive and brash to some degree. Oh, women can be too, but we only serve men here so that is our focus. Their tendencies along with their strength can cause issues if we do not bring them peace quickly enough. The smoke helps as soon as they walk through the door. What the smoke cannot cleanse, a bath and body rub can."

I frowned slightly, recalling my bathing experiences. The feeling of warm water surrounding me certainly did have a calming effect, but the water cooled so quickly it didn't stay soothing for long. Frowning further, I recalled Father's tendencies to wash with cold water from a bucket. When he did require a full bath, we typically left the cottage for a walk, and when we returned, he already had everything cleaned up and back in place.

"Do men really enjoy bathing?"

Aryana smiled while Ila took a turn explaining.

"New clients do hesitate, but when they see one of us rise from the water, they are usually willing to join us."

"Oh." In my mind, the experience turned from cleaning to frolicking in the open. I eyed the other tubs in plain view of this one.

"Make no assumptions, Benella," Aryana said. "State your thoughts and ask your questions. I wouldn't like for you to leave with incorrect notions."

"Do you have sex with your clients in the tubs where everyone can see?" I asked bluntly and without censor.

Ila laughed loudly, a deep sound that had me looking at her with concern. Aryana chuckled.

"I will certainly tell the other sisters you evoked a true laugh from Ila. Something that hasn't been done in a long while."

I opened my mouth to ask how what I said was funny, but she cut me off.

"We do not pleasure our clients that way within the tubs. It would be a messy experience, and require more water changes and tub washing than time would permit." She rose from the water and stepped gracefully from the tub. Holding out a hand, she helped me to my feet.

"Come. We will show you."

We walked through the room toward the curtain. On the other side of the curtain, a large stove radiated heat. The adolescent boy tending the stove gave my dress a curious look but said nothing.

To the side of the boy, a square stone trough, about a foot deep, sunk into the floor.

"Here we heat the water we need and drain away the old water." Ila pointed to the hole in the bottom corner of the wall at the base of the trough. "When we bring a client to the bathing chambers, we walk him through the bathing chambers so he can see others enjoying the communal bath. This is especially important for a new client. The sight of the sisters naked and bathing inspires cooperation where there might otherwise exist hesitation or belligerence. In this room, we have the client stand in the trough and give him a cool water scrub. It initiates our time together and cleans him within and without so he is ready for the tubs."

"I'm not certain I understand," I said hesitantly. "How would this clean from within? Wouldn't the cool water wake the client from the smoke just a little and bring back some of his..." the word she'd used before slipped from my mind a moment. "Aggression?"

"Yes, it normally would. But a man craves a woman's touch. When we begin bathing him, the sister providing the bath becomes his focus. During this part of the bath, the sister helps release the man's pent energies."

Finally, understanding dawned, and the image of the baker frantically tugging at himself under his apron rose to mind. Something must have shown on my face because Aryana spoke gently beside me and laid a comforting hand on my arm.

"I see you understand, and it doesn't inspire pleasant thoughts for you. What we do is not meant as an act of vulgarity but to bring peace."

"I understand. This interests me," I assured them. "Once a man has released his pent energies, then you move him to the tubs?"

Aryana gave me a relieved smile.

"If we are sharing too much information, please tell us. I would not offend our scholar's daughter on her first visit."

"Not too much information; just more than I've ever had before."

They both smiled knowingly and led me from the room. I could feel the boy's eyes on me as we walked away and wondered what things he saw in that room and why they allowed him there.

Ila continued the tour in the main bathing room.

"Since our clients only enter the waters clean, all we need do is keep the water warm and change it occasionally." She bent, again giving me a full view that I couldn't help but study, and pulled a large rock from the water.

I wondered what men thought when she did that.

"We heat these rocks by the stove and place them in the water throughout the day and night to keep the water warm."

The steam curling from the water called me to test it.

"May I?" I asked, stepping forward, pointing toward the water.

Ila nodded, and I dipped the tips of my fingers into the delightfully warm water.

"Oh, that is nice," I said.

"We do not have clients for a long while yet. We would be happy to send Gen away so you could bathe."

The tub we owned required a very uncomfortable position with my knees poking from the water. The beast's tub had been just as big as these, enough to fit two, but I hadn't been able to enjoy it. If they sent the boy away, I had no doubt I could have a real, uninterrupted bath.

"I..." I wanted to say yes, but what if I misunderstood and they required payment for the use of the bath. Accepting things from the beast had caused me trouble.

"Perhaps another time."

Aryana tilted her head.

"You wanted to say yes. What stopped you?"

"What do you want in return?"

"Nothing at all. We enjoy the company of other women. As a sister, we usually only speak with other sisters. Not many other women are willing to speak with us."

"Then I would greatly appreciate it. Though, I'm not sure my father would like it. I would prefer no one mention my extended visit unless he specifically asks." I wouldn't ask them to lie.

"We understand," Aryana said as Ila calmly led the way to the back bathing room.

While Aryana spoke to Gen, Ila quickly explained what I should do. Once they all left, I stripped to nothing, draped my clothes on the pegs lining the wall, and stepped into the trough.

Using the buckets nearby, I wet my skin then used the special scented soap that Aryana had brought down for her own bath. The light, sweet smell made my stomach rumble, reminding me that I hadn't yet eaten. I lathered my hair, enjoying the heat from the stove as I stood there covered in nothing but suds. Then I tilted the first bucket over my head, slowly rinsing it all away. As they directed, I used the second bucket to ensure I missed nothing.

Nervous, I peeked around the curtain before tiptoeing out and sliding into the first tub with a gusty sigh. The water stung my skin with its heat, but in a good way. I melted against the edge, sinking until my chin hit the water. Delightfully, my knees stayed submerged, too. My eyes fluttered closed.

"Benella," Aryana's now familiar whisper drifted to me. "May we sit on the cushions by you while you relax?"

I opened my eyes and nodded easily. These women strove to

bring a sense of calm to everyone they encountered. I knew they would do nothing to intentionally disrupt that. And after the way they moved around me, I felt comfortable enough with my submerged nudity to talk to them without shame.

Ila glided into the room with her, and they both sank to the cushions.

"We just replaced the rocks in the tubs. You don't find it too hot?" Aryana asked.

I shook my head lazily with a slight smile. She reached over the tub and tested the water.

"It would be best to only sit in it for a few minutes then move to one of the cooler tubs. Too long in the heat could make you ill," she cautioned.

"You have very pretty hair, Benella," Ila whispered, reaching out to touch the wet strands hanging over the edge of the tub. "Would you mind if I oiled it and brushed it?"

Mind? I vaguely recalled my mother doing that when I was young; but after that, I'd struggled with my own hair, often tearing through tangles to braid it without combing it.

"I wouldn't mind," I assured her. She stood smoothly, left the room, and walked upstairs.

"Come." Aryana stood. "Let's move you to a cooler tub before she returns. You're looking too red in the face." She held out her hand, and I hesitated. "I promise you, I've seen all manner of parts on my sisters, and yours are no different."

They might not be so different, but they were parts never seen before by anyone. She was right about the water, though. I could feel sweat beading my upper lip.

"Maybe another rinse bucket would be beneficial before going to another tub," I suggested, accepting her hand.

I stood and avoided meeting her gaze or moving too quickly. Everything they did was slow and measured. I didn't want to do anything they would consider aggressive or manly. I wondered what they would think if they knew I often wore trousers and a shirt. Inside, I laughed at the thought. They probably wouldn't say anything. They wore nothing, after all.

As I stepped into the trough, Aryana spoke.

"You are very beautiful, Benella, and when you fully realize that, I pity the men in your path."

The sincerity in her tone had me raising my eyes. She gave me a gentle smile then bent to pick up the rinse bucket.

"Ready?" she asked with the bucket poised over her head, her breasts lifted high, their rosy peaks taunting me with my own inadequacies.

I didn't think of myself as unattractive, just unendowed. Everyone else sported nice round breasts while mine seemed a bit smallish.

"Ready," I whispered.

The cool water rushed over my head, putting out a fire I hadn't noticed. I sighed in relief, and she laughed.

"I thought you looked too warm. Come, you still have time to relax while we oil your hair."

CHAPTER NINE

LONG BEFORE THE FIRST CLIENT STEPPED THROUGH THE DOOR OF THE Whispering Sisters, I found myself walking toward the estate's gate. After leaving the sisters, I'd known I couldn't go home. My hair smelled too nice for Bryn not to notice and start asking questions that I didn't want to answer. Father didn't like me knowing where he worked; I could only imagine how he would feel if two of his daughters knew.

If not for my growling stomach and the lack of food and coin at home, I wouldn't have come. The beast hadn't expected me today, and I wasn't sure of my unplanned welcome.

Standing inside the gate, waiting for the gathering mist that heralded the beast, I reflected on the new friends I had made. They'd taught me so much in a short period of time. When I'd left, they'd invited me to return any day before ten for another visit. I knew I would return. Their veils begged to be questioned.

"You have returned," he said.

I smiled slightly at his puzzled tone.

"I hope you don't mind. Do you have work for me? I'm really hungry."

The barest scrape of his foot on the ground behind me warned me where he stood. I'd grown so used to his cloaked presence that I felt no fear, just uncertainty. Perhaps the relaxing morning had something to do with my mood as well.

His hand touched my hair, and I heard him inhale deeply.

"No cleaning the kitchen today." His voice clicked with agitation. "Do you read?"

The question surprised me.

"Yes."

"The pages often tear when I try to turn them. Today, you will read for me. Come."

He led the way to the estate, his outline always just on the edge of my vision. We entered through the kitchen door. The mist swallowed all of the light indoors.

"I cannot see," I said. Hearing my own whispering voice, I wondered if I should try speaking softly to the beast. Perhaps he might growl less.

"Take my tail," he said with an agitated growl.

Something thick and heavy whacked against my side. I reached out and curled a hand around his thick, furry tail. He waited a moment before moving, walking slowly so I could keep pace without tugging on his appendage. While we walked, I couldn't help but bring my other hand to his tail to touch the coarse fur. When he'd carried me, I'd been too hurt to notice his fur, and I couldn't recall much detail from when I'd slept on it.

I spread my fingers and delved into his fur, stroking it the wrong way so the hair tickled between my fingers. Changing directions, I smoothed it back down. He neither growled nor spoke, so I continued with my touch as we wound through black hallways until we entered a large muffled room. We walked several steps in, and then he stopped. Reluctantly, I released his tail. It felt like the first semi-friendly touch we'd shared where my role involved more than holding still.

"Light a candle and sit facing away from the door," he said with a deep growl. "I will return shortly."

He left, taking the mist with him. A sliver of light shone straight ahead, and I cautiously shuffled toward it. Heavy drapery met my touch, and I tentatively pushed it aside. The large, glass-paned window framed a beautiful view of a very overgrown yard.

My mouth dropped open as a tree—of sorts—scampered into view. Its white paper skin marked with black dots and raised lines reminded me of a birch's bark. The fingers on her hands and the toes on her feet sprouted with leaves. Where hair should have streamed down her back, a cascade of wisp thin branches, heavily adorned with bright green spring leaves, grew instead. Her form looked very human, including two lumps on her main trunk to indicate breasts. A tree nymph.

Enthralled, I watched her spin and look over her shoulder with a smile. Another nymph came into view, this one obviously male, based on the short thick branch that extended from the area just above where the main trunk split into something resembling human legs.

The male nymph caught up to the female and spun her to face him. She tilted her head back with a wide smile, her leaf hair catching the light prettily. He grasped her behind the knee with one hand and drew her leg up over his hip. Between them, I could see his jutting root. The leg he had lifted melted into his trunk, solidifying the two into one. Slowly, he flexed forward, and I watched the root disappear. The scene left me warm as if I still sat in the hot waters at the Whispering Sisters. The male withdrew and flexed forward again. Both seemed to be enjoying it very much, and I felt a twinge of shame for watching.

Prying my fingers one by one from the curtain, I was about to let it drop when a dark mist came rolling in from the left. The male's head shot up, turning unnaturally to look at the mist. When he saw it, he broke away from his partner and immediately solidified into a tree.

The female, however, did not solidify. Instead, with a small smile, she glanced at the mist, then bent forward. The position brought to memory—in vivid detail—how Ila had looked when she bent to pet the cat. The mist consumed the back half of the nymph, pouring over her like an angry wave. Bent forward as she was, I watched the nymph's leaf hair sway as something pushed against her again and again.

Carefully, I let the curtain fall, hoping it wouldn't draw the attention of any of the parties outside, and scrambled to find a candle and a book. I flopped onto a sofa, kicking my feet up in a relaxed pose, just as I heard the beast enter the room.

"What book did you choose?" he asked softly, with only a hint of a growl. His hand found my hair and gently tugged it out so he could stroke it. I could smell a hint of outdoors on him.

I couldn't find my voice to speak. Lifting the book, I showed him the cover. I stared at it, too. A book on farming. My already thumping heart beat harder. Would he know now that I had seen them?

"This will be an enlightening hour," he said, and I felt him settle on the floor by my head, his hands still running through my hair. He breathed in deeply again, and I knew he was smelling the oil Ila had rubbed into the strands.

"Proceed."

After clearing my throat, I began to speak softly about a farmer's woes and how to alleviate them.

MORE THAN AN HOUR passed before I set the book on my chest. What most would find boring had interested me to the point that

I'd forgotten the time and the hands running through my hair. When I ceased reading, the beast halted as well.

"Why have you stopped?" he demanded in a growl.

"I haven't had anything to eat today and am thirsty," I said softly.

He grunted his objection, but I heard him stand.

"Can I hold your tail again?" I asked, thinking of the dark halls.

The mist in the room suddenly churned so darkly it extinguished the candle. I recalled the scene outside the window and regretted my request. I sat up in concern and tentatively reached out a hand. Almost immediately, I connected with fur, more than I could wrap a hand around. Unsure what else to do, I trailed my fingers along the fur until I understood I touched his hip. I carefully trailed my hand further back and clasped his tail.

Through it all, he held still and said nothing. I whispered a quick apology. He began walking, and this time, I didn't do more than hold his tail.

A few minutes later, we stepped into the kitchen.

"There is a tray on the block for you. Will you read more to me after you eat?" he asked impatiently.

"Yes," I whispered, trying to emulate the sisters to help calm him.

"Then, I will return shortly," he said, anger clipping his words.

"Wait," I called before the mist left. "I would rather eat in the library if you don't mind."

I'd noticed the number of books that lined the walls of the library when I'd raced to grab a book earlier. I wanted a chance to explore that space.

"Of course." The clicking quality was back in his voice.

I carried the tray in one hand while holding his tail in the other. He had barely stepped into the library when his tail tugged from my grasp. As he left, the candle flared to life so I could see. I sighed and set the tray down.

Curiously, I peeked out the window to see if the nymphs had resumed their frolic. To my surprise, the male remained frozen in the same position. The female sat at his feet, idly touching his root, which no longer stood out stiffly. I felt pity for her. Obviously, the interruption to their play had upset her partner.

As before, a black mist roiled in from the left, catching my attention. The female nymph stood slowly with a lingering sad touch on her partner before backing away a few steps. She didn't look as eager this time as she bent forward.

The mist rolled over her. In its depths, I discerned the shadow of the beast as he reared back on his hind legs. He braced his hands on her back and thrust forward into the nymph. He drove into her tirelessly, and I wondered how she stayed upright, until I noticed her feet rooted into the ground.

Troubled, I let the curtain fall. The enchantments on this place were a puzzle to me, often not appearing to adhere to any rules, such as the food that grew outside the wall. Now, I wondered if there were rules to the creatures here. Why hadn't the female nymph solidified into a tree to escape the beast? She hadn't appeared to want the beast's attention this time. Yet, instead of solidifying, she had rooted her feet in order to accommodate him. Why?

While I pondered possible reasons for what I'd witnessed, I went to my food and drink. Before the beast returned, I'd drunk my fill, eaten a bit of cheese, and then stored the rest of it in my bag to share with Father in the morning.

When the beast entered the room, I was exploring a small section of books.

"Continue," he prompted me softly, again with barely a growl.

I cautiously returned to the lounge, noting from my peripheral that no shadowy mist followed him.

Pent energies, I thought as I began to read. The beast seemed to have a lot of them. I knew the basics of the act I'd seen performed—after all, I'd discovered Bryn doing the same—but some of the finer details I'd yet to puzzle out. For instance, why a woman would want to do that? Obviously, the male enjoyed it. I recalled Sara's reaction to the baker and Bryn's noises. Both women made those noises from what I thought came from enjoyment; but afterward, both had been sad.

I read for a while longer before closing the book softly. The beast's fingers stilled in my hair.

I remained prone on the sofa, quietly thinking. He willingly traded my time for food, and he didn't seem to care how I spent that time so long as it was in his manor. If he truly wanted it cleaned, he would not have asked for me to read. Likewise, if he wanted to hear another's voice, he would have asked me to read from the beginning. Everything seemed to be on a whim with him, even his frolic with the nymph. Yet, each time I fulfilled my time obligation, he asked the same question and became agitated when I took my leave.

"Sir, why do you keep asking me to return?"

"That is my concern," he growled.

"It seems my visits cause you more anger than peace. Perhaps I shouldn't return," I said softly.

"No," he said with a harsh growl before sucking in a great breath. Slowly, the breath eased out. "I apologize for my anger. Return tomorrow, please."

"Will I clean tomorrow?" I asked tentatively. "I enjoy reading, but would like to earn more food to take home with me."

"You will leave with food today," he snarled at me as the mist swirled into the room and extinguished the candle again.

His tail bumped my neck, and I stood with my hand wrapped lightly around it.

I didn't understand his mercurial temper. Perhaps it was just his nature.

When we arrived in the kitchen, he stormed out the door without a word. On the block, I found a variety of cheeses and bread, which I stuffed into my bag.

THE NEXT MORNING, I waited until Father left before rising from bed. We hadn't discussed where he worked, yet, or that I'd brought him breakfast twice. I decided I would do the same for him, again, since I hadn't purchased oats with the coin I'd received in trade for a wheel of hard cheese. I had been given a full high silver. Twice the value of a blunt silver. I'd never held so much at once and honestly didn't know what to do with it. I'd slept with it tucked into my bindings.

When I arrived at the back door of the Whispering Sisters not much later, carrying a glazed pastry, I had a blunt silver and eighteen coppers still in my bag. The baker hadn't fussed about making change for a high silver, apparently having plenty of his own.

The guard at the door nodded and held the door for me to enter. I smiled and went inside, the smoke swamping my head almost immediately. However, Ila was waiting in the hallway with a cup of tea.

"How did you know I was coming?" I asked, after draining it.

"We watch from our windows. Another sister spotted you and let me know."

I delivered the pastry to my very surprised father who asked to speak with me in the hallway. Ila excused herself and stepped inside to speak with one of her sisters.

"I would prefer—"

I stopped him with a raised hand.

"You've raised me, taught me, and uprooted our family to protect me. Let me bring you breakfast when you forget to eat."

His shoulders slumped in defeat, and he nodded.

"I like the sisters," I said so softly that he had to lean forward to hear. "But you should rest easy when I'm here. Their life does not call to me."

He met my eyes with relief and gave me a brief hug to which the population of the room softly aw'ed, embarrassing him. I smiled at him as Ila joined me and closed the door. We retreated to the bathing room by an unspoken agreement.

"I can see the questions running through your mind," she said as we descended.

"Yes, but they aren't necessarily about the sisters," I admitted. "We've touched a little on the mood of men. What do you do with an angry man?"

"You want to know what we do, or would like advice regarding how you should handle an angry man?" Aryana asked, rising from the water in one of the tubs. She stepped over the edge and motioned to the back room.

Absently, I licked the glaze from my fingers as we moved. I didn't want anyone knowing about the beast nor did I want their questions if I admitted to having to deal with an angry man.

"What you would do."

Ila waved Gen from the room as she stepped into the trough and gave Aryana a concerned look. Aryana sluiced water over Ila and handed her soap without acknowledging the look.

"When our clients leave the baths, some choose to follow us

upstairs for muscle relief." They worked together to lather Ila's body, using languid strokes. I would have felt uncomfortable, but neither seemed aware of the other's touch as they remained focused on me.

"Many who visit us do physical labor that leaves them sore and strained," Aryana continued, absently smoothing her hand over Ila's right breast and leaving a soap trail. "A man with pain is more likely quick to temper. We can show you our techniques, but you must promise never to use them."

I eagerly agreed. The beast didn't seem to do physical labor, so I didn't think the information would benefit him, but I always sought to learn new things. Learning this could lead to other things that might eventually lead to knowledge that could help control the beast's temper.

Ila frowned while sliding her hand between her legs to wash her lower parts.

"Are you sure that's wise?"

Aryana helped her rinse.

"Better to have understanding of a room in the light before trying to walk about it in the dark."

Ila nodded and took a moment to stand before the stove to dry.

Aryana's remark made sense. What they had to teach probably bordered on inappropriate, but knowledge made choices easier. If I knew what obstacles to watch for, I wouldn't trip on them.

Aryana led the way upstairs to a room where Gen lounged on a flat sofa with no back. He didn't seem surprised when we entered.

"Gen, would you mind being our display for a skin and muscle touch?"

The adolescent, around my age, shrugged and nodded, but remained sitting.

Ila took me by the hand and led me back into the hall where we waited. "There are many aspects to a man. For you to fully understand them, we need to show you some of the dangers you might innocently overlook."

"What do you mean?" I asked, confused.

Aryana called softly from within the room, and Ila smiled.

"You will see."

When we walked back in, Gen lay on the sofa on his stomach with a light sheet over his head. Aryana caught my curious look.

"Just as we veil our faces to keep the focus on our bodies and our clients' needs, we must cover Gen's face to keep our focus on his body and our explanation. Gen's body, not his face, will tell us his needs."

Interesting, I thought, stepping closer. Gen still had the thin wiry muscles of youth, and I enjoyed looking at him.

"If releasing the pent energies does not remove a man's anger, we look at his body as a whole. Tension, which can cause anger, can be carried in many places throughout the body," Ila began her explanation, running her hand lightly over Gen's back and down his leg to the sole of his foot. She then ran her hand the opposite direction on the opposite side.

She explained the placement of certain muscles and what kind of touch to use to soothe the tension from them. When she'd covered the back of him, including the muscles of his butt, she asked him to flip over. She was careful to keep his face covered.

Immediately, my eyes drifted to his penis, and I thought of the poor wood nymph's wilted root. Gen's penis lay relaxed against the tangle of hair surrounding it. Under it hung a large sac with two obvious lumps. Ila chuckled at my long stare and gave me the names of each. I knew the term penis, thanks to one of my father's medicinal books, but ballsack was new and sounded odd.

Aryana took over the instruction of the front, starting with the arms and legs, then going to the chest. Their explanation of the tissue beneath the surface fascinated me, and I wondered if Father would be as interested.

"The soft area of the stomach, below the ribs and above the hips, should not be touched using any of the techniques we've shown you so far," Aryana said, trailing her fingers lightly over the skin.

I noticed Gen's penis twitch again as it had occasionally since he'd turned to his stomach.

"A man's rod will often respond with the use of any of these techniques; and that is what you must watch for because, instead of relaxing him, you may be causing an increase in pent energies."

She slid her hand over his stomach again in a firmer touch and trailed over the crease of his thigh. His penis jumped significantly. She trailed her hand lightly over his ballsack, and I watched in fascination as his penis stood upright.

"If it gets to this point, you can be assured, you are in trouble and should leave quickly before he becomes of a mind to have *you* release his pent energies for him."

She grasped Gen's penis firmly, and I watched the head of it turn red. Ila took a small vial from a nearby shelf and drizzled oil over the tip, which Aryana smoothed down its length. Then, she proceeded to stroke it in a smooth, slow rhythm. I couldn't look away.

Gen began to twitch slightly on the sofa, his hips thrusting forward to meet her downward slide. The room grew warm for me. The sac, which had been loose before, began to tighten and shrink. Aryana stopped, abruptly releasing his penis and stepping back. Ila used a gentle arm to nudge me back as well and motioned me to remain silent.

"Aryana," Gen rasped from under the sheet, his hips bucking forward. When she didn't answer, he bolted upright, whipping off the sheet from his face. He angrily glared at Aryana and Ila.

"I did not agree to this," he ground out, his face flushed.

Aryana held up both hands.

"A few moments more of your patience, Gen, might save our dear Benella from terrible mistakes," she said softly.

His eyes narrowed, but he nodded and lay back down, curling his own hand around his penis. He didn't stroke it as Aryana had. He held it as one would a bruised appendage.

"If a man's energies are pent and not released, he will become volatile, unpredictable. Tension will creep into his body and often stay there even after the energies are eventually released. If you touch a man, no matter how innocent the touch, watch for the signs," Aryana warned. "Be sure your touch is only releasing tension and not building pent energies."

Fascinated, I nodded my understanding. It did sound a bit like the beast. Even after his encounter with the wood nymph and he'd released his energies, he had still kept his tension. The sisters were right about the dangers. I would never attempt anything like what I'd just learned on the beast. I feared his response.

"Come," Ila whispered, taking my hand. "Some mysteries we will leave you to discover on your own."

She led me from the room as Aryana gently removed Gen's hand and replaced it with her own. Before we reached the end of the hall, I heard his loud groan.

THE DARK, rolling mist waited beyond the groaning gate of the estate. I calmly stepped into the shadows and walked forward until the gate closed behind me.

"What would you have me clean today?" I asked softly.

"The servant's quarters in the kitchen in exchange for as many berries as you can carry," he said in his typical aggravated tone.

"Lead the way."

In the kitchen, he left me to work, darkening the room occasionally to watch me after I'd changed from my dress.

The chairs stood in good repair, and a new table had taken the place of the damaged one. I dragged half of the broken table outside and tugged the mattresses out, one by one, for an airing. I even scoured the floor in the room and washed the window.

When I finished, I changed and wandered back into the kitchen to find food on the new table along with my bag filled with berries wrapped in two layers of soft cloth. No doubt, many would be crushed before I returned to the Water.

I ate my fill of bread, quail, and squash, then shouldered my bag. As soon as I moved toward the door, the beast returned in his shrouding mists.

"Will you stay?" he asked.

"I cannot."

He left in a fit of anger, and I found my own way to the gate. As I predicted, some of the berries did not survive the journey. Crushed by the weight of other berries, they bled through the cloth, my bag, and into my dress near the hip.

When I reached the bridge, a cooler wind gusted from the north and clouds drifted over the sun. The berries I carried would need either to be dried or eaten before they spoiled. Without the sun to help, drying would prove too difficult. I wandered to the market district and traded oats for berries.

Bryn was within the cottage, cooking dinner when I returned with the remaining berries and the small portion of oats. I let her know they were for Father when I set them down. She nodded and coughed lightly into her apron before telling me dinner had another twenty minutes.

Sitting in Father's chair, I perused a book, listening to the scrape of the spoon on the pan and the occasional light cough while thinking about the beast.

Perhaps tomorrow I should bargain my time for answers instead of food.

THE NEXT MORNING, Father remained near Bryn's bedside instead of leaving for the Whispering Sisters. During the night, her light cough had turned into a deep, grating whoop of air. None of us slept well from dusk to light, and nothing Father tried worked.

Dressing quickly in my stained dress, I took the coins I'd saved and ran to the business district to knock on the doors of anyone boasting knowledge of medicine. I finally found a learned doctor who claimed knowledge of the illness as well as a remedy. It took all of the coins I had to convince him to follow me home.

Bryn still lay in bed, rasping for breath when we arrived. The doctor asked Father to leave the room while he examined her. He cautioned Blye, who was already dressed for work, to remain until he concluded his exam. Several minutes later, he exited the bedroom.

"You should all remain in quarantine until this passes. Here is the medicine you will need once you start to cough. Take one dose a day. If you run out, I have more for purchase."

He and Father spoke quietly for several minutes before the doctor took his leave.

Father sat heavily in the chair before the fire.

"Blye, there is only enough medicine for three, should we all become sick. Do you have coin for another bottle?"

"I purchased cloth with the coin I had and am making my own dresses for the shop to sell. I have nothing until I finish them," she said with a worried quaver.

"Benella?"

I shook my head.

"I gave the doctor everything I had to get him here."

"He is going to tell the Head, and they will place us under mandatory quarantine. Take your bag and leave. Forage for what you can to trade should we need it. Go," he said sharply.

Grabbing my bag, I flew out the door, not arguing with the fault in his logic. If we were to be quarantined, no one would want to trade with me for anything I found. The whole point was not to spread the sickness.

Dark, heavy clouds hung damp in the sky, casting gloom over the town. I raced lightly to the Whispering Sisters and called to the guard that Bryn was ill and Father would not return until she recovered. I asked him to discreetly let Blye's seamstress know, too.

He nodded, and I spun away in a hurry to leave the Water behind me.

CHAPTER
TEN

On the outskirts of the estate, the sky rumbled and let loose a torrent of cold, spring rain to pound the ground. I sloshed the remaining distance to the gate, disheartened to see it raining inside, too. I'd hoped the magic would keep it out and let me dry.

No mist waited for me, so I found my own way to the manor, shivering as I let myself into the kitchen. A small fire crackled in the hearth, and I eagerly closed the door on the poor weather. Disregarding the trail of water I left, I crossed the room to warm myself. The heat from the flames barely heated my fingers and did nothing to reduce my trembling. Only dry clothes would warm me.

My boots made squishing noises as I walked to the servant's quarters. I closed the door, then struggled to remove my dress. Peeling off the wet mass wasn't easy. Shivering, I dug in my sodden bag for my shirt and trousers. The pants were soaked, but the shirt had escaped most of the water and only felt damp. I removed my wet binding, laid it over the footboard of the bed, and tugged on the shirt.

Sitting on the edge of the bed, I removed my boots and socks. The cold floor further numbed my feet while I gathered up my dress and pants. With my wet clothes draped over one arm and my boots in my hand, I opened the door to a mist filled kitchen. It was so dark the light of the fire didn't penetrate more than a few feet into the gloom.

"I didn't expect you so soon," the beast rumbled from the darkness.

Holding my dress to shield my bare legs, I hesitated in the doorway and debated if I should retreat into the room until I dried.

"My sister is sick. Father sent me to gather what I could to trade for more medicine. We were all told to stay in quarantine, so you might not want to come too close." I was less concerned about spreading sickness to an enchanted creature than I was about tempting the beast.

"There is washing to be done. Follow me, and I will show you to the laundry."

The fire snuffed out, and his tail bumped against me. I had no choice but to drop my boots and walk across the cold stone floor, holding his tail so I could follow.

It seemed that the winding path led behind the kitchen. Rain pinged against a window, and the sound echoed in the room. I continued to hold onto the beast's tail, unable to see anything.

"Stand here," he said gruffly as his tail pulled from my grasp.

In a moment, a fire burst to life on each end of the room, flooding the large area with light. At the opposite side of the room, two windows marked the wall with a door that led outside. Near the door, three wooden half-barrels squatted heavily beside the fireplace. Not far from there, a long table abutted the wall and racks for drying lay in a tumble. In order to wash anything, I would need to right the drying racks and fill the tubs. Both tasks requiring more bending than I would want to perform when dressed only in a shirt.

Turning, I eyed the mist just outside the arched entry I'd come through.

"May I have something to drink, sir?"

The mist receded, and I sagged with relief. I quickly tossed my dress over a drying rack and moved the rest of the racks into place between the tubs and the arch. To the left of the back door, lay a pile of dirty linens. By arranging several of those over the drying racks, I created a screen for myself before setting to work.

A large kettle and a cistern to the right of the fire gave me what I needed to start the process. The beast returned while I sorted through the soiled pile, his clicking growl announcing his presence. Arms around a mound of linens, I didn't turn to acknowledge him as I dropped everything into an empty tub.

The growling faded as I tested the heating water, so I braved looking around. A clay pitcher and a stout cup had appeared on the long back table. Cautiously, I tiptoed from behind my screens and poured myself some water. My throat felt dry and slightly sore, probably from walking in the rain. The cool water soothed it enough that I could focus on laundry.

It took a long time to fill the tub with hot water and even longer to scrub soap into the cloth. The soapy steam tickled my throat enough that I coughed occasionally. While I let the cloth soak, I filled another tub with cool water for rinsing. The heat from both fires warmed the room so much that I had to wipe the sweat from my brow. I no longer felt the chill from the floor.

Coughing made my throat sore, which made me cough more as I rinsed and wrung out the water. I changed the material screening me from the dirty ones to the clean ones and washed the second tub of linens.

A mist invaded the room again while I worked, easily two hours after I had started. He made no noise, not even a growl. I felt his eyes following me as I moved from the washtub to the rinse tub. As I twisted the material, sweating and coughing, I realized I would need to walk from my screen to hang the second string of bedding. But, the shirt I wore only hung to the tops of my thighs. As I considered the situation, I decided I didn't care as much anymore. I was hot and tired and wanted to finish, return home, and go to bed. With that thought, I realized I had Bryn's ailment.

Stepping from around the screens, I coughed harder and heard a slight wheeze as I inhaled. Yet, I continued to drape wet linens over a drying rack along with several shirts with torn button holes and missing buttons that I had found and washed. As soon as I deposited the last piece, I touched my still damp dress and looked toward the arch.

"Finished," I said softly.

Outside, the rain continued to pound against the door, so it didn't matter if the dress was dry. But would I make it home? Bryn had grown gradually worse in a short period of time.

"Will you accept my offer?" he asked.

"What exactly is your offer?" I asked. The heat I felt no longer came from the fires, but from inside.

"Stay with me, do as I command, and I will grant your every wish."

"And my family? Will I see them?"

He growled fiercely, giving me the answer I'd already known.

"I cannot accept your offer." A cough ripped from me, and I struggled to catch my breath. "But I don't think I can leave yet, either. May I stay in the servant's quarters until the rain stops?"

The mist swirled around me, blocking all light from the fires. His hand brushed my brow lightly, the touch brief. Suddenly, he bumped into me, knocking me into his arms.

"You may stay until you are well."

With him carrying me, we flew through the halls to the kitchen. He gently set me on one of the bare mattresses and left in a whirl. I shivered in the cool room, coughing so hard my stomach hurt. He returned with a thick comforter and covered me gently. I closed my eyes and asked for one more thing.

"Please send word to my father. I don't want him to worry."

HEAT BURNED THROUGH ME, and a crow cawed loudly. Wind roared through the room, making the beds shake. From the shadows a demon rose. Black with glowing red eyes, it opened its massive maw and bit down into my chest, opening me wide and tearing me apart with each cough. I faded.

"HELP HER!"

The roar filled the room, a distraction from the painful cough consuming me.

"Are you willing to pay the price?" a voice demanded sharply, sounding vaguely familiar.

"Wretched woman, haven't I given you enough? What more would you take from me?"

"Secrecy. Before she leaves, you must reveal yourself," the voice said in an angry, spiteful tone. "No mist to hide you. You deserve no respite. You've learned nothing."

A moment of silence reigned while the demon continued to devour me.

"Yes, I will pay the price and wish you to hell," he said raggedly.

"Here, give her one dose of this each day until she is well. Now, don't bother me again unless it's to give me what I want."

A cold wind rushed through the room, then a large hand burrowed under my head to lift me slightly. A cup pressed to my lips and liquid touched them. I swallowed convulsively three times before the hand lowered me to the mattress again. The liquid flowed down, burning through the wounds the demon had chewed, until I cried and begged for help.

The beast whispered promises in my ear. He asked me to give him my obedience, and he would stop the demon's feasting. I thought of my father and, hoping he didn't suffer the same fate, shook my head to deny the beast. The bed trembled with his anger.

THE DEMON LEFT at some point during the night, but the wounds he'd caused remained to fester and boil. Again, the beast lifted my head and forced me to drink the vile draught of water and medicine. It didn't burn as much when I coughed afterward.

He continued to whisper in my ear as I drifted in and out of sleep, making outrageous promises in return for my word to remain with him forever. His insistency didn't make any sense to me, and I shook my head to deny him each time.

WHEN I OPENED my eyes the following morning, I groaned at the sunlight streaming through the single window and wished I hadn't cleaned the glass so well. I coughed lightly and remembered the dreams I had of a creature ravaging my chest. Licking my dry lips, I turned my head to look around the room and found that I was alone and the door to the room closed.

I struggled upright and managed to bring myself to a sitting position. My bladder needed relief, and a chamber pot sat in the corner. The cold floor abraded my suddenly sensitive feet as I shuffled toward the pot. The shirt that I'd worn made it easier to do what needed to be done and get back into bed.

As soon as I pulled the cover over me again, the door crashed open and the dark mist rolled into the room.

"How long have I been ill?" I asked, not caring about courtesy.

"This is the second day," he said, sliding a hand under my head and forcing me to drain a cup of plain water. It sat cold and heavy in my stomach in a good way.

I felt sleep pulling at me.

"Did you send word to my father?" I asked.

"Yes. He knows you are safe and being cared for." His fingers touched my hair, and my eyes fluttered closed.

I slept several hours before waking again. The light through the window didn't shine as brightly. A chair near the bed held a cup filled with water. I reached for it eagerly and drained it before making another visit to the chamber pot.

My limbs shook less, but sleep still pulled at me. Again, when I returned to the bed, the beast reappeared in his masking mist.

"Are you feeling well enough to leave?" he asked angrily.

The thought of trudging home made me wince.

"If possible, I would leave and not exhaust your hospitality, but I'm afraid I wouldn't make it very far," I said, wondering if he would insist I leave regardless.

"Very well," he said, seemingly mollified. "Another night then, unless you'd rather stay indefinitely. There are many rooms much more suited to a permanent guest."

I opened my mouth to deny him, but he continued.

"Beds soft enough to sink several inches and drapes thick enough to keep away the deepest winter's chill. And wardrobes filled with dresses of supple cloth to caress your skin. You would want for nothing," he assured me.

"Why are you so desperate to keep me here?" I asked.

"Why do you refuse me so insistently?" he countered with a growl.

"Because you've given me no reason to stay," I said without meaning to. Perhaps being ill prevented my good sense from filtering what came out of my mouth. "You don't know anything about me. Now, tell me why you want me to stay."

He roared loudly, during which I caught a curse on all women, then he left in a fury. He slammed the door so hard it tore from the hinges and fell flat to the floor. I was glad the chamber pot wasn't near it. It would have been a mess to clean up.

I rolled to my side, facing the door, and noticed a tray with bread and a bowl of broth on the chair. Guilt swamped me for aggravating him so much when he'd obviously been taking care of me. I ate the bread, dipping it in the broth, while I tried to arrive at a reasonable explanation for his insistence that I stay.

Though he'd always seemed angry, he did provide for me. Yet, the night I'd run from Tennen and the vines pulled me to the estate—the night the beast had asked to see me naked—made me doubt that his care was due to compassion. However, since then, he'd asked of nothing improper from me, only that I clean...and one time that I read to him. Could he just be lonely?

What about the other enchanted creatures, though? And the old woman he'd brought me to when I'd hit my head on the pole? I recalled the conversation I'd heard while dreaming of the flesh-eating demon. Though I knew the demon was only a product of my fevered mind, I felt that conversation had been real. She'd given him the medicine I needed, and he had promised something in return.

The beast truly did provide for me. But why? I fell asleep before I could arrive at any conclusion.

WHEN I WOKE NEXT, I heard the crackle of a fire from the kitchen and noticed its soft glow illuminating the floor where the door had lain. Someone had removed the door while I slept. My stomach rumbled, and I looked to the chair, hoping for more broth. Instead, a gown draped over the back of it. The dress had more ruffles than I cared for, but I knew the beast meant for me to wear it as an example of what he could offer.

I pulled myself upright and quickly shed the shirt to tug on the dress. It fit snuggly, its supple material clinging and caressing my skin as he promised. When I stood, it fell to the floor in an overabundant cascade. It brought back memories of trying to run through the woods with Tennen right behind me.

Trying not to scowl, I treaded lightly to the kitchen. A crisp, white linen covered the new table. A feast lay out upon it, and the smells of roasted fowl, creamed soups, baked vegetables, and warm bread perfumed the air. Forgetting the dress, I moved to the only setting at the table and pushed back my chair, kicking my skirt slightly to move it out of the way as I sat.

Picking up the fork, I didn't hesitate to start eating. Everything looked and smelled so good my mouth watered with anticipation.

I didn't realize the beast had drifted into the room until he passed before the fire and momentarily blocked the light.

"Are you pleased?" he asked.

"The food is delicious. Thank you," I said after swallowing a bite. I broke off a hunk of steaming bread and smeared soft butter on it. My eyes rolled back.

"And the dress?" he asked.

"Suitably ruffled for such a fine meal," I said.

"Have you given my offer further consideration?"

Letting silence fall as I chewed a large bite, I wondered how to answer his question. Had I thought on his offer? Yes, but only to try to determine why he repeatedly asked, not to give it serious consideration. After all, I knew nothing of significance regarding the beast to give his proposal serious thought.

"Do you want to know why I consistently say no?" I didn't wait for him to respond. "How can I offer to stay, to obey your commands, when I see the considerable amount of cruelty and anger in you? How will you turn that on me when I am yours to command?" He growled ominously but didn't move closer to the table.

"You know nothing of my anger." A warning growl coated his words.

"I know that you resent this manor and would have gladly ripped it down if the magic here would have let you. And I know that you disregard most of the creatures here with you."

"Ridiculous," he roared. "I do not disregard those trapped here with me."

Trapped? I held onto that bit of knowledge but made no comment on it.

"I saw you with the nymph," I said, calmly taking a bite from the tender meat of the bird. "If that is how you treat those you care for, I want no part of it." His growl covered most of his cursing. "She seemed to want no part of you, the second time. Her man stood woodenly nearby watching your use of her. Tell me, would you have raked her trunk like you do to the wood in here had she turned into a tree?" I motioned to the furrows dug deeply into the wood in the kitchen. The black cloud of mist containing him churned with his wrath.

Suddenly, the table and its bounty of food flew away from me as if pulled by a gigantic hand. Dishes clattered to the floor and shattered at my feet, splattering the gown with bits of food. Fork still in hand, I popped my last bite into my mouth.

He raged while I chewed, my heart hammering at my audacity. Still, I felt certain he wouldn't touch me in anger despite my words.

He'd had opportunity to do so many times before. No, tonight was meant to tempt me to say yes to his offer. If he touched me, he knew the answer would never change.

"Thank you for the meal. I enjoyed the food, but the company could use some manners," I said lightly and stood, shaking what food I could from the dress.

I turned and carefully picked my way through the broken shards of dishware, navigating my bare feet to the safety of the bedroom. He growled, roared, and cursed the entire time.

Staying clothed, I lay back down in bed and stopped listening to his rant. The meal and his tantrum had exhausted me. I went to sleep.

AFTER PULLING on my socks and then lacing up my boots, I crept to the kitchen. Disaster still claimed the room. On the butcher block, I spotted the shredded remains of my dress and bag. A small sack, about the size of my fist, waited next to the pile. I loosened the tie and looked in at the fine granules of real sugar. The dull, light tan crystals were a rare treat this far north and worth their weight in gold. Two gold coins rested flat against the table near the piled remains of my belongings. I imagined his temper after I slept and his regret after he vented it on my things. Shaking my head, I scooped up everything and headed toward the door.

I still felt weak, but no longer sick. Unsure of the quarantine, I hoped my arrival back in the Water would not cause issue. The vial of medicine, which had been on the chair when I woke, now hid within my bodice. I'd sipped a small dose when I had wakened, as a precaution.

Walking out into the sunlight, I filled my lungs with the fresh air and let it out slowly. A crow watched from a nearby tree, and I bowed to it. It clacked its beak at me in return. Smiling, I ambled to the gate, enjoying the feeling of the sun on my face. It didn't seem to happen too often inside the estate.

Ahead, near the gate, a figure hid under the shadows of the trees. I halted as soon as I spotted it, wondering if someone had crossed into the estate without the beast's knowledge. I didn't have many friends in Konrall, and those I had wouldn't risk the beast's punishment for trespass.

"Will you not consider my offer?" the beast called to me angrily. "I've sheltered you, fed you, cared for you. You have no cause to deny me."

Hearing his voice eased some of my fears, and I started forward.

"Stay where you are," he commanded angrily.

I stilled, wondering what madness gripped him now.

"Your answer. I will give you everything you desire if you but stay and do as I command."

"Everything I desire?" I fought to keep from laughing as he swore to it. "That is a foolish promise when you have no idea what I desire. What if my desire was your death or to destroy the manor? Neither would be possible, would they?"

He snarled at my logic, and I moved forward. He called me a spiteful woman, ungrateful and cold to the plight of others, selfish and cruel in the face of giving and kindness. As I neared the gate, he moved back behind the underbrush, trying to stay in the shadows. When I stepped onto the dirt just before the gate, he began to beg.

"Please," he said. "Anything that is within my power to give will be yours. Do not take another step. Turn back and stay with me."

I shook my head and stepped forward again. The gate swung open as he struck the tree under which he stood. With a roar, he trampled through the brush, and I saw the beast with no obscurity a moment before I passed through the gate.

His pointy ears shot up from each side of his head. His dark eyes were set deep under a dark, shaggy brow. Claws tipped each digit, and fur covered his entire body. With lips pulled back, his very sharp teeth gave no illusions as to what he was. He truly was a beast.

I ran. When I reached the road, I stopped and loosened my grip on the sugar and coins to switch to the other hand. My heart pounded in my ears.

In the distance, I could still hear him. They could probably even hear him in Konrall.

Knowing I'd made the right decision to leave when I had, despite my weak and shaking limbs, I set out toward the Water.

CHAPTER
ELEVEN

A nail held a sign to the front door of our home. Ignoring the quarantine warning, I let myself inside. A dry hacking cough greeted me, and I saw Father at the stove, cooking a watery soup.

"Benella," he cried, backing away a step. "You should have stayed away."

"No, Father. I couldn't ever do that." I moved toward him and plucked my vial from my bodice and set it on the table next to the other very low vial. "How much longer are you supposed to take the medicine?"

"Seven days from the onset," he managed before coughing again. The wheezing rasp at the end worried me. He looked drawn and pale. The hand that stirred the soup shook. I pulled out a chair, took the spoon from him, then guided him to sit.

"Where are Bryn and Blye?"

"Sick in their bed."

I found it odd that Bryn still lay abed when she'd been the first of us sick. I was already up and walking about the countryside. Keeping my thoughts to myself, I went to the well out back to fetch fresh water.

"The Head warned us not to go out during the day," Father said.

"We need water," I replied tartly. I didn't see how fetching the water only at night would benefit anyone. It just meant Father worked when he should be resting. If the Head cared so much, he could enter our den of sickness to scold me.

"Did you take your dose today?"

He shook his head, and I knew it was because there was so little left. How could the doctor think this would last seven days for three people when only a quarter of the vial remained? Father caught my expression as I carefully measured a dose into a cup and added water.

"Bryn took the dose twice a day hoping it would work faster. I suspect Blye did the same, but in hopes it would keep her from catching it."

I cast a glance at their closed door, the only consideration I gave them, and ladled some of the soup to Father. As he sipped it, there was a knock on the front door.

We both exchanged glances before I called out a quarantine warning.

"I know," a voice called back. "I put it there. So I'm wondering why we spotted someone entering this building a short while ago."

My eyes narrowed, and I jerked open the door. The Head stood in the road a good distance from the door.

"Good morning, Head. Please, won't you come in and discuss this transgression? Better yet, I will come to you, and you can properly reprimand me."

"Benella," Father scolded behind me in a whisper.

"Please stay where you are," the man said. "Now that you've entered, you may not leave until the sickness passes."

"I am fully aware of that. I can read," I said, pointing to the sign right beside me. "We are running low on medicine. The doctor said he had more if we had payment. We also need supplies: oats, flour, any greens to be found. Can you arrange for that? I'd rather care for my father than have to run any errands," I spoke softly, watching him to see if he understood my threat.

He nodded slowly.

"We can leave it on the porch and knock when you can come out for it. You have payment for it?"

Nodding, I turned away from the door and grabbed the two coins I'd set on the table. Father's eyes rounded, having just noticed them. At the door, I flipped them so they landed at the Head's feet.

"Boil them before you trade with them."

The Head reached into his pocket for a piece of leather and wrapped the coins within before walking away. He would probably boil the coins and burn the leather.

"Where did those come from?" Father asked when I closed the door.

I smiled and sat by him.

"You will never believe the story," I said, knowing full well he would.

Just then, the bedroom door opened, and Blye shuffled out. She coughed weakly into an embroidered linen square, no rasp evident in her exhale.

"I heard voices," she said pathetically to explain her presence. Then her eyes widened at the sight of me. "Benella, where did you get that dress?" She rushed forward and touched the sleeve of it. "Exquisite," she breathed and tugged me to my feet. "What happened to the hem?"

When she met my eyes, looking for answers, I asked a question of my own.

"Why are you still abed? You seem fit enough."

Her air of excitement immediately left her, and she again coughed into her linen square.

"I think I'm well and come from the room, but too soon I feel worn and shaky and need to rest. The illness teases me, giving me a moment of normalcy, then robbing me of it all within the same hour."

Probably just long enough for her to eat, I thought nastily. I closed my eyes and pushed away my anger, knowing Father listened to us. It would do no good to pursue the subject.

"Then you should be back abed to rest. I will bring you something to eat soon. The Head went for supplies."

She nodded weakly and shuffled back into the room.

By dinner, I'd made a hearty soup with the supplies delivered by the Head. He'd put the two gold coins to good use, and we had plenty to hold us for four days, including more medicine. I ladled Father and I each a healthy portion. He rose from his bed to join me at the table. I felt his forehead when I noticed an extra shine in his eyes. He felt too warm, and I recalled how I'd burned with a fever. After we ate, I helped him to bed, giving him a drink before directing him to call for me if he needed anything.

Then I took what remained of the soup, added cold water, and served the tepid watery mix to my sisters in bed. They took their bowls without comment and drained them while I watched.

The next day Father grew worse. I gave him another dose from my bottle, promising that any pain he felt in his lungs would soon disappear, and left him to sleep. For my sisters, I gave them their dose for breakfast and promised them food, soon. I delivered the food several hours later. More watered down soup.

An agonizing day passed, listening to Father's racking cough. I sat by his bed, just watching him breathe, and wondered if the beast had done the same while I suffered through my fever. By the time the sun rose, Father rested easier, and I made him drink more water before bathing his face.

At no time during the night had either of my sisters crept from their room, so I went to check on them as well. Both slept soundly, each on her own side of the bed, and I felt a twinge of guilt at my assumption that they faked a lingering illness. I waited until I closed the door softly before I let a small cough escape. Had Father not been ill, I would have been in bed last night as well.

Tiredly, I sat beside him again and soon began to doze.

As the days passed, so did the supplies. We all managed a full seven days of medicine, but remained in quarantine until Father's cough subsided nine days after I had returned home. By then, very little of the salted stag meat remained. When the Head declared us fit to open our doors again, we all worked together to clean and air out the cottage. I avoided the chore of boiling the linens and thought of the beast.

With supplies so low, my sisters whispered to me about going for more. They didn't ask how I came by the dress or why the Head gave us the food he had. They only knew that I'd been the source of the good fortune that helped us through the sickness. When their incessant pleading became too much, I snuck away at dawn to visit the sisters.

Father had returned to teaching the day before. Though I hadn't been to the Whispering Sisters in over a week, the guard nodded when he saw me and let me in. Ila greeted me just inside the door with tea.

"What brings you here today? I heard about your illness and am glad you're fit again."

I nodded in agreement and followed her down the stairs to the bathing room. After so long away, her nakedness drew my gaze again, but she didn't seem to notice. Aryana already lounged in one of the heated tubs.

"My sisters are making my ears bleed with their—" I took a deep breath and then lowered my voice to mimic their husky whispers.

"Could I bathe today?" I asked, instead of complaining.

"You are so self-contained," Aryana commented. "You need to let your thoughts out more often so they don't sour you from the inside."

She rose from the tub, and I held out a hand to help her.

"If I speak my mind, I will sour my family. I've grown used to biting my tongue over the years. It usually doesn't bother me."

Ila made a neutral noise as she led the way to the back room. They shooed Gen out.

"Is this a new dress?" Aryana asked, touching the fabric.

I nodded and reached for the buttons running down the bodice.

"It's very pretty," she said. "I imagine Blye was quite jealous of it."

"How do you know Blye?" I asked, curious that she knew Blye well enough to know of her nature.

"Only what we hear from our clients," Ila whispered, helping me lift the dress over my head.

"Your clients speak of my sisters?" I didn't like that at all. Yes, I knew Blye could be a bit vain and jealous and Bryn a bit selfish and harsh, but they were my sisters. I loved them regardless.

"A few. They or their wives must see your sisters in the market district during the day," Aryana said on her way to fetch two pails of warm water while I discarded my underclothes.

Water cascaded over my head, and I raised my hands to wipe the water from my eyes. The touch of a hand on my back and another on my legs jarred me from my thoughts of a gossiping market street and to the reality of bathing with two relative strangers. My eyes widened a moment before Aryana slid her soaped hands to my shoulders. Her firm fingers melted my objection.

The past week of fetching, cooking, and cleaning had caused knots and strains, which had helped inspire the visit to the sisters to soak in one of their tubs.

"You're still considered new in the village, so people will talk about you. They've commented on your good trading skills, too. Many wonder where you find out of season produce."

In that moment, I was very glad I'd hidden the sugar under my mattress at home. Perhaps I needed to alternate where I traded and ask the beast for more common items. What was I thinking? Was I going back?

A hand slid over my breast, distracting me. A tingle of awareness prickled my skin. It felt odd, but not painful, just wrong. I'd washed myself plenty of times and never gotten such a reaction before.

"Here," Ila handed me the soap, having reached my upper thighs. I was thankful she let me wash myself instead of continuing upward.

"You have more tension than most men," Aryana commented as she worked her way down my back. "Perhaps after a soak, you'd like us to soothe your muscles."

I recalled how Gen had reacted and politely declined. I caught Ila's knowing smirk, but ignored it. They rinsed me, and the three of us walked to the tubs, picking three close together. We didn't talk much. Too soon, Ila was insisting we get out before we made ourselves sick. We went to rinse with cool water, and they worked oil into my hair again after I dried by the fire.

WHEN I RETURNED HOME, the lingering smell of eggs and bacon tinted the air inside the cottage. Bryn stood before the wash pan, scrubbing the dishes.

"How did you get more food?" I asked excitedly, my stomach grumbling and eyes wandering, looking for what my nose smelled.

"I don't know what you mean," she said.

"Eggs. Bacon. I can smell it," the words took on a harsh tone as they tumbled from my mouth.

"Oh, yes. There wasn't enough to share. Sorry," she said airily as she set a pan aside.

"Did you at least give some to Father?"

"Please. He sits all day. I'm here cleaning, cooking, running to the market. I needed the food so I wouldn't collapse," she replied irritably.

She refused to turn and look at me. I frowned at her back. We had no food and no coin. Again. Trading away the sugar would be dangerous, but Father wasn't eating again. I went to the mattress and felt for the sugar, but pulled out an empty hand.

"Don't bother," Bryn said. "I found what you were trying to hoard selfishly and traded it for the food."

My mouth dropped open.

"A handful of sugar for only enough bacon and eggs to feed one?"

"Just go and get more," she said with a shrug as if I had come by the sugar easily.

I thought of the beast and his last, frightening appearance over a week ago. In all likelihood, I would not be welcomed back.

"I can't," I said desperately. "That was the last of it."

"Every time you leave, you come back with something new. Don't tell me that's the last of it. Go." She picked up a bag and threw it at me, her face twisted with anger and her eyes filled with tears.

I took the bag and left with nowhere to go. The sisters were now accepting customers, and I wouldn't enter the estate again.

Walking to the outskirts of town, I found a new patch of grass near a tree and sat there until the sun started to crest the horizon. Stomach cramping, I started the walk home.

Bryn looked up expectantly when I entered. I set my empty bag on my bed and went to the well to drink my fill of cool water. It stopped the hunger pains, for now.

When Father came home and saw no dinner waited, he grabbed a book from his shelf and left again. He returned a long while later with some grain. Bryn divided it and cooked half for our dinner.

IN THE MORNING, Bryn boiled the remaining grain for our breakfast and, looking truly concerned, insisted Father stay to eat his portion.

As we sat at our table, quietly appreciating the meager breakfast, a sharp rat-a-tat on the door interrupted the silence. Father rose to answer it while we all spun in our chairs to watch. No one stood at the door, but a piece of parchment lay on the porch just outside. Father retrieved it and brought it back to the table after looking up and down the street.

He scanned the note briefly, then gave us a small smile.

"There is a traveling merchant who just passed through the Water. He heard I might have some books I no longer need and offered a fair price if I bring them to Konrall today. He must continue through Konrall south before nightfall."

He quickly ate his last few bites and pushed away from the table.

"I will cancel my teaching for today and return shortly. The merchant also expressed an interest in meeting my daughters. You will accompany me." His tone allowed no argument, though I could see distaste in my sisters' eyes.

Thoughts whirled. My heart ached that Father had to give up even a single book to feed us. After being ill for so long and not working, there would be no pay for several days yet. Most scholars would count themselves lucky to still have a position to return to after an extended illness. And a merchant wanting to meet us could only mean he'd heard of Father's desire to marry one of us off. One less mouth would relieve some of the burden.

Bryn tossed the dishes in the dry sink and hurried after Blye into their room. I ran my fingers through my hair before tugging it into a semblance of a braid, as usual. After Father returned, my sisters emerged from their room, looking fresh and well-groomed. Despite her illness, Bryn did not look as thin as the rest of us and still managed a healthy glow.

"Benella, can you carry these in your bag?" Father asked, plucking seven thin volumes from his shelves. Two were regarding the rudimentary teachings of mathematics, which I doubted Father even referenced anymore given his familiarity of the material due to repetitive teaching. Three regarded beginning reading and writing. The other two were rare pieces pertaining to flora and fauna. I didn't want to see them go.

"Did you procure a wagon?" Bryn asked, smoothing her dress.

Father gave her a flat look, and she dropped her gaze. The twit. We were selling his books because we had no coin. How exactly could he afford to pay for a wagon?

AHEAD, I spotted a familiar curve in the road clogged with a thick, unnatural fog. We were close to the place where I'd cut through the woods to go to the estate when I'd still traded with the beast. How long had it been now? Almost two weeks?

"Father," I began anxiously. "Doesn't it seem a bit too warm for patches of fog?"

"It depends," he said absently, his breathing slightly labored. Typically a sedentary man, the long walk after just recovering from illness taxed him. "There may be cooler water hidden under the trees causing it."

The fog loomed closer, and I blinked at it, trying to determine if we were walking faster or if the fog crept toward us. Still several feet away, I caught a slight movement within the mist. Before I could call out a warning, hundreds of vines shot out, wrapping around us.

The thick fog consumed us, hiding us from one another. I heard my sisters cry out, and my father call our names. I was unable to answer as a vine wrapped itself firmly, but gently around my mouth, effectively gagging me. I bit down on the vine to chew through it, but the acrid sap that ran into my mouth worried me, so I spat out what I could and remained mute.

The vines tugged us through the trees, up into the canopy, ever closer to the estate while the mist continued to keep us isolated. I heard the growing concern in Father's voice when I did not answer his calls.

Fear bloomed in my chest. Could I still try to claim refuge and would it work to protect all of us? How angry had my last departure made the beast? I felt the vines start to lower me and, soon, the mist retreated enough that we could see each other.

We all hung a few feet from the ground, tangled in vines. Bryn and Blye's eyes grew wide, and they began to struggle against their bindings when they saw we dangled inside the gate of the estate. Father calmly scanned the area, probably remembering his last harmless excursion behind the walls. The vines still binding my mouth worried me. I felt we would not leave this time without meeting the beast, and for a reason I couldn't guess, he didn't want me to speak.

The mist stopped retreating several yards away and then started to darken. Both my sisters began to cry. The pathetic mewling sounds had me pitying them and their fear. No one deserved to be tormented as the beast currently did to them. My eyes narrowed on the gloom, and I tried to speak around the vines, but it just sounded garbled.

"It would seem I have trespassers," the beast growled.

I snorted.

Father's face visibly paled, and he appeared to have lost his voice in the face of such menace.

"As the eldest, you shall take the punishment for the trespass, unless..."

I shook my head and attempted to speak past the gag, trying to tell the beast to stop his madness.

"Unless, what?" my father said.

"Unless one of your daughters agrees to stay with me," the beast said.

I ceased my struggles, seeing what the beast meant to do, the sneaky son of a—

"No," Blye wailed.

"It's not yet your turn to answer," the beast snapped harshly. "The eldest speaks first. It's only right I offer her the opportunity. And, she should be grateful I consider her at all when she's carrying a bastard child."

Blye's sniffles stopped, and she turned to stare at Bryn. We all did. Tears trickled down Bryn's face, her shame evident. The food hoarding, the moods, and the request for a wagon made sense now. Pity welled up for her, and I glared at the beast.

"Come now. Your turn to answer. I offer you the refuge of the estate in return for your immediate and complete obedience in every command I issue. And your father's life, of course."

Bryn sobbed and shook her head. Had my mouth not been full of vine, it would have popped open. How could she not save Father? My eyes fell to her middle. Of course she couldn't, and Father would never have wanted her to, knowing she carried his grandchild.

"Very well," the beast growled with little menace. "Good sir, you should consider marrying her to the first offer you can manage before the soon-to-be husband discovers her state."

Father paled further and would not look at Bryn.

"Now, the next oldest," the beast said without compassion. "Your father stands to pay the price for trespassing for each of you. As you are aware, he will be thrown from the estate. Once for each of you. How do you suppose he will fair after the second toss? Or third? Do you honestly think there will be much left to throw the fourth time?"

Blye's mewling cry won her no pity.

"Please grant us mercy," she sobbed.

"I *am* by offering you this chance to save your father's life. Agree to stay with me. You will have the finest silks you can imagine in return for your immediate and complete obedience in every command I issue."

She wailed and begged for several long minutes before rejecting his offer. Through it all, Father said nothing, his eyes growing more despondent.

"Now," the beast said. "For the youngest."

The vines slipped from my mouth as he spoke, and I interrupted him before he could go any further.

"Release me so we may speak face to face. I will not speak my answer to your cursed mist."

Immediately the vines flew from me, and I fell to the ground.

Straightening, I looked at my sisters and Father. They all had fear in their eyes.

"Benella," my father began. "Do not give up your life for—"

A vine slithered up from his chest to muffle his words.

Bracing myself for a confrontation, I walked straight into the mist and stopped when I felt a tug on my hair. My stomach gave an odd flip.

"What is your answer?" he rumbled softly as his fingers worked the braid free.

The heavy mist surrounding us muffled all sound, no doubt to keep my family from hearing. Though it also hid the beast from my view, I recalled every fang and claw in detail.

"Your terms are a bit steep for what you are gaining, and I would like to propose three revisions," I said bravely.

"How can they be steep?" he asked. "You gain your father's life."

"Do I? How do I know? That is my first provision. I must be allowed one day every week to leave the estate. If I'm not allowed to see Father, it will be just as if he had died."

The beast grunted in response. I felt him lean in to breathe the scented oil still clinging to my hair.

"What is your next provision?"

"I will ignore any command for my silence."

He didn't deny my provision.

"And the final?" he asked, instead.

"You may not touch me without permission."

His growl started low and grew in fury.

"Unacceptable," he roared. He fisted my hair and carefully pulled me against him so the fur from his jaw abraded my ear. "Why even keep you, then?"

I licked my lips.

"That's something I have been asking myself for many weeks. You've asked me so many times and offered so many things. Each time, I've said no. If you can't accept my terms, you will kill my father, I'm sure. Your temper will see to that. But you will lose any future chance of coercing an agreement from me. That I promise you."

He grew completely silent. I held still, waiting for his reply. Faintly, I heard Blye's continued sobs though Bryn tried to hush her, no doubt trying to hear what we said.

"A year," he growled. "I will accept your provisions for a year."

"No," I countered. "My silence cannot be guaranteed, and I will not lose my family. As long as I'm with you, you will listen to me and let me leave one day a week. In return for your gracious benevolence, I agree to reduce the touching restriction to six months." I had to raise my voice slightly so he could hear me over his own cursing.

Again, he stopped his rage. He didn't leave me waiting for long. "One week."

I snorted.

"One month. That is my final offer."

"Agreed," he said, triumphantly.

"I would like to say good-bye before you start commanding me, sir," I spoke in a rush.

His fist released my hair.

"Make it quick."

Obediently, I rushed from the mist just as the vines released Father and my sisters. I went to Father first and hugged him tightly.

"I will see you in four days," I whispered to him.

"Don't do this, Benella," he said fiercely, hugging me.

"I'll be fine and well fed here." Pulling back, I caught the hurt look in his eyes and quickly tugged the bag from my shoulders. "Here. I'll try to find some way to help."

I turned toward my sisters.

"Take care of him." There was a threat in my tone that I hadn't meant to let slip. "And yourselves," I added more calmly.

Something tugged at my foot, and I lifted my skirt enough to see a vine.

"I have to go."

Turning, I walked into the mist, away from my family.

DECEIT

DECEIT

CHAPTER ONE

Bryn's muffled sniffles faded as I stepped into the mists. I didn't go far before I hesitated. I could see the hand I held before me but nothing beyond that. Yet, visibility wasn't why I'd stopped. Fear held me in place.

The beast had always kept everyone at bay. Why had that changed? And, why with me? Knowing why he'd gone to such lengths to trap me within the estate might have assured me. Then again, perhaps his reasons were something to fear.

The beast's tail thumped against my stomach, a reminder of the bargain I'd made. To save my father, I had no choice but to clasp the tail and allow him to lead me through the mist. Walking away from my family was difficult, but walking toward my unknown future was harder.

Instead of leading me to the overgrown yard just outside of the kitchen, he turned slightly east. It wasn't long before gravel crunched under my feet. I frowned at the sound and at the sudden disappearance of his tail.

"Go where you wish within the boundaries of the estate. Do as you please, with the exception of leaving," he said, as he moved behind me.

The mist retreated with him and revealed a grand entrance to the manor that he so zealously protected. Three steps laid with large slabs of natural grey stone led up to a sheltered court. Great columns of the same stone supported a roof to protect guests who might arrive during inclement weather.

The claw-ravaged, large double doors stood open in invitation. Yet, instead of welcome, their gaping maw conveyed an eerie sense of desolation. With reluctance, I climbed the steps and entered the beast's home.

For the first time, I saw the interior of the manor clearly. Aged décor, perfectly preserved from the ravages of time, yet marred by the beast's anger and negligence, drew my curious gaze. Did he truly only need a maid?

"Should I clean, then?" I asked, knowing he still lingered behind me.

"Do as you please," he said irritably.

Taking him at his word, I went from room to room, studying the place I would now call home. Though I did not care for cleaning, a good straightening would make it a fair place to live. As I wandered, I took time to right a tumbled chair or straighten thrown papers. In some places, shards of broken objects dusted the floor, and I made note to come back with a broom as my boots crunched over them.

I lost count of the turns and rooms I visited while the beast trailed me, cloaked in his now small cloud of mist. Other than the library, I noted nothing of particular interest until I reached the second floor.

In the midst of the beast's destruction, a single room remained untouched, and I didn't blame him for avoiding it. Frills, perfumes, and pillows filled the room with their noxious pink shades. I had no issue with pink in small doses. However, what lay before me made my eyes hurt. The only exception to the overabundance, a set of black, glossy doors, called to me.

They were set into the interior wall to the side and begged for the beast's angry furrows. Yet, none decorated the surface.

I crossed the pink rugs and opened the door. On the other side, the wood bore the worst marks I'd witnessed, gouging so deep only a thin layer of wood prevented a hole. I gently ran my fingers over the marks, staring at the torn grains.

As I watched, a piece smaller than a hangnail twitched, slowly straightening itself to mend the gash. I would have watched longer, fascinated by the display of enchantment, but the mess inside the room distracted me. Everything from the mattress and bed hangings to the inlaid wood patterns of the floor had been shredded.

"My room," he said from behind me. "This room is yours."

I turned to look over my shoulder at the pink abomination.

"I'd rather we trade," I said under my breath.

I closed the doors and continued with my tour. For a while, I became hopelessly lost until I came to a hallway I recognized. It would take me a long while to learn the layout of his home. My home, I corrected myself.

Making my way toward the library, I decided to spend my day cleaning it, so I could turn it into my sanctuary. I wasn't sure what I would find. The day I'd read to him, I'd only caught a glimpse of it in the candle light. Today wasn't much different.

When I walked into the room, the curtains still covered the windows, making it hard to see even without his mist clouding the area. I found my way to the closest window and tugged the drapes wide open. Light poured in, and I turned to view the room. A small gasp escaped me at the vastness.

The large room boasted enough furniture for several sitting areas, though everything was knocked about haphazardly. Filled bookcases lined every wall, even above the two doors. The only interruptions were the four windows on the outer wall and a fireplace near the door from which I'd entered. Eager to see more, I moved to tug open each curtain and finally saw the library in full.

Ignoring the beast, I set to work righting furniture and shoving pieces across the wood floor to the positions I wanted. Whenever I found a book tumbled to the floor, I set it on the small writing desk near the center window. Until I had a chance to discover how the books were categorized and ordered, I didn't want to place anything onto the shelves.

I worked for hours until the sudden whoosh of the fire lighting itself distracted me. A tray of food rested on a table I'd placed near the first seating arrangement. Wiping my dusty hands on my skirt, I went to sit and eat while my eyes drifted over the room, seeking what I would work on next. The area near where I sat was restored to order. The far side of the room still needed much attention.

After devouring every bite of fruit and cheese, I went back to work. By the time the sun set, the library met my approval, and I began to study the books. I counted twenty-two floor to ceiling segmented bookcases. In each, there were at least fifteen shelves. Most were organized by subject, then author. However, several shelves seemed to be dedicated to a particular author.

Slowly, I began to see where the fallen books I had collected belonged and started to tuck them back into place. One shelf in particular gave me trouble as it towered just out of my tiptoed reach. Looking down at the lower shelf, I wondered if it would support my weight.

Rising to two legs, the beast stepped up behind me, plucked the book from my grasp, and then easily slid it into its place. Startled, I stared at his furred arm until it disappeared from view, not daring to turn around.

"Do not climb on the shelves," he said, having guessed my intent. "You will fall."

As quickly as he'd crowded me, I felt him move away; and I released the breath I'd held. When I looked around the room, I noticed him in the furthest, darkest corner, his mist obscuring him. I'd been so engrossed in the library I'd forgotten his presence.

"Thank you," I said softly.

A clock in the corner chimed for the half hour. I glanced at the face, saw how late it was, and yawned.

"Come. Eat. I will take you to your room afterwards," the beast said from his corner.

Again a tray with fruits, nuts, and cold water waited for me on the table. I ate everything then followed him through the dim, lamplit hallways, memorizing the path from the library to my room.

He opened the door to the room and stood aside to let me enter. As I passed him, my arm brushed against his torso, and he growled. A shiver of fear ran through me.

"Good night," he said simply and left me alone in the profusely pink room.

Giving the room a more thorough inspection than I had the first time, I found the bed soft and inviting, the wardrobe full of clothes, and a soft cloth waiting by the bowl of warm water on the washstand. I wiped the dust from my face and hands then went to the wardrobe and found several nightgowns, all sheer, with matching sheer wraps. At least they weren't pink, I thought as I undressed and slipped into a pale blue one.

I climbed into bed and thought of my family. I didn't doubt that the beast had freed them; he wanted me here willingly, for whatever his reasons. By now, I imagined my family had returned safely to the Water. Curling onto my side, I wondered how they would fare without me. Though I hoped that having one less mouth to feed would ease some of Father's burden, I knew he would rather have me home than here. Yet, the beast's manor didn't seem too terrible. I was free to roam inside the manor, regularly fed, and, so far, no demands had been made of me.

Sighing, I closed my eyes and wondered what I would do to occupy myself here. As interesting as this enchanted place was, if the rest of my days followed today, I would grow bored quickly.

THE NEXT MORNING, I rose late and reluctantly slipped from my warm bed—Father's mattress could not compare to the one I now called my own. Fresh, warm water again waited on the washstand for me to wash my face. I enjoyed not having to walk outside to fetch my own. However, when I turned to dress, I frowned in confusion at the empty chair beside the wardrobe. I was certain I'd draped my only dress there when I'd prepared for bed the night before.

I opened the wardrobe, thinking it had been magically placed in there while I slept. Inside, luxurious diaphanous gowns waited, a pale rainbow of colored skirts. No doubt, my dress had disappeared so I would wear one of his choosing. Sighing, I picked one at random. At least I had clothes. It could be worse, I thought, recalling his wish to see me when I'd bathed. He might have decided to have me walk about naked as the sisters did. I only wished I understood his purpose in having me here and dressing me in such a fashion.

The pale green dress I chose slipped over my head easily. The layered skirts afforded a shadowy glimpse at my legs. The bodice flattened my small breasts, making every detail clearly visible. Chewing my lip, I debated how to preserve some of my modesty. My eyes drifted to the wraps that I'd deemed worthless for cover.

I tore off both sleeves of the matching wrap and folded them in half to tuck the additional two layers of material into my bodice. It had the desired effect of blotting out the details while giving just a hint of what the bodice hid. I stepped into the flimsy slippers that matched the gown and left my room with the intent to spend the day reading.

In the library, a breakfast tray waited, but I ignored it to walk to the writing desk and retrieved the book on farming I'd set aside. It was the one I'd started reading to the beast, and I wanted to read to its conclusion. I settled on the sofa near the tray and absently popped a bite of chilled, cooked meat into my mouth as I found my place.

"Did you sleep well?" the beast asked softly.

My insides jumped from the start he gave me, but I only nodded to answer him and kept my eyes on the page. After a few minutes of silence, I calmed enough to eat and again lost myself in the book.

"Did you find the clothes to your satisfaction?"

"Not quite," I said. "I fear going outside will give me a chill and be the death of me. I hope in winter I'll have something with a bit more substance."

He snorted but made no comment.

Well after eating my last bite, I finished the book and closed it with a snap. Intrigued by the problems farmers faced and the solutions posed by the author, I wandered to the shelf on farming, replaced the book, and selected another thin volume, which I brought back to the sofa.

"You like farming?" the beast asked with a note of uncertainty.

"Not really. But I like eating, and the two are definitely related."

He made no response, and I settled in to absorb the new author's thoughts. On one topic they both agreed. Repeated plantings resulted in poorer harvests. However, their solutions varied. One suggested letting the field lay fallow for several years. The other suggested the annual slaughtering be done over the field to slow the soil depletion. I didn't like the idea of eating carrots soaked in year old animal blood. I sought out another's opinion and kept searching through the volumes until I had almost twenty books on farming lying on the table next to the tray. I referenced from one to another until I came to a conclusion based on several tried methods.

"Fish and certain animal waste," I murmured, thumbing through several pages. "Perhaps vegetation, too. Interesting." I wished I had a way to ask Mr. Kinlyn how he prevented soil depletion.

I turned my gaze to the writing desk. The thought of writing Mr. Kinlyn led to the thought of writing Father.

"May I write letters and have them delivered?" I asked the beast.

"You may write, but I will read your correspondence before sending it," he said.

I stood and moved to the writing desk. Outside the window, I caught the movement of the female nymph, kneeling before her no longer solid partner. Before I could fully stop to wonder what they did, the beast rumbled a quick promise to return shortly and left the room.

Worried for the nymph, I rushed to the window and tossed it open. Both nymphs froze at the noise.

"He comes," I quickly whispered in warning. Both solidified at the sound of my voice.

As the dark mists roiled into view from the left, I noticed where the pair remained joined and blushed deeply. Apparently, the baker wasn't the only one who liked to taste.

Leaning further out the window, I called to the beast, concerned about his temper should he find his nymph solidified.

"Sir, do all the trees on the estate grow so peculiarly?"

He slowed at the sound of my voice and growled menacingly but did not approach the trees. Instead, he came to the window, bringing me close to his height as he stood on two legs. Through the mist, I saw one of his ears flick in agitation.

"Why did you open the window?"

"To get a better view of the beauty outside," I said calmly. "I didn't mean to disturb your time away from me. I will look at the trees later. They bear studying." I kept the insincerity from my voice.

With a last look at the trees, I closed the window and moved back to the sofa.

Another tray waited for me. Anxiously, I nibbled at the food, only tasting it when the beast returned. On the pretext of writing a letter, I passed the window and saw, to my joy, the pair unmarred.

The beast rejected my first few attempts at a letter to my father. The version he finally accepted included very little detail, only that I had enjoyed a day reading about farming and my findings on the subject. In closing, I wished Father well and promised to see him soon. Similarly, I penned a letter to Mr. Kinlyn to ask what treatments he gave his fields at the end of each season.

The crow I'd noticed in Konrall came to the window when the beast called and took the letters in his beak before flying off again.

The afternoon faded to evening, and bored with the atmosphere of the library, I ambled through the house, the beast not far behind me. When I came to my room by chance, I decided to go to bed early and bade him good night. He growled and grumped but left me alone.

That night, the sound of my door opening roused me from my sleep enough that I lifted my head.

"Sleep, Benella," the beast whispered.

The bed dipped as he lay next to me and threaded his fingers in my hair. I slept.

A HOT BATH waited in my room when I woke. Naturally hesitant after my last experience bathing in the beast's lair, I stared at it before stripping. I couldn't avoid bathing forever and bathing once a week when I left this place didn't appeal to me, either.

Sinking into the warm water, I sighed but didn't waste time relaxing. After washing with an overly sweet smelling soap, I stepped from the water and wrapped a large towel around myself before opening the wardrobe. A lone garment waited within, a single panel of fabric which would leave nothing to the imagination. Turning to look for my nightgown, I noted that too had disappeared. I wrinkled my nose in frustration, until the garish pink curtains on the windows caught my eye.

When I stepped out into the hall, I wasn't surprised to see the beast waited. Ripped patches of pink discreetly hid my important parts, one long rectangle over my breasts and another uniquely shaped piece I'd tied at my sides to cover my backside and front.

The beast growled at the sight of me. I walked up to him, pressing through his mist until I saw his eyes inches from mine. He stood on all fours.

"Do you want me to fear you?" I asked, my breath moving his fur as I spoke.

He blinked at me.

"No."

"Then why do you keep growling at me? A growl in the animal world is meant as a warning and to inspire caution if not fear."

"I'm not an animal," he said with a growl still in his throat.

"Then stop acting like one," I said with a soft calm.

He blinked at me again then narrowed his eyes.

"I don't like your dress," he said.

"Much better," I said with a smile and reached out to pat his head. I knew I took a risk to treat him so; but if he insisted on playing games with me, I would play them back.

His eyes rounded at my touch, and I wondered if he'd growl again. Instead, he just watched me closely as I gave his head a final pat and turned away, not responding to his comment.

"May I have eggs for breakfast?" I asked pleasantly. "Oh, and bacon?" My mouth watered at the idea.

He answered with subdued approval and followed me through the hallways until I found the library. A tray already waited with the food I'd requested. Instead of searching for a book, I sat on the sofa and took a large bite.

"Do you eat?" I asked.

He'd pulled the mist around himself again, but not so fully that I couldn't see the outline of him.

"Of course," he answered.

"No need to sound so offended. Nothing else here seems normal, and you never eat with me, so I wasn't sure." I took several more bites. "What shall I do today?" I asked.

"Whatever you wish," he answered.

Finishing my meal, I found my way to the kitchen and wandered out the door. Every time I'd left the kitchen, I'd gone straight toward the estate's gates. This time, I turned left, hopefully toward the side of the manor with the library.

The dainty slippers did little to protect my feet as I tromped along, and my soles grew tender as I walked. Still, I pressed on until I walked the length of the front of the manor. Stopping, I looked up at one spot and counted four stories. Somehow, I'd missed seeing a staircase on the second story.

Rounding the corner, a patch of thick briars forced me away

from the manor and into the woods. I felt a snag on my dress a moment before I heard the material rip. A good portion of my thigh was now exposed.

"I don't care for my dress either," I said over my shoulder in response to the beast's earlier comment.

He said nothing as he followed me.

By the time I circled around the briars, I sported several snags and tears in the dress and truly appreciated the pieces of curtain I'd tucked inside of it. I bled from a few small scrapes, but it was nothing that slowed me down.

Finally, I came to the place where I'd spotted the nymphs, but neither remained. Disappointed, I looked toward the window. It would have been a much shorter journey to have climbed out from there. Shaking my head, I continued in the same direction and eventually found the door the beast had used to reach the nymphs the day I'd read to him.

With relief, I limped back to the library and sat on the sofa to tug off my slippers. This wouldn't have happened if he had let me keep my boots. The cuts were starting to sting.

"I need better clothes," I said. "Sturdy ones that will stand up to briars and stones."

"No. If I cannot touch you, I will at least look at you."

"That's why I have to wear this? Fine." I flopped back onto the sofa and put my feet up. "Touch my hair then give me boots, sturdy trousers, and a man's shirt."

A slight choked noise came from behind me, and I closed my eyes, not believing I'd let my temper escape.

"My apologies," he said. "Allow me to heal your injuries." It came as a demand rather than a request.

"I'd rather have trousers."

"Allow me to heal your injuries, and you will have your trousers when you journey outside."

"Fine," I said, knowing he'd neither offered boots nor a shirt. Trousers were a start, though.

His tongue lapped at my ankle, startling me from my thoughts. He moved higher, not needing to move the dress to soothe the cut on my knee. Warmth flooded me after his tongue found the light scrape on my thigh.

When he moved to the slight tear in the material on my stomach, I trembled, no longer certain of our deal. He ran his tongue over the tiny wound several times before moving upward. Then, he paused. His massive head hovered just above my breasts, the heat of his breath warming them.

Before I could think to panic, he continued upward toward my chin, and I recalled a branch that had snapped back at my face. The touch of his tongue so close to my mouth sent a shiver chasing through me. He licked me from just below my chin to my bottom lip.

"Touch me," he said.

My eyelids popped open, and I found myself staring into his eyes. Large, wide set in his shaggy head and deep blue, they held me in place with no mist separating us. I raised a hand and gently placed it against his neck, the soft fur warming my fingers. Underneath, I felt him shudder, and I wondered how often he felt anyone's touch. Probably never. The creatures here seemed to fear him as much as the townspeople.

"Tell me true, did I miss any?" he whispered.

Reluctantly, I nodded and rolled to my stomach, breaking our contact.

He laved the scrapes on the backs of my legs and arms and then the bottoms of my feet, which made me twitch and giggle involuntarily. When he finished, he moved away from me, retreating into the mist.

For the rest of the day, I contented myself with books and tried to forget his presence.

No trousers waited in the wardrobe the next day, just a selection of translucent gowns. Smiling at the selection, I picked the most modest dress from them and tucked another ripped panel from the curtains, which hadn't disappeared.

The beast waited in the hallway with less mist than the day before.

"I don't like the dress," he said again.

"Me neither," I said agreeably. "I thought I would be able to wear trousers today."

"If you would like to go out again today, you can change in the servant's quarters in the kitchen. Your trousers are there and are only meant for outside. Inside, I want you wearing the dresses you find within your wardrobe."

Nodding, I walked hurriedly toward the kitchen. True to his word, trousers waited on one of the beds as did boots and a cream shirt. I quickly closed the door and changed. The trousers were a bit snugger than I was used to, as was the shirt, but the boots fit well.

Eagerly, I stepped from the room and held out my arms to do a slow turn for the beast.

"Well?" I prompted with a smile on my face.

"Lovely," he said.

Happy with the clothes, I led the way out the door. As I slowly explored the area in front of the manor, the beast paced behind me. Near lunch, I sensed his growing impatience and knew my time outside would soon come to an end. It didn't upset me. It had been an enjoyable outing.

"Go change," he said. "Do not wear these clothes inside unless you want to lose them."

I went back into the servant's quarters and closed myself in to change. Immediately, I saw what he'd done. The dress remained where I'd set it, but my scraps of curtain were missing. I sat heavily on the mattress, its material too thick to tear without the help of a knife. There was nothing else to shield myself from his gaze. If I stayed in the trousers or tried to use the shirt in some way, I had no doubt they would be gone in the morning, and I would not see them again.

Defeated for the moment, I put on the dress and marched out the door. The table in the kitchen was laden with food.

"I'm not hungry," I said and turned to leave.

"Stop. Turn and show me your dress as you did when you changed this morning."

Teeth clenched to keep from telling him what I thought of him, I slowly turned a circle, keeping my arms at my side.

"If you're finished demeaning me, I'd like to go to my room."

He growled low and long.

"Sit. Eat. Or I will feed you."

Glaring at the swirling mist near the door of the kitchen, I marched to the table, spotted a bowl filled with meat and gravy, and stuck my hand in it. Pulling a fist full of dripping meat from it, I proceeded to shove it in my mouth in the most grotesque, unladylike fashion I could imagine.

His roar shook the windows, but I ignored him, swallowed the lump of meat, and reached for the roasted baby potatoes. With my hand. I crammed one in my mouth and chewed noisily.

"I said sit."

I sat heavily on the chair, not bothering to face the table. Never taking my eyes from him, I reached to the side and grabbed the next item. Stewed plums. Though a disgusting dish I usually avoided, I didn't blink as I shoved some in my mouth and dribbled juice down the front of my dress. The plums gagged me when I swallowed, and I lost the remaining threads of my temper.

Without standing, I grabbed the dish and threw it with all my might at the beast, whose form briefly appeared in the mist. The bowl hit him squarely, broke apart, and drenched him in the sugared plum sauce.

The mist disappeared, and I saw the rage in his eyes.

"Run," he whispered.

A shiver ran through me, and I bolted from my chair, my skirt floating around my legs as I ran for my room. I wouldn't make it unless he chose to let me.

Behind me, I heard a mighty crash and another roar.

He didn't sound like he was in the mood to let me escape.

My slippered feet slid on the wood floor as I changed direction to turn down the first hall I found. I kept running and turning until I was in the library. Shoving the window wide, I leapt out and landed on my feet, startling the nymphs who were back at it.

"Run," I whispered to them.

Inside, the beast roared. The male ran, but the female hesitated.

"Go!" I urged her as I turned toward the back of the manor. The female hooked my arm and turned me toward the east, giving me a little shove. I ran.

The beast's cries faded as I put distance between us. A stitch in my side grew to a cramp when I finally burst through the trees and fell face first into a familiar pool. I rolled onto my back and came up sputtering in knee-deep water.

After wiping my eyes, I tried to silence the harsh gasp of my breaths so I might listen for the beast. In the distance, I heard him calling my name.

"Child," a voice grated nearby.

I turned to look at the old tree, the face already formed.

"He will learn. Do not give up. Do not run."

The tree untwisted, closing its mouth and eyes just before the beast burst upon the clearing. My eyes widened at the sight of him as he stood at the pond's edge, breathing harshly and fully visible on all fours. His raised hackles and bared teeth sent a shiver of fear though me, as did the low crackling growl emanating from him. The tree wanted me to stay. I desperately wanted to run.

Trembling with fear and cold, I did what the tree suggested and stood my ground.

"Will you hurt me now?" The words barely escaped my tight throat. Yet, I knew he heard them for his growl deepened. Despite his anger, he remained on the bank.

I gripped my heavy skirts and exhaled slowly. Then, with my shoulders back, I bravely walked toward him. My heart thrummed in my chest. Certainly he could hear it; I could hear little else.

As I approached, his growl softened while the fur on his neck continued to stand up harshly. He glared at me as I stood before him. I cautiously reached out and smoothed his fur down.

He didn't move away. Instead, I felt the flesh under my palm quiver. The beast's gaze met mine, and I saw the storm there. The undeniable rage was still present, but I also saw sadness and frustration. My heart went out to the tortured creature, and I cautiously embraced him.

When I leaned my head against his neck, all noise stopped. Not just his growl, but the animated chirping of the birds, the rustling of the leaves, everything.

Plum sauce matted his hair.

"The plums were too disgusting to throw at you," I whispered. "I should have thrown the potatoes, instead."

I watched his hackles slowly relax.

"Why did you not want to eat?" he finally asked.

I snorted.

"It wasn't the food that bothered me. It's the clothes. I don't like pink, and I don't like dresses. When you run, they trip you; and I like to run. And I don't like being treated like a whore."

His teeth ground together.

"I do not treat you like a whore."

"How is making me wear these dresses so you can see all my personal parts not treating me like a whore?" I asked, keeping my head resting against his neck.

His hackles started to rise again, so I reached up and smoothed them down. He grunted in response and seemed to calm. I didn't touch him more than necessary, cautious of the sisters' lesson.

"Come," he said instead of answering me. "You will catch a chill if we stay here longer."

I moved away from him so he could lead. I didn't miss the long look he gave my wet, clinging dress. Biting my tongue to keep from whispering the word whore, I patted the tree as I passed, thankful for its advice.

IN MY ROOM, another bath waited along with a tray of food and a note that simply said *No plums.*

Smiling, I ate the food then peeled myself out of the clingy, damp dress. The plum juices had stained it, ruining the material. I felt no remorse as I dropped it to the floor.

CHAPTER
TWO

ON THE FIFTH DAY, THE WARDROBE REMAINED EMPTY. I SCOWLED AT it and whispered a single word. "Beast." And I meant his nature, not his name.

After the fight in the kitchen, I had thought he'd understood and would relent. Still he had insisted on the sheer clothes. Yesterday when I had woken, the curtains had vanished; and I'd torn a patch from my bedding to cover myself.

Now, I tugged a whole blanket from my bed to wrap around my shoulders before stomping to the hallway. Today was the day I was supposed to go see my father. I'd gone to bed early, so I could rise before first light, not wanting to waste any of the time I could spend with my family.

In the hall, the beast waited as usual.

"Why do I have no clothes?" I asked.

"Are you visiting your father today?" he asked much too calmly.

"Yes, I wanted to." His calm just upset me more.

"Then the dresses you have wouldn't suit. You can wear your trousers, which are in the kitchen."

The annoyance left me. Of course I couldn't wear the clothes he chose to town. I had assumed he wouldn't think of that on his own.

"Thank you," I said, turning to race to the kitchen.

He snagged the blanket, stopping my departure.

"Leave this here."

Normally, once I found a way to cover myself, he didn't order it away. Surprised, I glanced back at him.

"Now."

I averted my gaze and let the blanket fall to the floor. When I started to walk away from him, I wondered if he found the view of my backside as mesmerizing as Ila's had been that first time I'd seen it. The thought of Ila made me smile. I couldn't wait to see my friends again and wondered what Father had told them about my absence. I hurried my pace until I ran, eager to start my journey.

In the kitchen, I closed myself in the servant's quarters to change. As soon as I opened the door of the servant's quarters, the beast gave me a warning.

"We bargained one day a week. I grant that you may leave the gates after the sun rises and must return to them before the sun sets. Do not be late or I will fetch your father in recompense."

Nodding jerkily, I left him in the kitchen and raced toward the gate as the sky lightened. From the corner of my eye, I spotted one of the nymphs but it solidified before I could see which.

The gates swung open for me as the beast called my name. I stopped just inside the iron barrier.

The beast appeared beside me, his breath as heavy as mine.

"Will you return?" he asked gruffly.

In that question, I glimpsed his uncertainty of me. I didn't understand why he wanted me to stay. But, I understood that whatever his reasons, I mattered to him; and he worried that the fear for my father's safety wasn't enough to bring me back. Feeling a small measure of pity for him, I nodded again before walking out the gate.

Freedom flavored the air with a sweetness that I inhaled deeply as I alternated between walking and jogging. When I came in sight of the bridge, a crow that was roosted on one of the bridge supports shook the spray from his feathers and took flight, spiraling high over the Water. I didn't stop to see if it flew toward the estate.

With a light step, I walked through the market district, smiling at the early merchants as I made my way toward my father's house. At the Sisters' house, I caught a glimpse of someone and paused to wave up at the windows. Then, I continued on. When I stood before Father's small home, I paused for a moment and wistfully watched the smoke curling from the chimney. I had missed them all so much.

Without knocking, I pushed the door open, a smile on my lips. As I suspected, Bryn stood at the stove cooking something. She looked up at me, her eyes wide with surprise.

"Benella," she said, clearly surprised by my arrival. Her gaze touched my face then my clothes before clouding with disapproval. "You look fit and well fed. I hope you're not expecting to eat; there's not enough."

Her attitude did nothing to curb my joy in seeing her. I stepped in and closed the door behind me.

"How are you, Bryn? What happened after I last saw you?" I really wanted to know about the possibility of her being pregnant.

"We left the estate and walked to Konrall. Father still hoped to sell a book. He warned us not to speak of you or the estate." She turned away from me and poked at the meat sizzling in the pan. "He asked me if I would be happy in a forced marriage with Tennen. I said I would not; and we haven't spoken of anything, except you, since then."

"Me?" How could Father not ask questions of the baby? Obviously he'd deduced that Tennen had fathered it, but didn't he want to know how long ago? And, there were other questions that needed answers. How much time remained until the baby arrived? Did Bryn have other prospects? Had she felt the babe move yet?

"Of course, you. The beast took you. We all worried, thinking you wouldn't return to us. We should have known better," she said bitterly. Before I could respond, she continued. "Did you bring anything back with you? Things are not much better than they were those few days ago."

"I'm sorry. I did not." I hadn't thought of anything other than seeing them again. The next visit I would be better prepared.

The door burst open just then, and Father rushed in. He spun me about and caught me up in a tight hug. Finally, the welcome I'd hoped for. I wrapped my arms around him in return, smelling the faint tang of the sisters' incense.

"Father," Bryn said in surprise. "What are you doing home?"

"Someone told me they saw Benella," he said as he pulled back from me. A smile lined his mouth, but his eyes looked sadder than usual.

"But your work. Shouldn't you—"

"My employer has a fond spot for Benella and granted me time to spend with her this afternoon." Father dropped his arms from around me. "Benella, walk with me. Bryn, we will return for lunch." He turned and walked out the door.

When I looked at Bryn, I saw tears in her eyes.

"It'll be okay, Bryn. I'll be back later and want to hear what names you've picked so far for the baby." Her eyes widened, but then she offered me a small, sad smile.

I caught up with Father and wrapped my hand around his arm.

"Why are you angry with Bryn?" I asked.

"Her dalliance will cost her, robbing her of a marriage to a decent man."

Pulling back on his arm slightly, I stopped us in the street and turned him to look at me.

"Her dalliance will rob her of nothing because a decent man will look at her and see her worth and welcome the child she carries. The ones who won't see her worth or shun her because of the baby are not decent."

Father shook his head, but smiled at me indulgently.

"If only she had your sense of responsibility," he said.

"Father, how can you say that? Bryn has been responsible for all of us since Mother died. She's taken on so much responsibility so early it's a wonder her shoulders aren't curved from it. Despite that responsibility, she's still young and prone to a young woman's fancy. Tennen looked at her sweetly and played on her hopes. Don't fault her for her naivety of a man's character."

During my speech, my father's mouth dropped a bit. I probably sounded pompous.

"And don't hold me in too harsh a light when I make my own naïve mistakes."

"Wise beyond your years," he muttered, and we started walking again. "So what would you have me do?"

"Can't you see how frightened she is? She's probably wondering where she will be by the time the babe is born. Reassure her that you still love her and care. Ask about baby names or see if Blye has given her any tiny garments. I will try to find some way to help, too, the next time I return."

"You are not here to stay?"

I shook my head.

"He will allow me to visit you once a week. But I must have care to return before my allotted time."

He sighed and looked at me with concern.

"Just take care of yourself." We neared the Sister's back door. "I will want details when we eat lunch together."

I nodded and followed him in. He frowned at me slightly but made no comment when Ila waited with a cup of tea for me.

Ila remained quiet until Father walked away.

"We've missed you. Your father wouldn't say where you'd gone, even though Aryana pestered him constantly."

She led the way to the bathing chambers where Aryana lounged in one of the tubs.

"Benella," she spoke in soft delight. "I'm so happy to see you. Tell us where you've been."

I smiled as she stepped from the water and followed us to the back room. It felt like a ritual to bathe as soon as I came to the Sisters' house, and I wondered if this is how the men felt when they arrived.

"Employed," I said vaguely as Gen left the room. "Father came here because of me, so I wanted to repay his care of me. I'm granted one day in seven to return to visit." I let them undress me as I continued in a concerned whisper. "How has he been?"

"Distracted," Aryana answered as she set my clothes aside. She turned back to me and tilted her head in study. "You look like you gained some weight back."

I felt a blush creep into my skin, and she laughed huskily.

"Tell me about your new master," she said. "Does he treat you well?"

"He's confusing," I admitted. "And prickly. I think he's so used to everyone bending to his will, he doesn't know how to react when I start questioning him."

Ila poured water over me, and Aryana gave a small smile as she picked up the soap.

"Why do you question him?" she asked.

I laughed.

"Why does anyone question? To learn. All my life I have lived under the roof of a man I knew and understood. Now I find myself guessing and stumbling around in the dark. It's uncomfortable not being able to anticipate the direction of his thoughts. I've spent the last several days focused on his library. It's a lovely, large room filled with so many books. When I'd started, it had been a mess. Does he think I restored the room properly? Are the books in the correct order? Should I clean the adjoining room next or move to another wing entirely? When I start asking questions, I get irritable replies as if I'm bothering him."

I realized I'd started to raise my voice, so I took a calming breath again.

Aryana's hands soothed the muscles in my back while I tried to ignore Ila's hands washing my front. Ila's smirk told me she knew it, too.

"I am grateful that I'm no longer a burden on Father, but do wonder why my employer even wanted me there if he can't be bothered to give me direction."

"You are on the right path," Aryana murmured. "Ask questions; study him. You will learn."

Ila handed me the soap so I could finish washing as she fetched the rinse water. Rinsed of the soap, I followed them to the tubs, again noting how they walked with such ease.

"I'm curious," I said hesitantly.

"Of course you are," Ila laughed. "If you weren't, you wouldn't be in this house."

Smiling, I nodded in agreement.

"How do you walk about with such confidence and no clothes?" I asked as we each settled into a tub.

"What about clothes gives you confidence?" Aryana asked.

"A sound question," I said as I thought it over. "I suppose it hides our faults."

Aryana stood suddenly and held out her arms.

"Do you see faults?"

"Well, I'm not a good judge," I said. "I've not seen many women naked."

Aryana sat with a laugh.

"I have, and I will tell you that the men who come here have a hard time finding flaws in limbs or torso. They only see a body and not the person associated with it. So, we wear a veil to hide the person in which they might find fault."

I continued to think over her answer in silence. Is that how the beast wanted to see me when I wore his dresses? As a body and not a person?

Too soon, she insisted we leave the waters and dress again.

I RAN the last several yards to the estate as the sun sank below the tree line. I was cutting it close. The gate grated open for me, and I flew through the gap without slowing and collided with the beast, who had been waiting in mist clouded shadows.

"Returned as promised," I panted as I took a step back from him and bent to rest my hands on my knees.

In response to my announcement, he turned so the tip of his tail brushed my face. With a grimace, I straightened, clasped his tail, and allowed him to lead me, even though I knew I could find my own way. The fur of his tail stood out stiffly, and I surmised my return so close to sunset had given him concern.

Though I didn't like his threats against my father, I did feel a measure of pity for the beast. I could only imagine how lonely his life was within the walls of the estate.

My stomach began growling before we reached the kitchen.

"Change," he ordered after we walked through the outer door.

The mist pulled back to the small area where he paced.

Sensing his barely contained mood, I slipped into the servant's quarters and gently closed the door. The nightgown I'd removed just that morning now lay on the first bed. With a sigh, I put it on and thought again of Aryana's logic.

I didn't want the beast to only see me as a body. I wanted him to see me as a person, faults and all. After all, we all had faults. Why put me in a position where I would disappoint him when he discovered I wasn't what he wanted? But what did he want?

Knowing it would anger him, but unwilling to bend, I put the shirt on over the gown, wearing it unbuttoned like a wrap. When I opened the door, he growled loudly but didn't order the shirt away.

"Sit and eat," he said.

On the table, there was another full meal similar to the one I'd thrown at him. This time, I sat gracefully and politely consumed what was before me. I ate until my stomach stretched with pain, then used my napkin to dab my mouth. With a content sigh, I rose.

"Thank you," I said.

"Why did you wear the shirt? I warned that you would lose it if you wore it inside," he said, still in a poor mood.

"The gown left me feeling exposed and cold," I said.

"Take it off."

I walked toward him without reaching for the shirt. The rasp of his pacing silenced as he stopped to watch me.

The mist still obscured everything but his outline. Walking through it, I stopped when only an inch separated us. The mist tried gathering, but I stood too close for it to shield him. Looking into his eyes, I calmly shed the shirt and draped it over my arm. Then, I tilted my head and studied his pointed, furred ears, his very sharp teeth exposed by his pulled back lips, and his deep set blue eyes shot red with anger.

"Staring at the beast?" he asked with his clicking growl.

"Staring at the Benella?" I asked curiously.

He huffed a great breath that moved the hair loosened from my braid.

"If you want me to bare myself to you, be prepared to bare yourself to me," I said.

He turned away, his claws scraping harshly against the stone floor of the kitchen.

"Do as you like," he said as he tore open the door. It slammed closed behind him.

I wrapped the shirt around me again and made my way to my bedroom. Without hesitating, I opened the double doors to his room and walked to his wardrobe. There, I selected a new shirt, much larger than my own, and shed my gown. If I were to lose a shirt I wore, I'd rather that shirt be his.

Securely wrapped in a man's fine shirt, I curled under my covers and wondered what the beast would think of the gown and shirt I'd left in his wardrobe. I drifted to sleep with a slight smile on my lips.

AFTER WASHING MY FACE, I went to the wardrobe and saw it filled with a variety of gossamer dresses once again. I closed the doors and opted to walk about the manor in his shirt to see what he had to say about it. Though it bared my legs from just above the knee, it covered me more thoroughly than any of the dresses would.

The beast waited in the hall, as usual, when I opened the door, his thick mist protecting him.

"Good morning. What shall we do today?"

"Do as you wish," he said softly.

His calm voice surprised me. I'd been prepared for another rant or argument.

"Do as I wish? Don't you grow bored following me around?" I asked, making my way toward the library, listening to his soft steps behind me.

"That's not your concern."

"What exactly are my concerns?"

"Staying within the walls," he said immediately.

"Unless it's my day to leave, correct?"

"Of course," he said, his voice rough with agitation.

I stopped walking and turned to face him. We stood in the wide hallway just outside of the library. The mist acted as a wall separating us, but I saw him pace back and forth through it, backlit by a candle that quickly winked out.

"Do you intend to hurt me? Now or eventually?"

He snorted.

"No."

"You like watching me, no matter what I do; and after the month is up, you intend to touch me," I said as a statement of fact. "You've stated you do not want me to fear you. And you've kept me fed and sheltered. Yet through it all, I feel you growing angrier." I went on quickly before he could say anything. "Now, I admit, I've done several things—many, actually—to contribute to your ire. So I'm wondering if my presence is really providing you with any value. Undoubtedly, I am reaping more benefits than you. Why keep me?"

He growled, and I knew what he was about to say.

"I know," I sighed. "It is not my concern. But did you consider that if you shared the purpose of my presence with me, I might not be so difficult about what you request of me? That maybe I might understand your reasons and assist you as best I can in return for all the favor you've given me?"

Silence greeted my logic.

I turned and walked into the library, listening to the brush of his paws against the floor.

Not in the mood for anything particular, I browsed the shelves until a gilded book upon one of the highest shelves caught my eye. Tilting my head back, I stared at it. I had no hope of reaching it.

"Step onto my hand," the beast said from behind me.

I looked down and saw his furry paw extended forward.

"Won't I be too heavy to lift with one hand?"

He made a noise between a grunt and a laugh. I supposed he was very strong if he could throw grown men up and over the walls of the estate. I kicked off the delicate slipper and raised my foot, holding the shelf for balance.

"The other one, too," he said, offering his other hand.

I stood on his hands, and he easily lifted me as he shifted from the crouch in which he'd started to his full height. It brought me higher than the book. Placing a steadying hand on a shelf, I bent slightly to reach for it.

He lifted me higher, keeping the book just out of reach so I needed to bend lower. I rolled my eyes at his game and reached for the book again.

His tongue rasped the back of my thigh, and I froze.

"I changed my mind. I would like to get down."

"Not yet," he whispered, lifting me higher.

Still in his hands, I dropped to a squat and twisted to face him. I caught him with his tongue hanging out for the next swipe, and he licked my face instead of my thigh. We both looked at each other in surprise.

"You promised," I reminded him. "A month. You know this is a breach in our bargain."

"No more than the shirt."

I couldn't argue. He'd told me he wanted to at least see me if he couldn't touch me.

"What guarantee do I have you won't touch me if you do see me? I thought seeing a woman's body caused," I flapped a hand while my face grew warm. "Well, I thought it grew a man's desire to touch her. Wouldn't I just be putting myself in danger?"

"No," he said firmly. "If I see you, I wouldn't need to touch you. Only two days a week. The rest you could wear what you wish."

I narrowed my eyes at him. Why the change in our deal? Were we getting closer to the real reason for my presence?

"Please set me down. I need to consider this carefully."

He immediately set me on my own feet and followed me as I slowly moved to sit on the sofa. I remained quiet for several minutes, keeping my thoughts to myself, and he again began to pace in agitation.

Walking about without clothes might have seemed unsettling if not for my association with the Whispering Sisters. For them, it appeared completely natural and served a purpose. What purpose would my nudity serve, though, if not to entice as theirs did? I didn't know, and I didn't like not knowing.

There were several points in my life where I'd made decisions not based on logic or concern for my well-being, but simply based on curiosity. I knew this would be another instance. I wanted to discover his purpose. However, there were some concerns I couldn't put aside.

"I will agree, but I have a few conditions and some questions you must answer."

"No questions," he said with irritation.

"Come now, you don't even know what they are. How can you deny them? For instance, I've noticed several enchanted beings here. The wood nymphs, the crow. I'm sure there are others. I would like to know if you intend that they will see me naked."

He growled low, the click becoming so pronounced that it seemed the growl stopped and started in bursts.

"No one will see you but me," he said.

"See?" I smiled slightly. "Not such hard questions. May I choose the days?"

"Yes," he growled. His pacing grew more agitated.

"I'm not convinced I will be completely safe once we start this. If I should die at the estate, I want you to provide for my family."

He stopped pacing, and through the mist, I saw him turn toward me fully.

"You will not die." Then he added softly, "But I agree to your terms."

"Then one last thing," I said, taking a calming breath. He wouldn't like this condition, but I wouldn't sway from it. "No more mist. I need to trust that you will not harm me. I can't trust what you keep hidden from me."

"If you see me, you will trust me less."

Chewing my lip for a moment, I struggled to come up with a solution that would work for both of us.

"What if you gave me a few hours each day without the mist so I could know you better?"

He grunted his agreement, but the mist remained. I didn't mind. Trust took time.

"Go change," he said abruptly.

Or maybe time wasn't something the beast wanted to acknowledge. I stood reluctantly. I'd agreed to the terms. The only concern that remained was his treatment of me. Yet, even if something happened to me as a result of my folly, my father and sisters would benefit from it.

Without comment, he followed my slow progress through the halls until we reached my door.

"Pick what you like from the wardrobe. Your own this time," he said.

Clothes? I'd thought he'd meant me to run around naked.

I slipped into my room and rushed to pull open the wardrobe doors. Ruffled masses of pink horror filled the space. I made a face as I pulled one out. Blye would love to wear the dress I held. It laced up the front, and the layered skirt would cover all my important parts, so I couldn't complain.

Sighing, I let my shirt fall to the floor and tugged the dress over my head, lacing up the front. After sliding my feet into the matching slippers, I opened the door and turned for his inspection.

"I'd expected a happier face," he said with a puzzled note.

"I'm sorry, I'm just not used to wearing anything so...fancy." I had almost said feminine.

"That's the point. To provide you the things you couldn't have before."

"What if I liked the things I had before? Well, except the lack of food. I like the food here," I quickly added, hoping I'd get breakfast soon.

"If you could wear anything you wished," he asked slowly, "what would you wear?"

I grinned and answered promptly.

"Trousers and a sturdy shirt."

"Even indoors?" he asked.

I nodded and wondered what he thought of my preference. He didn't leave me waiting long.

"I would prefer you wear dresses, and in the future, I will offer you options that you might find more appealing than what you wear now. If you find you cannot adapt to them, we will see if there isn't perhaps some form of trouser I can tolerate. I have no issue with the shirts by themselves."

His words cheered me.

"Come, there is food waiting for you."

I SPENT the remainder of the day wandering around the manor and asking the beast questions about various rooms. Often he didn't answer or told me it wasn't my concern, but he made an effort to clear the mist when he spoke to me, and his growl faded as the day progressed.

The next morning, an unruffled day dress with no lace or other adornments waited hidden among several other options in the wardrobe. The drab brown color made me smile as I plucked it from its lace-bedecked companions.

When I stepped from the room, the beast made no comment. He followed me to the kitchen. Now, whenever I walked into the room, some form of food waited for me on the table. At the moment, eggs and thickly sliced bacon with mushrooms and cooked tomatoes waited on the tray.

"I never see you eat," I said as I sat at the chair. "When do you?"

"After you sleep."

I watched his eyes when he answered and saw them flick to the bacon.

"That seems a long time to go without food." Picking up a piece of bacon, I held it out to him. "Here," I offered holding it lightly.

He moved quickly, stretching from his mist and snapping it from my fingers in one bite that left me wide-eyed.

"I am not a tame pet," he said.

"Obviously," I said with a laugh. "A pet would have licked my fingers in thanks."

He made a choked noise, but I didn't look up from my food or offer him another bite.

After finishing every crumb on my plate, I stood with a content sigh.

"Is there a bag here that I could use? Like the one I used to own?" Before you shredded it, I thought sadly.

"I would like to walk the wall today and want something to carry the things I find."

"Look inside the servant's room."

I fetched the bag that I knew waited and held the door for him as we left. We spent the remainder of the day walking the wall, and he spent the majority of it without his mist.

CHAPTER THREE

I woke to a noise in my room and sat up abruptly. Weak moonlight and a dying fire cast shadows in the room, and I couldn't see more than vague shapes.

"Sir?" I called with my heart thundering.

Everything remained quiet, though I knew something had woken me. I held still for several long minutes until I heard the noise again. A rip and growl from the other side of the closed door.

I slipped from my bed and tiptoed toward the beast's door as noises continued from the other side. Carefully, I pulled the handle, and the door eased open. The fire in the room blazed; and within the light, I saw his massive form lying on the bed. He tossed about, his claws tearing the mattress as he struggled against a dream inspired foe.

"Sir?" I whispered again.

He shifted onto his back, and his struggles calmed slightly, but I saw his hands still twitched. Approaching the bed, I tentatively reached toward him to smooth the hair on his arm. It stood up stiffly, an indicator of his mood.

When I looked up at his face, I saw the glint of his eyes as he watched me.

"A dream troubled you," I barely whispered, wondering if he would roar at me for the intrusion. Instead, he closed his eyes; so I continued to stroke his fur. When the fur on his arm gradually settled, I shifted to his head where it still stood up wildly.

He sighed loudly, looped an arm around me, and tugged me onto his bed. When I landed, a cloud of feathers erupted around us. I squeaked in surprise and dread. I didn't want to be in his bed, I'd only thought to ease his troubled mind.

"Stay until I sleep," he said, closing his eyes.

I relaxed slightly and shifted in the loose feathers to again stroke my fingers through the fur on his head. Not long after, I felt his body relax and his breathing deepen.

The beast confused me. During the day, I attributed his ire to his isolation since he only had me for company. Once I retired each night, I had given little thought to what he did. Yet, I should have. The state of his room on my first day should have told me just how troubled his nights might be.

A feather tickled my nose, and I softly blew it away. What thoughts tormented him so much that he sought to destroy the comfort and extravagance around him?

Carefully, so I wouldn't wake him, I eased myself to the side of the bed and lightly touched my feet to the floor.

"She will never free me," he mumbled and rolled to his side.

"Who?" I whispered.

He didn't answer.

Looking at him, I decided he still slept. I withdrew from his room, leaving a trail of feathers. It was a long while before I slept.

SQUARING MY SHOULDERS, I dropped the beast's shirt to the floor and undid my braid.

After his comment the night before, I decided today would be the first day to try our new bargain. He'd let me wear proper clothes for two days and had let me see him without his mist. But it was last night, seeing him so disturbed by whatever he dreamt, that made up my mind. He had so many secrets, and no one to trust with them. I wasn't sure I wanted to be his confidant, but I didn't like being in the dark either. I hoped keeping my end of the bargain would open him up to a few questions I had. I wanted to know who wouldn't free him and from what he wanted to be freed.

As I stood combing my hair before the mirror, I began to shiver. This would never work. I would shiver the whole day through and wake up sick in the morning, I thought to myself. Yet, I knew if I didn't try to uphold my end of our new bargain, I would find myself dressed in his choice of clothes once again. Taking a calming breath, I smoothed my hands over my hair. Unbraided, it fell to my waist and could serve to shield me a little if I chose. But I didn't use it that way.

With one last worried look at myself, I turned away from the mirror. Each step brought more doubt, and by the time I reached the door, my hand shook. I paused and took a fortifying breath before setting my hand on the handle. I pulled open the door.

In the hall, the beast looked up from his usual waiting place. Without the mist, I saw the shock on his face. Before I blinked, a storm cloud of mist erupted around him, swirling with an intensity that stirred the air around me.

"Do not move," he said.

I stood frozen with my hand still on the door handle. His reaction and the violence of the tempest that surrounded him robbed me of my thin courage. My limbs shook with cold and fear. Several long minutes passed with the mist growing no calmer.

"Beauty," he growled. "Lead and I will follow."

My voice failed me the first time I tried to speak. After clearing it, I managed a whisper.

"I would, but between fear and cold, I'm shaking too badly. May I try again tomorrow?"

"No." The single word sounded like a desperate plea. "I will meet you in the library. Join me when you are ready."

He departed quickly, leaving me stunned and clinging to the door. I wasn't sure what I'd expected, but the disturbing storm that had surrounded him hadn't been it. That he'd left me as soon as I'd mentioned my fear helped calm me.

I went back into my room and looked in my wardrobe for a wrap. It was empty of everything. Even the shirt I'd dropped on the floor had disappeared.

Wrapping my arms about myself, I shivered and awkwardly walked naked through the halls until I reached the library doors. They stood ajar and glowed with orange light. Inside, I heard the roar of a large fire. I peeked around the corner but saw no sign of the beast. Or of his mist. However, the curtains were drawn, making it hard to see very far into the room beyond the circle of fire light.

Darting inside, I stood before the fire and held out my hands to warm myself. It seemed the temperature inside had dropped severely since revealing myself.

A whisper of noise had me spinning. A great black cloud churned just inches from me.

"Eat," he said gruffly.

Only then did I notice the tray laden with every sweet imaginable. My stomach growled. The tray sat low on the table, and I didn't want to bend to reach it.

"Could I see you please?" I whispered.

When he had shown himself during those brief periods over the last several days, he'd always appeared calm. The black air around him did not hint at calm. I needed to know what it meant.

"No," he said in a surprisingly gentle voice. "Eat. Do not fear me. You are safe."

I glanced at the tray. Everything on it tempted me, but it felt like a trap.

Taking a fortifying breath, I reached for a pastry glazed with sugar and stuffed with dates, ignoring the strawberries and grapes. I kept my eyes trained on the cloud the entire time, but nothing changed. It still swirled in the same position. I continued my wary study as I took my first bite. The sugar melted on my tongue, and the taste momentarily distracted me.

The mist moved away from me. I watched in surprise as it drifted toward the shelves and plucked the gilded book I'd wanted to read several days ago. The beast returned to the sofa and set the book on the cushions for me.

"Relax," he encouraged. "Read."

"I would prefer not," I said, not willing to turn my back on him.

He didn't become upset as I expected. Instead, he seemed to sense he caused my unease because he drifted from behind the sofa to the corner near the first curtained window.

"Please, sit," he said in a firmer tone.

Finishing the pastry, I licked my fingers and picked up the book. I sat as he bade and tried to read. I felt absurd sitting there naked while holding a book, and my mind drifted to my first glimpse of Father's classroom at the Whispering Sisters. Had he felt the same way sitting in a chair before a group of naked woman? Had they? I wondered if it became easier the more time they spent together.

The blaze kept the room warm enough that I didn't shiver, but it began to warm the tray of food too much. I looked up, noted the glistening moisture on the fruit, and reached for several. The tartness of the grapes and sweetness of the strawberries complemented each other. When I'd eaten those, I went back to reading. I'd only managed a few pages when my eyes drifted to the pastries. The heat from the fire had warmed them enough that they smelled freshly baked.

I glanced at the mist, but it remained the same. Since sitting, he hadn't made a sound.

I stretched forward and plucked another pastry from the tray. The tiny tart was no bigger than the palm of my hand. I nibbled at it slowly and read.

The gilded book contained a compilation of poetry from several authors. Most of the poems annoyed me as whining drivel from love struck fools, but a few provoked deep thought and required re-reading. After several chapters, I tossed the book aside and looked up at the cloud.

"I need a moment," I said softly, hoping he would understand.

He didn't move, so I stood and quickly left the library. I considered running to his room and getting a shirt but took a few calming breaths and made it back to my room to use the chamber pot, instead.

Away from the fire, I started shivering again. The cold didn't cause me to hurry, though, and my teeth chattered by the time I returned to the library.

I peeked around the door just to be certain the beast hadn't moved. The mist still swirled in the corner. I crept inside and stood before the fire, telling myself he was just sleeping and wouldn't notice me. Gradually, the shivers eased, and I sat on the sofa again. New food waited on the tray, cooled meat pulled from a bird and tender cooked vegetables.

I moved to the shelves to look for a different book. Since farming had held my interest for a while, I decided to read about animal husbandry. It amused me since I sat with a beast while reading it.

Losing track of time, I jumped slightly when the mist moved

toward me, nudging the table. It momentarily blocked the view of the fire. The crash of a log and crackle of new flames explained why he'd moved. I hadn't thought of feeding the fire. With the table so close, I settled back into the sofa and nibbled while I read.

Hours later, I unfolded my legs, which I'd curled under me at some point and stretched with a huge yawn. The food tray was missing from the table, and the fire had burned down again. I recalled the beast moving several times to add to it, but he'd remained in the corner for the last hour.

Other than feeding the fire, he'd not moved or spoken to me the entire day. I still didn't feel comfortable without clothes, but I wasn't afraid anymore.

"Come," he said softly. He sounded strained. "I will walk with you to your room."

I led the way through the hallway, feeling his acute gaze, and tried not to run. When we reached the door, he followed me inside. Another tray waited with a steaming bowl of soup. I still felt full from the last tray even though the pink light of sunset radiated through the windows.

"Thank you for today, Benella. Perhaps tomorrow I will be able to repay you as you deserve."

I turned to see him withdraw and close the door.

The day hadn't been what I'd expected. Because of the lesson that Aryana and Ila had provided, I'd imagined myself running from him when his pent energies became too much. At the very least, I'd thought he would leave to find the wood nymph.

I opened the wardrobe and found the shirt I'd taken from him and slipped it on, glad to finally have cover.

THE BEAST DIDN'T WAIT in the hallway the next morning when I exited my room, wearing another plain dress. I thought he might be tired of my company after the prior day. I would have grown bored watching me read, too.

Gliding through the silent hallways, I made my way to the kitchen ready to spend the day outside. Though I loved books, I loved being outdoors as well. When I'd peered out my window, the sun had been peeking through thin morning clouds, promising a mild day.

I entered a cold kitchen and glanced at the empty table in surprise. The beast paced before the door, his stormy mood apparent in his fur and bared teeth, which he chose not to hide from me. He muttered to himself quietly until I spoke.

"Sir?"

His head whipped toward me as if in surprise.

"I'm afraid yesterday was for nothing," he growled lowly.

I remained quiet, hoping he'd provide more information.

"In punishment for my failed attempt, she's blocked my ability to control the magic of this place since I could not control—"

He lashed out at the table in a violent rage. The wood split under the fury of his ravaging claws and a chunk flew toward me. In horror, I watched it tumble through the air. The wood piece struck my face just above the jawline, stinging as it gouged the skin before falling to the floor.

I gasped and pressed a hand to my face. The noise penetrated his rage enough to pause his destruction. His ragged breathing filled the room as tears filled my eyes, mostly from anger not pain. My fingers felt warm and wet, and I pulled my hand away long enough to look at the blood.

Without saying a word, I walked toward him. His angry gaze met mine.

"You hurt me," I said flatly. I turned away and pulled open the outer door.

He made no move to follow me.

I strode through the long grass and made my way toward the gate as I wondered what level of stupidity had possessed me to think I might actually have had a positive influence on the beast. It was that tree's fault. Teach him, it had said. Some creatures couldn't be taught kindness, patience, or civility.

Tears trickled down my face, and I stumbled over a tree root. The cut burned now, but no more than I deserved for my conceit. I'd been so certain I'd be able to figure out the puzzle that surrounded the beast.

A roar sounded behind me, pulling me from my thoughts enough to see that all of the vines and roots of the trees around me quivered oddly. The roots in the path ahead of me flattened to the ground as if trying to help ease my passage. Good, I thought, hurrying. Behind me, the beast roared again. This time, it sounded more like a curse. Ahead, the gates beckoned, yawning wide. As I stepped through them, the beast roared my name.

In the distance, the rattle of an empty wagon bed reverberated through the trees. I hurried my steps, and several minutes later, my feet crunched on the gravel of the road toward the Water. Just rounding the bend from Konrall, a wagon driven by Henick slowed to avoid me.

Henick smiled and called softly to his team as he pulled back on the reins.

"Benella, what are you doing here? I thought you left with your family to settle in Water-On-The-Bridge."

His familiar friendly smile sent a wave of relief through me just as the beast again roared my name. Henick's mouth firmed as he looked at me closely.

"What happened?" he asked with true concern.

"I'm sorry to ask this of you, but can I ride with you to the Water? I had a run in with the beast." Better that he thought the beast knew my name from a trespass than from an extended stay.

"Of course." He set the brake and jumped from the seat to offer me a hand up.

"That cut looks deep," he said as I settled onto the seat. He pulled a clean square of cloth from his pocket, and reaching into the bed of the wagon, he used a water skin to soak it before handing it to me.

"Hold that to the cut."

I took the cloth and pressed it to my cheek as he climbed back into the seat and clucked the team into action again. The beast's roars faded as we moved away. I kept a wary eye on the vines, but they remained dormant.

"What are you doing so far from home?" he asked.

I sighed and told him as much of the truth as I could.

"Things weren't going well in Konrall so Father moved us to the Water, but the house there is too small. That's why he wanted Bryn and Blye to marry. But he wouldn't force them into a decision they weren't ready to make. So, we all moved into a one room home in town. We're struggling for food. I thought I could gather near the estate like I used to."

He nodded.

"Did Bryn marry?"

"No."

"I offered for her," he said.

I nodded and turned the cloth over, hoping for a cooler spot.

"Do you think she might reconsider?"

I sighed, thinking of her current troubles.

"She might. But you should know she put her hopes in a man who left her with no promises, only a babe."

"Children are a blessing," Henick said firmly.

I hoped Bryn would open her eyes if Henick offered for her again.

THE WAGON CLATTERED to a stop in front of the small cottage, and Henick quickly leapt down to help me from my seat. My face throbbed, so I waved him toward the front door as I walked around back to get cooler water from the well.

When I walked through the back door, I only caught Bryn's reply to Henick's question.

"I want no part of dirt farming and scraping to live from season to season. Now that I'm in the Water, I see how much I like town life. I plan to marry up, not down."

Henick nodded and turned without a word. Bryn closed the door and turned to see me standing there with my mouth open. Saying nothing, she marched to her room and closed the door. I ran to the front door and pulled it open, calling Henick's name just as he moved to climb into the seat.

He paused and waited for me to run to his side.

"You should keep that on the cut," he said lightly, taking the cloth from my hand and guiding it to my face.

"She's a fool," I whispered harshly, raising my hand to his cleanly shaven jaw. "Marrying you would be marrying up no matter what kind of life to which your wife is born." I leaned forward and kissed the cheek opposite of the one I held.

He smiled and took my hand to press it against the cloth on my jaw.

"Truthfully, her answer doesn't bother me. When I heard two of the Hovtel sisters were to be married, I'd hoped one would be you." He brushed a light kiss on my cheek. A blush ignited where his lips had touched and spread outward.

"Tell your father to contact me when it's your turn. I'd gladly be the first to offer for you."

When he turned to climb aboard, I found my voice.

"Why did you hope it was me?" I asked.

"We, my brothers and I, thought you might finally be ready to notice we existed," he said, grinning down at me.

What an odd thing to say, I thought.

"Of course I knew you existed."

His smile only widened.

I didn't know how to respond to that so, instead, I chose to change the subject.

"Did your father ever take you fishing after our visit?" If possible, he smiled wider.

"He did, and it was the best fishing. Ma dried what we couldn't eat that night and said it would make a fine soup come winter. He also received your note and sent a reply to your father. He teases Ma about wanting to catch a crow to train to carry messages." His smile faded a little. "It might seem like we live from season to season, but we don't scrape. The land Da's clearing is meant to build a house for the first son who marries."

"If you find someone before it's my turn, she'll be lucky to have you," I said quietly and backed up a step. He shook the reins and pulled away.

Instead of walking inside, I started down the road after him, walking in his dust. From the neighbor's roof, a crow cawed and clacked its beak at me.

"Quiet," I muttered, not wanting to acknowledge anything related to the beast just yet.

Covered with a cloak, Ila stood at the door when I rounded the back corner of the house.

"What happened?" she demanded and nudged the guard. He

dutifully took a step toward me, but I held up a hand, motioning him to stay.

"I'm fine. I'm here because I need to speak with someone who still has an ounce of sanity."

She held out her hand and helped me up the remaining stairs. With the door closed, she shrugged out of the cloak then tugged me along. Instead of the basement, she turned down the hall to the right. Aryana waited inside a very clean room with a narrow bed.

"Well?" she said kindly.

"Well, what?"

"What happened to your face, dearest?"

"Oh. Carelessness. A piece of wood." I peeled the cloth away and showed her.

She tsked and motioned for me to sit on the bed. Using a clean cloth from a fresh bowl of water that waited on a nearby table, she washed the wound and pulled a sliver from the raw skin.

"I would say we should sew it, but I'm afraid there might be more splinters. If we sew them in, it would become infected. Best to let it heal on its own. It will likely leave a noticeable scar."

I nodded absently, thinking of Henick's comment. I'd always noticed him and his brothers when they'd come to town. They were a lively bunch that never let the baker or the Coalres bother them. When they'd smiled and greeted me, I'd always smiled in return.

Frowning, I realized I'd never actually said anything in return. In fact, looking back, I realized I'd spoken very little, content with my own thoughts and observations. I compared myself to the beast. He kept his own counsel, and it frustrated me. Was that how Henick felt when I'd done the same to him? Very seldom had I spoken my mind. It wasn't until I met the beast that I started speaking what I thought. Even then, I still kept much to myself, like now.

I felt Aryana's curious gaze.

"I met a friend on the road who let me ride with him in his wagon. He made a curious comment. He said that he thought I might be ready to realize he existed." I met Aryana's gaze. "I've always known he was there. I've never really spoken to him, but I've always smiled in return whenever he's greeted me. Why would he think I ignored him?"

Ila laughed huskily and left the room. Aryana sat beside me and clasped my hand in her own. I interrupted whatever she was about to say with another question.

"Isn't it uncomfortable sitting bare bottomed?" I blushed when I realized what I'd said.

She smiled behind the veil.

"You sound as if you are speaking from experience."

"Curiosity will be my downfall," I said with forced playfulness.

"Yes, it is uncomfortable at first. Then I grew used to it, and no longer even notice. As for your friend, I think he meant you never noticed him in a way a woman notices a man."

"That's silly. I remember thinking him handsome the first time I saw him."

"And?" she prompted.

"And what?" I asked confused.

"Did he make your heart flutter or your insides melt?"

"No," I said slowly. "That sounds uncomfortable."

She laughed and patted my hand.

"It is, but in a pleasant way. Come, let's tell your father you're here. He will want to spend time with you."

FATHER and I walked together down the market street while I told him of Henick's opportune arrival and Bryn's second rejection of his offer. We talked of Blye's success at the dressmaker's and her talk of opening her own shop in the south. I knew that meant she hoarded her coin and felt pity for Father.

He made no comment about the cut on my face, but I knew he still worried.

As the streets filled with people, Father sighed and said he needed to return to work. I realized I had nowhere to go. I couldn't return to the Sisters as they were now accepting customers, and I didn't want to face Bryn after listening to her rude refusal.

Hugging Father good-bye, I started the walk back to the estate.

THE BEAST WAITED within the gates, making no attempt to hide himself.

"You returned," he said in relief when I stepped through the opening.

"Of course," I said stiffly. "I wouldn't want you dragging my father from his bed tonight when I didn't."

I marched past him in the direction of the manor, but he caught my skirt and spun me around.

"I apologize for hurting you," he said gruffly. "Let me heal it."

"No. I want to wear it as a reminder for you. I'm a person, not an object that will withstand your fury and repair itself. I am not part of this estate."

"I will not forget again."

"Pardon me if I don't believe you." I tugged my skirt from his clawed grasp and heard a rip. Not caring, I started on my way only to be snagged again.

"I'm not asking. Hold still so I can heal it."

Slowly turning, I glared at him and crossed my arms. He approached me on all fours, a repentant look in his eyes.

"Bring back the wispy gowns. I will not stand before you without clothes again."

"Close your eyes," he ordered as if I hadn't spoken.

Exhaling angrily, I closed my eyes. The first swipe of his tongue over my jaw hurt, but the pain faded with each subsequent turn.

When he stopped, I opened my eyes and found the black mist surrounding us, too thick to see through. Something brushed over my collarbone. A knuckle perhaps? The gentle touch conflicted with the tumultuous mist.

"Rose, the enchantress, has cast a spell on me, and I'd hoped with your help to be free of it last night."

He turned away, and I quickly jogged to catch up, grabbing his tail. My curiosity outweighed my anger with him.

"How can I help free you?"

"I would rather talk inside," he said quietly.

The walk seemed to take longer. When he pushed inside the kitchen, I noticed that the table was still splintered but a loaf of bread was set on the block with a chair beside it.

"Sit and eat," he ordered.

"Will you tell me?" I asked, moving to the chair.

"She requires one night of pleasure," he growled, obviously agitated.

"And that is a problem?" After seeing him with the wood nymph, I wasn't sure how it posed a problem.

"Yes. If you recall, she's haggard and old," he replied dryly.

"I've met her?"

"Twice. I brought you to her cottage when you hit your head, and she brought the medicine when you were ill."

I vaguely recalled an older woman with missing teeth.

"How can I help?"

"If I could close my eyes and picture someone else, I thought I might have a chance. It worked until my first—"

I waited for him to continue but he did not.

"Your first what?"

"Never mind," he growled. "I should have known it wouldn't be so easy."

I ate quietly for several long minutes.

"You're trapped here and the only way to freedom is by giving this enchantress one night of pleasure," I said in summary, more for my benefit than his. "How long have you been here?"

"Over fifty years."

"You've been trying to pleasure her each night for over fifty years?" I asked in disbelief.

"Not every night. Several years ago she limited me to twice a week."

I felt a little gaggy on his behalf and understood why he would want to close his eyes and imagine someone else. Why me, though?

"It seems to me that if you've been trying the same thing for fifty years and getting the same disappointing results, you would try something different."

He sighed.

"That's why you're here. Now, I don't wish to talk about this anymore."

I immediately understood my role too well, but I doubted staring at me all day was enough to store up his energies to ensure an entire night of the old woman's attentions. But thanks to the sisters, I had a few more ideas.

"One more question," I said. He nodded reluctantly. "Will you allow me to help you?"

"I already have."

The humor in his tone was unmistakable, and I knew he meant walking around naked the day before.

CHAPTER
FOUR

"No. I can truly help you," I said.

The first thing I needed to do was calm him. His rages were dangerous to me, and undoubtedly disadvantageous to his goal to free himself. However, I felt the sisters' techniques for muscle relief, given Gen's response, might lead to another chase through the woods. Perhaps a bath, then?

I glanced at the beast and found him watching me closely. His fur stuck up in odd places and some burrs clung to his tail. No doubt, he would need convincing to get into a tub.

Standing, I marched toward him and leaned in to sniff.

"You need a bath," I said. "Come. I think you'll fit in one of the washtubs in the laundry."

"I'm not bathing."

"I'll help," I said.

The world spun, and I found myself clinging to his back. As soon as he lurched forward, I fisted my hands in his fur and wrapped my legs around his waist. He raced around a few corners and suddenly we stood in the laundry.

Sliding off his back, I grinned at the beast.

"That was fun. I'd expected there to be a fire and hot water when we arrived, though."

"I believe I mentioned she blocked my ability to use the magic."

"No matter," I said as I bent to start the fire.

Behind me, I heard him lifting the large pots to fill with water. We worked together for a long while before we had one of the tubs half filled with steaming water.

"In you go," I said.

He turned away from me and stepped into the water with a hiss. I quickly poured in another bucket of cooler water so he could sit. He sighed when he submerged up to his chest, his knees spread wide.

Using a dipper, I wet all of his fur and began lathering him. Once his fur was plastered against his skin, I could easily feel the hard ridges of his muscles. They distracted me from my purpose, and I found my hands idly wandering over their expanse. Recalling Ila's instruction, I began to wash him, rubbing the tension from the muscles in his shoulders and torso.

After I rinsed his back, I moved to the side of the tub and encouraged him to lift first one leg then the other out of the water. He watched me closely as I worked. I likewise paid close attention to him, ready to bolt if he showed any sign of pent energies.

Under the guise of scrubbing, I rubbed his calf muscles and as much of each thigh as I could reach under the water. Several times, I bumped into something under the murky depths, but didn't know if it was his penis or ball sack. Either way, the flesh did not feel firm, so I continued my efforts to ease his tension.

I didn't speak as I worked, preferring to adopt the sisters' silence. It gave me an opportunity to contemplate how to broach the subject of his failed attempts with Rose and what he might try differently. I hoped, after the bath, he'd be more open to suggestions.

When I moved to his head, he groaned and laid it back against the edge of the tub. He kept his eyes closed and his arms relaxed on the edge of the tub as I worked, and I felt certain I'd succeeded in calming him.

After rinsing him a second time, he rose from the tub and shook himself, sending water spraying everywhere. I gasped in surprise and felt doubly shocked when he laughed at me. A real laugh.

"Let's finish drying in the library," I suggested, wondering how long he'd stay relaxed and, hopefully, receptive to conversation.

He followed me closely and used the mist to cloak himself. In the library, I waited until he once again settled in the corner before speaking.

"I have a proposal. I know when aroused, you have certain pent energies..."

He made a choking noise.

"...that need to be released or you become tense and angry. However, have you considered that releasing these pent energies might be counterproductive toward your goal of a full night with the enchantress?"

"It crossed my mind as I sat in this very corner yesterday," he said sardonically.

"I'm speaking of a larger sacrifice," I said, excited that he understood and seemed willing to discuss the topic. "You've been doing the same thing for fifty years. What if you did not visit the enchantress for a week or two while letting your energies build? It might give you an advantage."

"A week," he scoffed.

"I'll help you. You just need to stay focused on the goal—your freedom."

He remained quiet in the corner for so long I began to pace. Perhaps, I'd assumed too much by speaking openly of his physical needs. It seemed that no one actually spoke of that in polite conversation, discounting the sisters of course.

"Perhaps, you're right," he said slowly. "This could work."

I stopped pacing and smiled at him.

"And, I suppose you want something in return for your help?" he said mulishly.

I fought not to roll my eyes.

"Not everything needs to be a trade or part of some deal. I'm helping to be helpful. That's all." And, maybe, by being so, I would win my own freedom.

He grunted, but said nothing more.

SEVERAL DAYS LATER, I struggled to maintain my temper as I faced the beast over breakfast. He paced back and forth in front of the door, his familiar mist cloaking him.

The day before he'd tried excusing himself often. However, each time I had quickly followed him, certain that he would try to find the wood nymph or some other substitute.

Now, he was surly and seemed to no longer care if I stayed at the estate or chose to flee. He had ordered me to take my day to visit my family.

"You can't order me to do that," I said. "I choose the day I visit."

For a moment, he paused his pacing to face me. An angry spark lit his eyes. When he resumed his pace, I set my fork down and quickly rose from my chair, ready to run if there seemed a need.

"You bore me, and I want time alone," he said with impatience and anger.

"Sir," I said, trying for a calm, soft voice. "It has only been a few days. Think of your freedom."

"I'm tired of thinking of it," he roared at me with such passion that his breath fluttered my hair.

"Let's go for a walk outside," I said, trying a different approach.

He spun toward me and took a step with each word he spoke.

"I do not want to walk outside. I want to fuck." He stood nose to nose with me, his breath fanning my face.

"Precisely why we need to calm you," I said, sensing my dangerous position.

He studied me for a long moment, then his tongue darted out to lap at my neck. I squeaked in surprise. He growled in response and stood on two legs, pulling me close. I only reached the bottom of his sternum when he stood, and his fur pressed into my face. I felt the length of his penis between my breasts.

He arched into me. I would have fallen backward if not for his arms holding me steady.

"Stop," I ordered him, trying to pull away. My movement only seemed to excite his thrusting. "You're hurting me." His root was bruising my ribs, and I felt a stab of pity for the wood nymph who had endured him. He was too large.

When he didn't listen, I stomped on first one paw, then the other. He roared but pulled away from me, dropping to all fours.

"There will be no fornicating," I yelled at him.

We glared at each other for a moment, then his temper erupted. He lashed out and flipped the table over, sending the dishes flying. This time, I covered my face to prevent injury. When he finished his fit and stood there panting, I retreated.

"I think I will visit my family," I said as I darted past him and out the door.

"Men aren't the only ones to suffer pent energies," he yelled at me as I ran.

I didn't know what he meant by that, but didn't slow to ponder it.

By the time I reached the gate, which swung open for me, I was out of breath and had a stitch in my side. The beast roared in the distance again. He still hadn't regained control of the estate, and it seemed to frustrate him as much as his pent energies.

I sprinted through the trees until I came to the gravel road and slowed to a hitched walk. Perhaps we were going about this wrong. He didn't respond well to self-denial. Perhaps I should have started with something smaller, like using the word "no" more often.

As I walked, I became aware of the sound of a wagon approaching from behind and turned to see Henick again.

I waved as he pulled up beside me.

"Going to the Water?" I asked.

Henick greeted me with a smile.

"I didn't think I'd see you again so soon." He jumped from the seat. "Your face is healed," he said in surprise and reached out to run a finger along my jaw.

"Yes, I'm very fortunate it didn't scar."

His touch left a slight tingle, and I blushed. Yet, the beast's parting comment rang in my ears. Why didn't I suffer from pent energies? Aryana had also hinted that I should feel my heart flutter or some such nonsense. Was I defective?

"Henick, why did you think I didn't notice you?"

He smiled again and lowered his hand, holding it out to me instead. I wrapped my sweat-dampened fingers around his warm, dry ones as I accepted his assistance and climbed up to the seat.

"Because you never lingered," he said easily, moving around the team to get to his side of the bench. "You never stopped to watch us like we stopped to watch you."

"Watch me?" I echoed, thinking of Tennen's words the night

he'd waited for me in the dark. Was this what he'd meant? He'd been angry because I'd never noticed him?

Henick laughed and shook his head at me.

"Everyone stops to watch you when you walk through the village, Benella."

That made me feel a bit uncomfortable.

"Is there something wrong with me?" He looked at me with worry. "Not that everyone watches me," I clarified quickly, "but that I don't watch back."

He smiled again, a small, soft smile.

"I don't think so. I think you're waiting for the right moment."

I frowned, and he laughed.

"You think before you feel," he said.

As I considered his words, I knew he was right.

We rode the rest of the distance in silence, and I asked him to drop me off by the mill so I could walk the rest of the way. When he slowed the team, I turned to kiss his cheek again. However, he turned at the same time and our lips met. A tingle of shock ran through me, and I pulled back in surprise.

Henick chuckled at my expression.

"Have you ever been kissed?" he asked.

"I have now," I mumbled.

"I'm honored to be the first," he said. He made no move to claim another one. I felt sure if it were the beast beside me instead of Henick, I would be fighting for my freedom.

Beside us, a crow cawed from a post bordering the mill. I stared at it as I licked my lips.

"Thank you, Henick," I said quietly, jumping to the ground before he could move to help me.

"Perhaps I'll see you on the road again," he said in farewell and encouraged the team forward.

I watched him disappear down the lane and, lost in thought,

started toward the market district. A familiar laugh drew me from my reverie as I passed a baker's stall.

Bryn stood with the baker's son in quiet discussion, leaning toward him and touching his arm lightly. He looked similar to Tennen. The young man's eyes repeatedly dipped to Bryn's cleavage, and his blush deepened each time.

Bryn spied me and said a quick, shy farewell to the man before walking my way. I waited for her, glad she wore a smile for a change. She looked much prettier for it.

"He's the one," she whispered, hooking her arm through mine. We walked toward home.

"What one?" I asked.

"The one who will offer for me. Edmund Rouflyn. His father runs the most successful bakery in the Water. It's just the two of them."

"I'm so happy for you, Bryn." I hugged her side. "Is he excited for the baby?"

She dug her fingers into my arm.

"Quiet," she hissed.

I frowned at her, not understanding her change in mood at first. Then, it dawned on me.

"You haven't told him?"

"He looks a lot like Tennen. He will never know it's not his because we've already been together," she whispered to me as she smiled and nodded to someone else in the market. "And he's much better than Tennen, too." She glanced at me from the corner of her eye. "You wouldn't know anything about that yet, would you," she said with a sigh.

Not knowing how to respond to that, I asked about Blye.

"She's doing well enough. Her dresses are selling, but slowly. Father's still trying to marry her off. She's getting offers but isn't in a position where she needs to settle like me."

Bryn was in a chatty mood and didn't give me any opportunity to excuse myself until it was well past ten. I knew the sisters were already taking clients, so I spent a long, boring day with my sister, who repeatedly begged me to bring something of value to trade the next time I visited.

When she began to prepare dinner, she politely told me there wasn't enough for four. I excused myself to meet Father on his way home.

I told him of Bryn's hope of the baker's son, and he nodded, sharing my concerns. He was disappointed he'd missed the opportunity to visit with me but was glad I'd spent time with Bryn. I left him with a kiss on his cheek and began the walk back to the estate.

WHEN I RETURNED, the kitchen was quiet and still destroyed. I skirted the wreckage and cautiously wandered the halls, speculating on the mood in which I would find the beast. Near the study, I heard an odd clicking noise. I stilled in the hallway, listening intently. It sounded like a tap of something against the glass.

Peering around the door, I watched in amazement as the beast threw open a window to let the crow in. The crow sat on the sill and cawed several times, clacking his beak in between caws. The beast watched him in silence, his fur slowly standing on end.

Beyond the crow, the sight of the wood nymph distracted me from the pair. Solid, she remained bent at the waist, her hair-like branches trailing the ground. As I watched, the spring green leaves from her hair fluttered to the earth in slow solidarity. The bark of her torso looked thin and curled in some places as if peeling away. The trunk of one leg glistened wetly. She looked broken.

The crow took flight, startling a noise from me as the beast rounded on me.

"You kissed him?" he roared.

The wood nymph trembled outside.

"You are mine," he growled, stalking toward me.

I stepped forward, meeting him without fear.

"Kiss me as you did him."

"No," I shouted, angry. He needed to be told no regardless of our agreement. "I'll end up broken or worse. Look at her!" I gestured at the wood nymph through the window. "If she were human, she would be ripped and bleeding. You are a beast. You don't stop and think how your actions might affect others. You have no regard for anyone but yourself and your own satisfaction."

He was no longer listening to me but stood before the window, staring at the nymph.

"Human," he said, before spinning from the window and racing from the room on all fours.

I glanced out the window in confusion. More leaves fell from the nymph's hair, and I wondered how many times he'd taken her.

The beast turned the corner at a run. When he reached her solidified form, he began speaking in earnest whispers. I couldn't hear the words, but the nymph came to life and collapsed to the ground. The beast scooped her into his arms and ran out of sight.

I shook my head. He needed to think with something other than his root.

I didn't see him again for three days. All the while, a storm lashed at the manor.

WHEN THE STORM FINALLY CLEARED, I grabbed the bag from the servant's quarters, dressed in my trousers and shirt, and strode out into the tranquil, dripping wet world. The sun made a valiant effort to break through the thick clouds above, but I knew it wouldn't succeed. It was magic that had made the storm, and only magic would clear it.

I left through the front gate with no intention of going very far. It wasn't my day to visit my family. I wanted to walk the wall as I used to and see if there was anything I could gather for Bryn. Since the beast wasn't there to ask, I decided to try it without his permission.

Turning west, so I would visit the enchanted patch of ground last, I started my long walk. A caw from above didn't surprise me, and I looked up to see the crow hop from branch to branch to keep up with me.

"I thought we were friends. How could you tell him I kissed Henick when you saw exactly what happened? It was an accident, and nothing came of it." I scowled at the bird as it cawed again. "I suppose you're going to fly off now and tell him I left. This, too, is innocent. Just a walk around the wall out of boredom. But go ahead, tattle." I waved it away, but it stuck to me doggedly. So, I ignored it.

The wall offered me a bunch of primrose on the north side and cabbage at the patch of raw earth. Happy with my findings, I rounded the wall toward the gate. The crow cawed loudly in warning, and I saw the beast standing just within the gates.

"Where have you been?" he demanded.

"Ask Mr. Crow," I said, slipping through the gates to walk past him.

The crow cawed once and flew away. The beast followed me back to the manor and continued to follow me for the rest of the day. I didn't speak again.

WHEN I WOKE in the morning, the gossamer dresses were back. I glared at them then went to yank open my door. The beast waited without his mist. I stood before him, dressed in his shirt.

"No." I said the single word with finality.

"Yes," he returned calmly. "Go put on one of the dresses. I will try again."

"I refuse," I said, crossing my arms. "The problem with your plan is that you're too used to getting your way. You need to learn how to contain yourself when someone refuses you. Until you can, I will dress as I please, not as you please."

He growled at me, an angry light filling his eyes. Then he huffed out a breath and rubbed a paw over his face.

"You are correct. I need to learn control," he said as a haunted look came to his eyes. "Dress as you please."

He turned to stalk away, but I stopped him.

"Were you so horrible as a man?" I asked.

"You know?" he asked, sounding strained.

"I guessed, but now I know."

He turned and walked away.

When I opened the wardrobe, it offered something of every style. The sheer gowns were there as were the plain ones that would cover me. But I also spotted trousers and shirts. I smiled and dressed as I pleased, knowing the beast's control of the magic had returned.

I FOUND HIM MUCH LATER, pacing outdoors near the place the wood nymphs had favored. He didn't seem to hear my approach, and I paused to study him.

Weeks ago, I would have considered his back and forth

movement a prowl. Now, I saw his frustration in the bend of his ears, his guilt in the droop of his tail, and his hopelessness in the weary set of his great shoulders. How could I not feel pity for such a creature?

"How is she?" I asked.

He stopped his pacing and turned toward me.

"Healing." Regret laced that single word.

"If I continue to help you, I need your word that Rose alone will be the recipient of your attentions."

His gaze dropped to the ground beside him. Tiny leaves dotted the area. Her hair.

"You have my word."

The words barely reached my ears, but it was enough. I cleared my throat and set my resolve. I would help him.

"Can I still do as I please?" I asked.

He snorted in response.

"Given your refusal to listen to any command I make, I would say yes."

"Perfect. I'll return before dinner," I spun away with the hope that he'd wonder what I intended.

I didn't walk very far, my bag gently tapping against my hip, when I heard him follow. There were a few things we'd misunderstood when trying abstinence to help his chances with the enchantress. His willpower and his boredom. He had too much of one and not enough of the other.

Now, I planned to coax him from his shadows of observance into the light of participation. It most likely wouldn't work, and he would roar and growl and leave in a storm, but the more we tried, the more I learned about him. I felt certain I'd eventually learn enough to truly help him.

Marching north, I ambled through fallow fields and quiet forests until I came to the wall. Unlacing my boots, I tossed them to the ground and began to climb one of the trees that stretched over the stacked stones.

"You're going to fall. Get down," he called to me as I climbed out of his reach.

Laughing, I kept climbing up and up until I reached the thinner branches of the canopy. I looked to the south, and far in the distance, I saw a bit of roofline. To the northwest, the moving waters of the river twinkled in the sunlight. I looked down at the beast.

"Are you able to leave these walls?"

"Yes," he said suspiciously, "Why?"

I crossed my legs around the branch and started scooting forward toward the empty space that separated me from my destination. I loosened my legs and dangled from the branch to squat on top of the wall.

"Then come on."

He looked up at me with concern.

I slipped over the wall and out of his sight. Slowly, I worked my way down the wall, one foot and handhold at a time. The beast sailed over the wall, his back feet clipping it with a thunk, before I reached the ground.

"Impressive," I said, looking up at the top of the wall that towered above my head. "You can clear it in one jump?"

"Yes, when necessary," he said, sniffing the air. "Why are we outside the estate? It isn't safe."

I scoffed at his concern. He was an enchanted beast. What had he to fear? I briefly thought of the stories of hunters and pillagers who'd tried to come for him in the past then quickly started walking away from the wall.

"You'll see why. It's a bit further. Come on."

We walked for another hour before the sound of the river reached my ears. My bare feet were starting to hurt, and I regretted not bringing the boots in the bag. But, I'd worried they would cause me to lose my balance on the tree.

Finding a quiet inlet, I stripped two branches for poles, attached the string and hooks I'd discovered in the bag, and handed one to the beast. I sat on a rock at the river's edge and dangled my feet into the cool water. The beast stood beside me, holding the pole uncertainly for a moment, then he joined me.

We sat in companionable silence for several hours while the fish ate our worms and laughed at our efforts. With the sun overhead, I pulled my hook from the water and opened my bag, hungry for the bread and cheese I'd taken from the kitchen.

Reaching to offer the beast half of the food, I watched him study the water. His eyes darted over the surface, following the shadows of the fish underneath.

"This is pointless," he growled.

I smiled at his frustration. "It's how most people eat every day," I said, handing him the food. "Haven't you ever had to work for your food?"

He scowled at me, but he accepted what I offered.

"There's something about it," I said. "A savory flavor to the food I gather with my own hands."

I watched him bite into the bread, and I considered it our first meal together. After eating, he grew restless, and I suggested we head back for a game in the library. He padded beside me, not commenting when I winced after stepping on something sharp. With sore feet, the climb back over the wall looked daunting.

"You control the vines, correct?" I said, staring at the high stone barrier.

"Yes," he said, watching me.

I turned to him with a mischievous smile.

"Toss me over the wall like you did the first time we met. Let the vines catch me."

He shook his head but gripped my waist with both hands a moment before flinging me up and over the wall. I laughed the whole way and landed on a loosely woven vine net. He sailed over the wall in one smooth vault.

"We should make a game of that," I said, still laughing as I jumped lightly to the ground and sat to tug on my boots. "It would be fun in water, too, when it's warmer. The splashes I could make." My mind wandered to the calculations of angles and heights needed until I caught his stare.

"You are not like other women," he said slowly, as if just realizing it.

Shaking my head at him, I stood and dusted off the seat of my trousers.

"A good thing for you, I am not."

DURING THE NEXT SEVERAL DAYS, I discovered something. The beast knew many games of chance, but very few intellectual ones. We studied a book of games and learned a few together. We made an odd pair sitting quietly in the library for hours, he on his haunches on the floor and me perched in a chair.

His mind was a beautiful thing to behold. He challenged me in a way that made me smile and laugh. But after mastering a game, he quickly grew bored with it whether he won or lost. The games of chance never lost his interest, though.

I studied him as he contemplated the wood board before us. He seemed relaxed and content, and I wondered if he knew how many days he'd gone without seeing the enchantress. Would it be enough?

Loathe to bring it to his attention, I continued to try to keep him constantly busy. As the days had stretched, I had watched for signs of growing agitation. As I'd guessed, boredom was his worst enemy.

Though four days had passed since I'd returned from my last visit to the Water, the games still served us well. However, I knew he would not tolerate another day of them.

"Have you ever wagered on a game?" I asked softly, not wanting to disturb his concentration.

"Certainly," he said absently.

"Would you care to wager on the outcome of this game?"

His gaze rose from the board to study me. "What kind of wager?"

"The food is delicious, but I think, if I should win, I want you to prepare my breakfast. By hand. Yourself."

"And if I win?"

I quirked a grin.

"Then I will prepare your food for you in the morning."

He chuckled and nodded, but I could sense his disinterest in the bet. I smothered my smile. It wasn't about winning or losing, but distracting him for another day.

I WOKE EARLY AND LOUDLY.

"I'm so hungry," I called as I sat up in bed.

From the adjoining room, I heard a thump and knew I'd woken him. Light was just starting to filter into my room. We'd stayed up late to finish the game, which I'd won.

Of one thing I was absolutely certain. The beast couldn't cook.

Smiling, I dressed in a plain gown—I'd been favoring the trousers and shirt since our hike to the river—and washed my mouth and face before walking out into the empty hallway.

Following the sounds of clanking and muffled curses, I found him in the kitchen. The fire roared, warming the room a bit much, so I opened the door to the outside before moving out of the way.

From the chair near the table, I watched him bumble around. He dropped eggs on the floor and seared one side of the bacon black. He lost a potato in the fire and singed his fur trying to get it back out.

When he set a plate before me, we both blinked at the mess that smeared its surface.

"It looks delicious," I said after a moment.

"I don't know how to cook," he admitted with a defeated note.

Finally, honesty from him. I grinned.

"Neither do I. Well, maybe a tad more than you, but not much. I think I saw a book in the chef's room that could help us."

We spent the whole day in the kitchen, making some wonderful mistakes. He even laughed once when he sampled my attempt at a pastry. That laugh marked the first time I'd ever seen him without a hint of his usual anger and frustration. A rush of pride filled me at my accomplishment. There was something more to the beast, after all.

As I grew tired and yawned, he determinedly kept reading and cooking until he caught me with my head on the table.

"Perhaps, that's enough for today," he said, walking toward me.

I stood with agreement and looked at the disaster we'd made of the kitchen.

"Do we need to clean this?"

"No."

Relieved, I kissed him affectionately on the cheek and turned to leave the kitchen.

He stared after me as I walked away, but he made no move to follow. The dull greys and purples of dusk painted the sky. Perhaps he would see the enchantress tonight.

CHAPTER FIVE

When I met him in the hallway the next morning, he wore pants and stood upright. I made no comment, but greeted him with a smile and my usual question about our plans for the day. His only remark was that we should eat first.

As he led me to the kitchen, I marveled at his full height. I'd seen it before but never for so long. He typically dropped back to all fours after several steps. He suddenly seemed more man than beast.

He motioned me toward the table where I saw two plates set. Scrambled eggs and bacon rested on each. A simple meal...but not. He'd cooked.

The eggs were a little moist, and the blackened edges of the bacon strips contrasted with the limp middle. Instead of seeing the improvements still needed, I saw the progress he'd made.

"This looks marvelous," I said, and I meant it.

He held the chair for me as I sat, which surprised me, and joined me at the table. The chair groaned under his weight, but it held.

The eggs were cold and a bit on the salty side, but I ate them all. I couldn't have done better. Though I preferred crisp bacon, I managed to eat most of that as well. Leaning back, I thanked him for the effort.

"I wanted to thank you," he said. "For your help. Five days..." He shook his head and sighed. "It didn't work," he admitted.

I reached across the table and touched his hand.

"I'm so sorry. We'll keep trying." I hesitated a moment, then asked a hard question.

"Can you tell me what went wrong? It would help to know what we might need to change."

He laughed self-deprecatingly.

"Your amusements and distractions worked too well. I went to her door; but when she opened it expectantly, I could only apologize and bid her good night."

"Nothing?" I asked, stunned.

"Nothing that could inspire me to cross her threshold."

I chewed my lip for a while. How to keep his arousal without the anger and tension? The question was beyond my expertise. I needed to talk to the sisters but didn't think it wise to leave him dejected again. It took too long to walk there and back. A ride from Henick would be nice, but I couldn't count on that coincidence.

"Do you own a horse?" I asked with idle hope.

"There is a horse, yes," he said, obviously curious why I'd asked.

"I would like to visit the Water before we try again, but I don't want to leave you alone so long, and I doubt I would find a wagon on the road again."

He scowled at the reminder of Henick and agreed that a horse would help me journey faster. He left the table to stalk outside, and I dashed to the servant's quarters to fetch my bag. The primrose I'd picked lay pressed between waxed pages of a small book I'd found. I hadn't forgotten Bryn's request and hoped to stop in Konrall at the candle maker before journeying to the Water.

Slinging the bag across my body, I stepped outside. The beast stood before a quivering horse, speaking to it in a soft growl.

When he saw me, he stepped away and offered me a hand. We never afforded our own mounts, but I recalled riding a horse in my youth and peered at this one curiously.

"No reins?" I questioned the beast while clasping his hand.

"Speak to him, and he will do as you say," the beast assured me.

I placed my right foot in the beast's free hand and sprung upward, swinging my left leg forward over the horse's neck and almost kicking the beast in the head.

"I apologize," I said quickly to both of them as I wrapped my fingers around the mane to keep myself upright.

Beside me, the beast rested a hand on my leg, his fingers heavy and twitching.

"Where are your underclothes?" he asked in a nearly unintelligible growl.

"I haven't the faintest idea. You haven't put them back in the wardrobe since I arrived. If you're willing to provide them again, I'm eager to wear them. I do feel a bit awkward without them at times."

The horse nickered and dipped its head. The beast reacted immediately, cuffing the creature upside its long head. It sidestepped from the blow.

"Sir," I cried. "What are you doing? Perhaps, I shouldn't go."

"I apologize. It would be best if you both leave for a short while." The beast spoke with slow effort.

He grabbed the horse's face in his large paw and brought its nose to his own.

"Protect her with your life."

The beast held the horse's gaze until it bobbed its head.

"Does he have a name?" I asked cautiously, still unsure of the beast's mood.

The beast released the horse and stared at it for a moment.

"If he does, I long ago forgot it."

"No matter," I assured him, patting the horse's neck to get its attention. "For this journey, I shall call you Swiftly. Please take me to the gate, Swiftly."

The horse pivoted and started down the path. Turning, I looked back at the beast.

"I will return shortly. If you feel angry, perhaps you would consider making pastries," I said with a smile. We had yet to master those.

The beast nodded and continued to watch us as I turned forward again. Despite my promise to return shortly, I wondered if he continued to have concern that I might not return. I hoped that he had gained a measure of trust in me by now. Still, I didn't want to take any longer than necessary.

Swiftly's current pace, however, would be a problem. He walked softly and slowly, as if not wanting to jostle me. An additional brief stop in Konrall wouldn't be wise if he couldn't move faster.

"Am I too heavy?" I asked, unsure if an enchanted horse could bear as much of a burden as a normal horse.

Swiftly shook his head.

"Perhaps we could try a trot, then?" I suggested.

He immediately picked up the pace, and I had to clench my thighs around him to keep upright. He skittered nervously at the touch but kept moving.

Once we reached the gate, I asked him to head south instead of west. He balked a bit but eventually did.

Seeing Konrall again brought forth a tiny bit of homesickness. The lewd attentions of the baker and the bullying focus of Tennen and Splane had faded from my mind, and I recalled the better times when I went to school with Father, and Bryn and Blye talked to me about boys.

"See the candle maker's sign?" I asked softly. One of Swiftly's ears twitched back, and I knew he heard me. "That's where I need to stop. Then we ride to Water-On-The-Bridge."

Swiftly stopped before the candle maker's home and knelt so I could dismount with ease. And probably so I wouldn't expose myself. I patted his neck.

"A true gentleman," I whispered.

He dipped his head, and I smiled.

"Do you need water?"

He shook his head, so I left him to go inside.

"Benella! Good to see you. Come in, sit," the candle maker said, greeting me as if I were an old friend. He rocked to a stand, his wispy hair fluttering with his efforts.

"Good morning," I returned politely. "I've brought you more primrose." Withdrawing the small book from my bag, I carefully removed the drying flowers and set them on his table.

"Perfect," he breathed, lifting one delicate flat bloom to his nose. "You've preserved their scent."

He shuffled to his shelves and searched until he produced a blunt silver and a few copper, which he brought to me.

"This is all I have for now. The merchant promised a higher sale for more of them, so I'll pay you more after he sells them."

"It's not necessary," I said. If he gave all his coin to me, how would he live until the merchant returned?

"Nonsense," he said, taking my hand and curling my fingers around the coins.

He gave me a narrow stare until I nodded. I dared not say more.

I thanked him, and we spent a few moments trading idle pleasantries. He asked after Father and any news from the Water. Awkwardly, I mentioned a few events I recalled Father mentioning during my last visit, but I left the details vague and hoped the candle maker wouldn't notice.

Though the nearby villages knew of the estate and avoided it, I wanted no one to know of my stay there. Too many coveted the riches they imagined the estate held, and greed motivated the kindest person to acts they might normally not commit.

Saying a hasty farewell and promising to return should I find more primroses, I escaped his innocent questioning.

Outside, Swiftly nickered when he saw me and knelt again to let me mount. Amused, I carefully swung my leg over his back and held on to his mane as he stood again.

"Benella," a familiar voice called from nearby.

I tensed on Swiftly, and the horse's left ear pivoted back in my direction as he swung his head toward the speaker. His flank quivered under me, and I ran a hand on his neck to soothe him as I watched the baker step off his porch to approach us. Despite the baker's extra girth, he carried himself with strength and speed.

"Good morning," I said with forced politeness.

"It's so good to see you, Benella," he said reaching out to pat my leg.

Swiftly sidestepped me out of reach and snorted at the baker. The baker dropped his hand, but not his eyes, which swept over me.

"You look well. You've gained some needed weight." He smiled slyly as his gaze lingered on my breasts. Swiftly's haunches quivered in earnest, and he backed up a step. The baker returned his gaze to mine and some of his humor faded.

"It's good to know you're being cared for," he said. His tone indicated otherwise, and I remained silent.

"I hope to visit the Water in two days and wanted to discuss some business with your father. Can you tell him to expect me for dinner?"

My stomach turned at the thought of what they might discuss. Thankfully, I wouldn't be there.

"Of course. Good day."

Swiftly took the cue and turned away from the baker.

"I will see you soon," the baker called in farewell.

"Not likely," I said as Swiftly picked up the pace, trotting north.

When we passed the smith's, Tennen stepped from the shadow of his father's forge with a rock in his hand.

"Run, Swiftly," I whispered urgently, leaning over the creature's back.

He didn't hesitate, but jumped into a full gallop. Clinging to his mane, I twisted to see Tennen pull back his arm. However, the sudden thunder of Swiftly's hooves had brought the butcher to his door; and he yelled for Tennen to stop. Caught, Tennen dropped the rock with a scowl.

Swiftly raced north and only slowed when we again neared the estate. I patted his neck and thanked him for his effort and protection. He bobbed his head in response, and we walked the rest of the way to the Water. Having a horse cut the travel time in half.

Worried that Swiftly would tell the beast of my activities, I brought him to the livery and gave a boy a copper to watch him for the short time I planned to stay. Swiftly nickered at me as if calling me back, but he remained with the boy, and I walked to the Whispering Sisters unobserved.

Ila met me at the door as usual.

"Benella, you look well."

"As do you," I said, accepting her hug while trying not to act self-conscious about where I placed my hands on her bare back.

"You have purpose in your eyes," she said when she pulled away. "What brings you here?"

"I seek advice," I said. "The kind only you and Aryana are likely to give."

She nodded sagely and led me to the bathing chambers. Aryana stood when I entered, but I waved her back to the water.

"Please sit. I would enjoy a bath," I said, thinking of the baker's stare and the ride to get there, "but I promised my employer my jaunt would be brief."

Aryana eased back into the water while Ila and I relaxed on a cushion. My skirts seemed so out of place, but they didn't appear to mind.

"What do you need of us?" Aryana asked.

"I need to know how to attract and hold a man's attention in a way to inspire arousal without the tension or aggression."

Aryana studied me quietly, her mouth turned down ever so slightly.

"Are you sure?" she whispered with concern.

"I'm sure of nothing," I replied with a slight smile. "But I'd like your advice regardless."

She considered me for another moment before speaking.

"Arousal is easy. A bit of flirting and an accidental glimpse of your breast or elsewhere would achieve that state. To prolong that state without tension is a bit difficult. You need to find a way to keep it light. Entertaining. A game, in which you both willingly play."

A game. He did well with games. Perhaps something with betting. I chewed my lip as I thought about the options. The biggest concern was keeping his arousal in check so the enchantress was the target and not myself. The image of the wood nymph rose to mind. This new game would be dangerous.

"Thank you," I said and stood. "I will see you again soon, I'm sure." I was embarking into unexplored territory, after all, and would undoubtedly have more questions.

"A moment," Aryana whispered, stopping me. "Benella, have you ever flirted?"

I couldn't see her eyes clearly, but I saw the amusement in her smile.

"No," I admitted. "But I've watched others. I'm sure I can manage a few unintelligent, insipid remarks."

Ila burst out in a deep laugh while Aryana snorted. I smiled sheepishly.

"I'm sorry. That wasn't polite." Turning around, I marched back to the cushion and flopped back down.

"I didn't mean it exactly the way it sounded. I do not think all those who flirt are unintelligent. Typically, when flirting, it seems a requirement that neither party behaves normally. The girl usually giggles and acts in a way I would consider below her typical intelligence, and the boy acts brasher than usual."

Aryana's teeth flashed at me, white and slightly crooked.

"You have it right, but you're speaking of youths. You're of an age now that you need to consider men. Brashness leaves, and intense cleverness remains. Be yourself. Do not hide your innocence, yet let this man know you are no simple maid to be manipulated."

I nodded slowly.

"The truth is easier than deception," I said in agreement.

"Deception is sometimes needed when truth fails," Aryana said sadly before clearing her expression. "Will you see your father?"

Recalling the baker's message, I gave a reluctant nod.

"Go see Bryn. We will tell him you're here for a visit and send him to you."

Ila accompanied me to the door and wished me luck. I would need luck and patience to deal with the beast while I played this game.

When I reached Father's home, Bryn surprised me by yanking

the door open before I reached it. She wore a dazzling smile. Taking my hand, she pulled me inside and revealed with barely concealed excitement that she would be engaged in just a few short days.

"The baker's son?" I asked, happy for her.

She nodded and hugged me tight.

"Then I have the perfect gift for you." I pulled back and dug the blunt silver from my bag.

Her eyes watered as she took the coin with heartfelt thanks.

"His father will host a dinner for us, just a few of the more prominent merchants. I have Father's newest shirt laundered for the occasion. Blye helped sew me a new dress so I'll look like I belong, but I worry about Father. Perhaps, I can use some of this for a new coat."

My smile congealed, not that she noticed.

"It shouldn't matter how one looks, but how one behaves. Father is an educated, well-spoken man."

"Of course," she agreed, tucking the coin into the pocket of her skirt. "It would be wiser to tuck this away in case there is a future need."

"I thought you wanted it for food," I said, trying to keep the exasperation from my voice.

"A week ago, I did. But I'll be married soon and will have plenty of food," she reminded me with a satisfied smile.

Biting my tongue, I said nothing about Father's need for food as I listened to her plans for the future and her dreams of socializing with the other merchant's wives. Father's arrival saved me from the complete history of each family invited to the dinner.

"Benella, I was beginning to worry," he said, hugging me. "Are you well?"

"Yes. But I do have some disturbing news. I saw the baker earlier, and he said he had business to discuss with you and to expect him for dinner in two days." We sat at the table together and Bryn moved to her room, not interested in our conversation. "His manner led me to believe he wanted to discuss me again, but I didn't mention I would not be here."

"I'll tell him you're employed elsewhere if I must, but I hope he won't be so direct." He looked down at his hands. "Does the beast treat you well?"

"Yes." I wanted to say more, like that I didn't need to clean or that I could eat until I burst, but knew Father would then wonder what I did there. So I settled for a plea.

"Please don't worry about me."

"I would be a poor Father if I did not," he said.

SWIFTLY WHINNIED with relief when I fetched him from the livery. He knelt so I could mount, then rose gracefully once I clutched his mane securely. Without needing guidance, he left the livery and picked his way through the market, turning us in the correct direction.

The sun had not yet crested the sky when we neared the estate. Swiftly's ears flicked with increasing frequency as we approached the final bend in the road, where he just stopped moving. I scanned the trees and hoped it wasn't Tennen who Swiftly sensed.

From the trees stepped an old woman. She wore a worn, patched gown and shuffled forward with her focus on the path. She leaned heavily on her staff for each small, mincing step and appeared not to notice us as she changed her course to follow the road toward us.

Watching her painfully slow progress, I knew I had to offer assistance. I slid from Swiftly and patted him when his flank quivered. His reaction seemed odd given how old and fragile the woman appeared. As an enchanted horse, I knew he possessed higher reasoning and wondered what about the woman worried him. Perhaps, because of his enchanted state, he didn't like strangers.

"Hello," I called.

The woman stopped her forward shuffle to look up at me. She looked vaguely familiar.

"Are you going to Water-On-The-Bridge?" I asked.

Her watery blue eyes stared at me, but she made no reply.

"It's a long way on foot," I said slowly, wondering if her hearing might be the problem. "Do you need assistance?"

Her sudden cackling laughter made me jump and Swiftly scream in terror. He bolted down the road, veering toward the trees opposite the estate to avoid her. Tendrils of fear wove through my veins and pooled in my stomach.

"We don't have much time," the old woman said.

I recognized her voice when she spoke but couldn't place it.

"Have we met?"

"Twice, but never officially," she said and started forward. This time her steps were not mincing; she strode toward me with an easy gait that did not match her apparent age.

"I'm Rose. Let us talk." She had a wild look in her eyes as she reached for me.

When her hand gripped my shoulder, the road disappeared; and we stood in the familiar room of her cottage. Having been in it once before, even befuddled, I would not forget it. My gaze wanted to wander the peculiar objects hanging from her walls, but I forced it to remain on her as she moved to sit in one of the room's matching chairs. She motioned for me to sit as well. The thick furs that draped the wooden frames provided a comfortable amount of cushion.

"You think to free him?" she asked bluntly.

I knew she meant the beast.

"I only seek to help him."

"If you want to help him, leave him as he is. He is better for it."

"Better?" I found that hard to believe. He was volatile as the beast, chafing at the loss of his true self.

"Without a doubt. Did he tell you everything?"

I eyed her for a moment and decided to speak as bluntly as she had.

"Hardly. He told me that you cast a spell on him, one he could win free of if he gives you one night of pleasure. I've determined a few other pieces on my own."

"Oh?" she said with a contemptuously raised brow.

"He was once human and, I believe, the Liege Lord. And he wasn't the only one affected by the spell you cast. I believe some of the other creatures here were once human as well."

"So wise," she said. "Have you determined why I cast my spell?"

I shook my head and remained silent, sensing her building anger.

"He was a man focused only on his baser needs. He drank when thirsty, slept when tired, and fucked when aroused, which was often. He ignored his responsibilities as Liege Lord completely. This area was overrun with thieves of all sorts and impoverished by his assumed entitlements. He turned a blind eye to the problems of the people who looked to him for protection and guidance. He even went so far as to appoint a Head that organized the thieves instead of ousting them. Had I not stepped in and cut the head from the snake, it would have consumed the north. For the safety of the people, he cannot return to power."

Her explanation was certainly compelling, but her requirement of him to win back his freedom bothered me.

"If you opposed his fornication, why require it for him to win back his freedom?" I asked.

"Why not? It should be easy for him, a man who would put his stick in anything. And, what a fine stick he has. Why not use it on me? He tried valiantly in the beginning, plowing into me until I was raw with it. I lay there willingly, yet, I wonder how many he took who were not so willing."

I felt ill, but Rose just laughed again, a low menacing sound.

Outside the cottage, the beast's roar filled the air. She snickered.

"He has learned a few tricks over the years and may eventually prove not entirely useless," she said. "Listen closely. I've trained him. When I first cast him to his true form, a beast, he would barge in here whenever his cock stood straight, thinking he would finally be free of me. Now..." she trailed off and glanced at the door with a small smile.

After a moment of silence, a fist banged on the door hard enough to rattle the hinges. I glanced at Rose. Her smile widened, and she winked at me.

"Enter."

The door eased open when I would have expected a crash.

"Rose," the beast growled, ducking through the door. "Why have you taken her?"

"I thought she and I should have a proper chat," she said, standing. "She had a few misconceptions of you, and I wanted to set them straight. Have you checked on Egrit, today? She can almost walk normally again."

My eyes widened as I realized she spoke of the wood nymph. Had he approached her again in my absence?

"Come," he said, holding out a hand to me.

My gaze lingered on his clawed paw then drifted to his face. He wasn't asking. He was commanding.

"Remember what I told you," Rose said as I touched my hand to his.

CHAPTER
SIX

THE BEAST LED ME FROM THE COTTAGE, KEEPING A FIRM HOLD ON MY hand until we reached the manor. My mind spun with so many observations and questions that I didn't notice the distance or time that passed. I'd already guessed the beast was once the Liege Lord, and the candle maker had told a brief bit of his history. A history I hadn't fully believed. Could I be certain I knew it now? Stories often differed depending on the view of the speaker. I wouldn't call the beast kind, exactly, but I did think he had the capacity for fair judgment. After all, he'd remained consistent with his punishment for trespassing...until me. He never truly harmed children. A bruise on the butt, at most, when they landed after being tossed. I'd witnessed worse in parental discipline. And as for women, I wanted to say he was kind to them too, but the wood nymph hadn't received kind treatment.

Rose's statement about the beast forcing his attention twisted my stomach, though; and I tried to distance myself from the problem so I could see it clearly. Facts. Observations. I needed to focus on those.

The beast had been a poor, perhaps horrible, liege lord. Therefore, the enchantress had improved the lives of the villagers dependent on the estate by casting her spell upon him. The candle maker confirmed both points, though he hadn't mentioned Rose.

I frowned, having noticed we walked the hallway to the library. Inside, the beast had another game ready for us.

"I need to think," I said, too confused to sit with him. Then I fled.

In my room, I paced. Rose's chief complaint had been his rule, but too much of our discussion had been on his lust. She claimed to be here to protect the people, but what of the baker and his manipulations? What of Tennen and Splane's unfair treatment of me?

If I'd been an enchantress angry at a liege lord for the poor care of his people, I would have made him suffer the same fates they'd been forced to endure. Fear of violence, rape, hunger...I imagined that over fifty years ago the villagers had experienced all of that with thieves populating these woods. Yet, she had put the beast in the estate, had given him power to protect and heal himself, an endless supply of food, and a tempting wood nymph upon which he could force himself. The only actual punishments, from my viewpoint, were the change in his form and having to fornicate with Rose.

None of it made sense, and it seemed to me that Rose played her own game. She not only punished him with a change in form but many others along with him. I felt certain the crow, wood nymphs, tree, and Swiftly had all been humans. What were their crimes?

I stopped my pacing and stared vacantly out the window.

The tree had asked me to teach the beast. When I'd reflected on what the beast might need to learn, I'd thought kindness, patience, and civility. Perhaps there was more. I cringed at that, though. Three virtues were hard enough to teach. Yet, in one thing,

Rose was right: the man who had come before the beast could return to Liege Lord.

Perhaps the tree wanted me to teach him to be a better person. I sighed, unsure how I could help with that when Rose still promoted all of the qualities that made him a poor lord. She complained that he had assumed entitlements. How did giving him such vast magical control over the estate teach him humility?

Frustrated with the beast, Rose, and the tree, I wanted to reach up and yank at my own hair. Why couldn't people just say what they meant? The whole thing felt like a deception.

Aryana's words sprang to mind. Deception is sometimes needed when truth fails. What truth failed fifty years ago?

"Benella?" the beast spoke quietly from behind me, bringing me back to the present. Light no longer shone through the window. The night sky sparkled with stars.

"I know exactly where I am, but have never felt so lost," I said, turning to look at him.

"What did she tell you?" he asked.

He stood just within my door, still dressed in trousers and standing on two legs. The mist pooled around his feet, ready to cover him if he needed it, but I saw his worried expression clearly.

How could a beast, a true beast, show such concern? Such uncertainty? It settled my mind. I would play a game of my own, a dangerous one that might earn the retribution of an angry enchantress, the wrath of a volatile beast, and the scorn of my family. No matter the ending, I would be the one to suffer. But my suffering could free a beast, who might not deserve it, and his servants, who most likely did deserve it.

"She told me what she thought would stop me from helping you," I said honestly. "But it doesn't matter. I will still try to help you."

He exhaled slowly, showing his relief. His reaction helped reassure me that I was making the right choice.

"We will keep going as we have, and eventually, if you hold to your word not to expend your energies on anyone other than Rose, you will be able to do what you must."

Now, I just needed to keep his hope of freedom alive while preventing him from breaking the curse until he learned how to be a better person in order to rule properly. The impossibility of the task was not lost on me.

THE BEAST WAITED outside my door the next morning.

"Let's work in the kitchen again today," I said and led the way without waiting for his answer.

He followed me quietly while I considered my plan.

I'd already shown him the pride that came from working with one's own hands, thanks to the bet about making breakfast. I planned to continue on that theme. Yet, I knew he would tire of cooking unless there was some type of reward to inspire him. Rewards always seemed to help promote the desired behavior. After all, Father kept his class quiet with the promise of earlier dismissal, and Bryn had taught the goat to hold still for milking by giving her carrots. I felt certain I could do something similar with the beast. Yet, I needed to have care about what I offered as a reward. I considered my options carefully and decided, sometimes, praise was enough of a reward. I would start with that.

In the kitchen, we used the chef's books to make an elaborate breakfast, which we didn't eat until closer to lunch. Covered in flour, a splattering of eggs, and some other unknown smears, I sat at the table with a sigh. The beast had willingly assisted the entire time and didn't look any cleaner.

"I will never again take for granted Bryn's skill in the kitchen," I said, eyeing the table.

The food before us looked questionable. The book had listed several different versions of an egg tartlet. According to the chef's writing, the egg would cause the mixture to raise high above the crust. Ours clung to the bottom of a very dark, stiff crust.

"I thought all women learned to cook," he said, poking at the egg.

"Perhaps most do. I wanted to learn my letters and numbers instead," I said. "I found there were many more interesting puzzles I could solve that way. Finding solutions is like winning a game, and it gives me an immense satisfaction. If I can't read, then I'd rather be outside, not in the kitchen, or worse, sewing."

Bravely, I tried to cut into the tartlet. I sawed back and forth to force the blade through the egg. Having won a slice free, I offered it politely to the beast.

"What were your favorite pastimes?" I asked, keeping the question to the past so I could watch his eyes as he thought about his past self. Did he like that man? Could he see any of his own faults?

"It's been so long, I don't recall," he replied just before he tried a bite. He grimaced as he chewed, but I didn't pay much attention to that.

I had noted the lie in his eyes. He did recall his pastimes but did not want to admit them to me. Did he find shame in them? I hoped so.

"Then you should try to discover them. Or find new ones. How is it?" I asked after he chewed for several moments.

"Horrible," he said bluntly, setting down the slice.

I laughed, stole his slice so I wouldn't need to saw through the tartlet again, and took a small bite. It tasted fine, but the texture ruined it.

"This isn't bad for a first try. I think we overbaked it or had the flame too high. Let's try again."

We made three more tartlets as the day progressed. The final one passed with both our approvals, though it was far from the fine dishes the beast could magic.

After finishing the last bite, I stood with a sigh. "We better start washing if we want to see our beds yet tonight."

"Wash?" he asked, staring at me in partial dread.

"The pots, pans, spoons, and every surface in here. I think we spattered eggs on the ceiling." I pointed up at a spatter I'd watch fly from the beast's mixing bowl during our first attempt.

"No," he said firmly.

"I understand."

While cooking, his cooperation had been easily gained by asking for his help and praising his efforts. Earning his cooperation for cleaning would require more than a request for assistance and a word of thanks.

I bent and started unlacing my boots. My feet hurt from standing stationary for most of the day, and I wanted to walk barefoot on the cool stone floor. But mostly, I knew how it would look to the beast.

"If you don't want to help, you won't upset me; but I do ask that you leave so you're not in my way." I pulled off one boot then the other. "If you stay, I'll put you to work."

I stood with a stretch and felt his eyes on me as I went to fetch some water. He watched me put it on the fire to warm. Knowing I had his attention, I stood before the flames for a moment and lifted my underskirt to wipe my face, exposing a leg all the way to mid-thigh.

Behind me, the beast's chair scraped against stone as he pushed away from the table. I dropped my skirt back into place. He hadn't moved fast enough to see anything; but without a doubt, he knew he'd missed some sort of view.

"Are you helping?" I asked, turning to arch a brow at him innocently. "If not, you're in my way."

"I will help for a while," he said reluctantly, glancing at my skirts.

I suppressed my triumphant grin.

We cleaned for a long while. When he did something especially helpful, I thanked him and did something innocently to reveal a bit of skin. In my mind, it was nothing he hadn't already viewed when I'd spent the day naked in his presence. But the glimpses seemed to have an even greater effect.

A glimpse of my bare calf when I stood on a chair while trying to wipe the ceiling had him watching me inconspicuously afterward. He always watched me, but his attempt to watch me without being obvious called his regard to even more attention.

When I moved the hot water from the fire, I used my outer skirt to protect my hand and left only my underskirt to cover me. He stood washing the butcher block, and I knew the fire glowed through my skirts and outlined my legs.

"We never addressed the issue of my underclothes," I said, turning toward him innocently. "Do I get them back?" I walked the water to the washtub and waited for his answer.

"They will be there when you need them," he answered hoarsely.

I thanked him and kept working.

For the remainder of the night, I focused on not displaying anything else.

THE UNDERCLOTHES DID NOT REAPPEAR the next morning, and I smiled as I picked out a dress to wear. Another plain one, though the wardrobe kept its usual variety.

Not wanting him to grow bored with any one task, I decreed we would try to discover some of his old pastimes. I knew what a few of those were and honestly did not want him to think about them once again, so I took him to the last place we would find them.

Connected to the library, a door led to the Lord's study. We breached the dusty room on the pretext of looking for clues.

On the desk sat an open ledger. I glanced at it casually when I walked a circle around the small room. Many of the books that lined the shelves were past ledgers or family accounts of daily life. A feminine swirl covered the open pages of the most current ledger. The last number noted had been underscored with force. Thirty-seven gold. An astounding amount to me, but for a vast estate it seemed a bit sparse.

"How many servants used to live here?" I asked, coming back to the study door, leaving the room undisturbed.

"Twenty, at any given time," he said, his eyes following me.

I caught a glimpse of something in their depths, but it disappeared quickly. It made me feel vulnerable, as if he knew my game.

I nodded, acknowledging his answer, but said nothing.

"Have you ever danced, Benella?"

"Yes," I said, wondering why he asked.

"I want to show you something." He reached for my hand and wrapped his fingers around my own.

Frowning at our joined hands, I followed where he led, to a large cavernous room with a polished wood floor. The curtains were pulled back and the windows thrown open. A pair of songbirds perched on the sill of one window and picked up a soft melody, and I added birds to the list of creatures who may have once been human. With a quick sinking dread, I thought of all the traps I'd set near the estate and hoped I'd never accidentally eaten someone.

The beast spun me about and caught me tight to his chest. I tilted my head back to look up at him as he swept me into a twirling dance that swirled my skirts around my legs. My feet skimmed the floor as he guided me through unfamiliar moves. The quick turns he executed made my head spin, and I laughed, which spurred him to twirl me faster. One of his hands rested on my lower back, its heat penetrating my dress until I could barely focus on the dance. I found the sensation...odd. Not disturbing, just different.

During moments like these, I liked the beast most. He seemed playful and earnest and willing to please.

The birds ended their song, and the beast guided me to a halt but did not release me. I looked at him expectantly, still smiling.

"I recall thinking dancing tedious," he said slowly. "A social requirement. I believe I may have misunderstood it. It has so much more potential." A small grin tugged his lips. "Especially when I know my partner isn't wearing her underclothes."

My brows shot up before I could stop myself.

Using the hand not anchored to the small of my back, he reached up and began to untangle my braid, reminding me he was no tame beast.

"What are you doing?"

"It's been a month," he said with a slight purr in his voice. "I can touch you now."

My heart froze and panic claimed me.

"Breathe, Benella," the beast said softly.

"Stop." The word came out strangled, but I found the strength to push against him.

His iron grip tightened for a moment before he withdrew his hands. My release eased my fears a little.

"You will not use me like you did—" I took a calming breath. "If you abuse me, I will leave," I vowed. "And no threat will incite me to return."

The beast scowled at me.

"You have the ability to ruin a perfectly good day," he said.

"How did I ruin it? I wasn't the one contemplating forcing myself on another." I glared back at him.

He growled at me then looked out the window, clearly frustrated but keeping his distance.

"You have Rose if you recall," I said. "Save your attentions for her. I'm only your inspiration."

"You haven't been very inspiring," he replied, referring to his last attempt.

"If I'm too inspiring, people get hurt."

He had the grace to flinch, showing he truly regretted his actions. He needed better control. How could I teach him self-denial, though?

"What is something you find completely uninspiring?" I asked.

He scowled at me and remained silent. I understood his meaning.

"If you can find something that uninspires you, something you can use to calm yourself and prove to me that it works, I will make an effort to be more inspiring."

I left him in the sunlit room.

He absented himself from my presence the remainder of the day and the two days following. I kept myself busy in the library, reading a book I'd found about fishing and the various baits to try depending on the weather and time of day. Occasionally, I would feel as if someone watched me; but when I looked up, no one would be there.

Trays would appear beside me at random times. Looking at the dishes, I knew he had made several of them himself, and I fought not to grin triumphantly. Cooking did not indicate reform, but it did show progress.

ON THE THIRD MORNING, I discovered the garden fully weeded and walked back inside, confused. After that, I began an exploration of the manor and found several things changed. Poorly washed linens hung in the laundry, there was a large supply of firewood in the kitchen, and it smelled as if someone had scrubbed the floor in the main entry.

"Sir?" I called loudly.

The mist rolled along the floor almost immediately.

"What?" The clipped word and his volume spoke his irritation.

"I'm curious what you've been doing these last few days."

He snorted.

"Trying to find something uninspiring."

"Any luck?" I kept any trace of humor from my voice.

"What do you think?"

I ignored his sarcasm.

"Have you tried reviewing the ledgers of past Lords to determine what in that year made the estate profitable and what lost the estate money? I wouldn't start with anything recent. Perhaps two generations back? Look for a pattern and try to determine what you would have done differently."

He didn't reply. Instead, he stalked off, taking his mist with him.

I endured another uneventful day.

THE BEAST WOKE me by barging into my room. He wore trousers and a mostly unbuttoned shirt.

"I'm ready to try again today," he said.

I sat up slowly, letting the covers fall away. The gossamer gown left little to the imagination.

"The ledgers proved uninspiring?" I asked as I lifted the covers off my legs and slid from the bed.

The mist quickly gathered around him.

"Yes."

I went to the wardrobe and picked out another plain gown.

"I'm ready to try again," he repeated as if I'd not heard him.

Smiling over my shoulder, I nodded then turned my attention back to the gowns.

"You may be, but I require proof before prancing about you naked again. Please excuse me while I change," I said calmly. "And no mist today," I added when he moved to leave.

He growled and slammed the door, leaving me to dress.

A few minutes later, I emerged. He paced in the hallway, the mist completely absent.

I smiled in greeting.

"I thought we could play a game in the library."

Not waiting for him, I moved down the hallway toward the library. His heavy footfalls sounded behind me after a moment.

When he saw me move toward the game board, he gave a slight growling groan of frustration.

"I tire of that game."

Sitting on a padded chair, I looked up at him.

"But I do not. Please, sit," I said, my tone more command than invitation.

His lip curled, but he sat. Several minutes into the game, I could sense his impatience boiling and decided it time to distract him. I'd selected the gown with care that morning. Most of the simple, appropriate gowns had two layers in the bodice, a finely woven soft underlay and a coarser overlay. The underlay, typically white, prevented the neckline from gaping if tied properly. I had tied it loosely.

Placing my elbow on the edge of the table, I leaned forward to rest my chin on my hand. After a moment, the beast ceased moving. I waited a heartbeat longer, then moved my piece with a satisfied smile before straightening.

When I looked up, his eyes studied the board intently.

In seven moves, the play had shifted to the far side of the board. I wanted to laugh at his wit. He could have ended the game but played his pieces for another purpose. I gave him what I knew he hoped for and stood slightly, bending at the waist to make my next move. He made a small noise, and I quickly looked up, a true frown on my face.

He met my gaze.

"Sir?" I questioned softly.

"Go eat," he said.

I looked beyond him and saw a tray on the table.

"We will continue afterwards," he said.

Only once I stood and moved away from him did I realize his growl had been missing. When I looked back at him, he was gone. Through the doors to his study, I caught a glimpse of him as he sat at his desk.

I grinned.

THE BED DIPPED, waking me enough that I rolled over. The beast's hand smoothed my hair from my face.

"Sleep," he whispered.

Instead of sinking back to sleep, his voice roused me further.

He sounded sad.

"Restless dreams?"

"Yes." He pulled me close to his side with a sigh.

I snuggled in, resting my head on his shoulder, and my hand on his chest. I gently patted him as I fell back to sleep.

I DEBATED over what to wear the next day and decided for normal. I'd tempted him enough with a bit of skin the day before. Today, I would try to tempt him through words.

Twisting my braid, I pinned it up in a knot at the back of my head then opened my door with a smile. The beast waited for me just outside, dressed again in trousers.

"No games today," I promised.

His mouth turned down in a slightly disgruntled expression, and I quickly turned away to hide my smile.

In the kitchen, I set about making breakfast and asked him to help in little ways: starting the fire, fetching a bowl, stirring the eggs. He did it all without complaint. When we sat to eat, I gave him a large portion and thanked him for his help. He said nothing in return. We ate in silence for several moments while I contemplated flirting and the sisters' advice. I struggled to find something to say.

"You're unusually quiet," he said, studying me closely.

"As are you."

He looked back at his food.

Aryana's recommendation to be myself made me want to wrinkle my nose. I decided on an honest compliment.

I reached over and lightly touched his arm.

"I think I'm starting to like living here," I said quickly and sincerely. "Without your growl...well, I like spending time with you."

His gaze bored into mine as if trying to find some hidden meaning.

"Do you?" he asked softly, but his tone hinted at anger.

I tilted my head with a frown.

"Was it wrong of me to tell you so?"

"Why are you telling me?"

My lips twitched at his suspiciousness, but my amusement quickly faded when a rumble started in his chest. I slowly withdrew my touch from his arm.

"How can I expect honesty from you if I cannot give it myself?" I asked, confused at his reaction. Instead of holding his gaze, I looked down and took another bite.

He continued his soft growl as I chewed and swallowed.

"Have you thought of any of your prior pastimes, yet?" I asked, trying to change the subject.

"In fact, I have," he said with a purr.

Before I realized his intent, he pulled me to my feet and sat me in his lap. I didn't react other than to glance at him. For some reason, telling him I liked it here had annoyed him. I didn't understand why but understood that his volatile mood couldn't be trusted. I reached for a misshapen biscuit and pinched off a bite, calmly eating it as if I were sitting in my own chair.

The pastime he'd recalled currently bruised my backside. I wondered what exactly I'd done to cause it. Whatever the issue, I did not intend to remain to see where his current mood led.

I pinched off a larger portion and met his hungry gaze.

"Open your mouth," I said softly.

Surprise lit in his eyes a moment before he did so.

Instead of putting the large bite in his mouth, I shoved in the remainder of the biscuit. He grunted then loosened his hold to cough into his hand. I quickly slid from his lap and stood by my chair, watching him warily as he continued to cough and sputter.

"Are you trying to kill me?"

"Hardly. But I am trying to reason out why I angered you."

He stood with menacing slowness, and I grabbed my plate of cold eggs and threw the contents at him.

"Would you stop throwing your food at me?" he roared.

The frustration in his tone eased some of my fear, and I laughed at my own audacity. His eyes narrowed. I squealed and scrambled for the outer door, barely closing it behind me. Something heavy thudded into it. I sniggered.

"I can still hear you," he bellowed.

He was truly angry, yet something possessed me to laugh again. It was an open challenge, and I took off at a sprint, barefoot through the weeds. Behind me, the door crashed open. I laughed louder and ran faster. A path around to the front of the house opened before me. Behind me, I heard it close and the beast's angry bellow as he tore through it.

"I recall a pastime from *my* childhood," I called, slowing. "I was fairly good at it. Let us see if I still am."

He roared in response, obviously still angry.

Moving forward, I burst into the front yard and onto the gravel drive. The stones bit into the soles of my feet, but I didn't slow. On the other side, the male wood nymph waved to me. I smiled and ran his direction. He pointed the way to another open path.

"Thank you. Warn the others to stay out of his way and to keep the path open, please." He nodded as I ran past.

I ran until I found a large tree right on the path, which I quickly climbed. Seconds later, the beast ran under the limbs, and I grinned at the egg that still clung to his fur.

I jumped from the tree and ran back the way I'd come. The nymph was nowhere in sight. I ran up the steps to the manor, eased open the door, and slipped inside. I didn't slow as I sprinted up the steps to my room or when I opened the doors to his room. I closed everything behind me before diving under his bed.

Long minutes passed. His roar from outside rattled the pane, and I began to doubt the wisdom of my impromptu game. There hadn't been any wisdom. I'd done something completely outrageous to distract him from his arousal. And where did that leave me? Under his bed. Just as I thought to creep out and find a safer place, the door to my room slammed open. I heard fabric ripping and furniture crashing. I trembled, regretting my spontaneity.

The door to his room flew open, and I held my breath. I heard him move around the room. I didn't try to look and follow his progress. I held completely still.

Suddenly, his hands closed around my ankles, and he yanked me from under the bed. I stared up in shock at the beast's face, which hovered just inches from my own.

"Found you," he purred.

"That's because you cheated," I said in a rush, unsure of his mood. "You didn't count the proper amount of time."

We stayed still, gazing at each other. So many emotions flitted through his gaze that I couldn't even begin to speculate their meaning.

"Go," he said suddenly, pushing away from me. "Leave me in peace."

Without hesitation, I quickly scurried to my own room. As soon as the doors closed, a thundering crash came from his side.

I'd thought to flirt with him but had only done so with honest praise. I stared at the doors wondering what had gone wrong.

CHAPTER
SEVEN

After two days of quiet avoidance—on his part, not mine—I finally found him in the kitchen, waiting near a set table. I approached cautiously and stopped a good distance away.

"Sit," he commanded. "Eat."

"No, thank you," I said softly.

He grunted in frustration but did not growl.

"Why not?"

"I seem to upset you no matter what I do or say. Then you upset me, and suddenly you're wearing more of my food."

He snorted and studied me for a moment.

"A bribe then? What price do you ask to sit and eat with me?"

"A full meal without any food decorating your fur?"

He nodded with a slight smile curving his lips.

"Answers," I said.

"To what questions?"

"I'm not yet sure. All I ask is your calm honesty. Instead of stating something isn't my concern, tell me why you do not want to answer the question."

I moved toward the table, knowing he would do as I asked.

"Why did my statement about liking it here upset you?"

"I thought it a lie."

"You no longer do?"

"No."

"Why not?"

He sighed gustily and pushed back his plate.

"Because...of so many reasons."

I took a bite and waited. He didn't disappoint.

"You don't hold back what you're thinking. And, you are willingly risking my anger to speak truthfully. Though I've given you enough cause to leave, you haven't yet done so. You do not act resentfully toward me, nor do you make outrageous or selfish demands when given the opportunity. What else can I think, but that you really do like it here, with me," he said softly.

I smiled widely at him.

"Well, there aren't many places I can go about my day naked," I teased. "Perhaps that is the draw."

He gave a half laugh and started eating. I dared to hope we were actually becoming friends. I reached for a covered plate to see what else he'd made.

"Wait, it's—"

Too late, I touched the hot dome and burned two fingers. I hissed in pain. The beast moved quickly to my side, kneeling by my chair.

"Let me see." Not waiting for me to move, he reached for my hand.

The tips of my fingers pulsed red. He brought them to his mouth, his tongue flicking out to swipe at the pads. My heart gave an odd flutter as my chest tightened. He licked the pads again, taking with him more of the sting. Heat crawled up my neck, and a strange warmth started in my middle. I frowned at him.

"Thank you," I said pulling my hand free. "They feel much better."

His gaze held me, and he slowly nodded, an unknown emotion lighting his eyes.

What did he see when he looked at me?

AFTER DRESSING in a plain dress for the day, I led the beast on a walk to visit the old tree that had spoken to me twice.

"What was your life like here before Rose enchanted everything?" I asked, sitting on the bank of the pond.

"I honestly don't recall the details. I drank fine wines and liquors, entertained many guests, played games. Why do you ask?"

"What of your family?" I removed my slippers then pulled up my skirts before stepping into the water. It chilled my skin.

"My father died long before Rose enchanted me. My mother...she left not long before Rose came." He cleared his throat. "Mother was ill and went south looking for help. She died years ago."

"You're alone."

"I was," he said.

My stomach grew warm at his sentiment.

"How deep is this water?" I asked, changing the subject.

"Not at all. Why?"

I grinned at him, waded a few feet out, then kicked water, hitting him fully in his face. He sputtered indignantly for a moment before chasing me into the water in a cascading splash that thoroughly soaked me.

Scooping more water to splash at him, I waged war. His splashes far surpassed mine for the next several minutes.

"I yield," I called, finally.

His matted, wet fur clung to him, and I shivered under my waterlogged dress.

"Would you kindly have a hot bath waiting for me in my room?" I asked with a stutter.

"Of course," he said, leading me to the front door. A trail of water marked our progress as we made our way to our rooms. He left me at my door with a bow and went to his own suite.

A large tub waited for me, steam rising from the water. I gladly peeled off the dress and sank into its depth with a sigh. Not a moment later, the door behind me clicked open then closed again.

"Do you mean to watch me bathe?" I asked, resisting the urge to turn around.

"I do," he answered softly.

I felt a twinge of pity for him. He meant to face Rose again. I nodded and submerged myself, rewetting my hair.

Bravely, I shifted to my knees, counting on his restraint. My top half cooled in the air as I reached for the soap. Closing my eyes, I lathered my hair, arms over my head. A soft noise on the carpet gave away his move to see more.

Blaming my trembling on the cool air, I rinsed my hair then started soaping the parts of me still out of water. Curiously, my nipples hardened when my palms passed over them. A tingle shot from my breast to my pelvis. I repeated the motion, analyzing my reaction. I'd washed myself before. Why was this time different?

A blush of pleasure warmed my face, and I rinsed the soap away, aware of my audience. When I opened my eyes, he did not stand before me.

Behind me, the door once again clicked open and closed.

"Good luck," I whispered in the empty room before finishing my bath.

I FELT him lay on the bed beside me at some point during the night. I rolled toward him and laid a hand on his chest, feeling the fur.

"What happened?" I murmured in sleepy disappointment.

"When I closed my eyes I pictured you but..." He sighed. "It wasn't enough."

Reaching up, I stroked my fingers along his shoulder.

"We will try again," I promised before giving into sleep once more.

I RODE to the Water just as the sun crested the horizon. Two gold coins rested in my pocket, a gift from the beast. This time I didn't bother with the stables, but rode straight to the Sisters' house. The guard at the back door nodded to me when I dismounted and tied Swiftly to the tree.

"Not a word of this," I whispered to the creature.

Swiftly nickered softly, his eyes on the house. In the shadows behind the guard, I saw a very naked Ila waiting for me.

"If you're good, I'll invite her to take you for a ride. She doesn't wear any underthings either," I said with a light laugh. He made an odd non-horse noise and shook his head as I walked away.

"We've been waiting for you to return," Ila whispered as she wrapped her arms around me in a warm embrace.

"I should have come sooner, but my master demands so much of my time."

"Things are well?"

"Yes. But I do have a purpose for my visit."

"Come, let us bathe."

I nodded and followed her down the steps.

Aryana did not wait in the tubs as usual, but Ila didn't seem surprised by it.

"I'd grown so used to Aryana down here that it's odd without her," I said as we walked through to the back room.

"She is still sleeping," Ila said.

As she helped me rinse, I broached one of the subjects on my mind.

"My master gifted me with some coin, and I had hoped to purchase some of the oil you used in my hair. I like the smell of it."

"Of course," she said as she poured water over me to rinse the soap away. "I make it myself."

"It's lovely."

Ila laughed lightly.

"I will make a new scent just for you."

I thanked her as we dried.

"I have another question," I said after a few moments of quiet. "You've explained pent energies. I'm wondering if a woman could have pent energies, too."

I'd watched their demonstration with Gen, and after my interaction with the beast, I deduced sight and touch of a woman and her body contributes to a man's energies. But would the same work for a woman? The beast had alluded that it was possible. But, if so, did the beast have the knowledge to try and build the enchantress's energies? I thought that might be the crux of the problem in achieving a full night of pleasure. The beast was certainly able to find his pleasure but could he find hers?

Ila smiled at me.

"Yes, we can. Though, we don't become angry like men do when it occurs."

"How do a woman's energies become pent?" I wanted to help the beast, but part of me was plain curious after his remark.

Ila made a slight coughing sound.

"Perhaps we can discuss this when you came back for the oil? I should have it ready by midday. It should give you time to visit your sister."

Reluctantly, I agreed and went to visit with Bryn.

Bryn excitedly spoke of all the people she'd met now that she'd engaged herself to the baker's son. She gushed about how the baker himself treated her as a daughter and often took her on a tour of the bakery to explain the business further.

I tried to ask about the babe, but it seemed to upset her otherwise bubbly mood so I quickly asked about the wedding again. She spoke of her wedding feast guest list and Blye's growing success as a dressmaker.

"She wanted me to ask if you could find her some more embellishments for hats or if you might have more of that thread," she finally finished.

"I'll see what I can do," I promised, standing to leave.

I walked Swiftly back to the Sisters. Ila again met me at the door and handed me a vial the size of my palm.

"You don't need to use much. Apply it when your hair is wet, and comb it through."

I grinned at her and gave her the two gold coins.

"This is too much," she said with a rough gasp.

"An advance for the next order. Please give anything that remains to my father." She seemed mollified by that.

"Do you have a moment to speak?" I asked, hoping she still might explain how a woman's energies become pent. Her appearance at the door, and the fact that they now had customers made it unlikely.

Ila glanced to her right, and Aryana stepped into view.

"We need to leave some mystery for you to discover on your own," Ila said. "If we reveal all of the secrets of seduction, it takes the magic from the moment."

"Seduction?" I tested the word, trying to recall a meaning.

"Not something generally discussed in polite company. The art of persuasion in which the end result is…" Ila looked to Aryana.

"I believe fornication would be the best word choice with our Benella."

Neither would say any more. With nothing further to discuss, I left.

When I returned to the manor, in my frustration, I slammed the door to the kitchen.

"This is unusual," the beast said as he entered the room. "What vexes you so?"

"Have you ever heard of the Whispering Sisters?" I asked.

"Yes, but why have *you* heard of them?"

"It is where my father teaches. And, I've made a few friends there. At least, I thought they were friends." I sat heavily on a chair. "They've been an invaluable source for information. There are things they know that have helped me understand—"

"You've been receiving advice from whores?"

His sudden upset surprised me.

"There is no need to yell. How else am I to learn about these things? Men are complex creatures on their own. Throw an enchantment on one, and he is impossible."

He took a slow, deep breath, and I waited for him to calm.

"Why are you upset with them?" he asked.

"As I mentioned, they've been open with their advice. Until today."

"What did you ask today?"

"How do a woman's energies become pent? I understand

fucking, as you put it, but don't understand where the appeal is for the woman."

He made a choked noise and immediately left the room.

"That's about the reaction they had," I yelled after him. "I don't think it fair that everyone is keeping this knowledge to themselves."

Really, how was I supposed to help him when I didn't know?

CHAPTER EIGHT

I stared into the darkness long after I blew out my candle.

"Benella," the beast whispered nearby, startling me. "Would you like to understand how a woman's energies become pent?"

"Yes," I said with frustration. I didn't see how he could accurately enlighten me, though, given his lack of success with Rose.

"It will take time," he said. "Several days perhaps. And I cannot tell you, I must show you."

Ah. So perhaps his lack of success with Rose wasn't due to his understanding but his technique. Showing would be beneficial.

"And I will need to touch you. With no restrictions."

I didn't like the sound of that.

"No fornication," I warned.

"No, Benella," he said with a softly amused calm.

"You have my permission, then," I said, very curious as to what exactly he would do. "But only on the condition that you will stop whenever I tell you."

He lay next to me and pulled me close like he'd done so many times before.

"Agreed. Now, sleep," he whispered, the furred tips of his

fingers stroking the skin of my arm. It felt so good, my eyes soon drifted closed.

During the night, I woke to his touch on my bare stomach. It remained feather light, but insistent. It traced a pattern skimming the bottom side of my right breast before dipping and barely brushing the curls between my legs.

I frowned, worried. His erection pressed into my backside.

"Relax," he whispered, moving his touch back to my arm where it caused less concern. Again, he lulled me to sleep.

In the morning, I woke next to him, my gown gone. His hands roamed over my stomach and arms. A burst of heat ignited in my stomach when his fingers brushed over a breast, just missing the nipple.

"Good morning," he said.

"Good morning," I returned, uncomfortable and ready to ask him to stop. But he stood without me asking.

His eyes ran the length of me, and my heart stuttered.

"I'll leave you to dress," he said.

With a slight grin on his lips, he walked to his room and closed the connecting doors.

I lay there for a moment, stunned. He'd touched me and walked away. His control relieved me. Yet, if that was an example of how he attempted to build Rose's energies, no wonder it didn't work.

Dressed in trousers and a shirt, I met him in the hallway.

"Interesting choice of clothes. What do you have in mind today?"

"I thought we might fish again."

"Lead on," he said willingly.

Remembering my comment from the last time we left the safety of the walls, he offered to toss me over the wall, which I quickly accepted. My stomach churned in delight as I sailed through the air. I landed with a light bounce in the vine net. Once it released me, the beast landed softly by my side.

At the river, I rolled up my pant legs, dangled my feet in the water, and sat back to think. The beast's skills were lacking and the Sisters wouldn't help me. I didn't have many other options to try to help him. Bryn would ask too many questions if I approached her, and I wasn't sure if Blye had the experience.

"You're very quiet," he said from beside me.

"I'm trying to determine our next course," I replied distractedly.

Did I dare speak with Rose to find out where he was lacking? She'd spoken very frankly regarding his efforts before. But what if asking upset her? Would I then end up as a beast, too? Not a very pleasant prospect. Speaking to her would be my last, dire resort.

"What do you mean?"

"To help you last a full night with Rose. I'd thought perhaps if we could improve your skill at building a woman's pent energies, we might succeed the next time, but I'm not knowledgeable—"

"Improve my skill?" he sputtered indignantly.

"Well, last night, you didn't inspire—"

"It was not supposed to." His exasperation was obvious.

"Then what was the purpose?"

"Did you fear me touching you this morning?"

I shook my head. Even naked I hadn't been afraid, just uncertain.

"Did you feel anything just before I left?"

The way he watched me had me wondering if he knew.

"A bit of warmth in my middle, but nothing lingering after I dressed for the day."

He reached over, plucked the pole from my hands, and set it out of the way. Then, he gently pushed me back so I lay on the bank. I calmly let him have his way, until he slowly began unbuttoning my shirt.

"Sir?"

"Shh. I want to prove a point and mean you no harm."

I wrinkled my nose, which made him smile, but he didn't stop. With my bindings exposed, he traced his fingers over my stomach again.

"So the warmth was here?"

My heart gave an odd flip again as I nodded.

"What exactly caused it?"

I blushed scarlet and quickly sat up.

"I'd rather not discuss this. I think my approach was misguided. Even if I had the knowledge, I don't think I could impart it without...well, doing this." I waved a hand at my flushed face. "Have you ever considered visiting the Sisters? Perhaps they would be willing to—"

He barked out a laugh. "An intriguing idea. But you're here now and can tell me what exactly I did wrong." He tugged on my shirt, encouraging me to lie back down.

I cleared my throat and attempted to ignore my heated face.

"I wouldn't say there was a wrong action. Nothing disturbed me or frightened me. Neither did anything inspire me," I said, using his words.

"I see. Please consider giving me another chance," he said softly, his fingers once again trailing my stomach.

"Honestly, I don't see how that will help. You have had fifty years of trying," I said softly and without censure.

"But if you're willing to tell me the effects of what I am trying, I can adjust my technique. Improve perhaps?"

Something about the look in his eyes made me nervous.

"And you will stop when I say?"

"Of course," he assured me.

I hesitantly nodded my agreement, and his grin widened.

"Close your eyes," he commanded, then softly added, "please."

In the obscurity behind my eyelids, I waited for something, unsure what to expect. What he gave was the same touch on my stomach as before. A slow swirl of his fingers over my skin. A circle that slowly expanded, until it almost touched the underside of my breast.

It grew warmer outside.

On the next pass, his fingers teased the edge of my bindings. My nipple tingled, and I found it difficult to breathe normally. His fingers left my skin. When I heard him sit up, I blinked in confusion. He reappeared above me a moment later, holding the pole.

"You have a fish on the line," he said, handing it to me.

A fish? I took a calming breath. My skin tingled from his touch. As I pulled the line in, I saw my error. He had lulled me and was slowly building a tension within me. His declaration for a few days now made sense. He would take his time pulling me further and further into a world I did not yet understand until...fornication. Of course. The beast. I scowled.

I strung the fish onto the line of another shorter pole and stuck the pole into the bank so the fish trailed in the water. My hands drifted to the buttons. His hands reached around me, closing over mine.

"Not yet," his rough voice tickled my ear.

"I would like to stop now." I moved his hands away and buttoned quickly.

He bowed his head at me and said nothing, staying close.

I caught another fish, and ready to leave his quiet, watchful presence, I declared our time outdoors complete.

AFTER CROSSING the wall and walking through the fields and hills, we came to the border of trees on the east side of the manor. Just at their edge, I caught movement. I stopped walking and watched the nymphs, unwilling to disturb a playful moment.

"I'm glad he forgave her," I commented as the nymphs chased each other.

"Forgave her?" the beast asked quietly.

"The first day I read to you and you dallied with her, he refused to talk to her afterward."

The beast's brow furrowed as he watched them as well.

"She looks well," I added softly, studying him instead of the nymphs.

"Yes. Quite," he said and turned away.

When I looked at the nymphs, she was again on her knees in front of her companion, his wooden penis in her mouth. I wondered how exactly that worked for trees. Then I wondered if the baker would like the taste of her sap.

"Must you study them?" the beast said with impatience, already a distance from me.

I hurried to catch up with him.

A SOFT TOUCH on my thigh woke me in the night. My skin felt hot and sensitive, uncomfortable, and my heart thundered in my chest.

I sat up abruptly, again naked.

"Stop."

His hand fell away as I turned to look at him. He lay beside me, watching me closely. I had the absurd urge to roll toward him and wrap my arms around him.

"What are you doing?" I demanded.

"Touching you."

He looked calm, but even the pants he wore couldn't hide his massive erection. Unknowingly, I'd started a dangerous game with his control. If he could not control himself, I would be the one broken and bleeding like the nymph.

"When I suggested it might be your approach, I didn't understand. Now, I have a better idea what continuing with this means for me. And it frightens me. I do not want to end up like the wood nymph. I do not want to be used and forgotten. Though you might not treat me as a whore, you would treat me as a body with no head attached. Have you given thought to how the pursuit of your game will make me feel?" I spoke softly, hoping to reason with him without angering him.

He leaned in.

"I hurt you once. I will not hurt you again. I swear."

"I'm glad we agree. Please leave."

He snorted.

"I think not," he said.

He reached forward, his fingers skimming my thigh again, first the outside, then the inside. He was just inches from where they met in the middle, his touch causing a slow burn. I desperately wanted to pull him closer, and that yearning scared me.

I scooted from the bed, grabbed a pillow, and dashed across the room. He stood but too slow. I quickly slipped into his room and locked the door. Then just as quickly, I locked the door coming from the hall.

He tried both calmly at first. When he understood that I'd locked him out, he pounded on the adjoining doors.

Raiding his wardrobe, I covered myself with one of his shirts then sat on his bed.

The pounding turned to rage. He didn't yell at me, only growled and slashed at the other side of the wood panels.

The urge to appeal to him, to calm him, held me fiercely. I hated hearing him so upset. Yet, I knew if I opened those doors, he would try to continue with what he had started. So, I remained on the bed, holding my pillow to my chest as I watched for a hint of the rising sun while listening as he tried to tear his way through. The doors held all night, repairing themselves before he could completely breach them.

With the sun, his racket quieted. I sat on his mattress, tired and wondering what to do. After several minutes, I eased from the bed and tiptoed to the doors leading to my room. I leaned my ear to the panel but heard nothing. I tried the handle. It turned, and I cautiously opened the door.

The other side of the wood panel was a patchwork of deep and numerous gouges. It was clear that very little material had separated me from the beast. As I stared, tiny wood fibers moved to mend themselves. If not for the magic of this place, he would have easily ripped his way through the wood. His temper was a frightening thing.

My room was littered with broken furniture and shredded dresses. I felt completely relieved that I'd put on one of his shirts. Nothing in my room remained for me to wear.

My stomach rumbled. Risking running into him and his anger, I tiptoed to the door that led to the hall and eased it open.

He paced in the hallway on all fours, an angry black swirling mist at his feet. Any semblance of the man he'd been during the night was gone. His head whipped toward me.

Before I could move, the mist enveloped me. Sightless, I groped for the door. Instead of the door, I touched fur.

I turned and tried to run, but he caught me up into his arms and started walking with me. I didn't try to struggle.

"You're still angry," I said nervously.

"Very," he growled.

"What do you intend to do?"

"Feed you."

He set me down on the lounge in the library. The mists receded from me while he continued to remain hidden. A food-laden tray sat on the low table.

"Eat," he ordered.

I nibbled at some food as I watched the mist pace back and forth with him. He moved to the shelves, and the rasp of a book sliding from its place made me curious.

"Eat," he said again.

I quickly took another bite of a tartlet while trying to determine his mood. Obviously angry, but driven, too. He had a goal in mind, but what? Light burst from the fireplace as flames suddenly appeared. He growled, and I finished the tartlet in two more bites.

"Drink," he said in a slightly calmer voice.

The cold spring water had barely touched my tongue when a book landed on the cushion next to me.

"Read," he said softly. It was less of a command and more of a plea.

The sudden shift in his mood made me suspicious. He moved behind me and lightly tugged on my braid to undo my hasty work. My eyes drifted to the book. The Medicinal Properties of Flora in the North.

My interest piqued, I picked up the book and read as his fingers trailed through my hair.

I WOKE with his fingers roaming my body. The mist surrounded me so I couldn't see a thing. His touch was completely unobstructed by the shirt I had been wearing. Heat flooded me. I'd fallen asleep reading. Warm, full, tired, and lulled by his fingers running through my hair, I hadn't had a chance.

The pad of his finger roamed over one nipple, and I gasped at the tingling sensation that spread down between my legs.

Opening my mouth to protest, he surprised me by covering it.

"Quiet and listen," he said, still touching me, fueling a fire that burned me from the inside. "You demanded I consider how my *game* would make you feel."

His finger crossed over my nipple again followed closely by his tongue. The tingling sensations spreading between my legs consumed me. He laved the tender peak for a moment while I panted for breath.

"I have considered it. Have you? How does this make you feel?"

Stretching out my hands, I curled my fingers in his hair and pulled him back down to my breast. He obligingly sucked it again, the scrape of his fangs adding to the pleasure. The heat spread out slowly, causing an ache in the other breast.

Finally, I understood why Bryn had lain with Tennen. Bryn. Pregnant and rejected. The realization of how this could end for me cooled the heat within me.

I yanked back on his head and sat up.

He growled loudly and pressed me into the back of the lounge. His head dipped to the other breast, giving it the same burning attention. My thoughts jumbled together and instead of pushing his head away, I pulled it closer again.

His hands gripped my legs and started easing the right one over the side of the lounge. His mouth drifted from my breast, and his tongue tickled a trail to my stomach, which dipped and clenched wildly.

With his semi-desertion, a clear thought penetrated the fog in my mind. Sara. The baker. Her crying in shame after he had tasted her.

"Stop!" I cried loudly, startling us both.

He pulled back, but I couldn't see him.

"Did I hurt you?" he asked, obviously confused.

"You selfish, single minded beast," I cried, swinging an arm out and connecting with the side of his head.

He grunted in surprise.

I quickly scrambled off the lounge and out of his reach.

"You *know* what I meant about feelings." My voice echoed slightly in the room, and I immediately took a slow breath. "You are so focused on you, you would even use the people who are trying to help you. You see something you want and take it regardless of feelings or if it is being given freely. You coerce and bargain to get your way."

The beast growled deep and long.

"No," I said firmly, cutting off his growl. "You are the Liege Lord still, despite your appearance. Remember your responsibility. Remember who you are supposed to be. *That* is why you were enchanted, your complete disregard of your every responsibility and obligation in pursuit of your own satisfaction."

His growl grew, clicking with his anger.

"You know *nothing* of me or my intentions."

The mist cleared the room. The beast was gone.

I let out my pent breath, glad to have escaped. My skin still tingled, and I looked for the shirt. It was gone. Narrowing my eyes, I made my way to my own room. It was neatly restored. The bedding and curtains now a soft green. The white wardrobe stood open and empty. I moved to his room. His wardrobe was also empty.

Sitting on his bed once again, I debated my future.

The progress I'd thought we'd made had evaporated last night with his fit. I'd voiced my concern several times that my presence seemed to make him worse, not better. To be fair, my goal had changed from wanting to free him from his curse to helping him become a better person. The two seemed counterproductive. After all, in his way of thinking, I was in his home to help him please another woman for a full night.

He'd made it clear to me that he expected me to walk around in nothing or next to nothing from the beginning, and I realized he had brought me here to be an object of gratification. I'd bargained for a month of no touching—which had long since passed—thus relegating myself to an object of inspiration. Only I hadn't known that then. Now that I knew what he really wanted from me, could I still help him become a better man?

Groaning, I flopped back on the bed.

Obviously throwing things, yelling, and hitting him didn't work. After his last attempt, I'd thought I could use the hair oil to help him associate a smell with me. Then, he could use that scent when he was with Rose. But before using the hair oil, I'd wanted to be sure he knew the correct way to build her energies. Combined, I'd been so certain it would succeed.

I should have never questioned his knowledge. Questioning it had been like a challenge. He didn't like to be challenged. I groaned again and used a pillow in an attempt to smother myself. It didn't work.

I made this problem. I needed to unmake it and earn back some clothes.

AFTER MAKING a simple meal of cheese, bread, and grapes, which I'd found in the kitchen, I carried the tray to the library. The doors to his study stood open, drawing my attention.

"Sir?" I called softly holding the tray.

"Go away. You annoy me," he called back flatly. Papers rustled.

I annoyed him? I carried the tray toward the door.

"I wanted to apologize," I said, entering the study. I set the tray on his desk, covering some of the papers he studied. I folded my hands in front of me, waiting for his attention.

"Go away," he repeated, not looking up.

I sighed.

"I shouldn't have questioned your knowledge on a subject of which I'm so obviously ignorant. Not that I want an education," I quickly added.

He still didn't look up.

"I understand why you would take that as a challenge to prove me wrong."

"I was doing nothing of the sort," he said in an exasperated tone.

I studied him as he continued looking at, and switching, papers.

"Doesn't it hurt sitting on your tail?"

"Yes. Will you please leave?"

"Why won't you look at me?"

"Because I will see your natural beauty and will be tempted to continue licking every inch of your skin."

My skin tingled again at the reminder, and I shifted uncomfortably.

"If you don't want me naked, why take all my clothes?"

"I thought your issue with being without clothes was my gaze. If I keep it averted, why clothe you?" he asked reasonably.

"I might catch a chill."

The fire in his study blazed to life.

"I doubt that," he replied.

Stubborn beast. My annoyance over his unwillingness to concede outweighed my amusement at his quick wit.

"What are you looking at?" I asked, determined not to leave until I figured out what game we now played.

"Estate records. Someone once suggested I might find it calming. Go away."

I refrained from stomping my foot.

"What have you found in them?"

"Just as you said. Practices that made the estate profitable. According to records, we sold flowers to candle makers in the south. You wouldn't perchance have seen any during your wanderings?"

"Actually, I have." Still he did not look up.

"I sold them to the candle maker in Konrall."

"There's still a candle maker there?"

"Yes, and a butcher, a smith, a tinker, and a baker. You know nothing of the people closest to your estate?"

Finally, he looked up.

"You've lectured me enough for one day," he said, rising from his chair and walking toward me on two legs.

I stood my ground as his gaze roved over my breasts then went slowly down and back up again. He stood inches from me, his gaze now resting on my pink face.

"Did you learn anything else of interest in the papers?" I asked to distract him.

"Several things, but nothing I'd care to discuss at the moment."

He reached out a finger and trailed the underside of my breast. My skin prickled, and my breast began to ache. His finger drifted over my nipple in a painful yet agreeable way.

"Please stop," I whispered. "I would like one of your shirts."

His hungry expression softened.

"I did not mean to take," he said gently, his hand moving to my face. "You are so beautiful, not just here..." His finger brushed along my jaw, then he leaned in to kiss my forehead. "But here as well."

His lips were thin and hard because of the teeth immediately behind them. Yet, I'd never felt anything more comforting. In that moment, I knew I was losing myself to the beast just as Bryn had lost herself to Tennen. Would I end up rejected, just as she had?

"When you're free," I said quickly, "you will forget me. You can't take everything I am because I need to be me when you're gone."

He pulled back and looked into my eyes, his expression closed off. I waited, bearing his scrutiny, hoping he would understand.

"Thank you for the food, Benella."

I nodded and walked away, feeling his eyes on my backside.

Hopeful, I went to my room, but I still didn't find a shred of clothing. Stubborn man. My stomach rumbled. And he had my food.

CHAPTER NINE

THREE DAYS LATER, I STILL HAD NO CLOTHES; AND THE BEAST continued to avoid me. Instead, he chose to close himself in the study.

Impatient with the stalemate and beyond bored, I sought him out.

"I would like clothes to visit my father."

"Would you mind delaying your visit for a few days, dearest?" he said. "I need to write a few letters and would like you to deliver them for me."

I blinked at him as my heart gave an odd flip. I had expected his refusal but not his explanation or the endearment. His request sounded reasonable, and he'd asked so nicely. With a small sigh, I nodded.

"Could I still have some clothes?"

"When it is time to leave, most certainly," he said distractedly, his eyes devouring the words on the paper.

I struggled for patience.

"The boredom is making me irritable. I would like to walk outside."

"I hardly think walking outdoors naked with all of the servants about is a good idea."

"That's exactly why I need clothes."

"Dearest, I will never get those letters written if you keep distracting me with conversation," he said.

Instead of leaving, I flopped in the chair opposite his desk, sitting sideways with my knees hooked over one arm while leaning back against the other. Although remaining would slow his work and prevent my visit, I couldn't stand the boredom any longer.

"What are the letters about?"

"Estate business." His eyes flicked to me and quickly returned to the papers.

"The estate has business?" I asked with humor.

"It might. If I can finish these letters."

I tipped my head back over the arm of the chair and observed the room upside down.

"If I can't have clothes and occupy myself outside, what else am I to do, but bother you?"

A sudden heat wrapped around my right breast, igniting an increasingly familiar flame in my middle. The suction tugged at an invisible string that led directly between my legs.

Jerking my head up, I saw the beast. He released my nipple with a wet sound and a lick before lifting his head and meeting my wide gaze.

He didn't speak, and I couldn't. We stared at each other in silence for several minutes. Then, he did something completely unexpected.

He closed the distance between us, and pressed his warm lips firmly against mine. But for only a moment. It wasn't a kiss, as in a warm press of soft lips, but a press of skin and teeth. Still, the gesture pierced something inside me. My chest ached with the sweetness of it and the uncertainty in his eyes when he pulled away.

"I'm trying," he said, straightening from me. "But what you did proved too tempting to ignore." He walked back to the desk. "Please find something to do elsewhere."

I sat up as he sat down.

He gave a pained groan.

"Do that again," he begged.

Frowning in confusion, I started to move back into the same position before I realized what I'd done. I'd removed my legs from the arm separately, giving a brief glimpse of the last part of me he had yet to see.

Blood rushed to my face, and I stood stiffly.

"I think I'll go take a bath," I murmured, trying to leave the room with dignity.

"That is not helpful," he said.

My thundering heart didn't return to normal until I stood in the laundry. I started a fire, filled the large kettle, and waited. The door to the outer court called to me, but I had no desire to frolic naked with the nymphs. Then, inspiration struck. He had removed anything I could use as a cover from his room and my own. Even the curtains tended to disappear if I looked at them too long. But what about the linen closet?

Excited, I ran to the small room and grabbed a clean white sheet from the shelves. Quickly wrapping it around myself, I ran back into the laundry, hoping he wouldn't know until too late. I checked through the window for any enchanted creatures then eased the door open.

Sunlight rained down on me as soon as I stepped outside the manor. I breathed in the air, tasting the freshness of it. With a smile, I ran away from the house.

I had almost made it to the trees when the female nymph came running toward me. She shook her head and pointed back to the manor.

"Not you, too," I said, slowing down.

She looked at me sadly with her wooden eyes.

"I wanted to check on you long ago, but he doesn't often let me out of his sight. Are you feeling better? I'm sorry for what happened."

She shrugged her shoulder and looked back into the trees. Her male counterpart waited there.

"Are you two together again?" I wasn't sure how else to word it.

She grinned widely, understanding, and nodded vigorously.

"I'm happy for that."

"Benella!" The vibrations of the beast's roar rumbled the ground, tickling the bottoms of my feet.

The nymphs shooed me toward the manor again.

With a sigh, I slowly turned around and walked back. He had sounded angry, but his mood didn't worry me. My slow pace was so I might enjoy more time outside.

He waited in the laundry room doorway. I clutched the sheet to me and stopped several paces away.

"What were you thinking, going outdoors without clothes?" he asked in a calm tone, but I could hear the frustration and anger underneath.

"I had the sheet."

He crooked a finger at me. I wrinkled my nose and didn't budge.

"I'm tired of being inside. I only wanted to walk around a bit. I was covered." I swept my hand down to indicate the sheet draped around me. "At least the important bits were covered."

He left the shelter of the doorway to stalk close to me. He circled me, inspecting the wrapping then stopped directly behind me. His breath tickled my hair a moment before his lips skimmed the exposed skin of my shoulder.

"All of your bits are important," he said, moving aside my hair to kiss the back of my neck before continuing on to the opposite shoulder. "I would like them all covered when you go out."

When he finished with the shoulder, he moved to the side of my neck. With guilty pleasure, I tipped my head to the side to give him better access.

He growled and pulled me against his chest. His erection pressed against me.

"If you can stay inside and out of the study unless absolutely necessary, I will have the letters ready by morning," he said, planting a kiss along my jaw.

His fingers closed around my hand, and he led me back inside where steaming water filled the largest washtub.

"Please wait until I leave before getting into the water."

He pressed his lips to my shoulder once more then quickly left.

I tingled all over. Pent energies, indeed.

THOUGH I'D HOPED to go directly to the Water, the beast insisted I ride to Konrall first. I had two letters to deliver there. I couldn't find it in myself to be too upset by the stop, however. I wore clothes; a plain dress to look respectable and underthings. I grinned to myself.

Swiftly brought me to Konrall in record time and halted before the candle maker's door. He knelt so I could dismount with grace and watched as I knocked.

It took a moment, but eventually the door opened and a familiar smile greeted me.

"Good day, Benella. Regretfully, the merchant isn't due for a few more days."

I realized he thought I'd arrived looking for payment from the last flower delivery.

"I'm actually here to bring you a letter," I said, pulling out the beast's note. It had the candle maker's name on it and a wax seal. Nothing else.

"Oh, from your father?"

"I'm afraid I don't know. I'm sure reading it will enlighten you. I have another to deliver to the butcher for the Kinlyn family, so I'd best be on my way."

The candle maker nodded absently as he stared at the seal.

The butcher was just as curious about the letter for the Kinlyn's that I left in his care, but I didn't say anything more to him than I had to the candle maker.

When I exited the shop, Swiftly was not where I'd left him. Tennen had his mane and was watering him at the smithy. The baker stood beside Tennen.

"Convenient for a quiet conversation with you," the butcher said from just behind me.

I nodded and looked back at him with a smile.

"Yes, if I were dull enough to march over there to claim my horse."

"Do you want me to fetch him for you?" he asked.

"No need."

I called for Swiftly, keeping my voice calm and pleasant so as not to upset the creature. However, it didn't seem to matter.

Swiftly pulled his head out of the water so abruptly that he yanked his mane out of Tennen's grasp. The horse then pivoted on his back legs and thundered toward me. In an instant, he stopped and dropped to his knees. The practicality of not using reins became very evident.

The butcher chuckled behind me.

"A well trained mount."

Already on Swiftly's back, I agreed.

"Keeps me out of trouble."

Swiftly stood as the baker called my name. I smiled my farewell to the butcher then leaned over Swiftly.

"I don't trust the pair of them. Best not to let them too close."

Swiftly bobbed his head and snorted in a very horse-like fashion. He closed the distance between the baker and me at a trot then came to a quivering stop, his ears laid back as he listened.

"Good day, Mr. Medunge," I said politely before glancing at Tennen, who still stood in the shadows of the smithy.

"Thank you for watering my horse," I called to him with a sweet smile. Tennen glared at me.

The baker took a step toward Swiftly, reclaiming my attention as the horse sidestepped.

"Has your father mentioned my visit?" the baker asked.

"I've been away and am just now going to see my father," I said.

"Away. Yes, your father mentioned you are an employed woman now. Such a shame for someone of your beauty to have to work so hard." He clucked his tongue. "I spoke to your father of several other options should you want a better life than a maid, but I'll let him discuss them with you."

I nodded farewell and tapped my heel to Swiftly. We quickly left Konrall.

The first letter I delivered in the Water was to the Head. Again, the man didn't receive me, but his assistant took the letter and assured me it would find its way into the Head's hands later in the day.

The last two letters I delivered in one stop. One was simply addressed to the Whispering Sisters and the other to my father. Ila greeted me as usual with tea at the door, but her smile was hesitant.

"You've been gone so long I thought perhaps Aryana truly upset you."

I hugged Ila close because I was so happy to see a friend.

"Not at all. Well, maybe at first, but my master's demand on my time is what kept me away so long."

"Everything is well, then?" she asked.

"Yes. I have a letter for you from my master and one for my father."

"I will take you to your father first."

We walked a familiar hall, and she stopped before his door. When she opened it, Father looked surprised, but happy, to see me there.

"Excuse me, please," he said, speaking comfortably now to the sisters he taught. He came to me and hugged me tightly.

"Had you not visited today," he said, pulling back, "I would have walked to you."

"I apologize for the delay." I reached into my bag and handed Father the letter the beast had penned. "He asked me to wait an extra day so he could send a letter with me."

Father glanced at the seal then tucked the letter in his jacket.

"I shall save this for later," he said, patting the pocket that hid it. "Have you spoken to Bryn?"

"I came straight here. I will visit with her before I go."

He nodded and promised to meet me at the house for the midday meal.

Ila led me to the bathing rooms where Aryana waited. Since I would join Father soon, I declined a bath and sat on the cushion beside her tub.

"What brings you today?" Aryana asked.

"I have a letter addressed to the Whispering Sisters."

I took the letter from my bag and held it out for either of them to take. Ila made no move toward it, and Aryana smiled at her before holding out her hand.

Unlike the rest, she barely glanced at the seal before breaking it and reading the contents. A moment later she laughed, low, rough, and amused. She handed the note to me, surprising me.

STOP EDUCATING HER. She is a smart, clever woman and should be left to discover the world and its pleasures first hand.

I FROWNED AT THE LETTER, then looked up to meet Ila's amused gaze as she too read the words.

"So you've spoken to your master about what you've learned here?" Aryana questioned lightly.

"I've kept my word," I said. "I've only mentioned that I visit my friends here. What I've learned has stayed with me."

She grinned.

"I think that's his issue. Has he tried to seduce you?"

I blushed.

"And thanks to our education, it didn't work?"

I shook my head because it hadn't been what the sisters had taught me that had kept me the most safe. I felt a slight sadness again for Bryn and Sara.

"It wasn't what I learned here as much what I've learned out there." They both made small noises of understanding. "I should go speak with Bryn," I said with a sigh and stood.

"No questions for us today?" Aryana asked.

"It might be better if I didn't. I wouldn't want to cause you trouble."

Aryana snorted.

"He doesn't worry me. I worry more about you under his roof. Take care. We are here if you need us."

I nodded and left.

Swiftly followed me to my old home and waited outside while I went in. Bryn sat at the table, speaking excitedly to a woman I didn't know. When Bryn saw me, some of the light left her eyes. The woman turned to me with an expectant smile.

"Dana," Bryn said, "this is my other sister, Benella."

"Another sister?" Dana said. "My, I didn't know there were so many of you. I don't think she was in the dinner count. I'd best go and add another place," she said, standing and leaning over to kiss Bryn's cheek.

"It's not necessary," Bryn said, standing as well. "Benella often doesn't have time for us."

Her words, though spoken politely, irritated me. She hadn't even consulted me to see if I might attend.

"Is this for your wedding dinner?" I asked.

"Of course," Dana said with a laugh. "Three nights from now, your sister will be married to my cousin. It will be a feast the Water will not soon forget."

How could Bryn think I would miss her wedding feast?

"Then I shall be there," I said, returning Dana's smile. She seemed truly excited by the dinner and the marriage.

"I'll leave you to visit," she said as she moved to the door.

After she left, Bryn turned on me. I didn't wait for whatever grief she intended to air.

"Are you well? How is the baby?" I asked.

She sighed, her expression between anger and excitement.

"The babe is fine, making my middle thicker. I told Edmund I suspected I might be carrying. He turned a bit green but assured me he is excited by the prospect." She eyed my dress. "Edmund's father is well connected with the most successful merchants in the

Water. Dana assured me it will be a formal affair. Blye has been working nonstop on our dresses. She won't have time to make one for you, too. Not this late."

Was that her only concern? The way I would dress?

"I'm certain I will not embarrass you."

She looked at my dress in doubt, and I distracted her with another question.

"Were you able to fix Father's coat?"

Her face flushed, and she glanced down at the table. Guilt painted her face.

"Someone in town saw Father going to the Whispering Sisters and discovered he worked there. Can you believe he would purposely tarnish our reputations like that? We spoke about it, and he agreed it would be best if he did not attend the dinner or my wedding."

"You suggested he not attend?" I asked in disbelief.

"It would have been awkward. His association with *them...*" She shook her head.

I couldn't believe my ears. She didn't want her own father to attend because he taught whores, giving them an education they could use to change their profession. The only reason Father taught there was to provide for us, for her. And, what about the merchants attending her dinner who visited the Sisters for other reasons? They were still good enough for Bryn.

"Who is paying for this dinner?" I asked, feeling disgusted with her.

"Edmund's father knows our situation so he offered to pay a portion."

"And the rest?"

She didn't meet my eyes.

"Father assured me he had been saving for just such an event."

I thought of the two gold I'd given for the hair oil. No doubt the change had gone toward Bryn's feast, but that wouldn't have been enough. I swung my gaze to the almost barren bookshelves. My heart broke for my father.

"You could have helped," Bryn accused. "When you forage, you always find something worth trading. I asked you to come back with something to trade, and you always return with nothing. It's as if you think you no longer have a responsibility to your family."

No responsibility? I'd sacrificed myself to save Father's life and set them all free.

"Tell Father I couldn't stay, but that I will visit again soon," I spoke through clenched teeth as I moved to the door.

"I understand if you don't want to attend," she called as I left.

So I was an embarrassment to her, too? I wanted to scream and hit something.

Swiftly sensed my mood and laid his ears back as I mounted.

"Home, Swiftly," I said harshly.

CHAPTER
TEN

STILL SEETHING, I CRASHED THROUGH THE KITCHEN DOOR AND
searched for something to throw. Bryn had gone too far. How could
she so publicly disassociate herself from our father? The man
who'd given everything to care for us. He never asked for anything
in return. He'd known about Bryn's interest in Tennen, her money
hoarding, and he accepted it. Accepted *her*.

Stalking into the room, I found a platter of fruit on the table. I
hefted the tray, ready to throw it into the fireplace when it was
plucked from my hands.

"And what, dearest, has you so agitated? Surely the letters
didn't cause this," the beast said quietly beside me.

I spun to face him.

"My sister told my father that she doesn't want him at her
wedding feast. Can you believe her? After all he's given. He's good
enough to pay for her wedding feast but not to attend." I tossed my
hands high into the air in my frustration then sat heavily on a
chair. "I think she meant to exclude me, too, had it not been for her
betrothed's cousin. Bryn hinted that the way I dress would
embarrass her."

He set the platter to the side and studied me intently for a moment.

"What do you plan to do?" he finally asked.

"What do you mean?"

"Revenge. Will you tell Edmund about the baby?"

"Of course not. It would only cause more pain to the people I care about." I paused and frowned at the beast. "How do you know his name?"

He gave a small smile. "I like to be kept current on what your family is doing. I wouldn't want any surprises to take you from me."

His comment struck a chord in me. And, I realized I wouldn't want to be taken from him either. Especially if it meant living with Bryn again.

"I wish my sister would see what she's doing," I said with a sigh.

"Perhaps you should tell her what a selfish bitch she is."

I gave him a sharp look. I might have been mad at her, but I still loved her and didn't like anyone speaking ill of her.

He gave a deprecating laugh and shook his head.

"It's the truth. I well know selfish."

"She won't listen."

"You are very persuasive," he said.

I sighed again.

"The feast is in three days. I do want to attend, and I want to bring my father. I will need Swiftly again. Do you have a coat that might fit my father? I would return it."

The beast nodded slowly.

"I can provide what's needed for both you and your father. But I need your word that you will return before sunset."

"Of course," I agreed easily, glad that he didn't mention it would be an extra visit.

As a precaution, I went to bed fully dressed. Having clothes again was nice, and I hoped to keep them. However, when I woke I was once again naked. The beast lay curled next to me, sleeping peacefully.

Warm and comfortable, I stayed in bed a moment. His dreams never seemed troubled when he slept beside me, and I was glad my presence gave him some measure of comfort; he seemed to derive very little elsewhere.

I studied his sleep-relaxed face. Where others might see a wild brute, I saw a bored, clever creature who had forgotten what it meant to be a man—if he ever really knew. I wasn't blind to his faults, just as I wasn't blind to his regrets.

Quietly, I slid from the bed and moved to the wash water as I continued to consider the beast.

His past misconducts had brought him fifty years of questionable punishment. A punishment that didn't inspire reform but, rather, loneliness.

I ran the cloth over my face and wondered if that wasn't the real reason he'd brought me here. Yes, he wanted to break the curse; but, perhaps, he had wanted a companion more. I rinsed the cloth and wiped my arms and torso.

The drag of cloth over my breast distracted me from my thoughts and brought forward the memory of his mouth on me. My nipples tightened. Since he'd first set his mouth on them, they felt more...alive. Perhaps I was only more aware.

I rinsed the cloth again, and a furry chest pressed against my back as if my thoughts had conjured him. I froze. His fingers trailed down my arm, leaving goosebumps in their wake.

"Beauty," he whispered.

His lips pressed against the curve of my shoulder as he stole the cloth from my grasp and set it against my stomach. I couldn't move. The cloth skimmed over my skin, from ribs to navel, while his breath tickled my neck.

"Allow me to help," he said.

The cloth sank lower until it swept over my curls. My breath hitched. He stopped and swept up over my stomach again and further still, until it smoothed over my breast. I leaned back against him and forgot to breathe as he gently circled one then the other.

When the cloth left my chest and drifted lower, I reached back and set my hand to his cheek. He turned his head and kissed my palm. All the while, the cloth continued its downward glide. My skin heated, and a burning ignited in my middle when the cloth swiped over my curls once more. Without meaning to, I widened my stance and then almost groaned when he retreated without exploring further.

"Please," I whispered, trembling.

He growled low and worked his way down again. This time, he parted me and gently ran the cloth over me. Once. I gasped. Twice. I panted. Thrice. My legs shook. He removed the cloth and set it on the wash bowl.

My insides had liquefied. I *wanted*, but I didn't understand what. I *ached*, but couldn't name an exact spot.

His fingers trailed over the skin of my arms and stomach. He swept my hair aside and pressed his lips against my neck, nuzzling and licking. The attention caused tingles and shocks to course through me, ending between my legs.

He prowled around me, his arm supporting my back. His hungry gaze held mine for a moment, then he dipped his head and suckled my nipple, causing a sweet ache that made me groan. He growled in response and nudged me back a step...two. I bumped against the bed.

He lowered me to the mattress, grasped my hands, and held

them slightly out to my sides. His mouth roamed my chest, then lower. Too consumed by heat, I didn't protest.

His tongue touched my curls, and I gave a soft whimper. My hips lifted of their own accord. He teased me, never going lower to the spot that ached so badly for his touch. My muscles tensed from anticipation. I whined and shifted when he skimmed by me again. Heat crested and ebbed, rolling over me in confusing waves. Gasping, I struggled for air as the tension coiled tighter.

Then his lips, his touch, left me. Cool air confused me. I lifted my head. The room was empty. Letting my head fall, I stared at the ceiling as I realized how close I'd come to letting him taste me. Oddly, the thought didn't disturb me.

Slowly, my breathing and pulse returned to normal. Though I physically recovered, mentally I replayed the encounter until I frowned with annoyance and understanding. Pent energies. He'd woken something inside me with patience and persistence. Whatever it was, I wanted something only he understood. Well, others might understand; however, he was the only one likely to tell me about it.

I stood and moved to the wardrobe, surprised to see he'd given me a full selection once again. Though I eyed the plain dresses and even the shirts and pants, I did not move to wear them. The remembered feel of his lips stopped me.

Moving around dresses, I found one of the gossamer types he'd first made me wear and grinned. Taking the dress and a shirt, I prepared myself for an interesting day.

Awhile later, I stepped through the study door, carrying a tray.

When he glanced at me, he froze. The shirt reached the top of my thighs just barely covering the v of my legs. I'd buttoned the hole just above my breasts and left the rest loose, exposing flesh from the valley between my breasts and everything downward each time I moved. Yet, the gossamer dress underneath the shirt gave the illusion of decency.

"Did you eat?" I asked politely, setting the tray on his desk.

He shook his head slightly, not taking his gaze from my body. I felt like stretching, to bask in his attention, which I thought odd since I'd always had it.

"What are you wearing?" he finally managed.

"A compromise, I hope," I said with a smile. "You want to see me. I want to feel covered. This is a little bit of both, don't you agree?"

I held out my arms, which inadvertently lifted the hem of my shirt by two inches and parted the edges. I executed a slow turn for him. Before I knew what had happened, he had me up in his arms, and we raced through the halls back to my room.

"It is better to wear nothing," he growled, setting me on my bed and stripping me of the clothes. The fabric tore in his haste. He sank to his knees and looked up at me.

"I'm begging you, stay in your room today. You will want for nothing."

I nodded, disappointed. I'd hoped for more from him.

His hungry gaze swept over my face, then he closed his eyes. In that moment, I understood that he'd wanted more from me, too.

Blushing deeply, I inched my knees apart.

With his eyes still closed, he gave a groan and kissed my knee.

I inched my knees further apart. He opened his eyes. His gaze locked with mine. Then, he leaned forward and kissed the side of my knee. Further still saw a kiss a few inches up. Barely breathing, I leaned back on my elbows and boldly drew up my legs and placed my heels on the edge of the bed, giving him the view he'd wanted just a few days ago.

My cheeks burned with uncertainty and wanting.

"I will not take," he said. "Tell me what you want from me."

"Taste me. No more," I begged.

He obliged, leaning forward to run his tongue along the crease of my hip and thigh. I fought not to squirm.

I felt myself part and his breath on my center. His tongue touched inside, just skimming to the left of my opening, missing the spot that burned for his attention. He shifted his focus to the right side, giving it the same. My hands drifted to his head. Then, his tongue touched my center. My hips bucked as he skimmed it lightly, at first, then with more urgency. When his lips closed over it and he suckled, noises escaped me. Moans and whimpers.

Gasping, I arched my hips. He closed his hands around my thighs. The firm touch of his fingers aroused me further. He left my center to tease my opening, dipping in for a small taste before plunging the length of his tongue into me. He lapped and sucked for a moment, all the while the area he'd left cried for more attention.

He seemed to sense my need because he returned to it and suckled with greater intensity. The tension inside me coiled tighter and tighter. By reflex, my legs tried to stiffen and close. His firm grip kept them open, enabling his feast until the coiled tension inside me broke free with a scream. I convulsed, thrusting up into his flicking tongue as my legs locked in their stretched position. Waves of pleasure coursed through me, tightening and releasing my muscles in slow rolling waves.

His licking eased as I twitched under him. I lay limp on the bed, a new world suddenly exposed to me. He kissed my sensitive nub lightly then the inside of my thigh. While I was still too weak to speak, he rose and left me there in a puddle of awe.

After several long minutes, I regained enough control to stand up and wash myself again. Every nerve ending still tingled. I felt relaxed and at ease. Sara's cry of delight and look of shame afterward made sense. To feel that way with the baker between her legs had to be deeply disturbing. But the beast. I sighed in contentment before I caught myself.

Sitting heavily, I gave my circumstances careful deliberation. If the beast freed himself, he would undoubtedly forget me. That he would probably disregard me easily made me uncomfortably morose. I certainly wouldn't forget him. Yet, once he was free, I would need to move on with my life. After Bryn wed, I would need to start my own search for a suitable man. However, the thought of marrying some unknown man caused my heart to lurch, and I realized just how much I'd grown to care for the beast. What I'd told him about leaving me a piece of myself was more true now, than ever.

I wouldn't be the same if he took everything I had. I wouldn't be able to walk away.

But, if he did not free himself, would saving a piece of myself be an issue? If he remained a beast, I could stay with him as long as I wanted.

Frowning, I considered his attitude toward Rose and amended my thought. I could stay with him as long as I had my youth. After that, I could still find someone suitable to wed. But, the prospect of doing so didn't fill me with any sense of anticipation.

Pushing aside the dread, I focused on the immediate possibilities and made a decision. I would stay here with the beast; not because of a threat I no longer believed him capable of carrying out, but because I wanted to stay.

Not bothering to dress, I stood with a smile and went to seek him out. To my dismay, both doors were locked.

A horrible thought struck, and I flew to my window. Thrusting open the glass, I leaned out and called for Egrit. She came into view after several moments. Relief flooded me.

She looked up at me and shrugged as if asking why I called.

"I'm so sorry to yell like that. I was worried. The beast has locked me in my room, and I wanted to be sure you were safe."

The nymph smiled and nodded. She waved me back inside, and I quickly obeyed, realizing I hung out the window with my breasts completely exposed.

Blushing, I sat on the bed.

"Sir?" I called after a few moments. "It's cruel to lock me in my room without telling me what I did wrong. I thought...what we did..." I sighed, suddenly uncomfortable with the thought that I may have asked him to do something he hadn't wanted to do.

"I apologize if I insisted on something that wasn't appropriate."

A mist filtered into the room, blocking out all light.

"Is this really necessary? We are capable of talking, aren't we?"

Just as quickly as the mists came, they left. Next to me on the bed, lay a tray stocked with food, drink, books, and a letter.

Dearest,

You did nothing wrong nor is there any need to apologize. I'm asking you to stay in your room for your safety while I work in the study on estate business. If you have further suggestions for distraction, please speak them aloud. I will need them.

Please refrain from hanging out windows unclothed. It upsets me.

Forever your servant.

I finished reading with a small smile.

"The ledgers and records are a fount of knowledge as are the books in the library. These lands used to be productive beyond the growth and sales of flowers. I think that is why there are so many books on farming and such."

Picking up a book, I reclined on the bed and settled in to read.

HE LEFT me in my room for three days. The relaxed ease I felt after he had tasted me quickly disappeared until I paced my room in agitation.

"This afternoon is my sister's wedding feast," I called, looking out the window at the colorful dawn. I felt like throwing something again. Instead, I marched over to his door and kicked it.

"You said I could go. You promised to provide me with everything I needed."

When I turned around, the large tub from the laundry sat near the end of my bed. Curls of steam drifted up from the water. Marching over to it, I slid in with a hiss and quickly washed, using the hair oil from Ila.

A towel rested on the edge of the tub when I opened my eyes. Rising from the water, pink from the heat, I toweled my skin. My mood improved only slightly with the bath.

I walked to the wardrobe and opened it. Inside waited a single dress, exquisite in its simplicity. On the floor was a pair of matching slippers. No underclothes were present.

I lifted the gown over my head and let the delicate material drift down my arms and body. It fit perfectly, but I frowned at the scooped neckline and the puckered outline of my nipples through the fabric. Though the material was not see-through, it was so fine it hardly seemed appropriate. Yet, he had given me no other options.

The door to my room unlatched and creaked open. I quickly stepped into the slippers and drifted to the door.

The hallway stood empty. Disappointed, I made my way to the kitchen and opened the outer door. Just outside, Swiftly waited. Again, there was no sign of the beast. It was so unlike him to allow me to leave without saying farewell and asking for assurance that I would return. Yet, given our last encounter, I understood his reason for staying away and applauded his progress in self-denial and control.

Swiftly quickly knelt, his ears flicking forward and back in apparent agitation. I smoothed a hand along his neck and mounted, wondering at his mood. However, his huff as my bare bottom settled on his back with only the skirt separating us wasn't a mystery.

"Sorry," I whispered. The creature shook his head and set off.

I rode straight to the Sisters. I needed help with my hair and assurances about the dress. Even though they didn't wear clothes, I trusted they knew what was fashionable.

Ila met me at the door with a wide smile.

"You look stunning. For your sister's feast?"

I nodded as I drank down the tea.

"Come to my room, I will do your hair."

Sitting on Ila's dressing stool, I relaxed as she wove my hair into several beautiful, twisting braids.

"Everyone there will forget your sister is the focus of the evening," Ila said, tucking the last braid. I smiled at her compliment and hoped Bryn would have no issue with my appearance...or Father's.

"Is Father here?"

"He asked not to work today. You will find him at home."

Standing, I hugged her and thanked her for her help. Before I left, I looked back over my shoulder.

"Is it too daring?" I asked, letting the uncertainty I felt show. "The dress?"

"The dress is beautiful, as are you," she assured me.

I glanced down at my breasts. Though the material was not transparent, I could still see details, not in color, but in shape.

"I don't want to shame my father," I said softly.

She smiled sadly and walked me to the door. Just behind it rested a fine black cloak that complemented the silver of the dress. "Here. Take this for today, until you feel comfortable. You will see that your dress is not so unusual."

I thanked her with yet another hug and placed the cloak around my shoulders before walking to my father's home. He answered the door with a happy smile. Thankfully, Bryn and Blye were both absent.

"I've been waiting for you." He pulled me into a tight hug. "I've missed you."

"I'm sorry I left before we could speak," I said, referring to my last visit. He waved off my apology and motioned for me to sit. I kept my cloak on, but he didn't comment.

"How have things been for you?" I asked, noting his healthy weight and complexion.

"I enjoy teaching the sisters," he said openly. "They are kind and gentle."

"And Bryn and Blye?"

He sighed.

"They are well but have learned where I teach. Blye has moved into a small room above the seamstress's shop, and Bryn is staying with Dana, Edmund's cousin, until the wedding."

"What a relief," I said with an impish smile. "Finally, you can eat your own food and relax in your own home."

He nodded, but a sad smile crossed his face.

"If only he would release you to come back home."

His comment caused an odd pang because, even for my father, I didn't want to leave the beast. Over the course of our weeks together, he'd won my affection; and through his progress to becoming a better man, he'd won my respect.

"The baker mentioned his visit," I said, changing the subject and pushing thoughts of the beast from my mind. "He said he spoke to you about several options if I didn't want to be a maid anymore."

"He offered for your hand."

I made a face, and he nodded.

"I know your feelings about the man and told him I could not accept his offer. He insisted I speak with you of his wealth and the position he would guarantee you."

The image of Sara on the dough table rose in my mind, and I knew with certainty that he offered a position I would not like.

"His wealth makes no difference in my aversion of the man," I said.

Father agreed, and we chatted for several hours before he asked if I was happy.

"I am, and will be even more so if you accompany me to the feast."

"I don't think I have a choice." He stood and fetched a box and letter. He handed me the letter.

GUARD *your daughter carefully in my absence. She must return to me before sunset.*

IT BORE the same seal the beast had used before. I looked up as Father opened the box. Inside rested a dignified suit coat, crisp shirt and neck cloth, and new pants to match. I smiled at the beast's thoughtfulness.

"When did this arrive?" I asked.

"Three days ago."

I insisted Father go dress. While I waited, a rapid tap sounded at the door. Opening it, I was surprised to see Mr. Crow hopping around on the ground outside. A small white piece of parchment was tied to his leg. I bent to remove it, ignoring his squawking.

The heavy scrawl on the paper was almost illegible with ink spills and rips where the beast had written too forcefully.

*R*ETURN AT ONCE.

I TURNED THE PAPER OVER, but the other side remained blank.

"I don't understand," I whispered to Mr. Crow.

He tilted his head at me and hopped forward. His beak gently worried my dress.

"He agreed I could go. He sent my father clothes. He can't ask me to return before the ceremony. Assure him I will return before sunset. I will keep my word."

The crow cawed loudly then took flight.

Closing the door, I waited for my father to emerge.

"You look so dapper," I said when he did.

He grinned at me and gave a little bow. No one would find fault in his appearance; the jacket was fashionable and fit him well.

"Let's dine together," he said, offering his arm.

We strolled down the market street to a small pub that served respectable families. Father offered to take my cloak as he held out a chair for me. Not wanting to draw attention, I surrendered it and quickly sat. When he took the chair across from me, his eyes swept my dress.

"I understand his warning now," he said.

I blushed and remained quiet. Though worry shone lightly in his expression, I saw no real rebuke. Cautiously, I glanced at the other women in the room. None wore a dress woven as fine as mine, and I caught their envious stares. No one's regard held any censure.

After our meal, we made our way to the Head's home. In the backyard, many had gathered to see Bryn wed Edmund. Near the back of the gathering, Father helped me from my cloak and caught my nervous look.

"Head high, Bini. You are lovely."

With his approval, I walked by his side to our seats near the pretty flower arch where Bryn would say her vows. Murmurs quieted as we passed. I kept a polite smile on my mouth and held my father's arm tightly.

Once we sat, we only had to wait a few moments before a sweet soprano rang out in a merry song about joining and love. When it quieted, the crowd turned to see Bryn and her fiancé walking down the aisle toward the arch. The Head followed them.

The simple ceremony didn't last long, but the well wishes and speeches took until the evening meal. I held myself still through it all, even though I wanted to fidget and shift on my seat to bring the blood and life back into my buttocks.

Bryn glowed with happiness as she clung to Edmund's arm. He looked equally pleased.

Father and I rose and followed the new couple from the Head's yard to the public room where Dana hosted the feast. I stopped to hug Bryn, bringing her attention to Father and me for the first time. Her smile hardened at the sight of us, but she did not turn away.

"I'm so happy you came. You look lovely," she said to me.

Then, she looked at Father and complimented him on his handsome garb. I could see the calculation in her eyes and suppressed a sigh.

Father and I sat and watched many others pour through the doors. Bryn hadn't lied about the merchants who would attend.

Many saw me sitting close to the bride and groom and asked for an introduction. Their unwelcome attention just served to irritate my sister further.

Finally, everyone sat and the meal began. Course after course slowly emerged from the kitchen. There was a time when I would have appreciated spending hours eating the wonderful dishes set before me. However, I couldn't find any joy in this meal. Instead, I watched the shadows shift in the room as the afternoon progressed.

With relief, I leaned toward Father when it was time for me to go. He guessed my purpose before I spoke.

"It is time for us to take our leave," he said softly to my sister.

She paused in her conversation with a merchant who had stopped to talk and nodded her farewell. It was brief and uncaring.

I turned to Blye and gave her a hug, whispering good-bye. At least Blye didn't seem resentful of my presence, though she didn't speak to Father at all.

On our way to the door, several men of influence stopped Father. He politely ended the conversation as soon as he could, but the sun never paused its sinking progress. When we finally reached the door, the golden orb hovered dangerously close to the horizon.

"I must hurry," I said, giving Father a hug outside.

"I didn't realize how late it was. Will you be all right?" Father pulled back to look at me with concern.

"I'll be fine." I kissed his cheek and gave him the cloak.

"Return this to Ila, please. Thank her for me." I turned away from him and called for Swiftly.

His hooves thundered nearby, then he was kneeling before me. I quickly climbed up and clasped his mane.

"Good night, Father," I said as Swiftly stood. "I'll see you soon."

I leaned low over Swiftly as he turned and galloped through the streets.

"Before the sun sets," I said, encouraging him to lengthen his stride.

The wind cooled my skin under my gown and tugged at my hair. I kept an eye on the sun the length of the journey. We made it through the gates just as the last light faded.

The sight of the waiting, roiling cloud of mist brought fierce joy to me. I'd missed him and hadn't known it until just then.

I slid from Swiftly and sent him away with a pat on the neck. He shied around the mist while I walked straight toward it.

"I'm going to fall and hurt myself," I said.

Suddenly, I was up in the beast's arms, cradled against his chest. I sighed and leaned my head against him, content to close my eyes and run my fingers through his fur. I was home.

He brought me into the kitchen and set me on my feet. The continued silence and mist worried me.

"No mist," I said, stepping forward to touch him. The mist disappeared instantly. His angry eyes swept me from head to toe.

"You look tumbled," he said, his growl garbling his words.

"Windblown from the race home."

"Home," he sighed and closed his eyes.

"Why are you so upset?"

He opened his eyes, his gaze sweeping over me.

"That is not the dress I gave you."

"Of course it is. It was in the wardrobe."

He exhaled slowly.

"Rose replaced the dress I had with this." He gestured at my dress. "When I discovered the change...what man who saw you in this would let you go?"

The insecurity behind his words made me ache for him, and I realized something vital that I'd overlooked. I'd protected my body from him but not my heart. And while I wasn't watching, he'd touched it, leaving me marked by his gentle caring. I could no longer imagine my life without the beast.

I stepped close and rested my hand on his chest.

"No man can capture me, only a beast."

He lifted my hand to his mouth and kissed the palm while his heated gaze searched my face. Was he so unsure of my loyalty?

With a hammering heart, I shrugged one shoulder, easing the sleeve down to expose the top of my breast. His gaze drifted down and stayed riveted on my skin. My nipples reacted, and I knew that he saw. He lifted a finger and traced the outline.

I closed my eyes and pressed my hand over his, holding him to my breast.

"No man," I said again. "Only a beast."

A pained sound escaped him, and he picked me up again and brought me to my room, gently laying me on my bed.

This time wasn't slow and teasing. He tore the dress from me and latched onto the peak of my right breast, suckling roughly. Each pull sent a sizzle of desire straight between my legs. He shifted his attention to the other breast. I sighed with pleasure and threaded my fingers in his fur. His mouth nibbled a quick trail down, and his fingers dug into my thighs as he spread me wide. His breath tickled me for a heartbeat then his tongue laved me from opening to curls. Again and again, a long, slow stroke that had my hips twitching. When he closed his lips over my nub and suckled, I moaned.

"Yes," I whispered, liking the feeling.

My tension coiled higher as he tongued my opening, licking and sucking as I thrust my hips to meet his plunge. I felt wild, uncontrolled. My legs stiffened, but his hands kept me wide. His mouth found my nub again to suck and flick. A cry burst from me as the tension broke in a torrent of fried nerve endings. I convulsed under his mouth, enjoying each pulse.

Finally, the sensation faded, and my hands fell to the mattress. What felt like hours of pleasure, took only minutes.

As before, he left me. This time, I fell asleep, legs spread wide and still dangling off the mattress.

I WOKE SNUGGLED AGAINST HIM. He kissed me softly but didn't touch me any further.

"Good morning," I whispered shyly. He'd tasted me twice, but this was the first time I'd actually faced him afterward.

"Good morning," he rumbled, combing his fingers through my unfettered hair.

I frowned at the feeling.

"Did you remove the braids?"

"I did...after I returned."

I blinked, understanding his meaning. "I'm sorry it didn't work."

He grunted then surprised me.

"It didn't work because I don't want it to work. I refuse to play her game any longer. I am content to stay as I am...if you will stay with me. Marry me," he said quietly.

My heart expanded at his unexpected proposal, and I knew I wanted nothing more than to say yes. Yet, I knew I could not. His revulsion of Rose held my tongue. Enchanted, he would never age; and one day, he would hold me in as much contempt as he did Rose. My heart broke at the thought, and I struggled to find the right answer to appease him.

I sat up, and he moved off the bed to watch me.

"I will leave something for your husband. I will leave you a virgin." He bent to a knee and placed a kiss on my bare stomach. "Will you marry me?" he repeated.

My heart jumped and fluttered in excitement despite my best efforts to quell it. If I married him, he would *be* my husband.

"Well, that's a convenient way to get around it, isn't it?"

He grinned, but it didn't reach his eyes. "I thought so." He remained on his knee. "And your answer?"

"I can't marry you," I said softly. After a hard swallow, I gave him the only reason I could speak aloud. "When I think of you, I have only these titles in my head: sir, master, liege lord, and beast. Where in there is your real name? I know too little about you."

He stood and nodded, surprisingly calm with my answer. Holding out a hand, he helped me to my feet. His gaze swept over me, bringing a light blush to my cheeks.

"Let's spend today together," he said.

"I need a moment first."

He nodded and left the room.

As soon as the door closed, I collapsed back onto the bed. What had I done? Somehow, along the way, I'd given the beast my heart. He would surely crush it within his too powerful grasp before he even realized he held it. Yet, I couldn't regret his keeping of my love. Because now, an imagined world without the beast seemed a horrible, lonely place. I was where I belonged.

After I relieved myself and washed, I went to the wardrobe. It was completely empty again. I smiled and moved to the door.

He waited for me in the hallway, as usual, and held out a hand. I wrapped my fingers in his and followed him to the library. A tray waited for us. He motioned for me to sit on the couch and proceeded to feed me bits of fruit.

"My name is Alec. When I was four, my father gave me my first horse, a pony really. I can barely remember what it looked like but remember thinking it enormous, until Father and I went on our first ride together." He chuckled at the memory. "I wish I could remember more of my life before he passed away."

"What about your youth with your mother?"

"After my father died, a large responsibility fell to her. She didn't have the advantage of a teacher for a father and struggled to learn so much in those first years. I didn't understand it then, but I see it now. Back then, I only knew that she was very busy."

"What did you do when she wasn't busy?" I asked, not liking the sad look he had.

We spent the rest of the day talking about our childhoods.

ON THE FOURTH morning since my return from the wedding, I ate in my room. The tray had been waiting for me beside my bed, and I knew he had slept with me at least a portion of the night. However, like the morning before, I woke alone.

Though we spent a good portion of our days together, and I remained naked, he had yet to touch me again. Instead, he spent his time telling me of his past, good and bad. I felt compassion for the lonely little boy he'd been but had a hard time understanding the selfish man he'd become. Though his mother had been busy, she'd loved him deeply.

I understood that he told me stories of his past so I could better know him, yet it didn't achieve his purpose. Those stories told me who he had been and gave some insight into how he'd become enchanted. Yet, they didn't tell me a thing about who he was now and what his hopes for the future might be. There were still so many questions I wanted to ask him. What did he like eating? What had he done to entertain himself since becoming enchanted? What had he thought the first time the villagers stormed the estate?

When I finished the food, I washed and left the room. Though we spent much time together, he excused himself often to work in his study. I didn't bring up the subject of my missing clothes, which I knew was the source of his need for distraction. I didn't want to diminish what he was achieving. Control over himself, regardless of the circumstance.

As I expected, I found him in his study, head bent over the estate records. He read them often, now. He even had pages of notes. Presently, he scratched something on a piece of parchment, lost to his thoughts.

"Good morning," I said from the door.

"Good morning." He lifted his gaze from his ledger to greet me but quickly returned to his reading.

"I was wondering...why did you spare me?"

"What do you mean?" he asked, maintaining his focus on the book before him.

"In the beginning, the first time you threw me over, I wasn't surprised by the net that caught me. The second time, I thought perhaps I'd just gotten lucky. But after...what was your reason?"

He looked up again and studied me with a peculiar expression.

"You didn't beg or stammer excuses. You accepted your fate but not with defeat."

Such a simple thing had saved me?

"Why did you offer me any one thing from the estate?"

A tension crept into his shoulders, and he looked down at his ledger again.

"Why are you asking so many questions?"

"I'm trying to know you better."

He sighed, and I knew he would answer.

"I wanted to give you a reason to return."

"And I did," I said with a smile.

"You did," he agreed solemnly. "The night you asked for refuge,

I watched you try to start the fire. You worked calmly, despite the shivers shaking your hands. You didn't ask for help or balk at the task like other women I'd known. It upset me."

His admission surprised me.

"You wanted me to balk and ask for help?" I asked.

"No, after watching you, I wanted to keep you. But you'd only asked for refuge. So, I left you to see if your father had returned."

"Why did you want to keep me?"

"You ask too many questions," he said without rancor.

"Is that why you sent the trunk? To lure me back?" I smiled at him, though he wasn't looking at me. "Blye was quite interested in the cloth. I wonder how you would have fared with her."

He grunted, and I knew I'd amused him.

I left him to his work, knowing that I'd bothered him enough. I studied the bookshelves. Unsure what I wanted to read, I wandered for a bit. A lower shelf near the door caught my attention, and I bent to study the titles.

Something thumped to the floor in the study. I straightened and looked over my shoulder. The beast leaned over his desk, completely focused on me. On the floor before the desk was the estate book he'd just had open.

"Benella, dearest, please pick a book from the other side of the room," he said slowly.

I frowned for a moment. Why would he want me to...I recalled Ila bending in front of me to pet the cat. Before the threatening grin could burst forth, I nodded and moved out of his line of sight. Then, I grinned foolishly.

A week later, I was feeling decidedly ignored and very unsure of myself. He'd stopped coming to my room at night and disappeared constantly; now, going so far as closing himself in the study.

I paced the library, trying to understand the turn in his behavior. It had started before Bryn's wedding. The first time he'd...I blushed and stopped my pacing to stare at the barred study. I'd thought his avoidance then might have meant we'd done something wrong, but he'd said we hadn't. Yet, his current actions seemed to suggest otherwise. Why else completely avoid me if not out of guilt?

Frustrated, I went and knocked on his door.

"Sir?" I still couldn't bring myself to use his given name.

"Yes," came his muffled answer. "Enter."

I walked in. As usual, he didn't look up. I nervously sat in a chair.

"I don't understand," I said.

That caught his attention. With a hint of worry, he looked up.

"What, dearest?"

"You said I didn't need to apologize, and you seemed to like tasting me. But you've stopped touching me completely. You don't look at me. You barely speak to me. I don't understand why."

He focused on his papers.

"Benella, now is not the best time for me to talk about—"

"Was it wrong? Are you ashamed of what we did? Should I be ashamed?" I couldn't get the image of Sara's shame from my head.

He stood abruptly and walked around the desk.

"No, Benella," he said, kneeling before me. "What we did should not cause you shame. I'm trying very hard to distract myself from thinking of those moments with you because I want to do it all again. But, I don't think I can taste you again and stop." He touched my face gently. "I want all of you. Please say you've reconsidered and will marry me."

I looked down at my hands, reflecting on what he'd just said. My fear remained. He would want me today or even ten years from now but certainly not beyond that. So I gave him the same answer as before.

"I know quite a bit about the old you, but still very little about who you are now. I know nothing about your hopes for the future beyond your desire to be free of the curse."

"The answer is still no, then."

Miserably, I nodded.

"May I please have clothes?"

He remained silent until I met his gaze.

"They are in your room."

CHAPTER
ELEVEN

Once I wore proper clothes, he spent more time with me. We talked for hours of inconsequential things and idled away our time with whatever struck our fancy. He no longer used his mist, and his growl was completely absent. I cherished each day spent with him but found time passed too quickly in his entertaining and courteous company. When each evening arrived, it always felt as if the sun had just risen.

At his insistence, I began to sleep in a plain white gown that stayed on me all night. He still came to my bed and held me while he rested, but only joined me once I already slept. When I woke, he was already gone, waiting for me in the hallway, ready to start a new, companionable day.

Through our time together, he began to share his hopes for his future as a beast; and he stopped trying to see Rose. However, he didn't ask me to marry him again. I thought he had perhaps come to the same conclusion I had. He would care for me easily in my youth, but not as I weathered.

I tried not to dwell on our future, and gave up trying to quell what I felt for him. I loved the beast and would never stop. I would stay with him for as long as he would have me.

Near the end of summer, an evening storm swept through the area, and the beast and I decided to linger by the fire in the library, one of our favorite pastimes. A warm fire lent a soft glow to the pre-twilight gloom as I reclined on the lounge. My bare feet were propped comfortably on the cushions, and the beast sat on the floor so he could idly run his fingers through my hair as I read aloud.

He stopped me occasionally to feed me some tidbit from the tray on the table or to ask a question about the text. I enjoyed both kinds of interruption.

When I finished the passage, I closed the book softly and sighed. Neither of us talked for a moment, both content as we were.

"I cannot recall when I have ever spent as pleasurable an evening as tonight," I said, twisting to look up at him.

He gave me a soft look and nodded. But I barely noticed. My words struck a deep chord, and the solution to his enchantment opened wide in my mind. I bolted upright with a jolt.

"Of course!"

He eyed me in concern.

"Did I witness an epiphany?"

I stared at him, torn. If I shared with him what I'd just realized, he could free himself and become a man and age like any other. Time would not make me leave. Yet, he wasn't any man. He was a lord. And what lord wanted a scholar's daughter, even in her youth? None. He would likely marry one of his own station. However, if I kept the information to myself, I would win a few more years of his consideration as a beast.

His caring gaze held mine, and I knew I couldn't keep the truth of my revelation from him. He'd suffered his punishment long enough.

I forced a wide grin and ignored the tightening in my chest.

"Yes, you did. A life changing one. If I asked you in what ways you might pleasure me, what would you say?"

"I would rather show you," he said with a playful growl and a leer.

"If I asked you what things please me, what would you say?"

"We are not talking about sexual pleasure any longer, are we?" he said. With a tender look, he studied me for a moment. "Books please you. Learning. Walking outside. Visiting with your father."

"So, if I were to ask you for a night of pleasure what would you do?"

His eyes widened, and I knew he'd come to the same conclusion. For the past fifty years, he'd been trying to sexually please the enchantress for nothing.

A storm grew behind his eyes, and I quickly scrambled to my knees and gently held his face.

"You've spent time with her over the years. You must know something of what she likes," I whispered. "Go to her. Try something new."

He hesitated, and I saw it was because of me. It gave me a small hope. Perhaps a lord could care for a scholar's daughter. I gently ran my hand along the fur of his neck.

"I am content to stay here with you just as you are, but you are not the same beast you were. Your people need you. You need to bring prosperity back to the north."

He rose reluctantly, kissed my brow, and left the room.

Feeling bereft, I went to my room and tugged on a nightgown. My heart ached with what the new day might offer. There was the possibility for great happiness and even greater despair. I hoped that once he turned into a man, he would not forget me, as I'd long ago predicted.

I'd thought saving my virginity would be all I needed for a future husband because I'd never considered the possibility that the beast would claim my heart. I knew my foolishness now. If he cast me aside, the beast would hurt me as he'd promised he never would.

Sighing, I tried to let my worries and heartaches free; and gradually, sleep claimed me.

BEFORE THE SUN YET ROSE, a distant clatter of breaking dishes woke me, and I realized our attempt had failed. As much as I wanted to keep the beast, I wanted to set him free to be the man he should be.

I rose from bed and followed the sounds that continued as I hurried through the halls. A rather loud bang came from the direction of the kitchen, and my heart broke for the beast. I rushed to the room, then froze.

Tennen stood with a sack in one hand, stuffing it with enchanted food. He spotted me and froze in shock as well.

I recovered first, pivoted, and took off running. His steps rang out behind me. Too close. He caught me by my braid. I cried out as he tugged me back against his chest. My heart hammered. I bent forward slightly, intending to hit him with the back of my head, but he spun me and tossed me over his shoulder. He sprinted out the door before I could inhale.

I kicked my legs and tried to twist from his grip, but he held tight. Bracing my hands on his back, I raised my head enough to see the vines move and felt a surge of hope. However, they didn't move for Tennen. They stretched for Egrit, who ran toward me, and tangled around her trunk and the trunk of her man. Swiftly came thundering toward us only to be caught in the vines, too. Mr. Crow took flight but was snatched from the air. Despair robbed me of my fight. Why would the beast do this?

In the predawn light, Tennen raced through the open gates. His shoulder dug into my middle. Nausea rose. Oblivious, or maybe uncaring, he continued on.

We reached the quiet village of Konrall with me on the verge of vomiting. Regardless, as soon as I saw the first house, I opened my mouth to scream, knowing the butcher and the candle maker would come to my aid. Before I could utter a sound, Tennen threw me to the ground and slapped my mouth.

"Not a sound," he warned.

"Piss off!" I cried as I tried to scramble away.

He used his body to pin me and stuffed my mouth with a cloth. Then, holding my arms, he tossed me behind his head and carried me like large game. My breath whooshed out of me for a moment. I still struggled, though. The effort earned me a sharp bite to my inner thigh.

He turned into the alley beside the bakery, and I started to panic. When he kicked his booted foot against the door, I struggled wildly. I tried to use my tongue to push the gag from my mouth as I yelled for help.

"Tennen," the baker cried in delight, eyeing me.

"Bread for life," Tennen demanded harshly.

I understood what he meant to do and thrashed about, hoping he would drop me.

"One loaf a week until the day you die, or one loaf a day for four months."

Tennen nodded just as I managed to wriggle one hand free. I clawed at his face, forgetting the gag in my desperation to be free.

"Inside, quickly," the baker panted.

As soon as the door closed, Tennen swung me from his shoulders and hit me. My ears rang, and I stumbled back, falling against something before crumbling to the ground.

The baker spoke, but I couldn't understand what he said. It

sounded as if I had water in my ears, making his words quieter and garbled. I blinked in an attempt to clear my cloudy vision. Tennen's legs passed in front of me. I traced them listlessly to the door. The room spun as the door closed behind him. I struggled to my feet then vomited.

The baker cried in dismay and wrapped a meaty hand around my upper arm to half drag me from the room. I struggled, knowing my pathetic attempts didn't deter him in the least.

He led me through the storefront, where his sister already sat.

"Help." Through my oddly filtered ears, my plea came out slurred.

She looked at me with concern, but the baker waved her aside.

"She…" The water garbled a few of the baker's words. "…to recover."

He opened the door behind the storeroom. It led to a sitting room. He guided me to a lounge and pressed me into the already compressed cushions. I batted his hands away, and he cuffed me upside the head. Not as hard as Tennen, but he hit the same spot and brought back the nausea.

His hand drifted along the line of my throat, down to the neckline of my pathetically thin nightgown. The palm of his hand skimmed my breast. The touch did not send a familiar tingle to my center, just another rolling wave of nausea. I encouraged revulsion with a forced gag.

The baker jumped back, giving me a moment's reprieve. I brought a hand to my head, rubbing the temple and blinking, trying to clear the fog.

"Let me go," I said.

"I don't think so." His eyes didn't leave my breasts.

I wanted to cry but, instead, looked for a way to escape. The baker used my distraction and pushed me back, pinning me down with his weight.

I couldn't breathe. Panic set in, and I pushed at his shoulders. I barely registered the feel of his hand as he shoved the hem of my nightgown up over my waist. I wore nothing underneath.

I twisted in an effort to move his weight aside enough to draw a decent breath.

The bruising force of his knee parted my legs. Air or not, I would not let him take me. I struggled harder, ignoring the spots that danced in my vision.

The door opened, and I sobbed in relief. But, the baker didn't pause. He began thrusting his hips at me. To my horror, I felt the head of his penis bumping my opening. However, he was unable to penetrate due to his massive stomach.

"Get off!"

He ignored me and pulled back enough to try to readjust his position. I craned my neck, looking to the door. Tennen, Sara, the smith, and the baker's mother stood there.

"Get him off!"

No one moved. The baker thrust forward again, and his penis came a little closer to my opening. He wiggled one hand under my hip and repositioned me with a grunt.

"Sara!" I screamed.

She looked away, her eyes filled with tears. Tennen smirked. The baker's mother looked deeply troubled, but did not move.

"Help me!"

The baker's mouth moved close to my ear. "Now you are mine."

I turned back toward him, ready to bite his damn nose off. He tilted his hips forward as I opened my mouth with an angry cry. He arched back to avoid me, and the head of his prick bumped to the side, missing my opening completely.

"I will never be yours." I gave up trying to push him away and clawed wildly at his face. My fingernails left a furrow along his cheek.

"Hold her hands," he panted, twisting his head out of the way.

"I think not," a deep voice said from the doorway.

The menacing rumble caused the baker to pause mid-hump. He looked up.

I used the distraction to claw the baker's face savagely. He cried out and tumbled off the lounge, holding his face in pain. I scrambled to my feet, smoothing down my thin gown as if it could protect me. My legs and arms shook.

"She is mine," the baker panted. "You saw us bedding."

"You stunted excuse for a man," I said, turning and kicking him in his soft middle. "I will never be yours."

The baker groaned and curled in on himself.

"You heard the lady," the newcomer said.

I raised my head from the baker to view those who had stood by so callously.

Patrick had pulled Sara to the side. Tennen stood close to them, his hateful expression still on me. I marched right up to him, balled up a fist, and hit him in the mouth. He cried out in shock, and I cradled my hand.

"Bryn was foolish to ever see value in a prick like you," I said, reigning in a sense of calm.

I looked at Sara with condemning eyes but said nothing. Her husband's hand rested on her shoulder. His face remained impassive.

Finally, I looked at the baker's mother, who glanced at her son with a brokenhearted expression. She removed a cloak from the back of a chair, shuffled toward me, and placed it over my shoulders.

While she helped me cover myself, I looked at my rescuers. The man stood tall. So tall he must have had to duck to fit through the door. His clipped dark hair missed his collar by an inch. His stern brow shadowed his deep blue eyes as his gaze remained on me.

His companion moved slightly, calling my attention. She stood just behind him, her soft hand on his shoulder, much like Patrick's hand on Sara's shoulder. I found that odd, and I ignored her compassionate, soft expression as I focused on her hand. Something seemed so familiar about that hand.

As I stared, my eyes rounded. I looked up at the face. The wrinkles and yellowed teeth were gone but there was no doubt. Rose's face. Aryana's hand.

I looked back at the handsome, stern man, my gaze sweeping him from head to feet. Alec. Liege Lord of the North. The beast had broken the curse.

My heart leapt with joy, until I realized he made no move toward me. I looked at him questioningly, and he grimaced ever so slightly as he met my gaze. Inside, I shattered. I'd known he wouldn't want me after he returned, but I hadn't expected his complete abandonment. My heart broke.

Beaten, nearly raped, and cast aside by the one I loved, I'd suffered enough.

"I want to go home," I whispered, averting my gaze from the pair. "My father's home."

"There is a carriage outside, waiting for you," the Liege Lord said.

He stepped aside, and Aryana/Rose copied his movement. Betrayed by the woman I'd grown to care for more than my own sisters.

Walking stiffly from the room, I left the bakery with my head high. Several people stood in the store's front room. I ignored them all.

Outside, a small, light carriage with a single horse waited; and the driver offered me a hand to step up. I sank into the plush leather seat and blankly stared at the man's coat as he sat in the driver's seat and encouraged the horse into a trot.

I saw little as we left Konrall. The devastation of my world blinded me. I'd lost the beast, the sisters I'd wanted, and the home I'd craved. What was left? I could think of nothing; and in my mind, the baker's weight pressed down on me once more.

DEVASTATION

DEVASTATION

CHAPTER ONE

THE TATTERED REMNANTS OF THE WORLD I'D HELD SO DEAR DRIFTED from my mind. Anger and hate clouded my thoughts.

I shook fiercely but refused to give in to the tears that so desperately wanted release. My stomach cramped from the recent abuse and the restraint to contain myself, and my face ached from the blows Tennen and the baker had delivered. Yet, the pain did not distract from the lingering feel of that grotesque, vile man as the carriage rumbled toward the Water. My skin crawled, and my lungs refused to work properly.

I remained so lost in the violent experience that I barely noticed when the carriage pulled up before my father's house.

The driver hopped down from his perch and offered a hand to help me down. I needed the help. The shaking in my legs had only grown worse.

Once I was on my feet, the driver turned to Father's home and knocked on the door. Trembling in Mrs. Medunge's cloak and my nightgown, I stood behind the man.

Father opened the door, took one look at me, and ushered me in.

"Benella, what's happened?" he said, wrapping an arm around me to steady me.

I could only shake my head. He tried quizzing the driver, but the man bowed and said to expect to hear from his master soon.

That penetrated my clouded mind. My stomach dropped. The returned Lord of the estate. The image of him standing so calmly burned my eyes; still, no moisture gathered.

As soon as the door closed, Father led me to a chair then quickly left to pull water from the well. When he returned, he dipped a cloth into the pail, wrung it out, and held it to my cheek. I flinched from the pain and the reminder of what had happened.

"I'll fetch the physician," he said, already turning away.

"No." I caught his hand to stop him.

I wasn't hurt so badly that I could justify what a physician would cost. I would recover. Yet, as Father faced me with concern, I knew he would insist unless I explained my abused appearance.

I averted my gaze as words spilled forth.

"I interrupted an attempted thievery at the beast's estate," I said, staring at the table. "The beast was...elsewhere. The thief carried me to the baker. The baker attempted to rape me. His grotesque belly saved me," I said in a broken whisper. "I'm shaken and bruised. Nothing that won't heal."

"Oh, my girl." Father knelt beside me and wrapped me in his arms. His compassion almost released the tears I struggled to withhold.

"I don't want to go back," I said in a tight, pained voice. "They all play cruel games. I thought Aryana a friend, but she's the enchantress who has held the beast this whole time. They were both there at the baker's." I lifted my head and met my father's agonized gaze. "Their presence stopped the baker, but they otherwise stood by indifferently."

"I'm so sorry, Bini," my father whispered with tears in his eyes. "I wish I knew how to fix this."

I knew he meant more than the attack I'd suffered. He pulled me back into a comforting hug, trying to protect me as he had from Tennen's bullying when he'd moved us to the Water. Yet, instead of Father making the sacrifice he'd intended, I'd been tricked into staying with the beast who I had thought would protect me as zealously as he'd protected his estate. Sadly, I had wrongly assumed his level of affection for me. The ache in my chest continued to grow, but for Father's sake, I withheld my tears.

Father pulled away and offered me the use of his room, along with some of his clothes. After I dressed, I sat on his bed with my elbows on my knees and stared at my folded hands.

All the advice Aryana had given or not given made more sense. She'd used me in her game with the beast. As Rose, she'd tried to dissuade me, thus steeling my determination to help. As Aryana, she'd given me the knowledge I'd needed to navigate a world I'd not understood. I recalled all the times she had said she worried about me. She had been sincere; I didn't doubt it. Yet, it hadn't been enough to stop her game.

Finally, tears fell hard and fast. With a muffled sob, I curled up on my father's bed. I cried until I felt empty and numb. Then I just lay there, remembering not the attack but my last days with the beast and his caring attentiveness. It made the pain I already bore twist bitterly. How could I miss someone who so easily watched my abuse and just as easily sent me away?

A knock sounded at the cottage door more than an hour later, jarring me from my thoughts. I recalled the driver's promise, and I felt a stab of pain through my chest. A small part of me wanted Alec to rush through the door. Yet, if he did enter, which Alec would it be? The mercurial beast or the cold lord?

A shiver ran through me a moment before Aryana strode into

my father's room without knocking. Though her unannounced appearance shocked me, I didn't sit up or acknowledge her. Instead, I continued to stare at the space the door had once occupied.

My heart continued to break as I realized Alec wouldn't come because there was nothing left to say. Bitterness began to eat the pain. He'd gotten what he'd wanted. His freedom. And by mere seconds, he'd made sure I'd left with the last piece of myself for my husband. I almost snorted. Husband. There would be no husband for me.

"Fifty years ago," Aryana said, pulling me from my musings, "Alec's mother came south looking for a way to help her son. She found me just before she died. Her story and love for her son moved me enough that I gave her my word I would help him become a better man, a man of whom she could be proud.

"When I came to the North, I could not believe the depravity. It was simple to open the Whispering Sisters. We serviced men, and I gained power from their lust. I used that power to shift the balance. I cursed the beast and drove out the dregs he had let in. Those of his servants who had stood by and let their Liege sink lower and lower without attempting to reason with him joined him in his enchantment.

"To give him hope, I set the price of his freedom on one night of pleasure. His earliest attempts fueled me so much that some of the energy seeped into the estate, making it possible for him to control some of the enchantments when I allowed it."

When she allowed it. The phrase struck me cold. She had been the one to control the vines, then. She'd allowed Tennen to take me, even after witnessing his past crimes against me. She'd sacrificed me so the Lord of the North might be free. Whatever friendship I'd thought we'd shared had only existed in my mind. The knowledge hurt me more than Tennen's fist had.

"When I saw you, time and again, bravely walk the mist surrounding the estate and boldly confront the local boys, I knew you were the one to help him." She paused for a moment. "I'm sorry for the lies and all you have suffered to free Alec. Yet, if he had been warned about your danger before dawn broke, he would not be free now."

I could feel her expectant stare but didn't meet her gaze.

After several long moments of silence, she stood. Did she think her story would justify how she'd used me? Anger and disbelief clawed at my insides.

"I'm sure his mother would be pleased with the result," I said in a raw whisper.

She looked down at me for a moment, her expression closed, before sweeping from the room.

Father came to look in on me, but said nothing as I continued to lay there and sort through my thoughts.

When Tennen and Splane had started chasing me, I hadn't hated them. I understood their angry reaction to my knowledge of what their mother had done with the baker. However, I struggled to see any possible explanation to excuse Alec and Rose from my burning resentment. The way she'd gone about trying to help him was a mockery. And, how could he have held me and listened to me read the night before, then make no move to help me when I needed him most?

When my father checked on me a second time, wringing his hands with worry, I decided I'd given those who'd hurt me enough thought. To think of them further would only allow them to harm me more. So I closed off my heart, sealing in the pain, and sat up and gave my father a small, reassuring smile.

"Is there anything to eat?"

He nodded and went to the kitchen to fix us a modest meal.

His attempt, boiled oats that looked more like paste, made me smile. We ate while laughing about it. The laughter didn't touch me inside. I doubted anything would ever again.

FOR THE NEXT SEVERAL DAYS, I stayed indoors, and Father remained my constant companion. When I asked about his teaching, he declared he'd educated the sisters as much as he thought possible for the time being.

I wondered if that meant we would be moving soon. The thought stopped me. Would I be moving with him? I was of an age where I should marry. However, where once I thought marriage something to look forward to, I no longer did. The memory of the baker pinning me to the lounge as he thrust down on me gave me shudders.

For how long could I ask Father to keep me as his dependent? I cringed, thinking of how he'd struggled to provide for his grown daughters so far. Yet, what other options did I have?

I contemplated the possibilities for my future often; there wasn't much else to do with my time.

Father left one morning and came back a short while later with a package. Inside, lay a plain, coarsely spun dress. Nothing fancy, but entirely suitable for leaving the house, unlike my shirt and pants. I knew my seclusion needed to end for his sake; so, I smiled my thanks and went to his room to change.

When I emerged, he offered to walk with me to the market street, but I declined. Content to keep my solitude, I left the house alone.

Memories continued to haunt me and not just of the baker. As much as I'd tried to lock away my thoughts of him, the beast dwelled in my mind. I'd always known he would forget me, but hadn't realized how quickly, and I missed his mercurial presence.

Needing a distraction, I walked to Bryn's new home to see how she fared as a bride. When I stepped in the storefront, I was surprised to see her wearing an apron and assisting customers. She looked tired, though it was still early morning. I moved to the counter to see if she would have time later to talk.

Bryn caught sight of me and marched over.

"Your kind is not welcome here," she said with a malevolent hiss to her words.

A woman next to me gasped and took a step back as if I were in quarantine again.

"My kind?" I asked, puzzled by my sister's hostile attitude.

"Whore," she spat. "We heard what happened in Konrall. How could you refuse the baker's offer after lying with him? Get out." She thrust out a finger, pointing toward the door.

I stared at her, my temper spiked and spiteful. She called me a whore? She had another man's babe growing in her belly. My gaze flicked there, and she paled. Her hand trembled.

"Have care with the titles you bestow me," I said, then turned to leave. Only the babe's future held my tongue. The innocent child she carried need not feel the sting of her parent's misjudgments and cruelties.

Word of the incident quickly followed me home. Father said nothing when I closed myself in his room once more to sit on his bed and consider my fate. I had no skills other than my education; and with my new reputation as a whore, no one respectable would want me teaching their children. The only unrespectable place to teach—the Whispering Sisters—was out of the question because of Aryana's betrayal. Discounting a teaching post, I reflected on my other skills. I could hunt and fish, but not well enough to make a profit to pay for a home. Enough to eat, though.

I shouldn't have shunned the occupations that my sisters had learned. Skills such as cleaning and cooking would have been useful to gain employment as a maid; yet, the effort I'd put into restoring the beast's estate made my incompetence at those skills painfully obvious. What did my future hold for me now?

After bundling my shirt and pants in a pack, I left the room. Father looked up at me with a slight frown of worry.

"You need to go back to teaching, and I need to figure out what I will do with my life," I said with determination.

He nodded slowly, opened his mouth as if he would say something, and paused.

"What is it?" I asked.

"I want you to be happy," he said with a sigh. "Would returning..." He cleared his throat. "Did he make you happy?" he asked tentatively.

A sad smile curved my lips. He had. While he was the beast.

"He made life interesting, but there was more danger there than I'd realized."

I left through the back door before he could say more.

Skirting around town, I headed south, wandering aimlessly through the woods until I felt I'd hiked far enough from town to set traps. I walked a long circuit twice, gathering as I went.

Time had passed quickly while at the manor, changing the seasons, so the forest provided several herbs and berries that I used in the traps. Three rabbits found their ends in my snares before I returned to an empty house.

Dressing the game brought back memories of my attempts at cooking with the beast. I smiled as I started a fire and brought out a kettle. I set two of the skinny hares in the pot and filled it with water. Then, determined, I wrapped the other and walked to the market street again.

Everywhere I went, I met censuring eyes. No respectable business would trade with me. Giving up, I turned from the market street and walked toward the less respectable trade district, taverns where women served men in several ways.

Houses of those working that area lined the next street over. I approached the door of one that had a small garden. The woman who answered greeted me with a smile when she heard my offer— the hare for two carrots and a small onion. She assuredly received the better part of the deal. When she hugged me in thanks, I saw two small children behind her. Their large eyes followed the game.

Happy that someone had welcomed the trade, I returned home and added the carrots and onion to the stew and left it to simmer. When the carrots were tender, I placed a portion in a much smaller kettle with a lid and walked to the seamstress where Blye worked. Living in a tiny room above the shop, I couldn't imagine she ate well.

A bell tinkled above my head when I opened the door. Blye knelt at the feet of a woman, pinning the woman's hem. When Blye looked up and saw me, her polite expression closed. She murmured to the woman, begging for a moment, before she stood and strode toward me.

"You can't come in here," she whispered. With a firm hold on my elbow, she turned me around.

"I just wanted to bring you some stew," I said as I offered the little kettle.

Her eyes shifted to the woman who watched us with disapproval.

"I can't accept anything from you. Just go, Benella," she said in a low, urgent tone. "Associating with you will ruin everything for me."

Disbelief coursed through me. I turned stiffly and walked out, hiding how her words hurt me. The lure of accomplishment and status had robbed my sisters of basic kindness.

My feet carried me to the houses close to where I'd traded for the vegetables. A thin child played in the dirt outside one of the homes. Inside I could hear moaning and knew her mother's work. I waved the child over and offered her the food. She nodded eagerly. Since there was no spoon, I wiped her dirty hands on my skirt and watched her use her fingers. After she finished, I showed her how to write her name in the dirt. She smiled brightly as I left her practicing.

I watched the faces of the people I passed and realized something. The pursuit of success and respectability hadn't just led my sisters astray, but many others as well. It shouldn't be that way.

WHILE I FETCHED water from the well out back that evening, a knock sounded at the door. I didn't move to see who it was. No one I knew wanted to speak to me, besides my father. Inside, I heard him move to answer the door. The quiet exchange as I hauled up the bucket had me wondering. When Father called for me to join him, I became even more curious.

Carrying the water inside, I found a young woman standing just inside the door. Dressed in a demure gown, with her dark hair pulled back, she watched me with an unsure smile.

"Hello, Benella," she said quietly.

She seemed to know me, but I could not recall her.

"Hello." I looked to my father, but he excused himself and walked out the front door, leaving me alone with her.

"Please, come in," I said, unsure what else to do.

She smiled once more and stepped in further, so I could close the door. She didn't move to sit, however. She lingered near the table, her hands tightly clasped before her.

"I wanted to thank you," she said. "We all wanted to, but we decided I would be the best to speak to you."

"We?"

"My name is Egrit. I understand if you want me to leave."

Egrit. The familiar name brought a bittersweet tingle to my nose. I blinked twice to ease the sensation then moved forward and wrapped her in a firm hug. She returned it with a sniffle.

"We weren't sure if you would be angry with us," she said, pulling back.

I looked into her bright hazel eyes and saw the nymph still there.

"Not at all. You all tried to help me when you could. I understand that."

"No," she said, shaking her head. "Not that." She looked down at her hands. "We are part of the reason the master was cursed." She sighed and uncomfortably looked around the room. "As a child he was a handsome handful, I was told. His teachers and nurses spoiled him as his parents ran the estate. His father passed away before the master's fifth birthday. His mother took over the estate responsibilities until he turned sixteen. I came to the estate before his fifteenth year."

I motioned for her to sit, and she did.

"As maids, we were told by the butler to give the master anything he wanted." She met my eyes steadily. "The older ones introduced him to women for his birthday. After that, all he needed to do was crook a finger. We all ran to please him, instilling in him an attitude toward women that caused many so much grief later."

She looked down at the table. "After the last time he was with me, he carried me to Rose. He knelt beside me and begged my forgiveness as she began to clean me. I told him there was nothing to forgive. I didn't blame him. I could have run. I could have solidified; he couldn't truly hurt me in that state. But I hadn't run. I'd stayed because, when he'd come for me, part of me had burst with excitement that someone like him would want me again. How could I expect him to value me when I valued myself so little?

"We all needed to learn what you had to teach us, and now we want to thank you and to beg your forgiveness for everything you suffered."

I listened to her tale with a heavy heart, seeing the beast in my mind.

"Egrit, his rough use of you, whether with your consent or not, was unspeakably horrible. You cannot forgive him. Your forgiveness is only for you. Your hate and pain are released with it, healing you, not him." She nodded slowly, a new light of understanding in her eyes. "And you can't take the blame for the choices he made, absolving him of all responsibility. That's what caused the curse. Hold him responsible. If you truly do feel no hardship toward him, give him the chance to make amends. Don't be easy on him." Only after I finished speaking did I realize the beast I knew, the one I spoke of, no longer existed.

Egrit smiled widely and stood.

"I have other errands to run. Do you know the name of the best dressmaker?"

Though I remained angry with my sister, I still wanted her happy. So, I gave her name. Egrit's smile changed slightly, but she nodded and took her leave.

LESS THAN A WEEK LATER, another knock sounded at the door. The man who stood outside looked slightly familiar, yet I could not place his name. He noticed my uncertainty and gave me a genuine smile.

"Egrit mentioned speaking to you. I wanted to stop and give my thanks as well."

He continued to grin at me. Could this be Egrit's man?

"Do I know you?"

"Swiftly, at your service." He bowed slightly, keeping his eyes on me.

I grinned and did the unexpected. Pulling him into a quick hug, I brushed his cheek with a kiss.

"I owe you my thanks for all the times you carried me to and fro and kept me out of the baker's hands."

His smile faded.

"Except the last time."

Suddenly, I placed why he seemed familiar. He had been the one to help me into the carriage and drive me to my father's home.

"Don't fret, Swiftly. The odious man's own fat saved me from the worst of his eager attentions."

"He no longer dwells in Konrall," Swiftly said of the baker. "His mother and sister have taken him south."

"That is good for Konrall."

Over Swiftly's shoulder, I caught the unexpected sight of a man turning toward our house.

"Henick," I said with surprised delight.

"Excuse me, madam," Swiftly mumbled.

With a bow, he quickly left. I thought to call him back, but Henick claimed my attention with a friendly wave. Henick nodded to Swiftly as they passed each other.

"Benella, I heard about the baker and wanted to tell you how sorry I am for it. And I wanted to remind you I am still here, hoping for your consideration...as are my younger brothers."

His words touched my heart.

"I haven't forgotten," I said with a kind smile, "but I'm not sure I'm still suitable for marriage."

"Don't," he said. "Your worth has not diminished because of a man's crime against you. Don't ever believe otherwise."

"I swear to you, I do not devalue myself. I only meant, I cannot submit to marriage as I once thought I could. Certain aspects would be infinitely distasteful to me."

Understanding lit his features, and a blush stole across his face.

"What if a husband promised not to touch you until you thought his touch no longer distasteful?"

"Henick..." I struggled with the words to explain myself. "When I see you, I feel light and happy because you are one of the kindest people I know. When you marry, it will be to someone who carries sunshine in her hair and rainbows in her eyes just for you. Anything less wouldn't be good enough." I glanced at the floor for a moment. He waited patiently.

"The clouds of my life have planted seeds of bitterness in me. I find myself looking at people with," my voice dropped to a whisper, "hate. It's burning me slowly from the inside, eating at me, and stealing the color from my life." I met his gaze and took his hands in both of mine.

"Do you see why I must say no? I would not have what I carry poison you, too. I would not poison anyone with what now dwells in my heart."

"What will you do?" he asked.

"Find a way to live," I said. I stood on my toes to kiss his cheek once more. "Perhaps I will see you at the stream sometime."

He nodded and left. I watched him walk away, and my chest swelled with pity. Twice rejected. The second time for his own sake. I hoped he would find someone worthy of him.

Closing the door, I turned back to stir the thin stew I'd made. Not long after, the door opened again, and Father strode in with a frown on his face.

"Benella, the Sisters have let me go," he said without preamble.

I felt a surge of relief. I'd worried that Aryana might try to manipulate my father in some way.

"We have a few options open to us that I wanted to discuss with you. We could move south, but because of your sister's wedding feast, I have very little coin. We would only be able to take what we can carry," his eyes flicked to his remaining books.

I didn't turn to eye the meager display.

"Is there another option?" I asked.

"Moving south would give us both a fresh start," he said, still trying to speak for the first option.

"Yes, but I've learned the baker has moved south. The North with all its snobbery and deceit no longer seems so bad."

Father's lips twitched for a moment before he grew serious and withdrew a letter from his coat. I recognized it immediately as the letter I'd delivered so long ago. He handed it to me and watched me unfold it.

For a moment, I could only stare at the beast's script. A pang of loss pierced me before I read the words.

Whether I return to my rightful form or not, the North still needs a lord to carry out certain responsibilities. During my youth, I ignored many of my lessons, especially those in mathematics, and need someone I can trust to help account the estate's expenses and so forth. Please consider my invitation for employment.

Regards,

Alec Ruhall, Lord of the North

"Why didn't you come?" I asked, meeting my father's gaze.

"I asked myself why he would invite me for employment when he had you, a person well able to account the estate's expenses. I thought that he perhaps sought to use me to coerce you as he'd done once before. Do you think this a serious offer for honest employment?"

I read the lines again and slowly nodded. "I do. But I wonder if the offer still holds."

"As did I. I went to see him," he said.

"What? Why didn't you tell me?" I paced the room, too restless to sit. I'd not spoken to the beast since...memories swamped me. Reading to him in the library, feeling his fingers in my hair. Then, running from Tennen and the baker's weight pressing the air from my lungs. It had been almost two weeks since I'd last seen the beast.

"I wanted to be sure before we discussed it as an option. He well knows my circumstance and that we come as a pair. He assured me of a place for you and a more than fair wage for my work."

My mind raced. I could see him again. Excitement surged for only a moment before I killed it. No, I couldn't see *him*. I would never see the beast again. He was gone. Lord Ruhall, the man who had watched with dispassionate eyes as the baker tried to force himself on me, had taken the beast's place.

"Is this why you asked if I wanted to return?"

"Yes. When I visited, people were coming and going through the gates at will. I don't think there would be any danger."

I considered the letter once more and didn't see that Father had much choice but to accept. The idea of returning made my stomach churn with anger. Yet, unlike my sisters, I would not make Father sacrifice any more of his books when there was a viable option to save them. His books meant so much to him. Books...I stopped my pacing and smiled at him excitedly.

"We most certainly should go, then. You will love the library, Father. There are more books than you can imagine." Of the beast and the Liege Lord, I forced myself to give little thought. One was dead and the other a cold stranger.

Father smiled and patted my hand, and we agreed to travel to the manor the next morning with the hope that we might return with a carriage for our belongings.

CHAPTER
TWO

THE GATES STOOD OPEN AS FATHER HAD SAID. AROUND THE IRON, vines curled, green, yet lifeless; the vitality the enchantment had imbued, gone. A man with a scythe hacked at the growth that crowded the drive. Another man worked not far from there, pulling out roots and picking up the cut remains the first man left in his wake.

Father and I walked the drive, each of us carrying a single bag. With the sun shining and the lane mostly cleared, the estate lacked the feeling I'd previously associated with it. A forbidden safety. Now, it seemed only a rundown estate.

When we reached the door, the man who swept the steps looked us over. There was no recognition in his eyes when he glanced at me, and I knew he was new to the Liege Lord's service. He directed us to the kitchen door. Familiar with the grounds, I nodded and led the way along the newly-made, narrow path. As I walked, I wondered how many of the original staff had remained after the enchantment had broken.

The kitchen door stood open, the hearth overheating the room as the three cooks set about making the morning meal. This room appeared much the same, yet with so many present, very different.

Those differences gave me hope that the memories of my time spent here would remain buried and that I might be comfortable here once more.

"Good morning," my father said to the kitchen staff.

One of the cooks looked up with a slightly disgruntled expression.

"We've hired the staff we can. Come back next fall. There might be more work then."

Father didn't even blink at her less than welcoming tone.

"I am his Lord's man of estate. Mr. Benard Hovtel."

The cook glanced at us once more then dusted her hands on her apron.

"I'm Mrs. Wimbly, Lord Ruhall's head cook. I'll have the maid inform him of your arrival." She moved toward the hall and yelled for Egrit.

The familiar name almost made me smile. So, a few had stayed.

"Have a seat," the cook said with a nod toward the table. "I'll feed you while you wait."

We'd barely seated ourselves when she set a coddled egg before each of us and moved away.

Behind us, someone strode into the room. Thinking it Egrit, I glanced over my shoulder. It wasn't Egrit, but still a face I recognized. And the sight of it killed my appetite.

The events that had unfolded at the bakery had overshadowed my glimpse of Lord Ruhall. Now, however, I saw him clearly. He was young and handsome with a strong jaw and a regal nose. His dark hair and thick brows made him appear a bit imposing while his blue eyes lent an air of cool detachment. He was dressed in fine clothes, his hair was neatly combed, and he appeared quite well.

Resentment clouded my thinking. How could he look so well when I felt so ill?

The Lord of the estate looked around for someone, presumably the cook, and froze when he saw me. Surprise colored his face as his gaze swept over me then moved to my father.

"I would speak to your daughter, with your permission, sir," he said to Father, not even looking at me again.

"It is not my permission that matters, but hers," my father said, looking at me in question.

"It is yours that matters at the moment," the Liege Lord said.

My eyebrows rose, and my hand instinctively closed over my coddled egg. Suddenly the egg sailed through the air and hit the returned Lord of the North in the chest. I couldn't remember throwing it. Yet, I didn't regret it.

"I think my permission matters most, sir," I said, standing. Despite his apparent disregard for me, I mattered.

His shocked gaze swung to me. Yolk dripped from his neckcloth onto his coat.

Several of the servants looked at me with rounded eyes as well. Of course, I'd shocked them. One of our rank did not disobey the Lord of the North or, at least, didn't lob an egg at him. The assistant cook moved forward to offer him a cloth to clean up. He accepted the rag.

"Sit," he said in an authoritative voice that rang in the kitchen.

While he looked down at the mess I'd made of his shirt, I ignored his command and marched from the kitchen toward the hall. I was wrong to think I could reside here. Wrong to think I could avoid my feelings of resentment and mistrust for him or that I might avoid him entirely.

"Benella!"

Anger laced his voice, sending a chill through me. My pulse leapt, and I instinctively lifted my skirts and ran. Egrit barely twisted out of my way near the laundry room.

Behind me, he yelled, asking which way I'd gone. I needed to leave. Quickly.

I slid into the entry where a weathered butler stood beside the door.

"Open the door," I said as I raced toward the man. His black eyes widened, and I immediately knew him. "Mr. Crow, open the damn door."

He hurriedly tugged it open. Just a few hand spans, but it was enough for me to squeeze through before the Liege Lord raced into the room.

"Why did you let her out?" I heard him demand as he pulled the door open.

"Because she was trying to escape you, sir."

I kept running but almost laughed. The servants who'd been enchanted had learned well.

Without warning, an arm encircled my waist, and I found myself tumbling forward. Something pressed against my back, and I turned in midair.

Facing the sky, I landed on something soft. Him.

I scrambled off and backed away a few steps as he slowly climbed to his feet. Poised to run, I glared at him.

"Why are you always throwing food at me?" he asked, his face red.

"You deserved it," I said, my temper freeing my tongue. He deserved far more than a lobbed egg.

His eyes flashed, and he took a step toward me. I backed up a step. He stopped his advance and threw his hands in the air.

"Why are you acting as if you fear me now?"

I almost snorted. When had I ever let fear rule me?

"How should I act?"

His expression softened.

"The same as you always have."

This time I did snort. "I thought you didn't like me throwing food."

He relaxed his stance. "You are correct. Act the same as you always have with the exception of the food throwing. Stop that."

"I cannot act the same. I am not the same person and neither are you. I thought I knew you, but I do not."

He frowned at me. "What do you mean?"

Bitterly, I eyed him. "The beast I'd grown fond of growled at me, ranted at me, and clawed through doors to get to me. He fed me. Cared for me. The Liege Lord stood in the doorway of the bakery and did nothing when that pig of a man rutted over me."

He paled and reached for me. I pulled back, and he dropped his hand.

"I am still that beast. Only Rose's restraining hand kept me from—" He closed his eyes briefly. "Benella, I wanted to kill him for touching you."

I struggled not to scoff.

He studied my unforgiving expression for a moment then took a slow breath.

"I need you here," he said. "I'm barely in control. Rose is watching me. She doubts I can be a lord in truth."

He needed my help, just as the beast had, but the pity I'd felt for the lonely beast didn't pertain to the man before me. I didn't want to help the Liege Lord. Yet, I knew I could give only one answer. For my father's sake and to avoid destitution, I had to agree.

"Of course I will help you, my Lord."

He stepped close again, and I quickly backed away several steps.

"Why do you keep doing that?" he asked, anger flashing in his eyes.

"It is not proper to stand too close to a servant. Haven't you learned anything?" I glanced at the lower windows of the manor, glad for the several faces that peeked out at us.

He followed my gaze and growled but kept his distance.

"We have more to discuss. Come to my study when you've finished your meal." Then, he stomped back inside.

I chose to walk around to the kitchen door. My heavy heart dragged my feet and slowed my progress. Seeing him had shocked me. And I realized my affection for the beast hadn't disappeared with the dear creature. Yet, it didn't extend to the man, either.

When I returned to the table, Father looked up from his eggs and studied me with a slight smile on his lips.

"How did your talk go?"

"Well, I'm not sure we ever got to the point of his request. He wants me to go to his study after I've finished eating."

"You have egg in your hair," Egrit said as she passed me.

AFTER WASHING IN THE LAUNDRY, I made my way to the library. Lord Ruhall paced in his study. As soon as I entered, he turned toward me. Some of his agitation faded as I approached.

"Sit," he said.

"Do you ever tire of giving commands?" I asked as I sat. Behind me, he closed the study doors.

"No."

He walked around my chair to stand in front of me. He still moved with the grace I'd grown accustomed to, walking with more of a prowl than a stride.

"Is it different? As a man?" I asked before I could stop myself.

"Yes. Uncomfortable, truthfully. I had more freedom before. Everything feels so restrained now. Not just my clothes, or how I move, but my own skin."

"How old were you when you were enchanted?"

"No more than twenty-three," he said.

"You are over seventy years old. Of course you'll feel a little strained." He grunted, but I caught the amused twinkle in his eyes so like the twinkle the beast had in his eyes in the weeks before I was taken. I felt an ache in my middle at the sight.

"Of what did you wish to speak?" I asked, not wanting to spend more time than necessary with him.

He leaned back against his desk and studied me for several long moments. I fought to remain still under his scrutiny. Finally, he sighed.

"I think estate concerns are the safest subject for the time being. As you suggested, I read up on farming and contacted your friend, Henick, whom you shall never kiss again, by the way."

My eyebrows shot up, but he continued without pause.

"There is no hope for planting any of the overgrown fields this year, but there are many ways to prepare them for next year. I need you to listen to my plans and point out any flaws."

He explained that he'd harvested several bags of primrose from the lands and contracted with the local candle maker for scented candles. He also contacted the traveling merchant to establish a permanent trade route, though he didn't state what he planned to trade.

For the candles that the candle maker had created from the flowers, the merchant paid the estate half of what was owed in gold and half in goats. The twenty goats now grazed in the overgrown fields, helping to prepare the ground for spring.

The remaining gold had been used to hire three cooks, two housemaids, five workers, a butler, a teacher, and a man of estate.

"Why three cooks?"

"I would slowly starve if I were left to feed myself."

The memory of the beast dropping eggs on the floor pressed against me, and I frowned. I didn't want reminders.

"I'm concerned with the expense. Surely one cook can handle simple meals through the summer."

"What of preparing food stores for the winter?" He tilted his head, appearing truly interested in my thoughts.

I recalled all the work Bryn did for the four of us and adjusted my thinking.

"Two cooks perhaps, but certainly not three. What are the five workers doing?"

"Two are clearing the drive so wagons with supplies can pass. Swiftly is repairing the stables. And the other two are gathering and re-sowing the seeds from the primrose to expand the field for next spring."

"How many horses do you have?"

"None yet."

"What of the one..." I couldn't finish the question. The image of Swiftly bringing me home in a horse drawn carriage also called to mind the baker. Lord Ruhall seemed to read my mind.

"Borrowed," he said quietly.

I struggled to think of something else.

"Have Swiftly help with the drive. With three there, as soon as it's passible, all five can work on the seeds. Re-sowing will give the greatest return next year. A horse, if you obtain one, can wait for stables to be repaired."

He rubbed his jaw as he listened intently.

"And having two maids seems extravagant when not much of the manor is being used," I said.

"But it will be soon. Some of the rooms haven't been touched in fifty years."

"Why a butler and a teacher?"

"Because they were enchanted with me. I owe them employment for as long as they want it."

I nodded in agreement.

"Is there anything else, then?" I asked, ready to leave.

"Yes. Konrall is missing a baker now. Going to the Water will be a hardship on many. I've contacted the bakers in the Water. Bryn and Edmund will be coming to take over the bakery. I thought you'd want to know."

Bryn's rejection still stung too deeply to feel any happiness for her opportunity. I inclined my head in acknowledgement and stood at the same time he straightened from the desk. The move brought us close. His breath fanned my face for a moment. Then, he leaned in as if to kiss me. I turned my head.

"I'm not here for that kind of help," I said. "I never was."

He sighed.

"Come back tomorrow morning to discuss more. You'll take your old room. It's the only one still ready."

I hurried away.

THE ROOM WAS JUST as I'd left it with the exception of the wardrobe. Two dresses waited within it, obviously meant for me. Pretty, yet practical creations made by real hands. I touched the taupe material of the first dress as I tried to understand the turn my life had taken yet again.

The Liege Lord confused me. I understood he depended on me to continue helping him. I could even accept the dresses as a gift of thanks. But why place me in this room? I could easily clean and air out another one for myself. And why had he moved so close to me in the study? Did he think I could continue with the physical side of the relationship I'd had with the beast? My breast tingled at the thought while my stomach lurched in a sickening way, giving me mixed signals.

I understood my reaction. Although I'd liked everything the beast had done, I had not liked what the baker had tried. Fornication wasn't for me. Perhaps if the beast were still here, I might eventually feel differently. However, if he were still here, I wouldn't have suffered the baker's touch at all.

I sighed and moved around the room, looking for something that might distract me from my dark thoughts.

Egrit saved me from boredom by knocking on the door a few minutes later.

"I'm happy you came," she said, stepping into the room. "Your father sent me with a message that he's left to settle your home in the Water."

I nodded, and she hesitated.

"Do you need anything?" she asked.

"No. Wait, yes. A way to occupy my time."

She grinned at me.

"I'm to clean the top floor and attic. Would you like to help?"

The thought of staying in my room for hours with nothing to do had me quickly agreeing. We walked to a dark and dusty section of a seldom used inner hall on the other side of the manor.

"Anything not of practical use or of sentimental value, we're to place in the main hall for trade," she said as she led me to a staircase I'd never discovered. Our skirts cleaned the cobwebs from the steps as we ascended.

"Most of the rooms up here are guest rooms and are seldom used, so very little should have sentimental value."

Dust danced in a beam of light that pierced the dirty pane of the nearest window. I sneezed twice and followed Egrit into the first room. We tried not to disturb anything until we had a window open. With the breeze, we started cleaning and sorting.

We finished two rooms by dinner. I grabbed a quick bite to eat from the kitchen, washed up in the laundry, then eagerly sought my bed before the sun fully set.

During the night, a sound woke me, sending me into a panic; I'd never learned of Tennen's fate.

"Shhh," a familiar voice whispered. The bed dipped, and a strong arm curved around me.

I froze for a moment then relaxed at the feel of fingers gently working my braid free. I kept my eyes closed and imagined the beast next to me.

Comforted, I drifted back to sleep.

A KNOCK WOKE me a second before Egrit opened my door. I sat up quickly, remembering the beast's visit, and turned to view the empty bed next to me. Not the beast, I thought. Alec. No, the Liege Lord. I wondered what it meant that he'd come to me at all. Did he still have trouble sleeping, even after the removal of the enchantment? If not that, then what? If he sought to use me again, he would be disappointed.

"Are you all right?" Egrit asked.

"Yes. It's just odd being here again," I said, slipping from the bed.

My dress from the day before waited draped over a chair. Dust streaked it, but I wasn't about to dirty another dress when we would be cleaning more rooms today.

"I'll leave you to dress," she said, walking to the bed. She set a napkin on the cover. "I brought you something to eat." She left the room and closed the door.

I quickly tossed aside my nightgown and slipped the dress over my head. Straightening the bedcover, I eyed the honeyed biscuit and wished for the magical trays the beast used to leave me. But, not one to spurn food in any form, I grabbed the biscuit as soon as the bed was made and took a bite on my way out the door.

When I located Egrit, she was already busy in a new room. I found cleaning a tedious chore best avoided under normal conditions. That we cleaned rooms untouched these last fifty years turned tedium into an exercise of willful perseverance.

Egrit and I had managed to complete two rooms before Father found me.

"Would you have time to meet in his Lordship's study for the midday meal?"

I had no wish to see his Lordship; yet, the need for air not clouded with dust had me glancing at Egrit.

"Go," she said. "I'll find my own food and meet with you here when we're both finished."

I nodded and left the room with Father.

"You seem to have found a way to keep yourself busy," he said.

"Yes. I can see now why two maids are needed."

Father made a noise between agreement and amusement.

"Lord Ruhall dismissed the other this morning."

Poor Egrit, I thought. Then realized I should have thought poor me for I certainly would not leave Egrit alone to deal with those rooms.

"Are you happy here?" Father asked as we descended to the second floor. "I could still seek employment elsewhere."

I loved him so much for the offer.

"I am content," I said, though I wasn't.

I followed Father toward the library. My nerves wound tightly as we neared. I swallowed hard as we entered the library and crossed the rugs to the study. Inside, a tray waited on a small table. Lord Ruhall sat behind his desk, reading something. He didn't look up at our arrival.

His dark head of hair was so dissimilar to the shaggy coat of the beast. Yet, I found similarity in the position in which he held himself in as he read. The connection brought an ache to my middle, and I had to look away.

"Sit, Benella," my father said. "I'd prefer you didn't touch the food." He winked at me and brought me my plate.

I sat and listened as Father and Lord Ruhall began to discuss estate accounts over our meal. Besides the maid, he'd let go one of the cooks as I'd suggested. The benign conversation and Father's presence eased my mind over the possible reasons Lord Ruhall had asked for my attendance. I remained quiet, enjoying the break and the food, and as soon as I swallowed my last bite, I excused myself.

Egrit had already returned to cleaning on the third floor when I arrived.

We finished four rooms that day, and my back ached when I made my way to my room. Dust coated my skin, and my stomach begged for dinner, but I didn't care. I barred both doors, stripped from my gown, ran the washrag over my face and arms, then crawled into bed.

Sleep claimed me quickly.

Again a noise woke me, the slight rattle of the door and a soft curse followed by silence. I smiled sadly and closed my eyes against the tears that wanted to run down my cheeks. I missed the beast.

MY DAYS SETTLED INTO A ROUTINE. Egrit and I continued to clear four rooms a day, I ate an amiable meal with Father and Lord Ruhall midday, and Lord Ruhall quietly tried my doors each night.

The pile in the main hall grew and shrunk as carts came and

hauled away things for trade. Spare chairs from already over furnished rooms, a few mirrors where there were duplicates, scented candles—many, many scented candles—rugs from rooms where they overlapped; I even placed a few questionable portraits depicting women in various nude positions on the pile. Egrit said nothing as I rid the manor of them.

The first week expired with little notice as everyone worked from dawn to dusk. On the following day, I went to join Lord Ruhall and Father for the midday meal and arrived before Father. Lord Ruhall sat behind his desk as usual but set his book aside as soon as I entered. He didn't mention my locked doors and kept the conversation strictly estate related as we waited for my father to join us.

Thankfully, Father didn't leave us waiting long.

"The third cart just left. The estate now has three hundred twenty-three gold, sir," Father said as he came into the room. "There were some portraits of value that the merchant was too eager to take. Egrit bargained the price higher than I would have thought to go."

"Family portraits?" Lord Ruhall asked, concerned.

A choked noise escaped me.

"I should hope not," I said.

"Ah." He changed the subject. "Now, what to do with that amount?" he said, looking at me. It was the first time in a week he'd directed a question to me.

I took a moment to gather my thoughts.

"The primrose seeds have been harvested and re-sown, and the drive has been cleared," I said. "I suggest bringing one hand inside. Egrit and I could use someone to carry the heavier items down the stairs. Then, set the other four to haying. There is enough time to put up a good supply for winter to allow for a horse or two, which we will need for tilling fields in spring."

"The estate records did show a savings by planting our own crops. Do you have a different suggestion, Benard?" he asked, turning to my father.

"I think Benella's suggestion the wisest choice and can offer nothing better than the purchase of a horse or two with that amount." My father glanced at me with a smile.

Lord Ruhall agreed to my plan with one exception. All five workers would attend the fields, and he would help clear the top floor. My back didn't care who helped so long as Egrit and I didn't have to carry anything more down the stairs.

However, my easy agreement to his assistance came back to haunt me the following day. Often, when I looked up from whatever task occupied me, I found him watching with a nearly indecipherable expression. At times, it hinted at anger and expectation. At others, remorse. He was courteous and respectful toward Egrit and cautiously cool around me.

I could find no fault in his behavior, yet it angered me. My conversation with Henick echoed in my ears. Inside, I had changed. A bitterness existed where none had before, and I had no idea what to do with it. So I sought jobs that would keep me away from his company as he walked to and fro, bringing items to the main entry.

Egrit and I were working together in one of the smaller guest rooms to hang a rug out the window to shake the dust from it.

"We might be better off rolling them up and taking them all outside for a thorough airing," Egrit said, eyeing the rug. Dust still stuck to it.

I nodded. I didn't want to carry the thing down the stairs, but holding that much weight out the window strained my back fiercely.

Behind us, I heard footsteps on the wood floor.

"It's time to eat," Lord Ruhall said.

"A moment, please," I said, helping Egrit pull the rug back in.

He waited by the door as she and I worked together to roll the rug. When I stepped toward him, he motioned for me to lead. We remained silent as we walked the halls.

In the study, Father waited for us. Lord Ruhall sat behind his desk as Father said there was nothing new to report. Our polite meal felt strained without estate affairs to discuss.

"Perhaps we don't need to meet as often?" I said after swallowing a bite of stew.

Lord Ruhall flushed noticeably. Father looked down, keeping busy with his meal as the Lord of the manor shot me a disapproving look.

"We will continue to meet as we have."

I nodded and concentrated on my own food, and as soon as I finished, excused myself.

ANOTHER TWO WEEKS saw the top floor cleared, the purchase of two horses, and the estate coffers steady at three hundred gold. The men worked to repair the stables with a few leaving to hunt. Stag, boar, and fowl occasionally lay on the butcher block in the kitchen as the two cooks put away stores for winter. Per Lord Ruhall's orders, they kept meals simple as their days filled with storage preparations.

With the top floor cleared, I convinced Egrit that we needed a day of rest. Before the house woke, she met me in the laundry where I had two fishing poles waiting; the same poles the beast and I had used so long ago.

"Are you certain he won't mind?" Egrit asked, doubt lacing her voice.

"I'm certain." We'd made significant progress, and we deserved a day of rest after the weeks we'd worked.

Egrit and I left through the laundry door. The light breeze teased stray strands of hair back from my face. Not a cloud decorated the sky. It was the perfect day to be outdoors. I stretched my stride, enjoying the walk. Egrit talked of her man, Tam, and the money they were saving to purchase a home off the estate once they wed.

"How old are you?" I asked. She seemed so young to be thinking of marriage.

"I was seventeen when I was enchanted. So, I must be sixty-seven now," she said with a laugh.

I smiled but said nothing. Even if she hadn't been enchanted, she wasn't too young. And neither was I. My seventeenth birthday was not far away. So much had happened so quickly that I felt much older in many ways. Still, marriage...I wasn't sure I would ever be ready for that. Yet, most girls my age were already planning weddings. If a girl saw eighteen unwed, it usually meant she had no hope of marrying. Out of love, my father had held on to us far past when he should have. I wondered what my life would have been like if he'd wed us off sooner.

Egrit didn't say anything as the silence stretched. We passed the newly planted fields and crossed many more that still needed attention.

When we reached the wall, I looked up at the tree.

"Can you climb?"

Egrit snorted. "I was a tree, living among trees for fifty years. I can climb."

"Toss your boots over first. You'll want to put them on once we reach the other side."

We sat on the grass to unlace our boots. In no time, we were up the tree and climbing down the other side of the wall. The wind on my face and rocks under my hands steadied me and quieted some of the unrest that had been building for days.

We spent the morning by the stream in the same spot where the beast had laid me back on the banks. My mind dwelled on the memory, and Egrit, sensing my pensive mood, left me to my thoughts.

In truth, I wanted the beast to return, and it shamed me. He'd spent so many years punished for his youthful pride and arrogance. Yet, I missed the beast's unpredictable moods, zealous attention, and his comforting presence.

My feelings toward Lord Ruhall were more undecided. He said Rose watched him still, judging his actions as Lord. I watched him, too. He left the maids alone and attended to estate business. His only overture to a female had been to me when he entered my room the first night I had returned. But, he'd done nothing more than lay beside me.

During the time we had spent together clearing the guest rooms, his watchful, aloof attitude had remained consistent with the man who'd stood in the doorway and watched the baker's thankfully pathetic attempts to compromise me. Had it been the beast, I knew without a doubt he would have charged into the room and ripped the baker from me. The enchantress wouldn't have been able to hold the beast back.

Egrit's excited squeal pulled me from my musings.

"What do I do?" she cried, holding the pole tight, fighting the fish.

I wished I could ask her the same. Instead, I moved to help her. She was thrilled at her first catch and swore she would take her man fishing if I would allow them the use of the poles. We stayed on the banks until six fat fish decorated the string. Our stomachs begged for food, and we gathered our poles to head back.

We rounded the estate before the sun hit its zenith and entered an empty kitchen. The butcher block waited, clean and empty, which I found unusual; one of the men typically returned with something by now. I laid the fish out, content to let the cooks clean them.

From somewhere in the manor, I heard a familiar, raised voice. Both Egrit and I shared a worried look before we hurried down the hall.

"Then look again," Lord Ruhall roared at the staff, who stood in line before him.

He spun at the sound of our steps. His red, angry face surprised me as our gazes met.

"Where have you been?" he asked, stalking toward me.

Egrit made a move to step in front of me, but I firmly grabbed her wrist and held her back.

"You wish to speak with me, my Lord?" I emphasized his title, trying to remind him he was no longer the beast, though his current tone and the prowling steps he took did remind me of the dear creature.

"I asked where you were." Despite his very human form, he growled.

Ridiculously, I almost smiled that he thought to intimidate me.

"Thank you for asking, my Lord. I shall certainly accompany you to your study to explain."

His eyes narrowed. He cocked his head to the side and studied me for a moment before waving for me to lead the way. I gave a gracious nod and leisurely moved past him. The servants all watched me with worry and trepidation. I stopped before the head cook, giving her a calm smile.

"There are several trout on the block. They still need cleaning."

She frowned but nodded slowly before she glanced at the man who impatiently waited just a step away.

"Thank you," I said.

He followed me through the halls, the angry click of his shoes puzzling me. I sincerely doubted he minded that Egrit and I had taken a morning from cleaning when we'd dedicated so many days to the task already. What then had made him so angry?

I walked through the study door and stopped in the middle of the room, preferring not to sit just in case I needed to leave quickly. The door closed. He walked around me and stood behind his desk.

"Well?" he said.

"We went fishing. I would think that obvious after telling the cook about the trout," I said with an arched brow.

His face, which had recovered its natural color, flushed again.

"My Lord, Egrit and I have worked tirelessly since I arrived. My back needed a rest days ago. Egrit would never complain, but I'm sure hers did as well. Certainly you cannot begrudge us a morning to relax. It wasn't a completely idle activity either; we brought back fish."

He looked heavenward.

"Fish." His regard settled on me once more. "You think this is about you fishing?" He rubbed a hand over his face.

"I honestly have no idea what would cause you, the Liege Lord, to start yelling at the staff in a most unbecoming manner and then to turn on me as soon as I walk into the room, in front of an already shocked staff," I said with annoyance. "You said Rose is watching you. What do you think she made of such beastly behavior?"

He had the grace to cringe. "I was less concerned about her than I was about you when I woke to find you missing."

"First, how did you know I was missing unless you tried to enter my room," I said in a harsh whisper. He snarled in return. "Second, my absence should not concern you. You hired my father, not me, if I recall. I should be free to move about as I please. I am under no obligation to stay locked in my room any longer. And don't even think about taking Egrit to task for some idle time. You owe her that and much more."

He opened his mouth, no doubt to shout back at me, when the door burst open. My father stood there looking flustered and slightly embarrassed.

"You summoned me, my Lord?"

Behind him, I caught sight of Egrit leaving the library.

"Father, you are just in time," I said, calming myself. "The boorish man behind the desk has spent too many years without the counsel of his father. Perhaps you can still help him despite his dotage."

My father's brows rose, and his gaze darted to Lord Ruhall, who watched me with a clenched jaw. I turned away from both men and stormed out the door.

"She gets her stubbornness from me and her intelligence from her mother," my father said.

His words made me pause in the library, just out of sight. I would argue that I had his intelligence.

"Books, the written word, captivate me. But I forgot them all when my wife first spoke to me. We were wed twelve years before she passed. I learned a few things in those years. When a woman leaves a room in a storm, best wait till the thunder fades before you walk out lest you risk being struck by lightning. Or worse, a frying pan."

Lord Ruhall said something too quietly for me to hear. With a smile, I left him to my father's sage advice.

CHAPTER
THREE

Just outside the library, the entire staff waited. Egrit flashed me a relieved smile.

"All is well," I assured them. "Mrs. Wimbly, the fish would be an excellent midday meal if there's time." It would also serve as a reminder to Lord Ruhall.

"Egrit, you should watch how they are cleaned if you plan on fishing again in the future."

Egrit nodded and, with a smile, left with the frowning cook. The rest of the staff seemed reluctant to leave.

"Swiftly, how are the repairs on the stables coming along?"

"I would be happy to show you," he said. Mr. Crow opened the door for us. The other men followed.

Swiftly's explanation of the repairs claimed my attention for almost an hour. I hadn't yet read anything about building but planned to in the future. The calculations needed to brace a structure's roof correctly astounded me.

My father caught me just as I entered through the main doors.

"Stop provoking the Lord. As you reminded him, he is the Liege Lord," he said.

"Father, truly, my intent wasn't to provoke him when I left this morning. I only wanted some peace and relaxation. Even with his help carrying the heavy items, I still think I might start walking with a stoop soon."

"Daughter, for such an astute girl, your ability to observe and learn concerns me," he said with a frown.

"How so?" I tried to think of what I might have done to upset him.

"Think of the last time you disappeared from his manor, daughter. You worried him."

My mouth popped open, and I struggled with how I felt about what Father was hinting at. Lord Ruhall, the cold man, cared if I disappeared? No, not me, but two people under his protection.

"Mrs. Wimbly announced the meal is ready. I'll fetch the tray." With a shake of his head, my father walked toward the kitchen.

That left me to face Lord Ruhall alone while we waited for Father. It sat wrong that I needed to apologize for an idle day of fishing. With slow steps, I made my way to the study. Lord Ruhall's bent head did not lift when I entered. He continued to read from the open book before him.

His hand rubbed his forehead, and his hair sprouted about in disarray. The set of his shoulders, tense and pushed back, told me enough. He was still angry with me.

Ignoring the chairs my father and I usually took, I walked around the desk and rested a hand on his jacketed shoulder to gain the attention I knew he wouldn't otherwise give. He sighed and dropped his hand. Leaning back into his chair, effectively removing my touch, he met my gaze.

"I'm sorry. We didn't mean to concern you."

He closed his eyes, not saying anything.

"We were safe. The baker's gone." To me, he and Tennen were the only ones that posed a real threat, and Tennen wouldn't have tried anything with Egrit beside me.

Alec snorted and opened his eyes to glare at me.

"Safe? You think the baker is the only man to look at you with lust?"

I refrained from naming him as one of the men to do so. But, no, it hadn't been him. It had been the beast, my sweet Alec.

"Benella," he said, leaning forward. A noise from the door stopped him from reaching for me. My father cleared his throat and moved to the desk with the tray.

"Fish," he announced.

"Of course," Lord Ruhall murmured, looking at me with a shake of his head. "Next time you'd care to fish, please take Swiftly with you and leave word."

I nodded and moved to my usual chair, ready to discuss estate affairs.

CARRYING the tray to the kitchen, I found the cooks at the table, enjoying idle conversation. The assistant cook caught sight of me and quickly stood. I smiled a greeting and set the dirty dishes on the empty butcher block.

"No game today?" I asked as the assistant cook moved around me to start wash water.

"No," Mrs. Wimbly answered. "The hands were out looking for you."

"Not my best decision," I said with a cringe.

She continued to scowl at me. So, I tried changing the subject after a moment of silence.

"Have you explored the cold storage yet?"

"When we first arrived. There's still ice in it from the winter so we've been putting the extra goat milk there."

"Is there cream?" I asked excitedly. I'd read a bit about making butter and thought the process sounded interesting. The cost of butter being too high, it wasn't something Bryn used. Lard was less expensive and easier to obtain.

After a moment, Mrs. Wimbly nodded.

"Might we make butter?"

She gave me an odd look before answering.

"If there's time. There are several buckets still in cold storage. Enough for a bit of butter."

"How long does the milk stay good?" I asked.

"We've thrown out several already that went sour."

The waste brought to mind all the times my family had dined on fresh goat's milk and nothing else while living in Konrall.

"Let's skim the cream we need and pour what's left in a large barrel to be taken to the Water. There are people there who could use the surplus instead of wasting it," I said.

Her expression grew more indignant as I spoke, and I wondered at the cause. I seemed to have acquired a knack for upsetting those around me.

"I'll need to check with Lord Ruhall," she said.

"Of course," I agreed. I didn't think he would disagree with my plan, though. "Do you know how to make cheese?" I asked.

"Of course," she said as she gave me a hard look.

"I meant no disrespect to your skills," I quickly assured her. "I was only wondering if we should do so here or perhaps trade a portion of the milk to the cheese maker in the Water for premade cheese." I tilted my head. "What do you think is the best use of your time? Storing food for winter or cheese making?"

She studied me for a moment, most likely trying to gauge if I mocked her with my question. She heaved an aggravated breath and started to explain the process of making cheese. It fascinated me, of course. Soft cheese would be easy enough for us, but hard cheese would require more ingredients, time, and space to cure.

"So it's not the preparing time we need worry about, but the items we need to make it. What do you think of making the soft cheese and trading milk for the hard cheese?"

"We won't get much in return for the milk," she said. "At least, not the goat's milk."

I nodded, thinking of cows, but decided the expense not yet worth the return given the small staff we housed.

"Please let me know what Lord Ruhall says. I'm very interested in assisting," I added.

She gave a single, curt nod.

With Lord Ruhall still annoyed with me, Egrit missing—most likely cleaning, which I wasn't eager to resume—and Swiftly and his men busy with repairs, I had nothing to do to occupy myself. I hesitated in the kitchen while Mrs. Wimbly left, presumably to speak with Lord Ruhall.

The assistant cook watched me closely.

"If anyone is looking for me, please let them know I've gone to Konrall," I said, deciding to check if Bryn had yet moved to the bakery.

The last time I'd seen her, she'd called me a whore. Yet, I refused to believe she would do so again. In her heart, she couldn't really see me as a whore. Most likely, she'd been afraid of losing her position among the merchants of the Water. But she wasn't in the Water anymore. Konrall was different, and I needed to see her again so we could mend things between us.

The assistant cook nodded and watched me leave. I decided the people at the estate an odd bunch. They didn't know what to make of me. Neither did I. I wasn't a servant, but not a guest either since my father was employed there. Yet, I slept in the Lady's quarters. Obviously, I was a nuisance. It made me smile.

Birds sang along the dirt and pebble drive. I found myself missing the vines and dark mist. Though eerie, it had felt safe, like my own place to hide with only the beast to trouble me.

A wagon rumbled in the distance. I waited on the shoulder and smiled at Henick as he neared.

"Your timing is impeccable," I said with a laugh. He smiled in return and braked.

"It looks like I'm traveling the wrong direction, though," he said. The wagon pointed north toward the Water.

"It's not the ride I'm after as much as it is the news. Has Bryn settled in Konrall, yet?"

"Yes. A few days back. The smoke's been pouring from the bakery. The new baker makes a fine tart and cake. His bread's not bad either."

"How is Bryn?"

He shrugged and looked down at his hands. "I know she thought she would have a hard life with me. But I don't think it would have been any worse than a fancy baker's wife."

My heart went out to him. "Remember to watch for rainbows, Henick. It's what you deserve."

He looked up at me and gave a small smile.

"Are you well?" he asked.

It was my turn to shrug.

"I think I'm still broken inside. Too quick to anger at times. Too scornful at other times, though I try to keep that hidden."

He looked sad for me.

"What a pair we are," I said with a small smile. My mother once told me time changed everything. In that moment, I realized what she meant. Nothing ever stayed the same.

"If you visit your sister, I hope it's pleasant," he said, nodding farewell.

I waved him off and considered his comment. I hoped, by the end, I would be able to call the visit pleasant.

But it wasn't meant to be. As soon as I walked into the bakery, Bryn's welcoming expression closed.

"Get out," she hissed, coming around the counter. "Whore," she spat. Thankfully, there were no customers to witness her clasping my arm and tugging me toward the door.

"Bryn!" Bryn froze.

"Go upstairs and calm yourself. Perhaps think on the names you choose to use."

Bryn released me, and I turned to see Edmund standing in the doorway to the bakery. He looked quite angry, and with reason. Tennen stood just behind him.

Bryn paled, and a sob escaped her. My heart broke for her, despite her name calling.

"Go," Edmund said softly.

Tennen smirked as she ran up the stairs, and a fire lit inside of me.

I stalked around the counter and pushed past Edmund as I balled up my fist. Without hesitation, I struck Tennen. Again, it wasn't hard enough to bloody him as I wanted, but his head still moved from the blow.

He growled and stepped toward me, but Edmund stopped him with a hand on his chest.

"You used her then come in here to boast about it to her husband?" I said to Tennen. "Her only fault was to believe your intentions honest."

"You're a whore just like her," Tennen said.

Edmund's hand on Tennen's chest fisted then flew to connect with Tennen's jaw. Tennen grunted as the hit drove him back a step. Edmund managed what I hadn't the first time. He made Tennen bleed.

Tennen narrowed his eyes at the baker, but he didn't move to retaliate.

"Get out," Edmund said between gritted teeth.

Tennen narrowed his eyes.

"Remember what I said. I'll tell everyone." Then he left.

"Let me guess. Bread for life or he'll tell everyone he's the father of the babe?"

Edmund nodded.

"Don't give in. As soon as you do, they have you," I said, rubbing my hand. Hitting someone hurt.

"I know. His mother was already here to see me."

I shook my head, troubled that the smith had sent his wife out again.

"The last baker was not a good man. I hope you're better." I glanced at the stairs before meeting Edmund's gaze again. "I meant what I said. Bryn's shame was in trusting Tennen. I know she's not perfect. She's selfish and lied to you about the babe, but she has some good qualities as well."

"Name one," he said flatly.

I felt badly for him. I knew what it was like to discover people weren't who you thought they were.

"She can cook well. For a baker's wife that's a good thing," I said with a small smile.

He gave a short, derisive laugh, showing just how much he was hurting.

"Everything she's been through has been hard on her," I said. "I don't think she knows who she is yet. She's been what we needed her to be. If you can forgive her, I think she'll forgive herself and maybe find out who she can be."

He studied me for a moment then looked away.

"Did you need any bread today?" he asked after a moment.

"No, I was just here for a visit. Is business doing well?"

"Not very. People here do not have the coin they did in the Water."

"I hope your fortune changes soon."

He nodded, and I left with nothing more to say. I wished Bryn would stop her whore nonsense. As her husband pointed out, we both knew I was not the whore.

Outside, I caught sight of Tennen, pacing before the smithy. I groaned. Being with the beast had made me impulsive. I shouldn't have hit Tennen. I headed to the butcher's.

"Hello, sir," I said as I walked through the door.

"Benella!" The butcher's glad smile lightened my heart. "I thought we might not see you again. I heard your father is now employed with the returned Liege Lord," he said, wiping his hands on his apron.

"He is. I'd hoped to visit with Bryn, but she holds me accountable for what happened with the old baker."

He made a sound of disapproval as Tennen walked past the butcher's door.

"And, I need your help," I said softly.

"It seems so. Why does he have such an issue with you?"

"The old baker hurt others as well, not just me," I said quietly. "I saw something I shouldn't have. Tennen knows. I think the smith knows, too."

The butcher heaved a pitying sigh.

"How can I help?"

"Speak with Tennen while I slip out the back door? I just need a head start," I said with a confident smile.

"Perhaps you should mention this to your father," he said.

I nodded with no intention of doing so. After all that Tennen had done to me, I still didn't have the heart to punish Sara by telling all. She might be sent away with her husband who would hold her accountable or, worse, make her do the same thing in another village. No, the punishment should lie solely on Mr. Coalre. As far as the son...well, perhaps he could be apprenticed to the south. Somewhere near the baker.

Slipping through the curtain that led to the butcher's kitchen, I listened to the butcher cross the store and walk outside. I waited a few moments, then I peeked out the back door. Seeing nothing, I sprinted to the trees and used my old route past the cottage toward the estate. It didn't take long for Tennen to shout my name, but thankfully it was in the distance. Then he shouted for Splane. Neither of them would have a chance.

I grinned too soon.

Splane stepped out in front of me, knocking me to the ground. He looked behind me nervously, and Tennen shouted again.

"You better have her, Splane!"

Tennen sounded closer, and I scrambled to my feet.

Splane watched me, but I could see he was torn. His gaze shifted behind me and then toward the estate. No matter what he chose, he would face either the wrath of his brother or of the beast. No, not the wrath of the beast. The beast wasn't there anymore to protect me, and Splane's brother was just behind me.

Lifting my skirts high to free my legs, I made an obvious feint to the right. Splane widened his stance to block me as we eyed each other. I kicked out, clipping him sharply between the legs.

"Thank you for the target," I said as I took off, not staying to watch his slow fall to the ground.

Tennen yelled again, much closer this time.

I kept my skirts high and ran as I hadn't in a long time. My side ached by the time I reached the gates. I flew past a very surprised Swiftly. There was only one place I felt safe.

Mr. Crow opened the door before I reached it, my pounding

footfalls probably giving away my presence. I sprinted up the stairs into the dark interior and crashed into a solid chest with an "oof." Strong arms and a familiar scent wrapped around me. In that instant, I felt safe.

"What happened?" Lord Ruhall asked.

The sound of his voice ruined my illusion.

"A moment...please," I gasped, dropping my skirts and sliding from his arms. I leaned my hands on my knees as the pain in my side clawed its way into my lungs. I'd found in the past the position eased the pain.

Swiftly entered just then.

"Is she all right?" he asked.

"She's out of breath," Lord Ruhall said, still close. "What happened?" he repeated.

"I don't know, my Lord," Swiftly said. "She ran past me full out. I looked behind her but saw nothing. There was fear in her eyes, though," he added.

I struggled to force slower breaths, knowing it would win me more air than the gasps.

"I feared," I managed, "missing the meal."

"Benella," Lord Ruhall said with unmistakable warning.

Straightening with effort, I kept a bland expression.

"Did I already miss it?"

He rubbed a hand over his face and remained curiously quiet for a moment. He cleared his throat three times before he spoke in a slow, calm tone.

"Do you recall speaking with me just a few hours past?"

I nodded, wondering at his point.

"Then why did you leave the estate without taking Swiftly with you?"

"Ah! Not just for fishing then. Sorry about that," I said. I turned toward Swiftly. "I promise to take you with me next time I go to speak with my sister. We'll try not to discuss anything too embarrassing."

Swiftly looked slightly uncomfortable. His gaze darted to Lord Ruhall, whose eyes had closed. A red flush was making its way up his neck.

I took the opportunity to leave. Mr. Crow gave me a slight smile. Perhaps he was on my side after all.

I COLLAPSED ON MY BED, sweat soaking my back and face. How I wished for a magical bath to appear. I needed a long soak and to think. I'd never before felt so lost and confused.

Konrall still wasn't safe. Poor Sara was still being used by her husband. Bryn had turned her self-hatred on me. Blye wouldn't speak to me, either. The Whispering Sisters no longer offered peace and guidance. Aryana, herself, had betrayed me. And above all, I missed the beast. I still had my father, but he had been burdened too much already in his life by trying to protect his daughters. Where did that leave me? With no one to talk to. Alone with my confused thoughts. Wondering what I should do with myself.

I stood and wandered to the adjoining doors, opening them. He didn't have his side locked. The room looked the same. Smelled the same. I opened the door of his wardrobe. The same shirts hung there. I took one and left, closing the doors behind me.

Stripping from the gown, I washed with the cool water in the pitcher and changed into his shirt. With his smell wrapped around me, I crawled under the covers, ignoring the sun.

Nothing ever stayed the same. But tomorrow had to be better.

CHAPTER
FOUR

THE SOUND OF MY DOOR PULLED ME FROM A LIGHT, TROUBLED SLEEP where Tennen and Splane continued to chase me through the trees. Before I thought my dream reality, Alec spoke.

"Benella, are you awake?"

Had I actually slept, his soft words would not have disturbed me. Still, I pretended to sleep, hoping he would leave and wishing I had remembered to lock the door.

The mattress dipped as he sat next to me. His hands found my hair, undoing my braid, and the wood creaked as he leaned back against the headboard. His fingers combed through my long tresses and helped me forget the day's chase, the dream, and my troubles.

At some point, he stopped sitting beside me and slipped under the covers. I woke with his arm draped over my side and his hand splayed over the skin of my stomach under my shirt. His deep breathing told me he slept. Yet, I frowned. His smooth skin wasn't right. It made my skin crawl and my breathing shorten with dread.

I rolled to my stomach, seeking a more comfortable position while remembering the pleasant touch of the beast's fur on my skin and fell back to sleep.

EGRIT WOKE me with a chipper good morning. I burrowed deeper and refused to open my eyes. She went on, undeterred.

"You've slept long enough according to Lord Ruhall," she said with a laugh in her voice. "He's waiting for you in the study."

I groaned. Despite his warm presence, I hadn't slept well. My dreams had returned to Tennen chasing me and the beast rescuing me.

"Please extend my regrets," I said, pulling the covers higher. "I'm ill disposed." To sunlight and men, I thought.

There was a moment of silence.

"I'll leave the tray. If you feel better, you'll want to eat."

She left the room, and I remained in bed. My problem was two-fold. I missed the beast, and I missed the direction my life had while I was helping him. My father's employment by Lord Ruhall was perfect. For him. Not for me. Seeing Lord Ruhall just made me miss the beast more.

Perhaps it was time I ventured into the world on my own. The thought terrified me as much as it did excite me. Yet, I wanted to feel useful again.

With a sigh, I rolled toward the window and opened my eyes. Lying in bed wouldn't change my future.

I washed with the cool water in the basin then removed a plain gown from the wardrobe. I dressed slowly, thinking of the possibilities. They were too far and too uncertain. I needed to speak with my father. While I refused to burden him with my troubles in Konrall, I saw no reason not to seek his guidance regarding options for my future. In the past, his counsel always proved helpful.

I left my room and sought him out in the library. He had a small desk set near the fire where he liked to work. If he wasn't there, he tended to hunt the kitchen for food or monitor the progress on the barn.

When I stepped through the library doors, he looked up from his ledger and smiled at the sight of me. He stood as I approached and leaned in to kiss my cheek.

"We missed you at breakfast. Are you feeling better?"

"I feel fine, Father. It's my thoughts that plague me."

He motioned for me to take a seat then sat beside me.

"Tell me," he said.

I clasped my hands and thought for a moment.

"I've lost my purpose and am struggling to think of a new one. Bryn and Blye have both found their way. I'm old enough to find my own." I hesitated for a moment. "I'm thinking of leaving." I watched his expression, afraid what I said might have hurt him.

"Leaving?" He looked troubled and glanced at the study door, which stood open, then back at me. "Do you seek my blessing or my advice?"

"Advice."

He sat back and stared at the flames for a while. I waited patiently.

"I believe the suggestion I would offer you now, might be selfish. I don't want to lose you. May I have some time to think on this?"

"Of course." I kissed his cheek. "That's why I came to you. As much as I want to leave, I want to stay," I said, standing.

My father remained there watching the flames as I walked away. I wandered the halls for a while, letting my feet choose their own path. Eventually, I found myself back in my room. I opened the window to let in the fresh air and leaned against the sill.

A crash followed by a string of cursing came from the adjoining room. I recognized Lord Ruhall's voice and walked to the door. Something hit it with a thud and fell to the floor on the other side. I laid my hand on the door and smiled. It reminded me of the time I'd locked myself in his room. But the beast was gone, leaving behind a man I didn't understand or very much like. Straightening my shoulders, I knocked.

The room on the other side silenced then the door swung open. Lord Ruhall's disheveled appearance shocked me. He'd ripped the seam on the right shoulder of his jacket, his neckcloth hung askew, and his hair stood on end. His chest rose and fell with his rapid breathing.

"You wear my shirt to bed then tell your father you want to leave. Why?"

I blinked at him. I'd forgotten about the shirt when he'd entered the room last night.

"I wore the shirt because I miss him," I admitted, tearing my gaze from his.

"Him?" he said with a confused frown.

A brief small smile lifted my lips, a sad offering of amusement.

"The beast. The very creature chosen to be your punishment, the one you loathed...the one I want back." I kept my eyes on the ground, unable to look at him to see what he thought of me.

"Why?" He didn't sound angry or upset anymore.

"He growled, threw fits, chased me about the estate, made all manner of inappropriate demands of me, but he also did something else."

"What?"

My chest ached with the truth.

"He made me love him," I said, finally meeting his eyes.

Joy lit his face, then after meeting my sad gaze, a somber frustration crept in.

"You stubborn girl," he growled. "I am still that beast!"

"No, you are not." It hurt speaking the words aloud. My heart ached with what I'd lost. The man before me was but a poor replacement for the beast who'd stolen my heart.

"You growl and yell at servants, yet you are stuffy and detached. The beast with all his anger and frustration didn't hold back his feelings. Well, not much," I added, recalling the many times he had in fact shown restraint.

"Are you calling me cold?" he asked, appalled.

I considered how he had stood in the doorway when he'd found me with the baker, how he'd helped Egrit and I clear the top floor, and how he'd sat through so many meals with me, speaking of nothing but estate affairs. His tantrum on the other side of the door just now wasn't his usual behavior.

"Yes, I think I am."

"I see," he said.

I expected him to walk out the door. Instead, he turned the lock.

"Sir?" I asked hesitantly.

"Alec," he corrected, removing his jacket.

"What are you doing?" I asked as he turned and stalked toward me.

"Changing your opinion of me." With a slight smile, he reached up and unknotted his neckcloth.

Panic flared in my chest as I understood his meaning, and I started to back away. He caught my wrist.

"I don't think so."

His thumb gently stroked the sensitive skin protecting my pulse, and my heart started to beat in fear.

"Please don't do this." My breaths started coming too fast. I felt the baker's weight pushing down on me again. "I won't let you do this." Panic and desperation pitched my voice.

Horror filled Alec's expression.

"Benella, no. I would never..."

Instead of stepping away, he wrapped his arms around me, pinning me to his chest.

"Never," he whispered in my ear as I shook.

He made no further move, other than to run his hand over my hair. I breathed in the smell of him and closed my eyes, imagining I had the beast back. He held me tightly until the shaking stopped.

When he pulled back, he looked as lost as I felt. He dropped his hands to his sides and stared at me.

"I don't know how to prove who I am."

"You don't need to."

"I don't need to because you think you already know." His gaze reflected the pain I'd caused him. He shook his head and left, slamming his door.

For some reason, my eyes began to water.

I hoped Father wouldn't need too long to consider my plight.

AN HOUR LATER, someone knocked, disturbing my musings. I opened the door and found my father standing just outside. Hope lit me from the inside, despite his grave expression.

"I cannot find Lord Ruhall. Do you know where he might be?"

Lord Ruhall? Keeping my disappointment hidden, I answered.

"Did you try his room?"

"Yes. Right after you left, a boy delivered this. I've been looking for him since then." Father handed me a letter.

I FULLY EXPECT you to hold with tradition and open the manor for the harvest feast with invitations sent to appropriate guests only. I will be watching. ~Rose

· · ·

"Harvest feast?" I said, looking up at Father.

"I don't have the details of what this means but with only three hundred gold to last until spring, I cannot see how the estate might host any feast. That she wants invitations sent…"

Invitations typically went to those of wealth. Those equal to Lord Ruhall's standing. For two heartbeats, happiness filled me. It was impossible to do, just as my father had suggested. The beast would return.

Guilt killed my brief joy. No matter how much I missed the beast, I could not condemn Alec to a fate he did not deserve. He had paid for his past sins and truly seemed to have learned from them. He didn't chase after women, drink, or gamble; and he was working hard to amend the poor affairs of his estate. He had suffered enough. Rose's game needed to end. And my father deserved steady employment without the threat of enchantment.

I tapped the letter against my palm with resolve and started to consider options. The three hundred gold currently noted in the ledgers needed to remain there for the estate to endure over winter and prosper once more in spring. Could a feast be hosted without spending estate gold?

"We need more information to know exactly what this feast entails. I'll find Mr. Crow; you keep searching for Lord Ruhall."

With purpose, I strode from the room.

Mr. Crow proved as hard to find as Lord Ruhall. His usual post by the door was vacant as were the library and study. I left Father in the study to wait for Lord Ruhall while I continued my search. Near the kitchen, I heard voices.

"If the food preparation is complete, then use your time to polish the silver. Idle hands will not be tolerated here."

"Yes, sir," Mrs. Wimbly said with a bob of her head as I entered. Her gaze met mine, and I suspected we had the same thought. My hands, when idle, seemed tolerated well enough.

Looking away, I spotted a kettle on the block and realized I'd missed breakfast and the midday meal. My stomach rumbled hungrily but I knew I would not be welcomed to eat just then. After Mrs. Wimbly turned away to find an appropriate task for herself, I moved toward Mr. Crow.

"May I speak with you?"

"Certainly, Miss Hovtel," he said formally.

He walked me to the cook's personal room. The cookbooks that the beast and I had combed through were missing, the floor was scrubbed, and the window was open to let in the fresh air. Mr. Crow sat behind the desk.

"Is this your study now?"

"Yes. I made the mistake of ignoring the day-to-day activities of the staff in the past and will not repeat it."

I wondered how an office in the kitchen helped that, but didn't ask.

"Can you tell me about the harvest feast that used to be held here?"

"Large affairs that stopped long before Lady Ruhall left for the South, just after the current Lord Ruhall invited several...unsavory guests."

That explained Rose's note about appropriate guests.

"How many guests usually attended? Were certain families typically invited?"

"The harvest feast wasn't as formal as the winter feast. The doors opened to whichever locals Lady Ruhall saw fit to invite. Music and dancing filled the ballroom, and the tables groaned with food in the dining room." He sighed and looked out the window for a moment. "So many looked forward to the harvest feast. It was a time when the Lord and Lady did not stand above the rest. They joined them, listened to their problems, made merry with them. From Konrall to the Water, everyone looked forward to seeing an invitation delivered to their door."

I withheld my cringe. Though inviting locals meant a less grand affair, it also possibly meant a larger number of guests.

"An estimate, Mr. Crow. How many guests do you recall hosting?"

"As many as would fill the ballroom."

I sat in the chair across from his desk and set the letter before him. Sharing the information was necessary as it affected them all.

"Mr. Crow, Rose is placing a condition on the estate's continued freedom. The tradition of the harvest feast must renew. When does the feast typically take place?"

Mr. Crow paled.

"After the harvests are complete. Another three or four weeks, perhaps."

Four weeks. Three hundred coin. I bit my lip, thinking.

"How many servants did you have then? Twenty, wasn't it?" I said, answering myself.

"Yes. That included the cooks, livery men, housemaids, and myself."

The hopelessness in his tone caught my attention.

"Mr. Crow, do not give up before we start. We need an accounting of the stores. Every last thing from milk to wine, from wilted carrots to salted pork," I said, standing.

"Where will you be, Miss?"

"The ballroom."

I left the room and called for Egrit.

"I sent her to milk the goats," Mrs. Wimbly said, sounding impatient.

"Please send Swiftly or Tam to milk the goats and have Egrit meet me in the ballroom," I said as I walked toward the hall. I stopped, suddenly. "Oh, did Lord Ruhall say anything about the excess milk?"

She raised her nose a notch in the air.

"I have not yet approached him. Who are you to say—"

"Mrs. Wimbly," Mr. Crow said, walking from his study. "Afford Miss Hovtel the same respect you would afford Lord Ruhall or you will find yourself without employment."

His words surprised me. I wasn't the only one. Mrs. Wimbly looked shocked, and it took a moment for her to give the barest of nods.

Mr. Crow turned his attention to the assistant cook.

"Kara, show me the cellars. We need an accounting."

I was glad he wasn't giving up.

"Mr. Crow, have all the milk from the cellar loaded into a wagon. Let me know when it's done."

"Yes, Miss," he said.

Mrs. Wimbly still hadn't moved from the cutting board.

"Get Egrit, please," I said.

She nodded stiffly and left the room.

I strode through the halls, my heels striking the floor with determination. Rose would not win.

At the ballroom, I pushed open the doors. It wasn't as I remembered it, and I wondered if Rose's magic had enhanced it. Now, dust drifted in the thin streams of midday light that filtered in from the curtained windows. The large room echoed with my footfalls as I crossed to the windows and pulled back the drapes, one by one. Two sitting rooms opened from the ballroom, and balcony doors led to a tangle of vines. A dust rag wouldn't be enough to set the rooms aright. It would take a shovel, several scrub brushes, and an army of help to fix fifty years of neglect.

"Benella?" Egrit said from the doors.

I pulled the balcony doors closed and turned to face her.

"Egrit, Rose expects the estate to host a harvest feast within four weeks." I held out the letter to her.

Her shocked, pale expression matched Mr. Crow's as she glanced down at the brief note. I looked around, and the same hopelessness crept up my spine.

"It will take us a week just to get this cleaned and polished."

"The men are making good progress on the barn. Perhaps we could have two help in here," Egrit said.

I shook my head and rid myself of any thoughts of futility.

"I have another idea. Where did the servants stay? The room off the kitchen has only four beds."

"There's room for three pallets on the floor. There are also rooms in the attic. That's where I stay."

"Will you show me?"

She nodded and led the way to the third floor. Once there, she pushed against a panel that matched the wall, and a door swung open.

"How do I keep missing these staircases?" I asked.

Egrit laughed. "They're meant to be missed."

She led me up a narrow staircase to an equally narrow hall lined with little rooms fitted with two beds each. At the end of the hall was a locked door.

"The attic?"

She nodded. The rooms were small and dusty but otherwise serviceable. Each had a small round window for airing. I reached for a window and opened it.

"Egrit, it's time for us to visit the Water."

THE WAGON RUMBLED past the market district. No one paid us attention until we turned onto the narrow path lined with the rundown homes of those who worked in trade. Children stood aside and watched us with wide eyes as we stopped before the house where I'd found a garden and someone willing to trade.

"Egrit, start knocking on the doors. A pail of milk for each house that wants it. Find out which homes have children between the ages of eight and twelve. Swiftly, stay by the wagon and keep an eye on Egrit." Both nodded and started working together to pour the milk. Children slowly drifted toward them.

I turned away and looked at the house I remembered. The soil in the side garden had been turned already. Nothing remained.

I knocked on the door, and it opened immediately. The woman looked a little thinner as did her children, and her eyes trailed to my hands. Her hopeful look faded when she saw them empty.

"Can I help you?" she asked, meeting my gaze.

"I think you can. May I come in?"

She nodded and held the door open. The children stood just behind her. Their neat clothes were well mended. Two rolled pallets sat near a cold hearth that was stacked with a few sticks of kindling.

"My name is Benella Hovtel. I'm here on behalf of Lord Ruhall."

Her eyes widened at the name.

"I'm Mrs. Palant."

"Pardon my question, but where is your husband?"

"We lost him last winter. He was a woodcutter." She didn't say more.

"How old are you two?" I asked, looking at the little boy and girl.

"Six and eight, Miss," the little boy said. He was the older of the two and held his sister's hand.

I looked at his mother. "The Liege Lord would offer your children an education in exchange for your work." She gave me a wary look. Many children were forced into work at an early age. Only those families with funds could see their children schooled.

"This is no trick. The children would attend private teachings at the estate six days a week from just after breakfast until just before dinner. All meals for you and your children will be provided by the estate. The children can do whatever tasks you give them to help you in your duties but will not be given work by any other member of Lord Ruhall's staff or by Lord Ruhall, himself. You would all live at the estate. There will be no other compensation for your labors," I said clearly. It was more than a fair deal while the children needed schooling.

She looked at her daughter, and I knew her thoughts. Most of the women in nearby houses traded their bodies for coin. If she stayed without a husband, it wouldn't be long before she found herself in the same position. What future could she then offer her daughter?

"There's a wagon just outside with enough room to carry what's needed. Take your time to think over the offer. I intend to return each week with the spare goat milk from the estate. It's not much, but it could help if you choose to stay," I said, standing and placing a hand on her shoulder. "I'll not play games with you. If you choose to accompany me, your children will not be ill-used and neither will you."

She nodded, still looking at her children. I let myself out.

A hand tugged my skirt, and I looked down at a girl no more than ten. Dirt dulled her pale blonde hair and streaked her left cheek. Her blue eyes darted to the wagon, then met mine.

"May I have milk?"

"Certainly. Did we miss your house?"

"I have no home."

"Where are your parents?"

She shrugged.

"Is there anyone here to care for you?"

She shook her head, and I felt a surge of pity for her.

"How old are you?"

"Eleven, Miss."

No one that age should be alone to fend for themselves.

"And your name?"

"Otta."

"Otta, I'm here to offer employment at Lord Ruhall's estate in exchange for an education. You would be required to attend school six days and work afterward. You will be fed, clothed, and given a warm place to sleep. You will be treated fairly and cared for. Does that interest you?"

"Very much, Miss."

"Then into the wagon with you. Ask Swiftly for a cup of milk while you wait," I said, pointing at the wagon.

Egrit met me by the wagon.

"There are three houses on this side with children those ages. Many more with younger."

I nodded and mentioned Otta, who already waited in the wagon.

"She will be returning to the estate with us."

Egrit nodded. I'd already shared my plan with her and Swiftly during our ride to the Water.

When she moved to the wagon to continue distributing milk, I went to the houses Egrit had indicated. To those houses, I offered the same opportunity I had Otta since the women already had a trade to support themselves. The children would be educated during the day but would be required to work before breakfast and after dinner.

Only two of the women agreed to release their children. The

third woman intended to introduce her twelve-year-old daughter to her trade. When she told me the price a virgin would fetch, I thought of the baker and struggled not to hit her.

I walked away from the house, not seeing the road I trod. Egrit caught my arm and pulled me toward the wagon.

"Horrid woman, that one," she said quietly.

"Quite," I agreed.

Two children already sat in the wagon. Mrs. Palant and her two children were working together to pack their belongings.

Watching them gave me an idea, and I stopped Mrs. Palant.

"What happens to your home when you leave it?"

She looked up and down the road at the other houses.

"One of them will claim it most likely."

Her house was in much better repair. All of the wood was solid, no rot, and there were no gaps between the boards.

"With your permission, I'd like to try trading it with the woman in that house," I pointed, "in exchange for her daughter."

"Meg has had plans for her daughter since she flowered. She's just waiting for the right buyer," she said quietly.

"Do you think your home might tempt her?"

"Not when all she needs to do is wait for me to leave."

"Yes, but so is everyone else."

Determined, I walked to Meg's door and knocked again. She answered with a surly expression.

"The house for the girl," I said without preamble.

Her eyes drifted behind me, and she laughed.

"I have no chance at that place. As soon as you leave there'll be a fight for who gets it."

"Unless we help the new owner move her belongings there and make it official." She glanced at the structure, her interest plain. "The girl will only be pure once," I said, the words souring my belly. "But that home will keep you warm for more than one winter."

"Retta, come here." A young woman stepped into the light of the doorway. A little girl held her hand. "You're going with this woman. Go." She waved her hand at me. The little girl started crying.

"Want both of them?" the woman asked, looking at the younger child with no obvious affection.

"Yes."

WHILE EGRIT LED everyone to the top floor to air the rooms and settle in before dinner, I went to find Mr. Crow.

He sat behind his desk, staring down at a piece of parchment. When he saw me, he wilted a bit and without a word handed me the paper. Scanning the list, I understood his despondency. We did not have enough to feed us for the winter, especially with the additional staff I'd brought.

Absently, I sat across from him and stared out the window. Surviving with meager supplies was familiar to me. But would that knowledge help produce an excess of food for a feast? It had to. I turned to Mr. Crow, who watched me expectantly. I gave him a reassuring smile.

"There are plenty of fish in the rivers to the northwest and southeast. On the estate land, a skilled hunter could also find more large game." We just needed the men to fish it and hunt it. "We will succeed." I stood. "I'll speak with Lord Ruhall about having three of the men hunt and fish every day for the next several weeks. It will keep the cooks busy. Meals will need to be simple. See if you can recall any of the families who may have attended in the past. We'll need to create a guest list quickly."

Leaving Mr. Crow, I went to search for Father or Lord Ruhall. As I approached the library, I heard them both.

"What good could milk possibly do?" Lord Ruhall's angry voice rang through the room.

"I'm sure her reasons are sound," my father said.

I caught a glimpse of Alec, pacing in his study. His wide shoulders were hunched and his head bent as he worked his path. I could imagine his expression. No doubt the news of Rose's letter had upset him.

"My reasons are quite sound," I said, walking into the study. His tense face swung in my direction. "Lord Ruhall, I'm sure Father's explained Rose's letter." I handed him the note I still carried. "I left with the milk and returned with several additional servants."

He studied me for a long moment, his anger fading to frustration.

"We can't afford to employ more," he said, bracing his fisted hands on his desk. "You, yourself, suggested trimming their numbers."

"Their wages will not be paid in coin. You have a teacher who is not teaching. So I brought a mother who could never afford an education for her two children and several older children who are willing to work in the morning and evenings in exchange for their education. It's a fair trade."

"Children, Benella?" my father said with shock.

"Father, here we will not ill-use them. They will have the sleep they need, a warm bed, food in their bellies, and an education in exchange for four hours of work a day. It is a far brighter future than what waited for them where they were."

Though Father continued to look troubled, he nodded.

"Benella, servants aren't enough." Lord Ruhall straightened

away from the desk and began to pace behind it once more. "What she's asking is impossible for three hundred coins."

I agreed, but I kept quiet. He already looked ready to yell. He didn't need me to further his despair. He needed hope, at least until I could look at the ledgers to discover the cost of past feasts. So, I walked toward the desk and leaned in until we met eye to eye.

"As impossible as freeing a beast from a fifty year enchantment, I imagine. Allow me a chance to try."

As his gaze swept over my face, the rest of the anger faded. Another expression took hold. Tenderness. I couldn't call it anything else. My stomach flipped, and my cheeks warmed in response.

"Of course," he said. "Tell me what needs to be done."

I straightened, putting distance between us.

"Please speak with your teacher and inform him he will have students starting tomorrow. There are seven aged between four and twelve. Most cannot read. He should start teaching after they've eaten. The children are not to be given work during their schooling hours, and Mrs. Palant's children aren't to be given work by anyone other than their mother.

"Also, if possible, we need three of the five men to focus on hunting and fishing. We need a larger quantity of game to store in the next few weeks."

Unable to maintain eye contact any longer, I cleared my throat, and met my father's gaze.

"Father, I need you to work with Mr. Crow and determine a guest list from Konrall and the Water. Mr. Crow said that, in the past, they filled the ballroom. I'd like to be conservative with the invitations while still meeting Rose's requirements. Next year, we can pack the room. As soon as you have a count, please let me know."

CHAPTER
FIVE

THE DAUNTING TASK OF CLEANING LOOMED BEFORE ME. EVEN WITH the extra help, cleaning the ballroom, parlors, dining room, and main sitting rooms before the feast would be difficult. But not impossible. Since Egrit, Mrs. Palant, and the children would remain occupied with airing the attic until after dinner, I meant to make some progress in the ballroom yet that day.

In the laundry, I filled several of the large, empty vats and started a fire in the pit under the first one. Everything in the ballroom and parlors needed a dusting and a washing. Hot water would make the task easier.

Mrs. Wimbly's voice reached me as I stepped into the hall.

"Seven more mouths to feed and she influenced Lord Ruhall to dismiss one of my staff? What is that woman thinking?"

I quickly moved away. Her tasks, to keep us fed and to store enough food for the feast and the winter, would not be easy. Yet, we couldn't afford more help for her. I hoped we wouldn't find ourselves missing a head cook.

In the ballroom, I stopped to look around and plan. The room needed more light to clean it properly. I checked the parlors and found the same problem. Though I was tempted to yank the curtains open, I did not. They were filthy like everything else and needed to be removed. I stared up at the hooks that held the drapes to the runner above the window.

"Need help?" Alec's quiet voice startled me. I turned and found him just behind me, scowling up at the hooks.

"The curtains here and in the ballroom need to be removed, beaten, and washed."

"Are you sure they will survive that?" He reached around me and plucked at the dust covered fabric. His arm brushed against mine, sending a tingle of awareness through me.

I moved away and studied the material.

"I hope so." The estate couldn't afford to replace them and winter without them would be chilly.

"I'll have one of the men come in with a ladder and remove them after sundown. Perhaps you can join me for dinner, and we can discuss the details of what you plan."

"Certainly. Father can join us and share his progress on the guest list."

He gave a small sigh before he left the room.

I had an hour at least until dinner. Best to put the time to use.

"He sent me looking for you," Egrit said from the door. Amusement laced her voice.

I straightened, and my spine made a loud cracking sound. The furniture of the first parlor now sat in the ballroom. It had taken much effort to pull the pieces out, and more effort still to roll up the large rug that dominated the space.

"I think he expects you to dine with him," she said.

"Yes. Of course." I brushed my hands on my skirts. "Are Mrs. Palant and the children settled in?"

"Yes. And fed." Amusement changed to barely contained laughter. "Are you going like that?"

Looking down at myself, I saw dust had made a muddle of my skirts. My sleeves, though rolled back, were dingy, and my bodice had finger streaks. I couldn't remember touching my bodice.

"I'm afraid I am. I plan to return here as soon as I finish meeting with Lord Ruhall. I have resolved to keep cleaning until I lose the light."

"Hmm," she said, eyeing the room.

I saw doubt in her gaze. In the time I'd spent in the room, I'd made no progress actually cleaning it, just emptying it.

I wiped away a stray strand of hair from my face as I moved toward Egrit. While I knew I'd eventually make progress on the parlor, I still wasn't sure what to do about the menu for the feast. Fish and game were only a start.

"I've been considering what foods to offer. In your jaunts around the estate, do you recall any fruit or nut trees?" I asked as we walked through the halls.

"Several actually. There is an apple grove and a couple stands of hazelnut trees."

"Perfect. Tomorrow, I want to see them. But I'll need you and Mrs. Palant to help in the sitting rooms and ballroom. Do you think Tam could show me the way?"

"I'll speak with him tonight. I'm sure he can."

At the library, she gave me a large smile then left me.

I strode through the doors and found Father's desk empty and the study door closed. The whisper of my boots across the rugs sounded loud in the silence. What could Father and Lord Ruhall be discussing that brought about such a hush? I paused to knock.

Lord Ruhall opened the door. His tense shoulders and tight jaw told me he was upset. His eyes swept over me, lingering the longest on my face.

"Benella, what happened to you?"

"I've been in the southern sitting room off the ballroom and am pleased to say I've made good progress." I didn't clarify that the progress only included furniture arrangement and not actual cleaning. His daunted expression told me he already worried enough.

He stepped back and motioned me in. Several paces into the study, I stopped short. A small table with two place settings waited before the fireplace. The room was empty, save for the two of us. Behind me, the door closed.

"Where's Father?" I said, turning to look at Lord Ruhall.

He scowled at me. There was no mistaking his surly mood.

"He has no progress to share yet and wanted me to remind you that he just started the list today."

I nodded absently and edged my way toward the table. Lord Ruhall slowly followed. Why was I feeling so wary? Perhaps it was his focused attention or perhaps the expression he wore was similar to the one he'd worn this morning after he'd thought to show me he wasn't cold. Right now, he looked anything but cold. His flushed face concerned me.

"Isn't it a bit warm for a fire already, sir?"

"Alec," he said, correcting me. "It was a little chilly in here after a day with the window open." He trailed me, making a game of slowly chasing me around the room. It reminded me too much of the way the beast had stalked me on more than one occasion.

"I believe I'm not yet hungry."

He stopped moving and narrowed his eyes.

"Benella, sit."

"I think not."

He ran a hand through his hair, looked ready to yell, but then took a deep breath.

"I made this myself," he said, gesturing at the covered plates.

Though his manner hadn't changed, that he'd cooked piqued my interest.

"Really? You cooked?"

"You know the extent of my skill," he said.

My gaze met his. I realized he sought to show me that he and the beast were the same person. My heart lurched. He didn't understand.

Logically, I knew they were the same. Yet, inside, I remained torn in reconciling the two. The man who had been held back by a simple hand on his shoulder, the man who had chosen his freedom over saving me from—I felt a heaviness on my chest and stopped the direction of my thought. That man was not the beast who had scared off Tennen and Splane so many times. Neither was he the beast who had risked Rose's wrath to fetch me from her cottage. One side of him wanted me above all else, and the other sacrificed me for his own desire.

I closed my eyes against the ache in my chest. It wasn't for loss of purpose that I wanted to leave the North. It was to avoid the pain of seeing the man who didn't want me enough.

Lips brushed my cheek, and my eyes flew open.

He pulled back enough to meet my gaze.

"As a man, I can finally do the one thing I craved to do as a beast."

"What is that?"

"Kiss you." He leaned in once more to the other cheek. His touch was infinitely light. Warm lips, soft compared to the beast's, yet still firm. A little bird took flight in my breast, beating its wings against its boned cage and robbing me of air.

His lips retreated.

"Sit. Please." He pulled out a chair for me.

Sitting, I watched him walk to his place. He seemed more

relaxed now. Why? Was it the kiss or that I'd agreed to dine with him?

He uncovered the plates, and I couldn't help the smile that spread across my face. The sad little egg tartlet wasn't as burnt as the last time we'd made it. He was getting better.

"It looks delicious, my Lord."

"Alec."

"How did Mrs. Wimbly react to the use of her kitchen?"

His puzzlement over the name I'd used disappeared as quickly as it had appeared.

"Ah, the cook. I sent her and her assistant away so no one would witness my attempt."

I took a bite. The flavor was there, and the texture not bad.

"Much improved," I said after I swallowed. "Where did you find the eggs?"

"Tam and I left this morning to search for the game keeper's cottage. I had recalled the estate having one. We found it."

I nibbled on the tartlet as I listened.

"The cottage is in good repair, spared perhaps by the enchantment. Beside the cottage is an overgrown, fenced pasture. The grass had grown so high we couldn't see the goats after we'd herded them in. It will help the winter hay last longer. On the other side of the pasture, we found a barn that can easily house the goats as well as several other animals. But the prize was the quail pen beside the barn. When we opened the door, Tam almost took a quail to the head. They flew out in a drove but didn't go far. No one has been out there in fifty years yet the birds seem tame. Tam is working on the netting for their side pen."

"This is wonderful news. Eggs and milk. The estate is on its way to self-sufficiency. How close is the cottage?"

"It's a distance, near the east wall. Tam and I believe we found the old path to it. We'll need to clear it again for a wagon."

"Egrit told me the estate also has apple and hazelnut trees. I've asked if Tam can take me to them tomorrow. I'm hoping we can incorporate the fruit into the feast's menu. If there's anything to harvest, we will need Swiftly and Tam to switch from the main barn to those efforts. I plan to keep our new help busy cleaning in here. I'm reluctant to pull the hunters from their task until we have a full cellar."

"A sound plan."

I took another bite of my dinner and considered how the addition of eggs and apples might help the menu.

"Do you recall the food you usually served?" I asked.

He shook his head and shame painted his face.

"My mother handled those details. The last few years, I didn't attend regularly; but when I did, I brought unsuitable company." His words grew strained. "I was such a fool. I miss her," he said.

I reached across the table and set my hand on his. I had no words to offer him. We were meant to make mistakes. We learned from them. But how did one console another for a mistake that cost him his mother? He turned his hand to hold mine. His thumb softly rubbed the back of mine for a moment before I pulled away. When he touched me like that, my heart felt too vulnerable.

We ate the rest of the meal in silence, and I was glad he didn't ask for any further details of what I had planned for I didn't yet have any.

If we had eggs, milk, apples, and nuts, we had the base for some simple fare. Father and Mr. Crow would handle the guest list, Mrs. Wimbly the cooking, and the rest of us the cleaning. Could it be that simple? What was I missing? I needed to look at his ledgers.

While I absently stared at the table and took a sip of my water, a missing piece fell into place, and I wrinkled my nose.

"Table linens, serving dishes, and something to drink." I

groaned as I thought of another piece. "And music. What kind of music?" I looked up and met his amused gaze.

"That wonderful head of yours never stops, does it?"

"As my father recently brought to my attention, when it does, I grow bored."

The relaxed calm fled his expression as his jaw tightened.

"And boredom doesn't suit you, does it," he said softly. He straightened in his chair and, with an almost accusatory glance, continued our conversation.

"The linens we have—if time hasn't damaged them—as well as the serving dishes. If there are enough apples, Mrs. Wimbly could press them for cider."

"A perfect harvest drink," I said in agreement. I itched to wander out to the grove now to see if there were enough, but I needed to start the actual cleaning of the southern parlor.

"Thank you for cooking for me, sir—Alec," I quickly corrected myself after a hard look from him. "I want to continue working in the parlor until the sun sets. Did you want me to take the tray back to the kitchen?" I stood.

"Go," he said with an annoyed wave. "I can take care of this."

I didn't try to guess what had irritated him. It was better not to delve too deeply. I felt his gaze on me as I left the library.

In the ballroom, just outside the sitting room, I found two buckets of ash. Inside the room, I found Egrit and Mrs. Palant hard at work. Soot no longer coated the fireplace, and the smaller rugs lay rolled up in the ballroom, leaving the sitting room floor exposed to their exhaustive effort. A good half of the area was clean.

"Thank you both," I said, stepping into the room. "I didn't expect you to work on your first night, Mrs. Palant. Are your children asleep?"

"Retta offered to put them to bed. I wanted to see what work needed to be done."

"Make sure Retta and the children know they can seek you out whenever they wish. This isn't a strict household and you working here should not deprive them of their mother."

I picked up a wet rag and joined their efforts. With three of us laboring, we finished the floor just a bit after dark. As we were leaving, Tam and Swiftly entered with candles and a ladder.

"We just washed the southern parlor floor," Egrit said to both of them. "Don't dirty it with your boots or dripping wax."

"Yes, ma'am," Tam said with a wink.

Egrit shook her head at him and turned to me.

"I saw Lord Ruhall refilling the kettle when I went for the last bucket of warm water. There should be plenty for us to bathe." She handed me a pail of dirty water. "I'll run and get us something clean to change into."

Mrs. Palant and I went to wait in the laundry where we worked together to fill a large washing kettle and the wooden tub with warm water.

When Egrit returned, she insisted I take the tub while they washed from a bucket. They'd somehow avoided wearing the grime I wore. I willingly stripped and slid into the water with a sigh. Once I finished washing away the dust, I forced myself from the pleasant water and dressed in a clean nightgown and wrap before throwing my dirty dress into the bath water. Egrit and Mrs. Palant threw in the aprons they had wisely worn. At Egrit's insistence, I left them to finish the laundry since Tam planned to take me to the woods at first light.

I padded barefoot through the halls but didn't go to my room. Though I had an idea of what the feast might entail because of Mr. Crow and Lord Ruhall, I wanted specifics. I needed to read the ledgers.

In the library only a glow of coals remained in the fireplace, which didn't surprise me. Father usually left after dinner unless Lord Ruhall requested something from him. Tiptoeing across the room in the moonlight, I focused on the dim study. An unlit candle waited on the desk, along with three ledgers. The three years before Alec's enchantment. Each held a bookmark on a page with the feast's accounting. Alec had obviously wondered the same thing and sought the answers in the ledgers as well. I quickly scanned the marked pages. The feast cost the estate dearly. Even the last year Alec's mother had hosted it. Three hundred gold. An impossible amount. I would just need to find a way to spend as little as possible and keep Alec from worrying.

I left the study and quickly made my way to my room. Someone had turned down the covers. I slipped under them and closed my eyes.

THE BED MOVED, waking me. Alec sat back against the headboard and ran his fingers through my damp, unbound hair.

"Please," he whispered, his voice raw.

My breath caught. Did he know he had woken me? I could think of only one reason he came to me in the middle of the night with such a pretty, desperate word on his lips. Panic took flight in my chest. Yet, he didn't seem to notice the change in my breathing as his fingers continued to run through my hair.

"Please. Please don't let her leave me."

The desperation in his whispered words stopped the panic. My heart broke for him as I suddenly understood his anger in the ballroom and at dinner. He had been in the study when I had spoken to Father and knew I meant to leave him.

He truly believed he needed me. Perhaps he did. Rose's letter regarding the feast made it clear she wasn't done with him. I would need to assure him I meant to stay through the feast. But not now when his mood was so volatile. I remained still as his fingers ran through my hair until he lulled me to sleep once more.

THE NEXT MORNING, I woke with a start and sat up. The bed beside me was empty. I stared at the spot for a moment, disoriented, then flopped back onto the bed. Alec thought I meant to abandon him before the feast. I'd need to tell him I meant to stay through the feast. But, how could I tell him without making him aware I'd been awake?

The door opened.

"Good morning," Egrit said in a chipper tone.

I groaned.

"You go to bed the same time I do. How do you wake before me?" I asked.

"When I set my head to my pillow, I immediately sleep. Do you?"

I used to. Lately, however, my mind raced long after I set my head to my pillow. It didn't help that Lord Ruhall interrupted my sleep as well. Egrit didn't wait for me to answer.

"Tam's waiting for you."

I didn't need further motivation to remove myself from bed. I hurried to dress.

The apples proved plentiful but not yet ripe, whereas the nuts had already ripened and most had fallen. With Tam's estimate of another two weeks for the apples to be ready, I gathered what nuts remained and took them to the kitchen. Given Mrs. Wimbly's continued surly mood, I kept the news of the apples to myself and went off to help in the ballroom once more.

While I assisted washing the large, long curtains, I pondered the menu. The unripe apples were a blessing as the kitchen could now remain focused on preparation and storage until just before the feast. Yet, would such a short timeframe be enough when they still had to cook meals?

I left Mrs. Palant and Egrit to wring and hang the material and went to the kitchen to seek Mrs. Wimbly's opinion. Hard at work with a stag on the block and several fish waiting on the table, she scowled at me when I entered. I left the room with my answer. She would not much appreciate additional work.

While the curtains dried, Egrit, Mrs. Palant, and I returned to the ballroom to move the furniture outdoors for an airing. The first piece gave us trouble as we moved it into the overgrown garden. Brambles tugged at our skirts and poked the old material covering the cushions.

"I'm going to tell Tam we need this weeded," Egrit said.

I nodded my agreement. If the ballroom became stuffy during the feast, we would need to open the doors for air. The tangle of vegetation would prevent anyone from stepping out.

The three of us stomped down what weeds we could and spent the rest of the day moving pieces outside.

After dinner, Retta and Lettie found us and explained that Otta had remained behind to watch the younger children; and Tom, the older boy, was with Mr. Crow. I'd forgotten they were to help clean but quickly found tasks for them to perform. Once we finished, they helped us move the pieces indoors. Though I knew the work they did was better than what would have waited for them, it did bother me to see the weary droop to their shoulders at the end of the day.

Yet, the children were no wearier than we were. Making the barest of efforts, I washed before bed and slid under the covers. It was only then that I recalled I hadn't spoken to Lord Ruhall about staying through until the end of the feast.

I briefly considered locking the door before I closed my eyes.

The next day Egrit, Mrs. Palant and I worked on the second parlor, and our progress moved slower than the passing hours. By dinner, the furniture and rugs were outside and beaten and the fireplace free of soot. This time Retta and Otta joined us.

"We'll take turns watching the little ones," Retta said. "If that's all right."

"It is. Did you two eat already?" They shook their heads. "Let's all stop for dinner."

We walked together to the kitchen and found the other children already at the table. They quietly watched Kara, the assistant cook, scoop a portion of dinner into their bowls.

Mrs. Wimbly stood at the block, scrubbing the surface clean. As she worked, she mumbled. I couldn't catch everything but enough to know that she didn't like that the children had come in for dinner. She moved a polished tray to the clean block then started to set it precisely.

She'd just set the food upon it when one of the men came in with a string of fish. She heaved a sigh.

"Set them in the basin. I'll deal with them in a bit."

"Is there somewhere the tray needs to be, Mrs. Wimbly? I'd be happy to deliver it so you can address the fish."

"It's a tray for Lord Ruhall," she said stiffly. She still didn't like me despite all the hard work I put in alongside everyone else.

"Then I'll deliver it for you."

She set the tray on the table and turned her back to me. Kara's gaze darted between the two of us. I smiled at Kara before I picked up the tray and left.

Father wasn't at his paper stacked desk or anywhere else in the library. From the study, I heard his voice.

"We've stopped at one hundred and twenty-five," he said.

Silence greeted him.

I stepped into the room and caught Alec's hopeless gaze.

"None of that now. Have you already gone through the list?"

"Is there a need?" Alec asked, watching me set the tray on the small table. I took the plate from it and set it before him but stole one of his biscuits before I turned away. I doubted the cook would save me any dinner. Alec could share.

Father shook his head as I bit into the biscuit. I swallowed with a grin and sat to face Alec once more.

"Of course," I said, answering him. "You will need to converse with everyone who comes. Wouldn't you like to know their names and a little about them?"

"Very well. Mr. Hovtel, would you be kind and read the list for us?"

Father read the list and added a few comments about each guest. I kept my expression neutral when I heard Bryn and Edmund's names. Blye's name didn't bother me as much. I smiled when I heard Henick and his family would receive an invitation. I hoped they would attend. Alec's scowl only deepened.

"We had better add Rose's name," I said when Father reached the end.

They both looked at me, clearly surprised. I shrugged.

"She said she would be watching regardless. Consider the invitation your official acknowledgement of her observation, nothing more; and perhaps she will see the invitation as a gesture of goodwill."

I stood, knowing I needed to return to the ballroom.

"Where are you going?" Alec said.

The thread of concern in his words stopped me.

"For now, back to the ballroom. There is much to clean in a very short time." I hoped that inference would be enough to assure him that I meant to stay through the feast.

He nodded, and I left the pair.

Mrs. Palant, Egrit, and the girls were already hard at work scrubbing the floor. Seeing the room well occupied, I took the ladder outside and started to wash windows.

THE NEXT MORNING, I woke with renewed ambition. At some point during the course of the night, I'd let go of my annoyance with Bryn long enough to realize Edmund might be the solution to Mrs. Wimbly's hectic schedule. Shortly after rising, I found myself walking toward Konrall to speak to him. This time, I brought Swiftly with.

"Benella, welcome," Edmund said when I walked into the bakery.

"Hello, Edmund. Allow me to introduce Swiftly. He is in Lord Ruhall's employ."

Above, the door to the second floor opened. I kept my smile on my face as Bryn descended. Her steps on the stairs slowed when she saw me, and her welcoming smile chilled. The arrival of another customer defused the tense moment.

"How can I help you?" Edmund said as Bryn moved to assist the other customer.

"Lord Ruhall is hosting a harvest feast. I would like to order two hundred pastries."

Edmund froze and Bryn stopped speaking to her customer to stare at me.

"I've had the sugar glazed kind from your bakery in the Water and enjoyed it immensely. However, I'm hoping you can work apples into a pastry for something out of the ordinary, something that would fit a harvest feast."

Edmund seemed to collect himself with a deep, slow breath, and Bryn went back to her customer.

"Apples...yes, I should be able to procure enough for two hundred pastries," Edmund said.

The customer left, and Bryn lingered by the counter.

"The estate has plenty, and I would be happy to send Swiftly back with the amount you need. They won't be ready for another two weeks," I said, knowing I'd just reduced the price he could charge. "Also, guests will be coming from the Water and a few even further afield. With so many guests sampling your sweet creations, you're sure to have new customers."

"This is for Lord Ruhall?" Bryn said, her voice heavy with disbelief. "Why would Lord Ruhall send you here to buy pastries?"

Since I'd already explained the reason behind the need for the pastries, I knew she was questioning why I was Lord Ruhall's emissary.

"Have you inquired after Father at all since you wed?" I asked. Her cheeks flushed, giving me her answer. "If you had, you would know he is no longer teaching but Lord Ruhall's man of estate. I'm assisting."

Bryn opened her mouth to say more, but a look from Edmund silenced her.

"Let's talk price in the back," he said, gesturing to the sitting room.

"No, thank you." I had no desire to visit that room again. "Perhaps the kitchen?"

Edmund nodded. When I moved around the counter, Swiftly followed; and I didn't mind his company. The kitchen had its own memories. Yet, when I stepped through the door, I couldn't recall them.

The back door stood open, letting in a breeze and light. No flour coated any surface. The old table was gone and a longer, thinner table had taken its place. There were also tall chairs near the high table. Edmund motioned to one and smiled at my questioning glance.

"It's easier on the back to switch from sitting to standing when working. The raised table helps, too."

"You look like you've quite settled in. Has business improved?"

"Not really. But perhaps this order will help."

"I think it will help both of us. I'll be honest, Edmund. After such a long enchantment, the estate struggles. It isn't what it once was, but Lord Ruhall is working hard to bring it back. Part of those efforts includes the harvest feast. It's not for the gentry, but for the merchants and common folk who depend on the estate."

"It feels as if you're trying to sell me something, Benella."

"In a way, I am. I'm trying to explain how you'll reach a larger market by baking for the harvest feast so when I tell you we can only pay a single gold for two hundred pastries, you won't kick me out."

Edmund sighed and his shoulders slumped, but he didn't kick me out. "That barely covers the cost of the flour, sugar, time to prepare—"

"I can also provide you with double the apples you'll need so you can produce the same pastries after the feast is over." He still looked troubled. "And promise a portion of next year's hazelnuts?"

His expression took on a speculative gleam. I sat quietly and waited for him to think over the offer. I was loath to part with a single gold piece but knew it only fair. If he didn't start receiving coin soon, there would be no baker in Konrall.

"You have a deal," Edmund said, offering his hand.

I shook it with a grin, feeling quite pleased with myself.

Swiftly and I left the bakery, together, after assuring Edmund I would keep him apprised of the progress of the apple harvest. I only hoped that promising him double the apples would leave enough for cider. If not, there was always spring water.

"He doesn't seem to like you any better," Swiftly said softly, interrupting my thoughts.

I followed his gaze and found Tennen watching us.

"His like or dislike is no bother to me," I said, looking away. "I've more important things to worry about."

"The feast will be a welcome respite because of your efforts," he said.

"I hope so."

We walked the rest of the way in silence. By the time we returned, we'd missed the midday meal. As I went to the kitchen for a quick bite, I heard a faint giggle. I walked slowly, listening. In the dim hall, just before I reached the laundry, I found a staircase leading up.

"I must be the least observant person here," I said under my breath.

At the top of the stairs, a hall led right above the kitchen and left above the laundry and formal dining room. Another faint peal of laughter came from the left.

A door opened to a large room. Inside, the children sat at small tables with the youngest in front and the oldest in back. A weathered man, dressed in a neat, yet worn, jacket decades out of fashion, wrote the letter D on the blackboard. He caught sight of me when he turned to his students.

"Welcome. Students, please welcome Miss Hovtel."

"Good afternoon, Miss Hovtel," they said in unison.

"What manners," I said with a smile.

"Manners, letters, and numbers, Miss Hovtel. I've found the letters and numbers do no good without manners."

I met the man's steady gaze, and he bowed slightly.

"Mr. Roost, at your service. I believe the last time I saw you, you were at the pond."

And, like that, I could see the resemblance in his features to those that had twice adorned the tree.

I smiled and gave a slight bow back.

"Do you have the supplies you need to teach this group?"

"Oh yes. The previous student did not use much of his supplies."

Alec had admitted to being a poor student.

"I'll leave you to your class then. Good afternoon children," I said, moving toward the door.

After leaving the schoolroom, I went to tell Father about my deal with Edmund.

Father sat at his desk, busily penning a letter. From the study, I heard a similar faint scratch of ink on parchment.

"Ah, Bini," Father said, looking up as he heard me enter. "How is the progress in the parlor today?"

"The second sitting room was almost finished yesterday. I hope we can start on the main ballroom yet today. How is everything here?"

"We've penned over half the invitations. By this evening, we should have two piles ready for the riders who will go out at dawn. I'll walk to the Water to hand deliver the ones in town."

"That is good news. I've made a deal with Edmund to make apple pastries for the feast. Twice as many apples as he'll need for two hundred pastries, for half the price he would normally charge. I'll need a gold to pay him when we deliver the apples."

Father nodded and made a note.

"Give my warm regards to Blye when you see her tomorrow," I said as I left.

Father nodded absently, already back to penning the next invitation.

Egrit, Mrs. Palant, and I used the rest of the afternoon to clean the parlor. Once we finished, Egrit went to press the curtains while Mrs. Palant and I set to work scrubbing the remaining windows. Once again, I skipped dinner and fell into bed exhausted.

When the bed dipped long after I'd fallen asleep, I barely roused. Gentle fingers began to untwist the braid from my hair. Sleep reclaimed me before he finished.

WHEN THE SUN hit my eyes, I groaned and rolled over. It took a moment to realize what the light meant. Sitting up, I looked at the windows. As I'd suspected, it was well past daybreak.

After a mad scramble of dressing and making my bed, I left my room and hurried to the ballroom. Both Mrs. Palant and Egrit were on ladders, using cloths tied to the end of long branches to dust the webs from the walls and ceiling.

"Why didn't you wake me?" I asked. Sun lit the room through the clean windows. The doors to the garden were wide open, and Tam whistled as he pulled up weeds from the immediate path.

"I tried. Lord Ruhall heard me and suggested I let you sleep."

Unsure how I felt about that, I changed the subject.

"I'm going to find myself something to eat in the kitchen and check on preparations while I'm there. I'll return to help."

The manor was quiet with everyone at their tasks. Father and the riders had left with first light, and Lord Ruhall was out hunting to replace the man who was helping Swiftly.

Mrs. Wimbly said little as I entered the kitchen and took a

biscuit from a sack on the shelves. Mr. Crow nodded to me. He sat at the table, polishing silver and, it appeared, sorting through linens.

A swell of satisfaction carried me back to the ballroom and invigorated my cleaning efforts.

It was well past dark before I sought my bed. Just as sleep pulled me under, I reminded myself to search out Father to see how his visit with Blye had gone.

THE BED DIPPED. His familiar fingers laced through my hair as they worked the braid free. I sighed, enjoying the feeling. When he finished, his arms wrapped around me and pulled me against his chest. His lips brushed the back of my neck. The sensation didn't disturb me. Instead, it comforted me; and I settled deeper into sleep.

CHAPTER
SIX

"You didn't need to bring me a tray," I said, untangling myself from the blankets.

"Lord Ruhall has noted that you haven't been eating enough and thought to prepare you a tray. I met him in the hall, and I insisted it wouldn't be proper for him to bring it himself."

I glanced at her face and saw she was entirely serious.

"I walked these halls shrouded in nothing but mist," I said. "I hardly think bringing me breakfast improper at this point."

"Don't you? Perhaps Rose isn't just watching him. This is our chance to show her we won't let him become the man he once was."

She made a valid point. She set the tray on the small table and moved to help me remake the bed. If she saw the dent in the second pillow, she didn't comment.

Four days had passed since Rose's letter. Though I felt we'd made fair plans toward a passable feast, I still worried about the food we would provide.

"Has Tam checked the apple trees lately?" I asked.

"We walk out each morning at sunrise," she said with a blush, and I suspected frolicking as nymphs wasn't something they would forget soon.

"We tried one this morning. They're tart. Another week or two will be needed."

"We might need to start picking a few days early than that so Edmund has the time he needs to make the pastries," I said.

"Mrs. Palant and I were talking last night about the menu. We think smoked fish would be a nice addition," she said, touching on a subject I'd so far avoided.

"Smoked fish is a good idea. I think Mrs. Wimbly is salting or immediately preparing the fish being brought to her. I'll have Mr. Crow mention the idea to her. Any ideas for the main course?"

Egrit shook her head, looking worried.

"We have time. We'll come up with something."

She nodded and left the room. I lifted the cover from the tray and smiled at the egg tartlet. We needed to work on a new recipe. But, I doubted there was much else Lord Ruhall could make with the ingredients we had in the kitchen. That thought took me back to the source of my dilemma for the feast. Grudgingly, I acknowledged the impossibility of hosting the feast without using some more of the estate's gold.

With a sigh, I dressed then returned the empty tray to the kitchen.

Mrs. Wimbly's voice reached me before I entered.

"I told you, we're not a market. Lord Ruhall has no use for—"

"Henick," I said as soon as I saw the man in the door.

His frustrated expression melted when he saw me.

"It's all right, Mrs. Wimbly. I'll speak with Henick."

Mrs. Wimbly turned to scowl at me. The woman might know how to cook, but her personality remained unpleasant.

"He's trying to sell us potatoes," she said in a huff.

I smiled at Henick.

"Would you happen to have onions, too?"

Mrs. Wimbly threw her hands in the air and stomped from the kitchen. Kara kept her head down as she continued to prepare the midday meal.

"I do, but not with me. Father thought you might be interested in some produce since the manor probably has fallow fields," he said, waving to his wagon that waited just outside the door.

"Let's see what you have." I stepped out, moving toward the back of the wagon. My skirts tangled with my legs when I attempted to boost myself up, and I missed the days when I went about in trousers and had freedom of movement.

With Henick's help, I stepped up into the bed. Four large sacks rested near the front. They were tied with twine, so I easily opened the first one and pulled out a potato. Dirt sprinkled off as I turned it in my hand.

"How much for a sack?"

"I'll give you two sacks of potatoes and half a sack of onions for a gold and a promise to dance with me at the feast."

"You received your invitation, then?"

He nodded, his eyes twinkling.

"Yesterday. It was one of the reasons we knew you might be interested in potatoes."

"Well, you have a deal," I said, dropping the potato in the sack.

Henick reached up, and with a firm grip on my waist, helped me from the wagon. Inside the kitchen, something crashed. That woman...I sighed, pasted a pleasant smile on my face and motioned to the drive that wandered to the estate's gate.

"Shall we walk and discuss delivery?"

The corners of his eyes crinkled as he smiled knowingly.

"Yes."

We strolled side by side in silence until we passed the front of the house.

"Are you well?" he asked.

"Much the same. Memories plague me. I was thinking a fresh start in a new place might be the adventure I need to lighten my spirit."

"You want to leave, then?" Disappointment laced his statement.

"Not just yet. I'll be here to honor my promised dance."

"A dance I will look forward to."

We'd reached the gate and turned around. Walking from the manor to the gate took much less time without the tangle of living plants to impede a person.

"I can leave the sacks of potatoes and return with the onions in a few days."

"That will work perfectly. Thank you, Henick. I'm grateful that you and your father thought of us."

When we reached the wagon, he lifted the potatoes from the bed and set them by the door before climbing aboard. I waited beside the door and waved as he left.

"Benella." Alec's angry, clipped voice had me turning in surprise just as Henick rounded the front of the building. "What are you doing?"

Behind him, I caught Mrs. Wimbly glaring at me with an overly satisfied smirk.

"Purchasing potatoes and onions. Now we can serve individual meat pies."

Alec's gaze drifted to the direction in which Henick had disappeared.

I turned to Mrs. Wimbly.

"Please see the potatoes stored. Henick will return later with the onions."

She glanced at Alec expectantly as I moved to walk inside.

A moment after I cleared the door, Alec followed. He didn't speak as we left the kitchen; but in the hall, he caught me by the waist and pulled me into the laundry. His arm remained fixed over my stomach, anchoring my back to his chest. He leaned forward until his lips almost touched my ear. My pulse leapt.

"I said he was not to touch you." The low words spoken so close to my ear almost made me shiver.

"No," I said slowly. "You said he wasn't to kiss me anymore. And he didn't. Now, I need to let my father know of the deal Henick and I struck so Henick can be paid when he returns."

Instead of releasing me, Alec tangled his free hand in my hair.

"I don't want him touching you, either," he said. The menace in his tone had me submitting to the insistent, steady draw on my hair. His lips found the column of my neck. A tingle spread where his mouth touched. "From the first day you entered my lands, you were mine. No other will have you."

I shivered.

"Don't continue my torture, Benella. I miss you. I miss the way we spent our days together."

My heart skipped a beat. The memory of his mouth on my skin, of his hands gripping my thighs, dimmed the memory of the baker's touch. I missed the days we'd spent together too.

"Marry me," he said, surprising me.

"I cannot."

He dropped his hands and yelled his frustration. The sudden noise startled me. I spun to face him. His angry gaze pierced me.

"I asked you when I had nothing to offer but myself, and you refused me. I ask again, now offering you a title and modest wealth. But you refuse me still. What exactly am I missing?" He paced before me, his relentless scowl never turning away.

"My answer remains. I do not know you."

"How do you not know me? You know I can barely cook an edible meal, abhor arithmetic, and irritate easily. You know you need never fear me, that I would never harm you." He lifted his hand to stroke my cheek where he once had hurt me. "That I cannot sleep unless I am beside you. That you can calm me with a touch or a word. That I search you out just to hear you. You know there will never be another for me. That there is only you." He dropped his hand. "Yet, you say you cannot...I say you stubbornly *will* not. What is left to know?"

I stepped back from him and looked about the room.

"I gave up my freedom in exchange for my father's life, and the more I learned about you, the more I wanted to stay. I saw something in you worth helping, and my heart broke for you each time you tried to win back your freedom and failed.

"You say you need me. I've always known that. You asked what I still need to know..." I took a breath and pressed on. "When faced with the decision of saving the people here from re-enchantment or saving me, you choose your people. I understand your reasons. I'm not angry. Yet, I do not believe you can ever love me as much as I have loved you."

Alec turned scarlet, his gaze thunderous.

A cough echoed outside the laundry room, and Egrit stepped in.

"Lord Ruhall, Mr. Hovtel wants to speak with you."

Alec didn't glance at me as he stormed from the room. Egrit gave me a look I couldn't quite decipher then left.

I quickly made my way to the ballroom where I spent the rest of my day scrubbing the floor and avoiding Lord Ruhall. I would speak to Father about Henick tomorrow.

A WARM HAND on my abdomen woke me. My stomach lurched sickeningly at the same time a tingle of awareness crept through me. I took a moment to remind myself it wasn't the baker touching me. He was gone.

Alec held me from behind with his arm draped over my waist. His hand didn't move but rested possessively on my bare skin just below my navel. He slept peacefully with me, just as he'd said.

Yet, knowing it was Alec didn't lift my unease at being touched by a furless hand. Breathing slowly through my nose, I tried to focus on a more pleasant memory than the baker. I remembered the beast kissing his way from my breast to my stomach and lower still. My breathing quickly grew shallow, and I warmed considerably. Perhaps that wasn't the best memory on which to dwell. I struggled to push away the recollection, but the feel of his tongue rasping between my legs lingered.

Dislodging Alec's hand, I rolled onto my stomach. Though I'd successfully banished my unease, it took a while for the new sensations to fade and for sleep to find me once more.

THE FOLLOWING MORNING, I woke before Egrit arrived. I quickly dressed and left the room. Wary of Lord Ruhall's mood, I chose to clean and forgo breakfast. The ballroom and connecting parlors were spotless, and Egrit and Mrs. Palant had agreed to start on the main sitting room at the front of the manor. However, the room remained empty and untouched.

Just as I was leaving, I collided with Swiftly.

"I'm sorry, Miss Hovtel," he said, quickly reaching out to steady me.

"No need for apology. I'm right and well." My heart still hammered from the unexpected impact, though. For half a moment, I'd thought him Alec.

"Meaning you can release her, Swiftly," Alec said from somewhere behind me.

Annoyance laced his words, and I recalled his reaction when Henick had walked with me. I inwardly cringed, and Swiftly immediately dropped his hand.

"Was there something you needed?"

Unsure to which of us he spoke, I remained facing Swiftly. Swiftly stepped away from me and looked at a point beyond me.

"I've run out of nails."

"There's a smith in the village, according to Miss Hovtel. Take this and get what you need."

A coin flipped through the air, and gold glinted in the early morning light. Swiftly caught the coin easily. He nodded and was about to turn away when I realized I'd be left alone with Alec.

"I should help," I said, moving to catch up to Swiftly. "I'm better at wheedling a fair price."

Alec remained quiet behind us.

It wasn't until we were halfway to Konrall that I realized what I'd done. I'd offered to face the people who'd been present at my near rape. My steps slowed noticeably.

"Miss Hovtel?"

My stomach clenched, and I struggled to breathe through it.

"Benella, you look pale. Are you feeling faint?"

Exhaling slowly, I shook my head.

"Not in the least. Just settling a moment in my mind."

"I can negotiate the price of nails," he said softly. "You need not accompany me."

"I swear I'm right and well. Besides, I must visit the candle maker. We'll need large, tall pillars for the feast. Bigger than anything we have."

"Then I'll take you there. You can inquire about candles while I speak with the smith. I'll return for you when my business is complete."

I nodded, glad I didn't have to return to the manor just yet and equally glad I could avoid the Coalre family.

The candle maker greeted me with a smile when he opened the door.

"Benella, welcome. Come in, come in." As soon as he stepped aside, Swiftly turned away to go to the smithy.

"It's been too long, dear child. How are you?"

"Well, and you?"

He snorted.

"Well? I doubt well. I heard what happened." He patted my hand and led me to the chair near the fire. "Sit."

"You heard? From who?"

"Your sister. She needed candles. She's a mean one, that girl. Silly twit to try to put the blame on you. A harsh tongue for one carrying another man's babe."

My eyes rounded, and he laughed at me as he sat in his chair. "I'm old but my eyes and ears work well. There is plenty of yelling coming from the bakery of late. Edmund's a good man. Shame he didn't know about your sister before it was too late."

I had no idea what to say, so I remained quiet for a moment.

"Did you receive your invitation to the harvest feast?" I asked finally.

"I did. I hear we'll have some fancy apple pastries."

"And cider, meat pies, and smoked fish. The menu isn't set yet. Like everything at the estate, it needs work."

"So what can I do for you?"

"I need pillars to light the ballroom once the sun sets."

"Do you have stands?"

"How tall would they need to be?"

"About five feet to keep the flame away from the children. And wide to keep the flame from a lady's hair."

"We don't have them yet, but we will."

"I'm guessing you'll need a dozen big pillars. The fire will be lit, most likely."

"Yes."

He hummed to himself and looked at his shelves.

"I can do it, but it'll take all the wax I have. When the night's done, I'll collect the remaining wicks and wax. Since I'm taking more than half back, I'll halve the price. A blunt silver for each candle."

A little over a gold for a dozen pillars.

"The price is more than fair. Since you'll need to stay until the end, I'll have a room readied for—"

He laughed.

"There is no need for that. I'll walk home and sleep comfortably in my own bed."

"Then, I insist Swiftly bring you home. You'll have too much wax to carry safely in the dark."

"Very well."

Swiftly's knock ended my visit, and before I left, I promised to send payment the same day.

After we returned to the manor, I sent Swiftly back with the required coin while I helped clean the front sitting parlor. I was content to lend my assistance and avoid Alec. I'd upset him with my rejection and with my reason for doing so. No doubt he felt there was more to say on the topic. In my mind, there wasn't.

The next day, I successfully managed the same evasion. Though he did almost catch me alone in the laundry; however, his distinctive stride had given me enough warning to slip out the door. I'd waited around the corner with bated breath until he quit the room once more, cursing softly.

The nights proved more difficult as I continued to leave the door between our rooms unlocked. I'd debated locking them but thought it would only aggravate him further. Since he didn't accost me as I slept and only held me close, I continued to allow his nightly visits.

My feelings toward Alec were confusing. With a glance, he could change my pulse or just as likely annoy me. I found his dedication to returning the estate to its former glory admirable; but at the same time, I resented that he'd put it before me. I pitied him his continued scrutiny from Rose but wanted to shake him senseless for his close observance of me.

Rather than attempt to resolve how I felt, I chose not to think of it at all and drifted through my days, keeping busy with feast preparations.

Before twelve days had passed, much of the lower floor shined from our collective efforts.

"Two weeks before the feast," Egrit said as she entered my room.

I groaned and burrowed under the covers.

"Come now. You have things to do today. Lord Ruhall needs you to go to the Water with Swiftly. The carriage is waiting for you out front."

I sat up in bed, pushing down the covers with the motion.

"Why am I going to the Water?"

"He didn't say." Egrit moved to my wardrobe and pulled out the dress she'd washed. She tossed it to me as I slid from bed. "But I'm sure it has to do with the feast. Swiftly probably knows more."

"Instead of the carriage, see if we can take the wagon," I said, unabashedly stripping from my shirt in my hurry to dress. "If we're going to the Water, we should take the spare milk we have."

"A sound plan."

"Have Swiftly meet me in the kitchen," I said as my head cleared the neckline of the dress. It took a moment for me to right myself and notice that Egrit was no longer there.

After quickly washing my face and teeth, I left my room. The rapid click of my boot heels echoed in the hall. It had been over a week since we'd last delivered milk. I wondered how much milk we had in storage and hoped it would be enough to give some to each home as we had before.

Swiftly waited in the kitchen and stood when I entered.

"Good morning," I said with a smile. "I apologize for the change in plans but thought we could take the milk as promised."

"I've plans for the milk, Miss," Mrs. Wimbly said from her place at the butcher's block. She was kneading dough and didn't look up as she spoke.

"Plans?"

"For soft cheese."

"How much cheese do you plan to make?"

"As much as the milk in storage will give me." A hard note had crept into her voice.

I studied her for a moment. She always seemed so busy with the food preparations she currently maintained. I wondered how she would find the time to make cheese, too.

"I see. How much milk is in storage?"

"Sixteen small barrels, Miss Hovtel," Kara said. Mrs. Wimbly's movements stumbled then resumed. Sixteen seemed a bit much for our small household.

"Thank you, Kara." I focused on Mrs. Wimbly. "How much soft cheese do you estimate a single barrel will provide?"

"Miss Hovtel, I have duties assigned to me by Lord Ruhall. I can't stand about chatting with you all day. If you'll excuse me..." She left the room in a huff, and I stared after her.

Despite Mr. Crow's admonition to treat me with respect, she seemed to be having a hard time of it. The why puzzled me as I'd been nothing but courteous to her.

"If you take all but three, there should be plenty," Kara said softly, watching the door.

"Thank you."

Once we had the wagon loaded—thankfully without Mrs. Wimbly returning—Swiftly helped me into my seat and clucked the horses to start our journey. While we navigated the drive, I kept a close watch on the barrels tied in the back to ensure they didn't jostle overly much. After we reached the main road, I turned toward Swiftly.

"What business would Lord Ruhall have at the Water?"

"We are buying a dress," he said with a slight smile.

"A dress? Why would Lord Ruhall need a dress?"

"He doesn't. You do."

"I have no coin. And if I did, I wouldn't use it for a dress. I have two, which is twice as many as I'd like."

Swiftly laughed.

"No need to worry about the coin," he said, reaching up and tapping his chest. Metal jingled.

"Whose coin?"

"Lord Ruhall. He asked that I remind you the purpose behind the feast is to help support the community by paying for local goods."

A concept I understood. However, supporting the community by impoverishing the estate would benefit no one. Rather than pointing that out, I decided to wait and see how much a new dress would cost. Since Blye had always made mine for me, I had no idea.

When we reached the trade street, the homes with children eagerly accepted the milk we offered. Barrels empty, we climbed aboard once more and rattled our way to the market district.

"Lord Ruhall thought you might want to try the seamstress at the end of the street," Swiftly said as we approached my sister's shop.

"No. I'd like to speak with Blye about the dress."

Swiftly made an odd face but slowed the wagon before her shop. He helped me down and followed me to the door.

"I'll wait here," he said, opening it for me.

I nodded and stepped in. Blye stood folding handkerchiefs on a small table. She looked up at the sound of the door, and the welcoming smile on her face faded when she saw me. She was probably hoping for a paying customer. Which I was. I smiled at her.

"Hello, Blye. I've come to see if you have time to sew a dress for me."

"Benella, I thought I said—" She glanced at the curtained door that no doubt led to the sewing room and started again. "No, I don't have time."

She'd been folding handkerchiefs. I doubted lack of time the reason. I studied her hard expression.

"Why?" I asked, unwilling to leave without hearing a reason for her attitude.

She released a slow breath with a shake of her head.

"Because I won't associate with loose women."

A small choking noise escaped me.

"And you consider me loose because a pig of a man almost raped me?"

"Benella, please. Just leave," she said with another nervous glance at the back room. She lowered her voice. "And it would be better if you never came back."

Her complete abandonment pierced me. I'd thought Bryn cruel; Blye was more so because she had no cause. Hers wasn't misguided self-recrimination but rather the shallow concern of what her peers might think of her.

Without another word, I turned and left.

Outside, Swiftly spoke to a beautiful woman with long blonde hair. His scarlet face and averted eyes distracted me from my anger.

"Swiftly?"

"Benella," the woman said with a small smile. Her voice sounded raspy and familiar. I studied her mouth and recognized Ila dressed in a simple, normal gown.

"I saw you and hoped we might talk."

"I'd rather not," I said with a glance at the Whispering Sisters' house. The place I had once thought filled with friends now seemed a house of lies. And it made me wonder why Ila sought me out.

"Not there," she said, following my gaze. "Just a walk if you think it suitable."

"I'm not concerned with suitability as much as I am preservation. Aryana has done enough—"

"I'm not here for her. I'm here for you."

Swiftly had watched our exchange; and when I looked at him in question, he shrugged.

"I will follow wherever you lead, Miss Hovtel."

"Well, then. Come, Ila. Let's walk."

Side by side, we slowly paced north along the street.

"Are you well?" she asked softly.

"Well enough, I suppose. How are you? I'm surprised to see you about at this time." It was nearing the hour when their clients would arrive.

"When news spread that Aryana was responsible for Lord Ruhall's curse, many of our customers did not return."

"I can hardly fault them."

"Nor do I. But now, many of us find ourselves idle. Without Aryana there to ensure our future, some have left for other occupations, thanks to their education. Two had offers of marriage."

"What do you mean? She's not there?"

"She gave us all a small fortune and disappeared not long after..." Conversation halted for several moments. "I heard some of what your sister said to you and am afraid you will find the same welcome at many of the seamstresses here."

"They condemn the wrong party," I said with a frustrated exhale.

"They do."

"It's just as well. I wasn't looking forward to another dress. I long for the days when I walked the woods in my sturdy shirt and trousers."

Ila chuckled.

"If you're willing, I would be glad to make your dress. We've grown adept at creating our own dresses because we've found the same welcome at most shops here."

I stopped walking and turned to Ila. The sincerity in her gaze and her words filled me with enough compassion that I answered more kindly than I would have previously.

"I would be honored and will wear it proudly."

She seemed relieved, and I wondered if boredom hadn't prompted the offer.

"What does the future hold for you, Ila?"

She shrugged and looked around. "I wouldn't mind finding a man willing to take me as I am."

"I wouldn't think that would be an issue. How old are you?"

She gave a small smile. "Almost twenty."

"Plenty of time to meet a decent man."

"Not here."

I looked around and caught the long glances aimed our way.

"No, not here," I said in agreement. "Come to Lord Ruhall's feast and be my special guest. There will be many faces there that I think you might not yet have seen."

Her smile widened. "I would be honored."

"Now, do you need my measurements?"

She laughed. "No need. I know them well."

"Payment?" I glanced at Swiftly.

He handed her the gold.

"I hope that's enough," I said with a question in my voice.

"It is. Your gown will be lovely."

With nothing more to say, I nodded farewell and followed Swiftly back to the wagon.

He and I rode back in silence. My thoughts were heavy and unsuitable for company. My sisters shunned me; and though Ila sought me out, I wasn't ready to trust her or count her among my friends. I could count Egrit as a friend to an extent; however, she didn't treat me as a peer. Her affection for me ran closer to savior and part errant ward. I realized I was quite friendless. Now, more than ever, I wished I could leave the North.

Swiftly dropped me off at the front door and clucked the horse to bring the wagon to the barn. I let myself in and closed the door behind me. Though I wanted nothing more than to escape to my room, I turned toward the laundry to help press the table linens. Neither Egrit nor Mrs. Palant commented on my subdued responses to their active conversation.

Lord Ruhall had Father fetch me for a stilted dinner where Father glanced at me often, a knowing sadness in his gaze. I wondered what Blye might have said to him when he had gone to the Water. No doubt she'd accepted the invitation well enough, just not Father's presence. My heart was heavy for him as well.

Alec remained quiet throughout the meal, the set of his jaw becoming more tense with each moment until I finally excused myself.

With relief, I sought my bed.

THE SOUND of steps roused me. Someone moved about in my room. Before I could panic, Alec spoke softly.

"Why do you refuse to see I'm here?" Frustration laced his low words.

I knew he was speaking to himself. He didn't understand. I did see him. I knew he was there. And my longing for who he used to be was destroying me.

The pacing stopped and the bed dipped. He wrapped me in his arms, and I stayed awake long after his breathing lulled.

I LAY in bed after waking. My heavy heart wouldn't let me stand. I hated the need for the feast and my commitment to stay to see it through. I wanted to speak to my father and flee.

Pushing aside my despondency, I slid from bed. It was only when I stood and felt the air on my bare legs that I recalled I still slept in his shirt. Wrinkling my nose, I pulled it off over my head. It needed a washing. Though Egrit hadn't commented on it during the many times she'd come to wake me, I thought it better to return it to Alec's dirty laundry than to wash it myself.

After I washed and dressed, I strode across the room with the shirt. Perhaps it was time to put aside my memories of the beast.

His return was unlikely, and my continued hope for it, unfair. Twisting the handle, I pulled the door wide and froze.

Lord Ruhall reclined in a bathing tub on a rug at the foot of his bed. The wide expanse of his bare shoulders had me staring stupidly. I'd never before seen a man without his shirt. Not true. I'd seen all of Gen at the Whisperings Sisters. My stomach dipped and heat flooded my face as I recalled every detail of that particular lesson.

At the sound of the door, Alec turned his head and caught my gaze. The move brought more of his back out of the water. I swallowed and averted my gaze slightly to his shoulder and the tiny red marks there. Deeply puckered scars. As I stared, the small crescent shapes took on meaning, and my world pitched.

"Benella? Are you all right?" His words broke through my revelation, and I struggled to recall my purpose.

"Yes. Quite. I wanted to return your shirt. It needs a wash."

"Take a new one," he said, leaning back in the water once more.

The wardrobe stood just a few feet from the tub. My mind in a jumble, I absently dropped the old shirt to the floor and went to the wardrobe to select a clean one from the several waiting within. As I closed the doors, something tugged on my skirt. I turned. Alec had an arm extended from the tub and held the material in his hand. He looked up at me, his expression masked.

"Could you bring the soap for me?" He pointed to his dressing table near the wardrobe.

I absently nodded, and he let go of my skirt.

What did the scars mean? Could I have been wrong?

The well-used cake of soap was small and made me feel so guilty that I couldn't find a way around using estate gold for the feast. Soap in hand, I turned and brought it to Alec. The water did little to hide the strong length of his legs or the hard planes of his chest and stomach. He was so much bigger than Gen's lean frame. So much more interesting to study.

"The soap?" Humor laced his words.

I shook myself and handed over the soap before rushing from the room. In my own chamber, I went to the window and stared out.

The marks were unmistakably fingernails. Only one person had set her hand on Alec's shoulder. Rose. The morning the baker had almost raped me. Had Alec truly wanted to come to my aid? Though Rose posed no threat physically, her nails would have served as a reminder of what she could do with her magic. Why stop him, though?

The sun traveled the sky as I debated the possibilities. I needed to talk to someone. The only person left to me was Father. I knew he would listen, yet the reason behind the lackluster rescue of my near rape would be a potentially disquieting topic for him.

Sighing, I left my room and felt a small measure of guilt that I'd done nothing to help that day. Many of the rooms I passed had open doors and windows. Fresh air swept through the first and second floors.

I met Otta at the bottom of the steps.

"Otta, what are you doing out of the schoolroom?"

She looked nervous. I reached out, smoothed back the hair on her head, and gave her an encouraging smile.

"We stopped for the midday meal. Mrs. Wimbly had me deliver a tray to your father. I'm to return straight to Mr. Roost."

"I'll speak with Mr. Roost and Mrs. Wimbly. You should have no tasks during the day."

"Thank you, Miss Hovtel," she said before she scampered away.

As I continued toward the library, I heard what sounded like someone stomping on the floor. The sound came again. Not stomping. Something hitting the floor.

Lengthening my stride, I rounded the corner of the library door just in time to see a book sail from the study. It landed not far from the door with a loud bang. Cursing followed, punctuated by something hitting wood.

Father half-stood behind his desk, his shock clear. We looked at each other before I hurried to the study.

I ducked to dodge another book that Alec threw without seeing me. He was in a rage, his face red and his jaw clenched. He grabbed his chair and began to lift it high over his head.

"Alec," I said. Shock robbed my voice of volume, yet he heard.

He froze at the sound of his given name and turned his angry gaze on me. His chest heaved, and his eyes were dark. My pulse leapt at the sight. How many times had I faced him like this?

Cautiously, I walked into the room.

"Set it down," I said softly.

He yelled loudly and half-slammed the chair to the floor. I stepped further into the room and carefully approached him. I almost smiled. His mood reminded me so much of how he'd acted the time I'd locked myself in his room.

Once I reached him, I gently touched his face.

"What upsets you so?"

He closed his eyes, heaved a breath, and leaned his cheek into my hand. He stayed like that until some of the flush faded from his face. Pulling away from me, he reached for a crumpled piece of parchment and handed it to me.

HAVING a woman assist with your bath is not a wise decision. I am watching and will take from you all you hold dear if you continue with these transgressions. ~Rose

. . .

"I SEE," I said, though I didn't. How did fetching soap mean I had assisted with a bath? Aryana had assisted with my bath in a far more physical manner at the Whispering Sisters. Her assessment of the situation remained far from just. Then again, all her assessments seemed to run toward unjust. I thought of the marks on Alec's shoulder as I glanced up at him.

He looked ready to start throwing things again. He didn't seem cold at all, now, and I wondered if he ever had been. Could it be that he had only been trying to maintain control of himself? A control he still hadn't mastered by the looks of it.

Though I agreed he had a reason to be upset, his way of showing his disagreement needed to stop.

I glanced at the door and saw Mr. Crow and Father there.

"Mr. Crow, would you bring some spring water to the library?" He nodded and left. "Father, would it bother you if I read aloud while you worked?"

"No. Not at all," he said.

I turned back to Alec. "Would you care to listen to me read for a while?"

His gaze searched mine. So much anger and resentment churned there. Yet, I didn't think any of it was for me. Should it be, though? Perhaps I had misunderstood him. Or perhaps regaining my affection was another game. After all, if I'd misunderstood, why hadn't he come to see Father as Swiftly had said that day?

Instead of answering, Alec motioned for me to lead him out. I went to the couch before the fire and waited. He joined me with a book on farming. I smiled at the topic, recalling better times, and took the book from him. I reclined on the couch so my braid draped over the arm, and Alec sat on the floor. A moment later, I felt a tug on my braid, and I began.

Mr. Crow arrived with the pitcher and cups before I'd progressed more than a page. He quietly set everything on the table next to the tray already there, then withdrew as I continued reading about selective animal husbandry to create a stronger herd.

Alec's fingers combed through my hair as I read, and I hoped it soothed him as much as he soothed me.

Finishing the chapter, I closed the book with a snap then waited.

"Thank you," Alec said softly, removing his hands.

I sat up, moved over, and patted the spot beside me. He rose from the floor and took the seat.

"You have every right to be upset," I said, reaching to pour him a cup of water. "However, destroying your study resolves nothing." I handed him the cup and watched his expression.

His jaw clenched, but he nodded.

"She seems so fond of writing you notes. Write one back." I helped myself to a meat pie and waited for his reaction.

"And what would I say to defend myself? She is correct. I shouldn't have—" He looked down at his water.

"Alec," I reached out and took his hand in mine, "you're not the man you were. Don't let her keep punishing you for a past you've already paid for."

His hand tightened around mine a moment before he released me and walked back to his study, picking up the ejected book on his way.

I let out a long slow breath, then stood.

"I'll take this tray back to the kitchen. Do you need help with anything today?" I asked, looking at my father.

"No, Bini. We'll be fine here."

I left, carrying the tray to the kitchen, and once again not speaking to my father as I'd planned.

CHAPTER
SEVEN

"Would you like me to return the tray for you?" he asked, stepping forward.

"No need. I haven't eaten yet," I said.

He nodded and let me continue with the tray.

When I entered the kitchen, Kara kneaded bread at the block. Her nervous glance at me, then at the stairs to the cellar, only left me puzzled for a moment.

"Where is the milk?" Mrs. Wimbly shouted from the cellar.

"Sorry, Miss," Kara whispered as Mrs. Wimbly thundered up the steps.

I set the tray on the table and braced myself for a confrontation. However, when she saw me, she stopped in her tracks. Her face turned red, and the disapproving set of her mouth tightened. With a glare, she turned on her heel and left the kitchen.

"She'll go to Mr. Crow to complain," Kara said.

That Mrs. Wimbly went to Mr. Crow didn't bother me. She would likely find an unsympathetic ear there. However, it did concern me that she was spending time on worrying about milk.

"How are the preparations coming along?" I asked as I browsed the pots for any leftovers. I'd missed breakfast because of Alec in the bath and Rose's nail marks, and now I'd missed lunch because of his temper. I wasn't about to go hungry until dinner.

"By the fire, you'll still find some fish stew," Kara said quietly. "There are biscuits in the oven, too. We've stored a good portion of stag, boar, and fish for the winter. The menu for the feast still needs to be settled."

"Have we smoked any fish yet?" I skipped the stew, though it did look tasty, and helped myself to a biscuit.

"Not yet. Mrs. Wimbly plans to start that closer to the feast."

"Will that interfere with all the meat pies she needs to make?" I took a quick bite.

"I believe she hopes one of the girls from the schoolroom will help us in the days just before the feast."

"Perhaps in the evenings, but I'll stay true to my word. They will remain in the classroom during the day."

Kara nodded but I saw the doubt there. I needed to find Mrs. Wimbly and set her straight regarding the children and their roles. Still nibbling my biscuit, I left the kitchen.

Neither she nor Mr. Crow were by the closed front door. Wandering further, I heard faint voices from the library.

"...will not tolerate any more interference," I heard Mrs. Wimbly say from the study as I entered the library. "You hired me as the head cook, a position that requires me to complete preparation and planning each week."

I glanced at my father who sat at his desk. He met my gaze briefly then focused on his book once more, his expression set. Whatever the discussion in Lord Ruhall's study, Father did not approve.

Mrs. Wimbly continued in her agitated tone.

"My preparation and plans fall apart when others take it upon themselves to remove supplies without approval."

The woman had admitted to me that she threw much of the milk to waste. Why was she so upset? And why bring such a petty grievance before Alec? I continued toward the study and caught sight of Mr. Crow beside Alec.

"Mrs. Wimbly, who is taking it upon themselves to remove supplies and what supplies were removed?" Alec asked. Though his tone was calm, the tension from Rose's last letter remained in his hard expression.

I caught Mr. Crow's attention as I neared the study door, and his troubled gaze found mine. Nodding to Mr. Crow, I stepped into the study before Mrs. Wimbly could answer.

"I beg your pardon, but I believe I've upset Mrs. Wimbly by taking milk from the cold storage."

"You believe? Yes, you've upset me. You have no regard for—"

"Mrs. Wimbly," Alec said, "I would like a private word with Miss Hovtel. Thank you for bringing this to my attention."

"Very good," she said. She shot me a satisfied look and strode from the room. Mr. Crow moved to follow her.

"A moment, Phillip," Alec said.

Mr. Crow paused his departure and turned to look at Alec.

"Mrs. Wimbly is to leave my employ immediately. See her packed and delivered to wherever it is she came from."

"What? But why?" I asked as Mr. Crow moved to leave. "Wait, Mr. Crow." I held up a hand to forestall him and turned to Alec. "We need her. The feast is just weeks away. We can't possibly manage with just one cook."

Mr. Crow glanced at Alec who waved him from the room. An edge of panic grabbed me as I realized my plea had fallen on deaf ears.

"Alec, please be reasonable. She's done nothing to deserve dismissal."

He stood and moved around the desk. His carefully blank expression unnerved me.

"She has done nothing?" He stopped before me and lifted a hand to brush a strand of hair from my cheek. "Phillip said she's rude to you and refuses to treat you with the courtesy you deserve."

Very few had lately. The thought brought the hurt of my sisters' rejections dangerously close to the surface, and I quickly turned away.

Alec caught my arm and brought me back around.

"What's this, now?" he said, studying my face. A second later, he pulled me into a firm hug. "Surely, Mrs. Wimbly's dismissal isn't that upsetting. Even your father finds her disagreeable," he said against my hair.

Secure in his arms, the hurt from Blye's latest rejection eased. His hold felt so right. I leaned into the protection of his arms, allowing myself a moment of shelter from all life had been throwing at me lately. I wrapped my arms around his waist and breathed deeply of his familiar scent.

"You can speak to me, Benella," he said softly. "I'm here to listen. Always."

I sighed as I realized how much I needed just that.

"It's not your dismissal of Mrs. Wimbly. It's my life. I can't—"

His arms tightened around me so much that I looked up. His closed eyes, red face, and clenched jaw surprised me; and I knew I'd upset him. Removing my hold from his waist, I cupped his face.

"Alec, you're no longer listening."

He exhaled slowly, and his turbulent gaze found me.

"I am. You still want to leave. Don't." He closed his eyes once more and set his forehead to mine, a tormented man seeking sanctuary. What a poor pair we were, both seeking the same thing.

"I've made up my mind to stay and help with the feast. I won't abandon you."

"Say ever. Say, 'I won't abandon you ever, Alec.'"

I soothed my fingers over his jaw. His breath tickled my neck. When I said nothing, he opened his eyes. From the study, my father loudly cleared his throat, and I surmised we'd been quiet for too long.

"About Mrs. Wimbly?" I said, trying to step back. Alec's arms tightened, and for a moment, I thought he might not release me. Then, they fell to his sides. He studied me intensely, and I wondered what he searched so hard for in my expression.

Finally, he shook his head.

"Phillip will search for an immediate replacement. I would like you to help interview whomever he finds."

"Of course."

That night, I didn't sleep until Alec came to my bed and wrapped his arms around me. I waited until his breathing deepened then turned in his arms. Lightly, I ran my fingers over the marks. The hard, puckered skin rose from the sculpted curve of his shoulder. Rose had marked him deeply.

As I lay there, I again struggled with how he'd stood there and calmly ordered the baker off of me. Were these marks enough to absolve him of his inaction? No. But they were enough for me to start questioning what happened after Tennen took me from the manor. Questions that I would never speak because I trusted no one to tell me the truth.

The most important in my mind was, why hadn't Alec come for me like Swiftly had said he would?

IN THE MORNING, Egrit woke me with a letter and a coddled egg.

"A letter is never good news in this place," I said, sitting up.

Egrit grinned at me. "You're very perceptive." She left the room before I could say more. Sighing heavily, I unfolded the note.

BENELLA,

Bryn and I have heard Lord Ruhall is in need of another cook. I know Bryn deserves less after her treatment of you, but would you perhaps mention her for consideration? Business remains slow enough that I manage the store and the stove well without assistance.

Yours,

Edmund

UNGRACIOUSLY, I did not want to endure my sister's presence on a daily basis. Yet, I knew her skill in the kitchen and knew we could do worse. However, it wasn't a decision I wanted to make without Father's input.

I dressed and carried my egg and the letter to the library.

"Good morning, Bini," Father said from his seat at his desk.

"Good morning, Father. I received a letter this morning."

"Letters bode ill here."

"My sentiments as well. I cannot ignore this one. Yet, I do not know how to respond."

I handed him the letter then sat on the chair near his desk. While he read, I ate the egg, enjoying the deliciously soft yolk.

"Hmm," Father said, sitting back. "What were your first thoughts after reading this?"

"That Edmund was correct. Bryn doesn't deserve my consideration. Then, I immediately felt guilty for having such uncharitable thoughts. Even if Bryn doesn't deserve the opportunity, Edmund does. For him to reach out...I think he truly needs help."

"So you'll speak to Lord Ruhall."

"Speak to me about what?" Alec asked, walking into the library. His gaze went to the empty eggshell and spoon that I held. "How was it?"

"Did you make the egg?"

"I thought with Mrs. Wimbly gone Kara might need some assistance in the kitchen."

A laugh escaped me. It couldn't be helped. The image of him wandering into the kitchen and offering aid...

"And her reaction?" I asked.

"As you might imagine. But after the initial shock, she gave me direction on how to soft boil the eggs for everyone's breakfast."

"Well done. You might not need to return to the kitchen tomorrow, though," I said, holding up the note.

He took it from me, scanned the contents, and frowned, studying first me then Father.

"You are both considering this, aren't you?"

I sighed and nodded. Alec looked at Father.

"With respect, your eldest daughter has shown her true nature again and again at the expense of both of you. For you, I will allow this, but if she causes trouble, she will leave as quickly as Mrs. Wimbly, family or not."

"I completely agree," Father said.

"Then, I should go speak with Edmund and Bryn," I said, standing.

"Take Swiftly with you," Alec said.

I agreed and left. Before seeking out Swiftly, I found Kara and Mr. Crow at the table in the kitchen. If they had been conversing, they stopped when I arrived.

"Good morning," I said. "Do you both have a moment?"

"Of course," Mr. Crow said.

I sat beside him.

"It seems word has spread of our need for a cook. I received a letter this morning with a possible replacement but wanted to speak with both of you first. Mrs. Wimbly wasn't agreeable, but she cooked well. I'd like to see an agreeable and competent person fill the position." The sister I knew now was not that person. I wondered at my reasoning, then, for considering her. Because we needed help. Any help. Yet, I would not subject Kara to another version of Mrs. Wimbly. If Bryn would only reserve her bad temperament for me alone, things would be fine in the kitchen.

"Miss Hovtel?" Mr. Crow said.

"My sister's husband has asked that we consider her for the position. However, I do not think she would be suited for head cook. I would prefer to see that position go to Kara."

"Me?" Kara said, her shock plain.

"Yes. You understand the workings of the kitchen and the staff. You work well with others. My sister has never had to direct anyone else." Not true. She had directed me plenty. But I wouldn't allow her to use Kara like that.

"My greatest concern as we approach the feast is keeping the expenses low. I propose that all kitchen purchases go through Mr. Crow, who can report weekly spending to Lord Ruhall." My bigger fear was that Bryn would find a way to filch coin from the estate, and I faulted that concern on my tarnished esteem of her character.

"Bryn does know how to cook and, with the knowledgeable direction you can provide, will be a fit addition."

"I look forward to meeting her," Kara said.

"As do I," Mr. Crow said, standing. "May I walk with you for a moment?" He offered me a hand up and indicated the outer kitchen door.

He didn't speak until we were on the path outside.

"Miss Hovtel, your presence here is an honor and a delight."

I smiled at his kind words, until I noted his very concerned expression.

"With respect, I watched your family for several days before you came to live here the first time, and I saw your hesitation just now as you spoke in the kitchen. Surely I am not alone in my concern regarding your sister's employ."

"Mr. Crow, you are far from alone. That is why I will not offer her the position of head cook and why I want purchasing to go through you. I trust her to cook, but little else. If you find her manner offensive or abrasive, Lord Ruhall and my father both insist she then be dismissed in the same fashion as Mrs. Wimbly."

He exhaled in relief.

"Very good."

"We need the help, Mr. Crow. If not, I would not choose her."

"I understand."

At the front of the house, I caught sight of Swiftly.

"If you will pardon me, I best catch Swiftly and visit my sister. The sooner she arrives, the sooner we will have the help we need."

After parting ways with Mr. Crow, I caught up with Swiftly and told him of my need to visit Konrall immediately. He turned and walked with me toward the gate.

"And what so urgently calls us to Konrall?" Swiftly asked.

"I need to speak with Edmund. He would have Bryn work in the kitchen with Kara."

"Do you think that wise? I mean no disrespect with the question..."

"It is only right that you question what concerns you. The enchantment taught you that, and I find no offense in it. It is wise to replace Mrs. Wimbly immediately. Time will tell if Bryn was the wisest choice."

He nodded, and we walked the rest of the distance in silence. Konrall seemed quieter than I remembered. Possibly because the schoolhouse remained closed. I needed to speak with Alec about that. The bakery doors stood open, but we found the front store empty when we stepped in, just another element to the uninhabited feel of Konrall.

I rang the bell at the counter and waited.

Edmund appeared from the kitchen after a moment, and he smiled widely when he saw me.

"Benella. Welcome. Did you receive my letter?" His hopeful expression firmed my decision.

"I did. It's the reason behind my visit. Lord Ruhall and Father were agreeable to hiring Bryn, not as head cook but as an assistant. Is she here?"

"Bryn," he called in answer. She came down the steps a moment later. When she saw me, her face closed of all expression.

"Yes?"

"Lord Ruhall will hire you as an assistant cook," he said. Where the news excited him, she revealed no emotion.

"When does he want me to start?" she said, looking at Edmund when she reached the bottom step. Her middle was just a bit thicker.

"Immediately if you can," I said.

"She can," Edmund said firmly.

Bryn turned away from him, still without even a glance at me and marched out the door. There, she stopped.

"Where's the wagon?"

Swiftly arched a brow at me. Edmund caught the look and flushed.

"Pardon us for a moment," he said before he strode out the door, grabbing Bryn's arm on the way. They moved off to the side to speak in hushed tones. Her shoulders stiffened to whatever he said, then she pulled her arm away and started down the road.

Edmund watched her for a moment before he came back in.

"Thank you for giving her a chance, Benella."

"I didn't do it for her," I said with a slight smile. "Enjoy your day, Edmund."

He smiled in return.

"I will."

Bryn had managed a healthy distance by the time Swiftly and I stepped out, and I was glad to let her keep it. We trailed her, and I witnessed her first glimpse of the estate. Her steps faltered for only a moment then doubled their pace toward the front door. Mr. Crow opened it before she reached it. When he closed it behind him and pointed to the left, I knew he would see her settled in the kitchen.

"Thank you for accompanying me, Swiftly."

"Whenever you have the need, Miss Hovtel," he said with a wink.

I grinned and moved to the front steps as Mr. Crow and Bryn disappeared around the side. For the rest of the morning, I helped clean wherever Egrit pointed.

Midday, I eagerly joined the others in the kitchen where a kettle of stew and a stack of bowls waited on the table. The children and Mr. Roost were already there. Mrs. Palant spoke softly to her son and daughter while Egrit sat by Tam. The mood of the room was relaxed and pleasant. Mr. Crow stood near the butcher block, watching Bryn as she ladled portions into three bowls and set a loaf of bread on a tray. As soon as she finished, Mr. Crow picked it up.

"I can take it," Bryn said quickly. Mr. Crow frowned at her, but she didn't seem to notice.

"There is a setting for you," he said, looking at me, "if you would care to join your father and Lord Ruhall."

I nodded and followed him from the kitchen.

"How did she do?" I asked.

"Fair. She questioned Kara about Lord Ruhall but asked nothing about you or your father."

I chuckled. Lord Ruhall was of interest in her eyes, and we were not.

"How did Kara deal with her inquisition?"

"Her standard answer was, 'Why should a cook know that?'"

"I like Kara."

"As do I," he said with the barest of smiles.

When we reached the library, Mr. Crow set the tray on the table and left.

Father, unaware of the world around him, continued to read. I doubted estate business kept him at his seat all day. The rows upon rows of books would tempt even the dullest scholar. Leaving him to his peace, I made my way to the study.

Alec likewise focused on a book and didn't immediately look up at my approach. With his brow furrowed in concentration, he absently rubbed his jaw. A healthy coating of stubble rasped his fingers. He'd removed his jacket and loosened his neckcloth. The sight of him thus made my middle warm, and I wondered again about the marks on his shoulder.

"Mr. Crow brought a tray," I said softly.

He looked up and warmth filled his gaze for a brief moment before it disappeared.

"Did you visit your sister?" he asked, standing.

"Yes. She helped prepare the midday meal under Kara and Mr. Crow's instruction. Instead of biscuits, we have bread."

He looked mildly interested.

"What were you reading?" I asked as he marked his page and stood.

"A book of basic arithmetic your father borrowed from Mr. Roost."

"Ah."

"Yes, ah. I have a man of estate who insists I must know the arithmetic to check my own records."

"I won't live forever," my father said from the other room. "And your next man might not be as honest."

"He hears everything," I said in a mock whisper. "Years of teaching."

Alec chuckled and walked around the desk toward me. When he reached me, he set a hand on my lower back and guided me to the library.

"I'm ready for a break. Let's eat."

AFTER A PLEASANTLY DRAWN out meal with Father and Lord Ruhall, I carried the tray back to the kitchen.

Bryn was washing dishes, and Kara was absent. I brought the tray over to the sink and set it near the other dirty bowls.

"What is it you do here?" Bryn asked without looking up.

"I clean," I said, surprised she spoke to me.

"And eat meals with Lord Ruhall."

"With Father. Lord Ruhall chooses to join him."

She nodded slightly, straightened, and wiped her hands.

"Could you wash for a bit? I need to sit," she said.

"I'm afraid, Miss Hovtel is needed elsewhere," Mr. Crow said from his office, making me start.

Bryn gave an almost inaudible sigh and went back to washing. I turned to look at Mr. Crow, and with a conspiratorial wave, he shooed me from the kitchen.

THE NEXT MORNING I woke with a stretch. Exhausted from a day of beating mattresses, I'd collapsed on the bed fully dressed. I had no recollection of Alec joining me; yet a blanket covered me, and my stockings were off.

I washed my face and went in search of food. In the kitchen, Kara and Bryn were already hard at work.

"Good morning, Miss Hovtel," Kara said when she spotted me.

Bryn looked up and frowned at me.

"Really, Benella. Your dress is wrinkled like you slept in it. You're in a Lord's house now. Go change so you at least *look* respectable."

I pressed my lips together. I was respectable, wrinkled dress or not.

"Bryn, go see if Tam has fresh milk for the children," Kara said.

Bryn dusted her hands on her apron and walked outside.

"Are you hungry?" Kara asked once we were alone.

"Very. Is there anything ready?"

"I can boil an egg for you. The biscuits will need another half an hour. There are also a few apples Tam picked yesterday. They should be ready for harvest tomorrow or the day after."

"I'll take an apple and come back later for a biscuit."

She grabbed the apple, and I held up my hand. With a grin, she tossed it to me.

"Thank you, Kara." Before Bryn could return, I hurried out of the kitchen and found Egrit in the laundry room.

"What will we work on today?" I crunched into my apple. The juice was only slightly tart and, in my opinion, perfect.

"Mrs. Palant is dusting the parlors in the ballroom so they remain clean. You can dust the front sitting room if you'd like. I am going to go through the second floor bedrooms that have been aired and cleaned." She had three of the large vats filled and lit a small fire under each.

"What is the water for?"

She straightened with a laugh.

"Benella, you are wearing yesterday's dust. It's for our baths tonight."

The idea of a bath in one of the large vats had me eagerly heading toward the sitting room. The sooner I finished the day's work, the sooner I could bathe. Once I eyed the room and recalled it had taken three of us more than a day to clean it, my enthusiasm faltered. With a sigh, I took my dust rag and set to work.

Several hours had passed when Mr. Crow found me.

"Miss Hovtel, your assistance is needed immediately."

I eagerly set down my rag and followed him from the room, hoping the assistance brought me to the kitchen. The apple had long since disappeared.

My anticipation of food dwindled as I neared the kitchen and heard a familiar voice. Blye stood in the center of the kitchen with her back to us when we entered. But she quickly turned at the sound of our steps.

"Why can't Bryn stop to talk to me?" she asked me. Annoyance painted her face.

I glanced at Mr. Crow who stood just slightly behind me and to my right. His focus remained on Blye. Why had he brought me here to deal with her? Facing Blye, I forced myself to relax and tried to forget our last, hurtful encounter.

"I'm not in charge of what Bryn chooses to do."

"He says if she stops working, she stops being paid. Why is it you can stop working?"

I laughed. At her. At the question. At the absurdity of the moment.

"Because I'm not paid."

She eyed me for a moment then seemed to decide I was telling the truth. With one last irritated glance at Mr. Crow, she began to explain her presence.

"I'm making Bryn's dress for the feast. I rented a carriage for two hours to bring it to her for a fitting because of the babe."

I sighed and glanced at Mr. Crow again. This time, we shared a calculating look. I didn't want to encourage either of my sisters to abuse Bryn's position. Yet, I couldn't ignore Blye's reasoning or her unspoken plea.

"A quarter of an hour should more than suffice," Mr. Crow said. "Miss Hovtel, I will leave you to show your sisters to an appropriate room."

Bryn and Blye shared an exuberant embrace that made me feel hollow. I turned away and listened to them follow me.

"If you're not paid, why are you here?" Blye asked as we passed the laundry.

"I'm here because Father is here, and I have no money to see me elsewhere. Would either of you care to visit Father?"

"I only have a quarter of an hour," Bryn said.

"And I must return to the shop as soon as I've finished," Blye said.

My face flushed with annoyance, but I said nothing as I led them to one of the smaller sitting rooms near the dining room. Egrit and Mrs. Palant had recently cleaned and aired it. I lit several candles and drew the curtains closed while Blye went to fetch the dress. Bryn closed the door and started undressing.

"What is he like?" she asked.

"Who?"

She rolled her eyes.

"Lord Ruhall." She stepped out of her dress and stood before me in her underthings.

"You've met him. Don't you recall what he's like?"

"That was when he was cursed. What is he like now? Is he handsome?"

The door opened and closed quickly as Blye stepped in with a sturdy, large bag.

"Who is handsome?" she asked as she set the bag on a lounge. She opened it and pulled out a pretty, lavender dress with a hint of lace trim.

"Lord Ruhall," Bryn said. Then she studied the dress Blye held out for her. "Isn't there more lace?"

"Not for the price you paid," Blye said. Bryn took the dress with a scowl and began to slip into it.

"Why would a married woman care about the handsomeness of a man?" I asked, watching the pair of them.

"Don't be dull, Benella," Bryn said. She laced up the front of her dress and adjusted the panel there. The clever design would allow the dress to grow with her.

"I wonder how many high ladies he's invited to the feast," Blye said. She tugged here and there and stood back to eye the dress critically.

"It's a feast for the local community. Why would he invite high ladies?"

"To start looking for a wife, of course. He's wasted enough of his life because of the enchantment and needs an heir for the estate," Blye said as someone knocked on the door.

I went to open it and found Otta in the hall.

"Mr. Crow sent me to tell you the quarter hour is up."

I smiled at the girl and gave her hair a gentle tug.

"And you should be in the schoolroom."

"Yes, Miss." She scampered off.

I closed the door and turned to face my sisters. Blye was already closing her bag, and Bryn was undressing. It didn't take her too long to change back into her normal dress.

"See if Benella can hang it for you until you leave tonight," Blye said as Bryn carefully laid her dress over the lounge.

"There is a spare room at the top of the stairs," I said to Bryn. "You can hang it in the wardrobe there."

"Good." She picked her dress back up and draped it over her arm. "I might need to leave it until just before the feast, so I can change at the last minute."

As I opened the door and stepped from the room, I heard a strange commotion, like the frantic rearrangement of furniture.

"Surely you're not working feast day," Blye said.

Bryn's reply escaped my attention as I hurried my steps to the end of the hall that opened to the front entry. The noise from the right almost covered Mr. Crow's arrival from my left. He glanced nervously toward the sounds then at me.

"Lord Ruhall, wait," Tam said distantly.

"Mr. Crow, see to my sisters," I said, just as something crashed. I lifted my skirts and dashed toward the sound.

I found Alec in the dining room. Several chairs lay in a broken heap already. Tam stood guard over the undamaged seats. But Alec wasn't eyeing those anymore. He was eyeing the stack of fine glazed plates at his side.

Mrs. Palant knelt near the fireplace, a forgotten bucket of dirty scrub water beside her as she stared at Lord Ruhall in shock.

I snatched up the bucket and hoisted the contents through the air in the general direction of Alec. The grey water doused him, just as he moved for the plates. The silence was immediate. Soot chunks stuck to his cheeks and forehead and littered his once white shirt.

His dark, angry eyes found me. His jaw remained locked, and his fists clenched as our gazes held.

"Mrs. Palant," I said calmly. "I apologize for the mess I've made on the floor. Would you fetch some rags so I can clean it?"

She said nothing, only rushed from the room. Under Tam's watchful and anxious presence, I approached Alec.

"This is unacceptable and beneath you," I said.

His eyes narrowed dangerously. I narrowed mine in return and leaned in so only he could hear me.

"I shall lock my door at night if you choose to lose control again." When I pulled back, his eyes were closed. He shook with his rage.

I looked at Tam.

"Lord Ruhall has sat behind his desk for too long. He needs fresh air and exercise, an abundance of it. And I have just the task. I need pillar stands for the feast. I thought tree trunks about this high would be just the thing," I said, leveling my hand to the height of my chest. "Make sure the limbs are thick and that Lord Ruhall does all the chopping."

When I finished speaking, Alec opened his eyes and left the room. Tam hurried after him.

Beside the door, I noticed a crumpled piece of paper on the floor. Another note from Rose based on Alec's reaction. I picked it up and straightened it as Bryn walked into the room.

"I just saw Lord Ruhall. It looked as if someone had dumped ash water on him."

Her words barely registered. They certainly weren't important. Nor was Mr. Crow's response.

"Mrs. Rouflyn, please return to your duties in the kitchen."

My heart continued to sink as I reread the brief message.

IT IS plain to see you cannot manage the estate alone. To continue as you are, a man, you must wed by winter solstice. Choose your bride with care. ~Rose

I CRUSHED the note once more, truly feeling Alec's anger. She was punishing him because of my help? Help she'd instigated. The longer I stood there, the more I seethed. She'd played her game long enough.

"Mr. Crow, I have business in the Water and will return before dinner."

"Yes, Miss. Is everything in order?" he said, glancing at my hand.

"I'm not certain," I said, giving him the honesty he deserved. "If Lord Ruhall returns before I do and asks for me, say nothing of my leaving. We cannot give Rose more reason to doubt him."

Mr. Crow nodded.

CHAPTER
EIGHT

ILA HAD SAID THAT ROSE WASN'T OFTEN AT THE WHISPERING Sisters. Yet, I had nowhere else to look for her. Well after the hour when the Sisters opened their doors to customers, I approached the back door. The guard who stood there let me through. Ila waited within. But she wasn't dressed in her veil, and smoke no longer clogged the air.

"Benella," she said warmly. When she stepped toward me to impart a hug, I eagerly accepted it.

"I'm not yet ready to show you your dress," she said, releasing me.

"I wish I were here for a fitting. I'm here for Rose. Aryana. Whatever we're to call her now."

"She's not here."

"Then, I'll wait and hope she returns."

Ila nodded and started to lead me down the familiar hallway.

"Where is everyone?" I asked.

She smiled at me over her shoulder.

"The men? Their numbers continued to dwindle until they stopped completely."

"How long will you stay?"

"At least until the feast. I want to see you wear your dress."

We went to the room where my father used to teach the women. A lounge and chairs now adorned the room. We'd only settled when the door flew open.

"Now, you want to talk to me?" Rose said, striding into the room. She wore a displeased expression, and she did not look old in either form or face. Seeing her so, angered me. It brought back the misery I'd suffered and continued to suffer.

"Silence didn't achieve the result I'd wanted," I said as Ila stood and left the room.

"And what result would that be?"

"For you to go away. You're punishing Lord Ruhall because of my help. That hardly seems just. If I leave, will you withdraw your demand?"

"Not at all. Your help proved that he cannot hope to manage his affairs on his own. Whether you remain or not, he needs a wife. Actually, if you leave, I shall be forced to move up the deadline to the feast. We wouldn't want him failing."

"Ha. I think you do want him to fail. You continue to punish him though he has paid for his past failings. Withdraw your edict."

"No. It remains. He has several months to woo his future bride. That is not a punishment; that is a kindness. Request that I change my mind again, and I will choose his bride for him and see them wed this night."

"Hateful woman," I said, standing. "I hope never to see you again."

The hurt that crossed her features was almost laughable. Did she think I would thank her for her cruel meddling?

When I reached the door, she spoke quietly.

"Thank you for talking to Ila. She was upset to think you might hold her to blame for anything that has transpired."

"Unlike you, I don't punish the innocent," I said without turning.

"When have I punished an innocent?"

With a scoff, I faced her.

"You've confessed that your manipulations brought me to the estate where I met with many manners of ill-use, disregard, and danger. The final event was your refusal to let the estate come to my aid, allowing the baker to nearly rape me. Was my time there not punishment? For surely I suffered more so than the enchanted beings of the estate who had the freedom to frolic and fuck without consequence or care during the duration of their stay."

Her eyes widened slightly, and her face flushed. "You would see no one punished. Instead, you label the guilty as innocent and let them carry on with their crimes."

I left, slamming the door behind me. My visit accomplished nothing but angering us both. I strode through the halls with clenched fists. Ila stood by the back door, waiting for me. Sympathy softened her features.

"Do you still wish me to attend the feast as your guest?"

I exhaled slowly and gave her a weak smile.

"I do. You are welcome to stay the night as well."

A DOZEN CANDLE stands were now scattered throughout the ballroom. Large, and thicker than my waist, they would work beautifully to hold the pillars the candle maker would bring. But it worried me that Alec had felled them so quickly. I hadn't been gone long. Two hours, perhaps. The purpose of the task had been to allow him to vent his anger in a suitable manner. That he had completed the chore in such a small amount of time could mean that Tam had helped him. Or...Alec was still very angry.

Whisking out of the ballroom, I went in search of Alec. I found him in his study. He sat behind the desk and stared at his arithmetic book. He still wore his soot stained shirt, but his jacket and neckcloth were missing. Sweat dampened hair stuck to his forehead.

"The stands are very nice. Thank you," I said from the doorway.

He didn't look up, and the furrow in his brow did not ease in the slightest. I felt pity and sorrow for him. I wished Rose would leave him alone. He'd suffered through so much, already. And the injustice of her latest decision only added more.

"I saw the letter from Rose."

His jaw clenched and the grip on the book tightened.

"I'm sorry, Alec. I went to her to see if she would rescind her edict. She would not."

His gaze remained locked on the pages.

"There is time," I said, trying to console him.

He threw the book aside and rose from his chair to stalk toward me, his temper unsubdued by the recent hard labor. When he reached me, his expression shifted through emotions too quickly for me to attempt to understand his precise mood. He was angry, but more. Frustrated. Desperate. Weary. It all flashed in his gaze.

"Time for what? For you to change your mind?"

I swallowed hard and looked away. He still wanted me as his wife. Though I'd told him I didn't trust him to love me, which still held true, there was much more.

"Alec, the idea of marrying anyone upsets me. I cannot endure what the baker—"

He pulled me into his arms and hushed me. Cautious of his turbulent mood, I allowed it for a brief moment before I pulled away.

"You're spending too much time in here," I said. He was too

active a man to remain sitting and studying for so long. He needed to moderate his pursuits to include activity each day. It might help with his temper.

"Would you consider helping with the harvest? According to what Egrit said, the apples should be ready any day."

"Will you be harvesting?"

"Of course."

A curious expression flitted over his features then disappeared.

"I will help. Will you read to me tonight? We can eat in the library."

I nodded. "I'll let Kara know we'll need a tray." I turned to go but looked back. "Don't give up hope."

I left him by his desk and went to the kitchen. When Kara saw me, she pointed to the table.

"Sit. You never came back for your biscuit and left before midday meal. I saved you some food."

Her concern had me smiling and dutifully following her order. While I sat, she went to the oven and pulled out a plate full of fish, carrots, and biscuits. My mouth watered as she set it before me.

"Thank you," I breathed just before taking a large bite of warm fish.

Bryn moved quietly about the kitchen, ignoring me. Her disregard allowed me to focus on my meal. It was only when I had a few crumbs left that I recalled why I'd come to the kitchen.

"Kara, Lord Ruhall has requested a tray for three for dinner."

Kara nodded and came for my plate. As I rose, I noticed Bryn's annoyed glance in my direction. I left without giving it thought.

MY BELLY WAS STILL satisfied when I joined Father in the library a while later. Alec read in the study.

"I heard there was a disturbance this afternoon," Father said discreetly.

I nodded and sat near his desk.

"Rose told him he needs to marry by winter solstice or suffer enchantment once more."

"We'd best start considering what preparations need to be made. Two feasts in a season will be a strain on the estate."

"The wedding feast must be simple, then. There were no requirements made by Rose. Only that he marry."

Father nodded and studied me for so long I looked away. Thankfully, Alec joined us and spared me from further scrutiny. As we ate, we discussed the estate coffers, which hadn't changed and shared reports on the feast's progress.

"I sent a note to the Head asking for suitable family entertainment," Father said. "He referred several local musicians who are happy to play for food, drink, and a bit of coin."

Relieved we'd managed yet another piece of the affair, I reported that the lower level was clean and ready for guests and the menu was tentatively planned.

"Tentatively?"

"Smoked fish, meat pies, apple pastries, and cider. I haven't thought of anything else we might offer without incurring an unreasonable expense."

"I think the menu will suffice," Alec said. "She seems to know exactly what we do. If it wasn't sufficient, we would have heard from her."

I knew he referred to Rose.

As soon as I finished, Alec stood.

"Would you read to me, Benella?"

He handed me a thin volume, and Father moved to go back to his desk.

"Of course," I said, accepting the book. I went to recline on the lounge, and Alec took his usual place on the floor. His hands tugged at my hair before I began.

He'd chosen poetry, sad pieces that brought melancholy more than cheer. I only read a few before closing the volume.

"Finished already?"

"Egrit has bath water heating. A warm bath would be more welcome than a cold one," I said, sitting up.

He accepted the volume from me.

"Will you read to me again tomorrow?"

I nodded and left, wondering what Father thought of how we behaved. It wasn't inappropriate, exactly. Yet, I still felt Alec's fingers in my hair.

THE BED DIPPED. Alec pulled me close. I sighed and sank deeper into sleep as his fingers trailed my arm.

TAM HAD baskets waiting at the base of the trees when Alec, Swiftly, and I joined him. The other men were fishing, trying to catch as much as possible to smoke for the feast. With only four of us to harvest, the task before us was daunting.

Alec stripped off his coat and neckcloth and rolled up his sleeves as Tam started to explain how to use the poles. I found myself glancing at Alec too often and missing bits of the instruction. The marks on his shoulder and the reason behind them were never far from my mind.

Tam handed us our poles, and Alec followed me as I selected a tree on which to start.

Within minutes, it was obvious I would be of little help with the pole, so I set it aside and picked from the lower branches. Alec worked the top branches. He never moved far from my side, and our time together was reminiscent of our times before the enchantment broke.

It was well past midday before we had our first tree picked clean.

"We'll carry the baskets to the wagon," Alec said, looking at me. "Will you ask Kara to prepare us something to eat? We'll join you after we finish."

I willingly left them to carry the heavy baskets and walked the distance to the manor. Kara wasn't in the kitchen this time. Hiding my reluctance, I turned to Bryn.

"Could you please prepare four servings of something? We've finished with the first load of apples."

She glanced at me, marched to the stove, and pulled four biscuits from the oven. Setting them on a single plate, she handed them to me.

"Perhaps you should have eaten a few of the apples."

I will not break this plate over my sister's head, I thought to myself. I took a calming breath before I spoke aloud.

"I'm sure Lord Ruhall will be grateful for the lunch you've provided."

Her eyes narrowed slightly, and she snatched the plate back.

I watched as she grabbed three more plates and put a biscuit on each. Then, she sliced thick wedges of cheese and placed them along with pieces of smoked fish on the plates. By the time she finished, Swiftly had joined us.

"I'll bring them to the table, Miss," he said to me. "Go sit."

He joined me at the table and set a plate before me. Tam and Alec came in a moment later. Alec sat beside me. Bryn brought us water and fawned over Lord Ruhall, asking if he'd like more of anything. She had obviously forgotten his disdain of her when he'd been a beast and had us all hanging in vines.

As soon as we finished eating, Tam, Alec, and I returned to picking while Swiftly delivered the apples to Edmund. It didn't take Swiftly long to return with the empty baskets.

"He said that was more than twice what he needed and thanked us for it."

I eyed all the trees that still hung heavy with fruit. Letting the harvest fall to waste on the ground wasn't an option. What we couldn't use, we would sell.

Alec came to stand behind me as I stared up at the heavy branches.

"Are you tired?"

"A little," I admitted.

"We can continue without you."

"No, I prefer this over dusting," I said, reaching for my next apple. In truth, I didn't want the men having to work harder because of my absence.

When we returned to the manor several hours later, Alec went directly to the study, assured by Tam and Swiftly that they no longer needed his help. The two then brought the baskets of apples around to the kitchen, and I followed. Kara knew of our plans to press them for cider and directed the men to take them into the cellar. While Bryn prepared a tray for me to take to the study, Kara pulled me to the side.

"Your sister is very helpful. However, with all these apples, I'm not certain the two of us can prepare meals, smoke fish, press cider, and—"

"I will speak with Egrit and see if she and Mrs. Palant can help. The rooms on the first floor are clean, as are a few on the second floor. It should be enough to suit our needs."

With relief, Kara thanked me and went down to the cellar to check on Tam and Swiftly.

I turned to get the tray from Bryn. She stared at the door in shock. I followed her gaze and found Patrick and Sara there. Sara kept her attention on the ground.

"We're here to see Lord Ruhall," Mr. Coalre said. "My wife is seeking a position."

Anger heated my face. They'd stood idly by as the baker rutted over me and now wanted help? Hate had me clenching my fists at my side as I stood there stiffly.

Mr. Crow stepped from his office and eyed the pair.

"There are no positions currently open," he said.

Sara's face fell while the smith's grew red.

"I asked to speak with Lord Ruhall."

"Mr. Crow handles Lord Ruhall's staff," I said, drawing his attention. "There is nothing for Sara." Her face flushed. I noted the tears starting in her eyes, and I hated myself for the pity I felt. "However, there is work for you and your sons."

"And what would that be?"

"There are apples to harvest. We'll pay a copper for a filled basket."

"My time at the forge is worth more than that. As is Tennen's. I'll send Splane to help. Sara, too."

"It's the three of you or none. The forge lies cold most days, and Tennen has too much time on his hands."

The look Mr. Coalre gave made my knees weak with fear, but I didn't stop.

"Work for your bread or don't eat." I turned and left the kitchen before he could respond.

When I reached the laundry door, I stopped to lean against the wall and catch my breath. My hands shook.

"Miss Hovtel?" Mr. Crow approached me with concern, and I quickly straightened from the wall.

"Yes?"

"The smith and his sons will be here in the morning. Why did you offer them work?"

"Why did you and Father invite them to the feast?"

"Your father suggested them. I had the impression he was unaware of their involvement in what transpired and didn't speak out against it, fearing he'd want to know why." He glanced down. "I'd thought it the right thing to do. Was I wrong?"

I knew his doubt not only stemmed from his worry about me, but also from his past silence.

"I apologize if I sounded harsh. You were not wrong. I chose not to burden my father with all the details. I am glad you did not, as well." I sighed as I considered how to answer Mr. Crow's original question. "I offered them work because they should feel what it's like to labor for so little. The smith has not been a good husband and helpmate to his wife, and his sons are learning from his lazy and disrespectful ways. If they work hard, they could easily earn a blunt silver tomorrow. The choice is theirs.

"But warn Tam and Swiftly to keep close watch on them at all times and have Kara prepare a simple meal for Tam and Swiftly to take with them in the morning so they have no reason to leave the Coalre men unattended."

"You're concerned they will do something?"

"My past experiences have taught me to be cautious of them."

"Very well. I'll bring the tray to the library, Miss, if you'd like to wash first."

He left to fetch the tray; and after a hasty wash in the laundry, I joined Alec and Father in the library where the tray already waited.

"We've made such wonderful progress harvesting that Kara has asked for extra help in the kitchen tomorrow," I said, sitting. Father served me a plate, and we began eating. "And, interestingly, I also found help to harvest tomorrow. The smith and his sons." I held Alec's gaze as I said it and witnessed his grip tighten on his fork. "I agreed to pay them a copper per filled basket. After we press what we need for the feast, we can bring the rest of the apples to the Water to sell, making the expense of their labor profitable."

Alec studied me for a moment then nodded.

"A splendid idea, Benella," Father said. "I was thinking of having Kara press three times as much as we might need or as much as she can before she thinks they will go bad. I've come across a book on making wine and spirits, and it has detailed instructions on making hard cider. We could use the drink for future feasts or sell it to local taverns."

He was thinking of Lord Ruhall's commanded wedding. Such a celebration usually required wine, but a hard cider would do.

"You're right. We should use whatever we can. I plan to stay here to help Kara in the kitchen tomorrow."

"I'll do the same," Alec said. "With five men harvesting, it will likely take the three of us pressing the apples to keep up."

"Three?" Father said.

The genuine smile Alec gave my father warmed me.

"You have the knowledge, sir. We wouldn't know what to do without you. Kara and Bryn would be able to keep on their tasks with our help."

We ate the rest of the meal; and after reading to Alec, I excused myself and retired early. The day had exhausted me. I had barely lay in bed before sleep claimed me.

I only roused slightly when Alec joined me. And again later, when the languid caress of his fingers shifted from my arm to my exposed stomach. Too tired to speak, I simply rolled away from him, and his touch returned to my arm.

FATHER, Alec, and I ate early in the study. We listened to Father explain the pressing process and then went to the small courtyard outside the laundry. While Alec brought up the baskets, Father and I worked the press. It was an interesting contraption with a large metal wheel and connecting crank. The apples went into the top holding chute; and as the wheel turned, the apples fell into the inner workings that crushed them. The juices and fine pulp slid down the exit chute and the peels and seeds fell into the waste bucket.

We all took turns working the wheel and feeding apples into the chute. When it was my turn at the wheel, my arms grew weary quickly, and I paused to watch the ease with which Alec lifted a full basket closer to the chute.

He caught me watching him and gave me a quick grin. Looking away, I tried to ignore the warmth that spread in my middle from his simple smile.

Tennen and Swiftly returned around midday with more apples, which they left outside the kitchen.

"How many baskets will we need to do?" I asked, feeling the burn in my arms.

"I've noted that we gain a bucket of cider for every three baskets. Estimating the servings for the evening, we need to press at least one hundred baskets. More would be better."

"How many trees were out there?" I asked Alec when he carried out some of the baskets the men had just delivered.

"Perhaps fifty in that field."

I stopped turning the handle.

"That field? There are more apple trees?"

"Tam mentioned there is another grove. A different apple.

Green. Too tart for cider but he thinks they might store well over winter."

Even if we didn't need to turn the green apples, we still had the rest of the red to consider. I did the calculations in my head and decided I would end up pressing cider until my arms ceased to function.

"Interesting," Father said. "I'd like to try just a few baskets of green apples to see how they taste as a hard cider."

Something must have shown on my face because Alec stopped loading apples and walked toward me.

"Let me turn the wheel for a while," he said. "See if Kara knows where the old barrels are to store the cider."

BY NIGHTFALL, we had several barrels of cider stored in the cellar and many baskets waiting for the press the next day. Mr. Crow had paid the Coalre family and reported that the men would return the following day.

I went to bed weary. My arms didn't want to cooperate enough to undress, so it took much longer than usual, and I was still awake when Alec quietly entered my room. I pretended to sleep as he pulled me against his chest.

His fingers trailed along my arm. I sighed sleepily, soothed by the motion...until I felt my shirt lift. A moment later, his fingers trailed lazily along my stomach. They moved from bellybutton to ribs, blazing a little further south and north with each pass.

My thoughts scattered, and my pulse quickened as I recalled the last time he'd touched me like this. Remembered sensations swamped me anew, and my breathing grew shallow as my body heated.

His fingertips skimmed the underside of my breast. The raw

need that ignited startled me enough that I sat up in bed and twisted to stare down at him.

The moonlight glinted in his eyes as we watched one another.

"What are you doing, Alec?"

Slowly, he lifted a hand and lightly brushed a knuckle over my nipple. My chest tightened with longing.

"Do you fear me?"

"No," I answered, honestly, wondering why he would think that.

He lifted his hand and drew his palm under my shirt and up along my side. My breath caught at the need I felt. He tried to pull me toward him, but I resisted. I had to because I wasn't thinking straight.

"Leave, Alec. Leave now, and I won't bar my doors. Persist, and I'll call for help and bolt the doors every night until the day I leave."

Because I would need to leave, I reminded myself.

I saw his temper flare, but his only reaction was to withdraw his hand and leave my bed. He stalked across the carpets and quietly closed himself into his own room.

It was a long while before I fell asleep.

As soon as I opened my eyes, I hurried from bed and dressed. With the feast so close, we couldn't afford to have Alec losing his temper after my rejection the night before.

Instead of finding him upset, I found him reading in his study. When I hesitated in the doorway, he glanced up at me.

"Are we to press cider so early?" he asked as he set the book aside and stood. He looked completely relaxed and not a bit upset with me.

"Uh...yes. Have you eaten?"

"Not yet. And you?"

"No."

"Then we'll see what your sister can offer us before we begin today's work."

He held out his arm, and I hesitated. Once before, I'd mistaken his courtesy and patience for coldness. Yet, according to him, it had been a mask to hide what he really felt. What was he hiding now?

"Perhaps I shouldn't," I said, considering the courtesy he offered.

"Perhaps you're right."

His accepting, genial mood worried me.

He motioned for me to lead the way, and I did.

In the kitchen, the table was set with bowls, and a kettle of oats waited with a pitcher of fresh cream. Kara and Bryn were absent. I spooned us both a portion and saw they'd added apples to the oats. Topping the bowls with cream, I sat across from Alec.

"You seem in a good mood today," I said carefully, watching him eat with enthusiasm.

"I am."

"Does that mean you've accepted that you need to wed soon?"

He paused eating to look at me. A serious light crept into his gaze.

"I have."

My stomach gave a nauseating turn.

"Very good," I said softly as I lifted the spoon to my mouth.

Bryn walked out of the dry pantry just then. Though she didn't acknowledge us, I knew she'd heard he needed to wed. Tonight, everyone in the village would know. Within a day or two, many in the Water would know as well. My face flushed at the thought, and my stomach continued its sickening churning. I struggled to remind myself that Alec wasn't the beast I'd once loved. It was kinder to let him go and start anew. Kinder for us both. And, having those around us know about his need to wed might not be a bad thing. If Alec had settled his mind on wedding someone, he needed to start meeting his options. And once the female population heard he meant to wed, his options would come to him. I struggled to continue eating.

He finished his food first and stood.

"I will see you outside," he said.

Bryn stopped adding things to her kettle and stared after him, no doubt waiting for him to leave so she could question me. However, Kara came up from the cellar, carrying a half basket of apples. Alec passed her with a polite nod.

"I hope it's all right to take some," she said, looking at me after he left.

"Certainly. We'll have more than I'll care to press. Plenty to make cider for the feast and any future entertaining the estate may need to do."

I forced myself to finish breakfast quickly and fled the kitchen.

Alec was already outside pressing the baskets of apples we'd stored in the laundry. Father joined us not long after, and we spent a companionable morning and afternoon together making more cider.

Bryn finally caught me alone as I washed in the laundry before dinner.

"Is he truly seeking a wife?" she asked in a hushed tone. She didn't wait for an answer. "Did you tell Blye?"

"Tell Blye? Why? Both you and Blye were quite clear in your refusal to speak with me ever again."

"We didn't understand you were in Lord Ruhall's confidence."

I stopped drying my hands and turned to stare at her.

"Your selfish ways continue to astound me," I said.

"Me, selfish? Hardly. You should have told Blye when she was here. She could have introduced herself as a prospect. In fact, you should invite her for tea and introduce her yourself. If they married, we'd be related to the Lord. Edmund and I wouldn't need to work like this, then."

I threw my hands in the air.

"Do you have any idea how futile that would be? Do you honestly think he doesn't remember you or Blye? He knows your characters and wants nothing to do with either of you. He tolerates you here because Father and I asked him to. Stop thinking of yourselves. Start thinking of your babe and your husband. He likes and respects his occupation, and you did too once. Change your ways, Bryn, before you find yourself alone and unloved. Never forget you have another man's babe in your belly and that Edmund could choose to annul your marriage."

She paled and trembled, but her fear didn't stop her anger.

"I hope Lord Ruhall weds soon. You preside over the staff and sleep in the Lady's room as if the role was yours. But you're too stupid to take it."

She turned and left. I didn't move.

She was right. If Alec did meet someone, what would she think of me occupying the Lady's room? Many of the bedrooms on the second floor had been cleaned now. There was no reason to remain where I was.

Instead of joining Alec and Father in the library for dinner, I went to my room and gathered my things. I looked around the room with sad eyes. It had been my home for so long.

Father found me as I left the room with my arms full.

"Will you dine with us?"

"Yes, let me just set these things in my room."

He made no comment when I picked the room next to his and placed my few possessions there. The spare dress, my shirt and pants, which I hadn't worn in ages, and my hairbrush and hair oil.

After straightening the Lady's room, I closed the door behind me for good and joined them for dinner.

A CRASH WOKE ME. Lying still, I listened with a hammering heart. Another crash followed.

"Damn her!"

Alec's roar echoed in the hallway. Cowering under the covers crossed my mind. Instead, I rose and tiptoed to the door. Something crashed again, and I jumped. He would wake the house if he hadn't already. Nibbling my lip, I opened my door.

"Bini?" Father said quietly. His door stood open, and he held a lit candle.

"Yes," I said, just as softly.

Suddenly, all sound stopped. I turned to look down the hall and saw Alec standing just outside his door. As soon as our gazes met, he started toward me.

"Perhaps you should fetch your wrap," my father said. "It appears he would like to speak to you."

Then he withdrew from the hall, closing his door. I blinked at his abandonment.

"Benella," Alec said, startling me. I spun and found him just inches from me. "Why are you not in your room?"

I swallowed and stood straight.

"I am in my room. If you recall, I only took the Lady's room because no other had been cleaned. Most are now clean, so I could choose."

He opened his mouth, ready to argue, and without thinking, I stepped closer and pressed my hand over it.

"Listen. Many people will be here in just a few days. Some might ask to spend the night. How would it look if I slept in that chamber? Especially, when most who attend know what the baker tried to do."

He growled and grabbed my wrist. Then, he surprised me by licking my palm before pulling my hand from his mouth. The tingle almost distracted me from what he said next.

"Marry me, and you need not worry what they think."

I curled my hand into a fist. I stared at him for a moment, confused. He had told me just that morning he'd resolved himself to marriage. Had he meant to me?

"I cannot," I said. But I struggled to remember why. His abandonment of me after the baker attacked. Yes. I questioned if he truly cared for me.

Even in the dimly lit hall, I caught the scarlet hue of his face.

"Then I damn what they think and damn the feast. If I cannot have you, I will have no one." He turned and strode back to his room, slamming his door.

Surely, he did not mean that.

ALEC SAID nothing when he joined us outside at the press. Though he was late, I was glad to see him. Many baskets lined the laundry. So many that Tam, Swiftly, and the Coalres ran out. On their last delivery, they had created a small mountain outside. Father and I fed the apples in as Alec turned the wheel with aggressive force.

His gaze tracked my movements, yet he made no comment. It wasn't until near lunch, when Father walked inside for a drink, that Alec moved away from the press. I stood quickly, dropping the apples I'd been about to place in the bucket.

"Return to your room tonight."

"That is not my room."

He snarled and ran his hand through his hair. I backed away a step and tripped over the bucket. Before I could fall, he wrapped his arm around me and pulled me tight to his chest.

A shiver stole through me at the contact. His frown faded as he studied me. He brought his other arm around me and slowly smoothed his hand up my back. When he reached my neck, his fingers speared into my hair. My breathing became irregular as I realized he intended to kiss me.

I lifted my hands and gripped his coat.

"No," I whispered.

"Yes." He started to close the distance.

"Ah-erm."

The noise gave me the motivation I needed to pull myself from his embrace.

Father stood by the door, looking decidedly embarrassed. He held two cups.

"I thought you might both be thirsty."

"I am. Thank you. If you'll excuse me, I need a private moment."

I took the cup from him and left, heading toward my room for some quiet and perhaps a nap. However, it wasn't meant to be.

The door opened to a disaster. The mattress lay shredded on the bed frame, and for a stunned moment, I just stood there. Then I realized what had happened and stomped my foot. Alec's late arrival wasn't due to sleep but manipulative destruction. He thought to drive me back into the Lady's room. I wouldn't go back, and the estate couldn't afford for me to choose another room. I would need to sleep on a ruined mattress.

Breathing through my anger, I left my room just as I'd found it. When I rejoined them for lunch, Alec watched me closely. I gave nothing away then or through our dinner.

"Will you read to me, Benella?" he asked softly just before we finished.

Father excused himself to look at books on one of the far shelves.

"I've slept poorly these last few nights and pressing cider is tiresome work. I would prefer to retire early."

He bowed his head as if in acceptance. I knew better. He hid his smile.

SLEEPING ON A TORN, lumpy mattress made my slumber restless and light. The slightest noise roused me as did the slamming of Alec's door at some point during the night. I lay awake a long while after, straining to hear the slightest noise, but all was silent. The quiet was worse than the previous night's rage. What was he planning?

The next day, he glared at me over breakfast and maintained his surly mood throughout the morning. When he excused himself from our midday meal, I wondered what he would do next.

Later that evening, when I stepped into my room, I discovered a large space where my bed and torn mattress had once existed. I hoped he hadn't destroyed the bed further when removing it. Backtracking, I went to the laundry and took what blankets and bedding I could to make myself a nest on the floor.

Exhaustion did not aid me to sleep. My mind refused to calm. I considered Alec's anger over my change in rooms. He had agreed he needed to marry. Surely his comment about only marrying me was false. He would do what was needed in order to maintain his freedom. Wouldn't he?

CHAPTER
NINE

My back objected when I rose the next morning, and my arms begged to be left alone as I dressed. Had I an actual bed, I would have remained in my room several more hours and ignored my protesting stomach.

I opened my door and squeaked at the sight of Alec. He hadn't made a sound in the hall to warn me that he stood just outside the door. His eyes were bloodshot, and he wore the same clothes as the prior day.

He scowled at me.

"I vow, tonight you will sleep where you belong."

He turned and walked to his room. I stared after him and hoped he would stay in his room to rest nearly as much as I hoped he would continue to help us press the apples. After his door slapped shut, I quietly left my sanctuary.

When I entered the kitchen, I found Bryn and Kara hard at work. Bryn rolled out thin sheets of dough while Kara sliced apples, equally thin.

"Good morning, Miss Hovtel," Kara said with a smile. "Would you care to sample one of the apple tartlets we're making?"

"Please. I'm starving and will sample anything you set before me."

She smiled as she went to the warming oven where she withdrew a full plate.

"I'd hoped you would be hungry," she said as she brought the food to me.

On the plate, she had several types of tartlets, bits of apple that looked brown, and a serving of thick oats mixed with more brown bits of apple.

"May I sit with you?" she asked.

"Of course."

She studied me closely as I sampled everything, and I knew she was waiting for my opinion.

"The tartlets are delicious."

"Good. With Lord Ruhall's intent to marry, Bryn and I thought we might need some form of refreshment in supply for any callers."

Bryn was a gossip. I'd known that. Yet, it still irked me that she'd told Kara.

"A sound plan. This bit here," I said, pointing to the brown apple pieces. "It was surprisingly sweet. I'd thought it burnt at first glance." I popped the last morsel into my mouth and chewed.

"We set some of the slices in the warming oven last night to dry them. Often, stored apples rot too fast. Dried apples last much longer. I used the dried pieces to sweeten the oats to show you how they could be consumed."

"It was very tasty," I said.

She smiled broadly.

"I'd hope you would say that and allow me to dry some more."

"Take as many apples as you want. The fewer to press, the happier I will be."

She thanked me and took away my empty plate. Sated, I walked out the laundry's door and found Alec already at the press.

He cranked the handle ruthlessly. Knowing him to be in a mood, I carefully did not turn my back to him as I filled a bucket with apples. He watched me approach and narrowed his eyes as I dumped the fruit into the chute. The way he acted reminded me of our earlier attempts to pent up his energies in the moments just before he would run and find the wood nymph.

However, Egrit was no longer his target. I wasn't sure what to do about him.

Father joined us before I'd added the fourth bucket, and I almost sighed with relief. He moved to help me fill buckets, and Alec continued with his wheel.

We worked a long while that way before Father offered to take a turn at the wheel. Alec quickly agreed. Neither Father nor I could compete with Alec's endurance, but we tried to help.

As I bent to pick up more apples, something brushed against my backside. A hand gripped my hip. I straightened with a blush and glanced at my father who busily turned the wheel. Glaring at Alec, I pushed him back a step.

"Stop this," I whispered.

"No," he said, not bothering to lower his voice.

"Beast," I hissed.

He grinned at me.

"I need to rest," Father said suddenly. "This work is taxing me."

And faster than I could blink, he left me alone with Alec in the courtyard.

As Father's steps faded, Alec's grin widened. He'd rolled up his sleeves at some point during his labor, and his shirt was damp with sweat. My heart skipped a beat. He took a step toward me, and I retreated in time as if we danced. His eyes narrowed, and he reached out to grab me. I ducked under his arm and sprinted for the door. Behind me, I heard apples tumble and his curse. A glance showed him on the ground due to a tipped basket. I didn't hesitate but fled to the kitchen.

Kara looked up in surprise as I burst into the room.

"Kara, do you have a pitcher of cold water?"

"Yes, right th—"

I rushed to where she pointed and snatched up the pitcher just as Alec stomped into the room. His gaze immediately landed on me. We stared at each other, both of us breathing heavily but for different reasons. Anger and lust fueled him. Fear had me tossing the contents of the pitcher in his face.

For a moment, stunned silence claimed the kitchen.

"Benella!"

I ignored Bryn's censure and stared at Alec, awaiting his reaction. Mr. Crow stepped from his office.

"Is there a problem, Lord Ruhall?" he asked.

Alec's eyes narrowed on me briefly.

"No problem. I think I'll go change." He turned away and said over his shoulder, "Have Miss Hovtel take a tray to the library."

I swallowed hard, glanced at Mr. Crow, and shook my head slightly. Alec wasn't done with me; but, I wasn't foolish enough to enter into whatever game he saw us playing.

Mr. Crow turned to Bryn who stared at me with her mouth open.

"Mrs. Rouflyn, please take a tray to Lord Ruhall."

She nodded and started preparing a tray. I watched her for a moment, knowing Alec would only become more impossible when he saw Bryn.

"Mr. Crow," I said, "how many pitchers do we have?"

"Several, Miss Hotvel."

"Good. Each room needs a full pitcher of water. When we run out of pitchers, use buckets just inside the doors."

"I will see to it myself," he said with a bow before he left the room.

I left the kitchen and tried to decide where Father might be. Most likely the library, the very place I did not want to go. Hoping Alec still changed, I cautiously hurried through the halls and paused outside the library door. When I peeked inside, I found Father reclined on the lounge, comfortably reading a book.

"With respect, you're not so old as to be taxed enough to warrant an afternoon nap," I said, entering the room. "Why did you abandon me? Twice now."

"Abandon? Never. I trust Alec to keep within the boundaries you've established with him."

I snorted. I didn't even trust Alec to keep within the boundaries.

"Bini, you've upset him."

"He has upset me." I crossed my arms.

"He told me you've rejected his proposal more times than he has toes. His words."

My arms fell to my sides. Counting the times he'd asked me as the beast, I had rejected him that many times. Father sat up and patted the lounge next to him.

"Why, Bini?"

I sighed and sat beside him.

"Because of so many reasons. What happened with the baker makes marriage a less than appealing state, and it broke my trust in Lord Ruhall. I also thought I didn't know him; but lately, I'm wondering if I say no because I don't know myself."

He wrapped an arm around my shoulders and hugged me to his side to kiss my temple.

"Of all of us, you know yourself best. Trust your heart and your head to lead you to the right choice."

Mr. Crow entered the room and discreetly set a bucket of water just within the door.

"Thank you, Mr. Crow," I said to him.

He gave a single nod and left.

"Should I ask?" Father said.

"Probably not."

A few moments later, Mr. Crow returned.

"There is a caller for Lord Ruhall. I've put her in the front sitting room."

A caller? So soon?

"Please have Bryn provide refreshment and let Lord Ruhall know. I believe he's in his room, changing."

Mr. Crow didn't move. I watched him glance at Father before focusing on me once more.

"It's your sister, Blye."

"Don't bother with the refreshment."

"Benella," Father said chidingly.

"I understand you must love your children, but I will not encourage what she intends with pampered attention and sweet treats."

Mr. Crow nodded and left the library. I stood, too.

"I should try to dissuade her. In Alec's current mood, I don't believe he will tolerate her attempted manipulations well."

"I quite agree," Father said after a weary sigh.

I left him on the lounge with his book and sought out my sister. I found her sitting serenely in a new dress, drowning in yards of pink lace.

"Hello, Blye."

"Benella," she said indifferently. "Is Lord Ruhall on his way?"

"I haven't the slightest idea. Why are you here?"

"As if you don't know. You've always been close mouthed, but how could you keep such news as Lord Ruhall's need to wed to yourself? You weren't hoping he'd marry you, were you?"

The heat of anger colored my cheeks as she continued in a patronizing tone.

"You're not precisely the model of a lady. Pants, fishing, hunting, foraging..." She shook her head.

"You didn't so disregard those skills when they kept you from starving. And what skills do you possess that you think might tempt him to forget your groveling pleas for mercy when he asked you to stay with him in exchange for Father's life?"

She didn't look the slightest bit put off by the reminder. Instead, she fluffed her skirt and smiled serenely.

"He's no longer the beast."

"He is the same, only changed in form. He's forgotten nothing. Spare yourself humiliation or worse. Leave."

A throat cleared behind me. I turned and saw Mr. Crow.

"Miss Hovtel," he said, looking at Blye. "Lord Ruhall is unable to take callers today."

"Will he be available tomorrow?" she asked, crossing the room to stand before Mr. Crow.

"He will be unavailable to all callers until after the feast. He begs you understand the time and attention it takes to coordinate such an affair."

"Of course," she said serenely.

"Might you want to see your father?" he asked.

She waved a hand negligibly.

"I haven't the time. I must return to the shop."

"I will see you out," he said with a bow. Since he left her no choice, she followed him from the room.

With effort, I pushed my sister's visit from my mind and focused on the problem at hand. Alec was angry with me; and if he hadn't already realized I wasn't in the library waiting for him, he would soon. Thinking quickly, I went in search of Egrit.

I survived the rest of the day by sending Mrs. Palant to help with the press while I helped Egrit dust. Egrit didn't comment on the change. However, she did ask if I was well several times throughout the afternoon because I jumped at the slightest sounds.

By evening, I'd exhausted myself with worry over what trouble he might cause next.

When I went to my room, the nest of blankets remained as I'd left them. I carefully locked the door and undressed for bed. It didn't take me long to fall asleep.

FINGERS TRAILED OVER MY SKIN, tracing a burning path from navel to knee. I woke with an aching need that smothered any sense of worry. Turning my head, I found Alec beside me. I blinked at him, trying to focus. How had he gotten in?

His dark gaze held mine as his fingers barely missed the v of my legs. My breath hitched, and I almost forgot my question.

I closed my eyes and turned my head away to escape his focus. The pillow shifted under me, and I became aware that I lay on a bed, not the floor. I opened my eyes once more and saw his wardrobe. He'd moved me.

His lips suddenly skimmed along my neck. I sighed, and my eyes drifted closed. His fingers continued their languid strokes, tempting me, begging me to part my knees and give them access. I wanted nothing more than to give in to his seduction. My need almost robbed me of thought and will, as did his fingers and mouth.

I needed to deny him. Why? I couldn't remember...

He nibbled his way from my neck to my shoulder. My skin tingled with fire and life. Then he licked my collarbone. He lifted his head and moved so his mouth hovered over my left breast. He exhaled, the hot air creating an ache. I knew what he intended, and I wanted it more than I wanted my next breath.

"You are mine," he breathed against my skin. His fingers continued to dance along the v of my legs. His tongue brushed against my nipple then disappeared, leaving me unsatisfied. I whimpered and arched.

"Agree to marry me, and I will give you what you desire."

The words chilled me as if a pitcher had doused me. Marriage. He needed to marry or be re-enchanted. I balled up my fist and swung at him.

"Manipulator. Beast," I cried as my fist connected with his cheek. He grunted and grabbed both my hands. I pulled back hard and tumbled from the bed.

Tired and frustrated, I couldn't prevent the tears that welled in my eyes.

"Why? Haven't I been punished enough?"

"Punished?" He sat up and looked down at me. "Do you really see my touch as punishment?"

"Do not twist my meaning. It's not your touch but your cruel manipulations to gain your own ends. Stop this, Alec. I want sleep."

"As do I," he shouted at me.

"Then why are you awake touching me?"

"How else am I to get you to stay?"

The tears spilled over.

"That is the problem, Alec. You cannot force me to stay. You can only ask and leave the choice to me."

His shoulders slumped, and his hopeless expression tugged at my heart.

"Please stay the night with me, Benella. I cannot sleep without you by my side."

I considered him a long while. Saying yes would ease whatever madness gripped him now, but it would not ease my conscience. He would marry soon. Sleeping with me like this was wrong. Yet, his desperate expression and bloodshot eyes moved me to compassion.

"I want my nightshirt back. And my underclothes."

"Yes," he said quickly. He rose and retrieved them from the bottom of his wardrobe.

Once I had the shirt about me, I sat on the edge of the bed.

"Lie down," I said.

He immediately obeyed but then pulled me down with him. He tucked me close to his chest and rested his chin on the top of my head.

I held still and waited for his breathing to slow. Once each exhale came in an even rhythm, I eased from his arms. He didn't stir. I covered him with a spare blanket and quietly left his room.

THE NEXT DAY looked as if it would play out no better than the prior day when I heard Alec pacing in the hall. He whirled at the sound of my door opening. I hesitated near the threshold, close to the pitcher of water Mr. Crow had considerately placed within.

"You left me," he said with an angry scowl.

"It wasn't my place to stay. I should not have been there to begin with."

He opened his mouth to argue, and I stepped close to take his hands in mine. The action stopped the forthcoming rant. He gripped my hands firmly and watched me with mixed emotions.

"Alec, have patience. The feast is a mere five days from today.

You might meet someone then." He made a sound of disagreement. "Or perhaps officially announce your intent to wed. If you can just hold yourself for a few more days, your life might unexpectedly change for the better."

"I don't want my life to change unexpectedly. I want you."

He pulled his hands from mine and left me in the hallway.

For a brief moment, I considered finding Egrit to see if she would consider helping with the press. Then, I slowly followed in Alec's wake. Hiding from him did no good. Avoiding him made things worse. Perhaps if I did the opposite, things would then improve.

We worked together throughout the morning. He watched me continually and used any opportunity to touch me. When he invited me to join him in the library for the midday meal, I accepted after he also invited Father.

The meal didn't last long. As soon as Alec finished his portion, he stood and began pacing just behind my chair. I felt as if the beast was back, waiting to pounce. I took my last bite and set my plate back upon the tray. Before I could swallow, Father quickly excused himself to return the tray to the kitchen.

The sound of Alec's pacing stopped. I stood and turned. With a determined glint in his eyes, he waited, poised just behind my chair. Instead of finding an excuse to leave, I stayed where I was. He seemed to calm when he saw I wasn't about to bolt.

"Thank you for a lovely meal," I said softly.

He exhaled slowly. If he still had fur, I had no doubt I would have witnessed his hackles lowering.

"Will you read to me after dinner?" he asked.

"Yes, if you will tell me how you entered my room last night."

"So you can bar me from entering?" he asked with a scowl.

"I won't need to bar you if I have your word that I will remain in my room all night tonight and have no cause to lock my door."

He considered me for a moment then reached into his pocket. He withdrew a key and handed it to me.

"I asked Phillip for the master key. I had to wait half the night for him to leave his post outside your door." The petulant way he said it almost made me smile.

"Mr. Crow is a good man. I'll return it and let him know he need not worry tonight?" I ended it as a question because I wanted Alec's agreement. When he nodded, I smiled. "Then, I will read to you for as long as you like."

AFTER DINNER, Alec brought me a tome of enormous proportions, and I read until my voice objected. The whole while, he sat on the floor and ran his fingers through my hair. When I closed the book, he stood and offered me his arm.

We walked together to our rooms, and he bade me goodnight at my door. His civility eased my mind enough that I kept my promise and did not turn the lock.

In the morning, the warm place in the blankets beside me told a truth. He'd come to me, and slept beside me, but had left me unmolested.

The next three days followed a similar pattern. If I behaved in an accommodating manner, he adhered to the boundaries I'd set, with the exception of sleeping in my room. He continued to let himself in, though I had asked him to cease.

In those three days, the stacked barrels of fresh cider lined one full wall of the cellar, and the men completed the harvest of the red apples. Mr. Crow paid the smiths their due and let them know there was no further work for them. If they were smart, they would hold tight to their coin.

Bryn and Kara continued to cook and prepare everything

brought to them. Cloth-covered, wooden platters of smoked fish crowded the cellar on every spare surface. Kara even managed to turn a large amount of herbed soft cheese from the goat milk that I'd neglected to take to the Water the week prior.

The day before the feast, we finished pressing the remaining apples early in the morning while Bryn and Kara started the meat pies.

Everything was progressing nicely, and I felt a sense of calm until midday.

Alec, Father, and I were in the library, eating and discussing last minute details when Mr. Crow interrupted us.

"Lord Ruhall, a guest for the feast has arrived early. Egrit is showing her to a guest room...near her father's."

Blye. Mr. Crow and I shared a look before I glanced at Alec.

"Perhaps you should lock *your* door tonight," I said.

Alec ignored me and turned to Phillip.

"Let Kara know we'll eat in the dining room tonight with our guest. Nothing formal, just a change in scene."

Mr. Crow nodded and left.

"I'll take the tray to the kitchen," I said, standing. "Alec, will you help me in the ballroom? We should start moving the tables and chairs in."

He seemed pleased that I'd asked him and nodded.

We met a few minutes later in the ballroom. Alec had brought Swiftly with him to help. I directed them where to place the food and drink tables, then helped bring in some of the lighter chairs for the older guests like the candle maker.

Less than an hour had passed when Mr. Crow found us again.

"Miss Hovtel, there is someone here to see you. She gave the name Ila."

I was elated she'd decided to come early.

"Thank you, Mr. Crow." I turned to glance at the tables. "Can you bring Kara in here to see if this will be enough room for the food? I'd like to set it all out right away tomorrow so everyone can join in the feast."

He nodded, and I left him in the ballroom so quickly that he had to call after me.

"She is in the sitting room, Miss."

I waved to show I'd heard and kept going. I desperately needed a friendly face and an escape from my troubled thoughts. I hoped Ila would provide both.

Ila didn't sit on a chair as Blye had but wandered around the room to study interesting objects here and there. When she heard me enter, she turned with a hesitant smile.

"Ila, I'm so happy you're here. Will you be staying the night?"

I hugged her warmly when I reached her, and after a slight hesitation, she hugged me in return.

"I'm glad you're happy to see me," she said. "I wasn't certain."

"Nonsense. I'm delighted. And I would like you to stay. Blye is here early as well, and I would enjoy a companion who doesn't ignore me."

Ila laughed, a husky sound and a bittersweet reminder of our shared past, as she pulled back from our embrace.

"I will stay, then, and protect you as I am able." She turned and gestured to a small trunk just inside the door. "I brought your dress."

It was hard to keep the joy on my face. The extravagance of having a formal dress still annoyed me. Even my serviceable dresses annoyed me at times. What would I do with a lace-ridden dress? Owning something that could only be worn once, maybe twice, made little sense.

"Don't look so cornered," Ila said. "Through your visits, I've grown to know you. I think you'll be happy with what I've brought. Would you like to see it?"

"I apologize if I looked unappreciative, I'm nothing but grateful. Yes, please do show me."

Ila moved to the trunk and opened it. With her back to me, she lifted something from within, shook it out, then turned. The cream dress adorned with golden and burgundy threads stunned me. No lace trimmed the square neckline; the parallel patterns of the threads were enough of an adornment. The pattern continued down the length of the skirt as well. From a distance, it would appear a solid cream color. Only on closer inspection would someone realize the beauty of the material. The only lace on the creation hung from the sleeves that stopped at the elbow.

"It's beautiful," I said, reaching out to touch it. The fine, thin material reminded me of the dress I'd worn to my sister's wedding.

"There is an underskirt if you want more volume, or you can wear it without."

"I cannot wait to try it on," I said with honesty.

"Not until tomorrow." She smiled at me, then turned to tuck it into the trunk once more.

"You're sure it will fit?"

"Yes. I have no doubt."

After asking Mr. Crow for a tray, Ila and I enjoyed a quiet afternoon talking. Before dinner, I showed her to her room then walked with her to the dining room where we found Alec, Father, and Blye already seated.

"I apologize," I said. "I didn't think us late."

Alec stood as we approached the table and pulled out the chair to his right.

"You're not. We were early, Miss Hovtel."

Blye, who sat beside Father, narrowed her eyes at my placement next to Lord Ruhall. I sat and let him push me in. He gave the same courtesy to Ila, who sat beside me and across from Blye.

"Hello, Mr. Hovtel," Ila said softly.

Father smiled at her.

"It is good to see you again, Ila. How are your sisters?"

"Well, thank you. A few have found husbands since we last saw you."

Blye's gaze bounced between the pair before understanding dawned. Her lips thinned in disapproval. I ignored her.

"You should see the dress Ila made me, Father. It is truly stunning."

"I look forward to seeing it tomorrow," Alec said, his eyes on me.

Mr. Crow's arrival saved me from needing to respond. He entered the room slowly, carrying a heavily laden tray. I stood quickly and went to help him.

"Thank you, Miss," he said. "It wasn't heavy when I left the kitchen."

"I had the same problem with the press. The handle turned with ease the first few times."

I set it on the table and moved aside so Mr. Crow could serve us.

Alec again helped me sit. This time his arm brushed against mine. No one seemed to notice as Mr. Crow began to set our soup bowls before us.

"This looks delicious. Thank you," I said when my bowl waited before me. Orange and thick, the aroma hinted at squash and onion.

The table grew quiet as we ate. I was surprised when Mr. Crow returned a short while later and held the door open for Kara. She carried in a large platter with a roast surrounded by peeled potatoes.

She set the dish on the table as Mr. Crow took our bowls and replaced them with plates. The first slice of roast she set to the side. The second slice she set on Alec's plate. The smell made my mouth water.

"Thank you, Kara," Alec said after she added potatoes. He waited until we each had our portions before picking up his fork. I beat him to the first bite. The last time I'd eaten roast escaped me. While enchanted, the estate or the beast usually fed me finger food.

I chewed slowly, savoring the flavor and remembered. It had been at the Kinlyn's. Mrs. Kinlyn had served us roast, and I'd met Henick for the first time. I smiled and took another bite.

"The roast pleases you," Alec said. I noticed he no longer ate but only studied me.

"Very much. It's been a long while since I last tasted roast." I took another bite.

"Roast isn't typically served here?" Blye asked.

With my mouth full, Alec answered her.

"A stew is much easier for the kitchen to prepare while they try to shore the winter stores."

"I'm honored you had a special meal prepared for us, Lord Ruhall," Ila said.

Blye's lips thinned again. Her distaste for Ila was obvious, and I wanted to kick my sister under the table.

"I'm honored you could join us, Ila," Alec said. "Tell me what news you have from the Water."

And with that, he let Ila lead the conversation and Blye sulk quietly in her chair.

EGRIT WOKE me with a knock on my door. The place beside me still held Alec's heat. He always managed to come and go without being caught. Too many years prowling as a beast had honed his nocturnal skills.

"Good morning," she said softly when I opened the door. "I started water heating in the laundry so the children can wash before the feast. Tam is bringing bath water to Lord Ruhall's room. Would you like him to bring some to your old room, too?"

"Would he mind?"

"Not at all. Mr. Crow said that we have no duties today other than setting up for the feast. Tam and I still milked the goats and collected eggs, though."

"Tell Tam thank you for his hard work. You too," I said, reaching out to touch her arm.

"You're welcome, Benella. The water should be in your room in an hour."

I nodded, and she walked away. Down the hall, another door opened and Ila stepped out to wave to me. I joined her and saw my dress laid out on her bed.

"Should we take it to your room?"

"I'm going to use the Lady's room to bathe. Let's take it there." Better she thought me overreaching than for her to see I had no bed in my room. She picked up the dress, and I carried the underskirt and matching slippers.

"This is truly amazing." I spoke softly in the hallway, not wanting to wake Blye or Father.

"I cannot wait to see you in it. Let me know as soon as you have it on."

I opened the door to the large room. It was just as I'd left it. We set everything out on the bed, and I pulled the tub out from under its table.

"Let's see if there's anything to eat in the kitchen," I said, ready to leave the room before Alec heard something.

Ila agreed, and we left the room to search out food. Giggles echoed in the laundry as we passed the room. I caught sight of Otta in the doorway and waved.

Kara was alone in the kitchen, frantically moving about.

"Where's Bryn?"

"She hasn't arrived yet."

I hoped everything was all right.

"Can I help?" I said, moving to stir whatever bubbled over the fire.

"Please. I have biscuits in the oven, eggs boiling over here, stew boiling over there for the remaining meat pies, I need to roll out the dough…"

She looked ready to cry. Ila stepped forward.

"I'll watch the biscuits and eggs and set the table for the children. You roll out your dough."

Between the three of us, we settled the kitchen to its typical morning rhythm. In no time, we had the table set, the eggs in a bowl, a pitcher of fresh milk ready, and the biscuits from the oven. The children started to trail in; and when Egrit saw us, she shooed us to the table.

"Eat," she said. "I wonder where Bryn is. I saw her walking down the lane earlier."

I frowned, wondering what might have happened to her, and sat at the table. The children were excited for the feast. Otta and Retta spoke in quiet tones about the possibility of dancing with boys their ages.

"I promise there will be a few in attendance," I said, thinking of the Kinlyn boys.

As soon as Ila and I finished, we started the trek back to our rooms. When we passed the dining room, I stopped short at the sound of both Bryn and Blye's voices. I waved Ila to go without me and waited until she was out of hearing before I stepped into the room.

They both sat at the table, one on each side of where Alec usually sat.

"Is breakfast almost ready?" Blye asked.

They were waiting to be served breakfast. I closed my eyes and took a calming breath.

"Benella? Are you well enough to fetch Blye and me a tray?"

I opened my eyes, looked at them once more, then turned to leave, swallowing what I would have liked to say to Bryn.

When I spotted Mr. Crow in the entry, I hurried to his side.

"Bryn is sitting in the dining room while Kara is struggling to prepare the feast."

"I will address the issue immediately, Miss Hovtel."

"Thank you, Mr. Crow. If more help is needed in the kitchen, please let me know. Kara looked near tears this morning."

I stalked to the ballroom, seething because my sisters were so arrogant and selfish. After closing my eyes and counting backward for several moments, I calmed enough to view the progress within the room. Tables lined the wall near the north parlor. Linens already covered the tables. A mountain of napkins and small plates waited at one end.

Chairs lined the wall near the fireplace and several more near the garden doors for the musicians. Someone had thoughtfully gathered fall's last wildflower blooms and placed them in vases on the tables and around the base of each wooden candle stand. The simple decorations were beautiful.

Satisfied everything was ready, I went to my room to grab my brush and hair oil. With the items in hand, I returned to my old room. The tub waited, full of steaming water. Setting everything within reach, I stripped my clothes and slid into the water with a sigh. Less than a minute later, a door opened.

I turned my head and met Alec's gaze. While he crossed the room, I cursed myself for not thinking to lock the door. Ila's company had too successfully distracted me from my troubles with Alec.

"Stop there," I said quietly.

"It has been more than two months since I watched you in the bath." He stepped close and circled the tub.

I crossed my arms to shield what held his attention. It only encouraged him to squat beside the tub.

Keeping my gaze, he leaned close.

"You are most precious to behold as you are, without clothes and pink from the water." Closer still he came, his intent clear when his gaze dipped to my mouth.

I lifted one hand and flicked water in his face.

Angrily, he leaned in, held the back of my neck, and pressed his lips to mine. I turned my head, unwilling to part with a single bit of affection for the impertinent man, and splashed him again. He quickly stood and stepped out of danger.

"Behave yourself tonight," I said in a harsh whisper. "There will be plenty of cider for me to douse you."

"Me?" He plucked at his wet shirt. "I will behave if you behave," he said.

"What do you mean?"

"If you cause issues, such as throwing anything at me, or disagreeing with me in front of the assembled, I will ruin the feast."

With that, he left me. I frowned after him, trying to understand his threat. What did my behavior have to do with the feast? His was under scrutiny, not mine. And why threaten with the ruination of the feast when that would result in the return of the enchantment?

Still puzzling over it, I continued my bath.

I DIDN'T ATTEMPT to put on the dress until I'd combed my hair dry, which seemed to take ages. The soft material danced upon my skin as I let it fall down my raised arms and over my head. The bodice had a double panel, so I went without my bindings. The lacings, once tightened, pushed my breasts up so they mounded ever so slightly over the top. Even through the stretched material, I could see the shape of each breast. The full underskirt provided a bit more modesty.

After stepping into my slippers, I left the room to show Ila. She opened the door after my first knock. Her dress was equally beautiful. Dyed a deep red-brown, the fine material was edged with cream lace at her sleeves. White threads created a swirling pattern along her hem.

"It's beautiful," I said. "Perfect for fall or winter."

She smiled, stepped aside, and waved me in. "Your dress fits nicely. Come in. Let me braid your hair."

I sat on a low stool while she stood behind me and patiently created braid after braid within my loose hair. Then she swept the mass up and started pulling out the braided sections to weave them into unbraided sections. When she finished, she handed me a mirror.

"Ila, you are very talented. I would offer to help braid your hair, but it would look nothing like this."

"Don't worry. I plan to wear mine in a simple braid. You should go now and check that everything is ready."

CHAPTER
TEN

Mr. Crow stood ready at the door but waved me over when he saw me.

"You are most lovely, Miss Hovtel."

I smiled at his sincerity.

"Thank you, Mr. Crow. You look very fine yourself." He wore his usual dark jacket and pants but had taken care to polish his shoes until they reflected even the tiniest bit of light.

"I want to keep you apprised of your sister's behavior. She has been warned. If she ignores her duties again, she will be dismissed. She also lost half a day's wages."

"A fair consequence for her actions," I said. "I'm going to check on the kitchen and see when Kara thinks we should start bringing out the food. How much longer until you expect guests to arrive?"

"Within minutes, Miss. There are always those who want to be early."

I hoped the candle maker was among them. While heading toward the kitchen, I checked the rooms I passed and found everything in order. After weeks of preparation, it seemed the estate was ready to hold its first feast in fifty years. I hurried my steps.

Kara stood alone in the kitchen. Trays of carefully stacked meat pies crowded the table.

"I sent Bryn to get ready with your other sister," she said as soon as she saw me. "I'm just waiting for this last batch of pies to come from the oven."

"It smells like heaven in here," I said, leaning over the pies. Heat radiated from them. "How did you get so many done so quickly?"

"I under baked several batches yesterday, so I would only need to brown them today. I had crust ready in the cellar, too, for rolling this morning."

Flour dusted her apron and face.

"I will watch the oven. Go ready yourself. Mr. Crow says he expects guests soon."

"I have everything right in here," she said, pointing at the servant's room. "Call out if you need anything."

After Kara ducked into the room, Ila entered with her hair plainly braided. I was glad for her company. Worry over Alec's threat kept churning through my head, and I needed a distraction.

"I thought you might be here," she said, studying the meat pies as I had.

"Though I have no love of cooking, I do so enjoy eating," I said with a grin. "Kara is dressing while I watch the oven for her."

Ila kept me company until Kara reappeared. She wore a plain, light grey dress very similar to the one she'd worn before. Her hair remained in its typical bun.

"Do you have any hair ribbons?" Ila asked.

"Yes. A black one and a grey one. Do you think I should use one of them?" She reached up to touch her hair.

"Yes, but not in your hair. Let me show you." Ila stepped into the room with Kara and a moment later Kara reappeared with a black ribbon tied around her neck with the bow in the back.

"Lovely," I said. "That such a simple thing can so enhance one's appearance amazes me."

"I agree," said Kara. "Where did you learn this?"

Ila gave a small smile.

"I have many sisters who are well traveled."

"You are lucky, then, to have them."

"I agree," Ila said.

"Are we ready to start carrying the food to the ballroom?" I asked.

"Yes," Kara said. "The cider should probably go first. I imagine the guests who choose to walk will be thirsty."

Ila stayed in the kitchen while I went off to find help. Tam and the other men returned with me and carried up more than a dozen small barrels before starting on the trays.

Outside the kitchen door, I heard the rumble of a wagon and went to see who had arrived. Edmund waved at me then set the brake and jumped down from his seat. Beside him, the candle maker held several thick pillars in his arms.

The men, having just returned from the ballroom, helped Edmund unload his pastries and took the pillars from the candle maker. Satisfaction coursed through me at seeing everything coming together so nicely.

"Where's Bryn?" Edmund asked after the last of his trays disappeared. Kara and Ila were carefully arranging the last meat pies on a tray.

"Dressing with Blye."

"Shouldn't she be helping?"

"Kara said she could dress."

"You're dressed and helping."

"I am." I patted his arm. "How have things been going without the extra help in the bakery?"

"Fine. It's quiet, though." His expression said he missed her.

"If you'd like, perhaps your wife should stay home with you for the next few days. I expect it will be quiet enough here."

"I would like that. I think she would, too."

"Go find her and tell her. And enjoy yourself tonight, Edmund."

He walked out, leaving Kara, Ila, and me in the kitchen.

"Are we ready?" I asked them.

"We are," Ila said, coming to hook her arm through mine.

"Thank you for your help. I truly appreciate it."

"It's what a friend would do."

We walked out of the kitchen and soon heard the buzz of voices from those guests who had already arrived. In the main entry, I gave a warm greeting to the butcher and introduced both Ila and Kara. His daughter found Retta, and the pair went off to the ballroom.

The general gaiety of the crowd had me smiling at everyone who stopped to say hello. I spotted Sara and her family in the crowd and followed Tennen's narrowed gaze to Bryn, who stood beside Edmund. Edmund had his arm around Bryn's waist, and she was looking up at him with complete focus.

"Miss Hovtel," Alec said from behind me, "you look lovely."

I turned to look over my shoulder and found him just inches from me. He wore a dark jacket and matching pants. Like Mr. Crow, his shoes were highly polished. His neckcloth was precisely tied and set against his neck. He was devastatingly handsome and looked every inch a lord. However, the heated gaze he raked over me stole the respectability given by his clothes. And it made my pulse flutter.

Tonight he must announce his intent to wed, I reminded myself. The sting of that realization helped ground me in the reality of our relationship. I would leave, and he would wed. Hopefully, in that order.

"Might I return the compliment, Lord Ruhall," I said politely.

"Lord Ruhall," a man I'd never met before said, claiming Alec's attention.

I quickly moved away and spoke with several of the students my father used to teach.

Before long, the sounds of music drifted from the ballroom, and the crowd slowly migrated that way. As we moved, I caught sight of a woman in a pale pink dress tiered with ruffles. The volume of the skirt was so much that no one could walk too close to her. Though the dress was pretty—if one had an affection for ruffles—it was far too overstated for such a simple gathering.

The wide neckline set the sleeves from the woman's shoulders, and her side swept hair bared her neck, which she held regally erect. She turned her head, and I caught sight of her profile. Blye.

Her sewing must be lucrative, indeed, to afford such a dress. When would she ever wear it again, though? I watched her glide into the ballroom and look around. Her gaze slid right over me and settled on someone not yet in the ballroom. I turned to look back in the hall and found Lord Ruhall walking slowly as he listened to what the man beside him said. I wanted to shake my head at my sister for her wasted efforts.

"Would you care to dance?" someone said as he gently tapped my shoulder. I turned to find Bolen, one of the Kinlyn boys, bowing to me.

"I would be delighted, sir," I said, returning his humor and pushing Blye from my mind.

Bolen led me to the floor, and we joined the others already there in a simple dance. He kept his hand politely at my waist while he held my other hand.

"How have you been?" I asked. "I heard you were able to fish."

"I am well, thank you. We've been fishing more now that the crops are in. Parlen finally got his wild pig with Da's help." He regaled me with their story and had me laughing. "He wanted to dance with you so he could tell you himself, but Ma said..." A blush painted his cheeks.

His mother hadn't wanted Parlen to dance with me. But why? I could think of only one reason. The baker. Yet why then let another son dance with me?

"Did your mother think me unsuitable to dance with?"

"Not at all," he rushed to assure me. "She said it would be improper to dance with a woman so much taller than him."

I puzzled for a moment then laughed aloud as I realized young Parlen would have been level with my breasts.

"Well, there are many girls here who are very close to his height. I hope he asks some of them."

The dance ended, and before I could leave the floor, I had another offer to dance. I vaguely recalled seeing the boy while I'd attended school but could not recall his first name. His family lived on a patch of land to the south, like the Kinlyns.

Another song saw a new partner waiting for me; and as I danced, Blye's words about how unsuitable I would be rang in my ears. How could I be so unsuitable and dance with so many while my perfectly suitable sister stood on the side without a single offer to dance? Blye circled the ballroom, chatting to those she knew and casting long looks at Lord Ruhall.

When the song ended, I found myself facing Henick. He took up my hand and gently held my waist as I rested my palm on his shoulder. A new song began, and he led our moves.

"Did you know there is a line to dance with you?"

"Surely not," I said, looking around. I caught Alec's thunderous frown before Henick's laugh returned my attention.

"It's true. Not an obvious line, but it's there all the same. Bolen was smart to grab you first."

"Your brother was a fine dancer. As are you. I hope the other women here find the same attention as I've received."

He smiled.

"A few might. But none are as pretty."

I blushed and glanced away. My gaze collided with Alec's again. He tracked my dance with Henick, clearly unhappy. When he saw me looking at him, he jerked his head to the side, a motion to show me he wanted me to leave the floor. I returned my gaze to Henick, determined to ignore Alec and his threats.

"Perhaps you'll allow me to introduce you to a friend who might be one of those few?" I asked.

"I would be honored."

On the next turn of the room, Alec wasn't where he had been. Before I could worry, the dance ended; and I asked Henick to walk me to the drink table rather than let another partner sweep me into the next set.

Drink in hand, I turned back to observe the room and caught sight of Alec weaving his way through waiting dancers. Unbeknownst to him, Blye moved toward him from his right, their paths set to intersect. She stepped in front of him just as the music started. He frowned at her then, glancing about, held out a hand.

Ila approached Henick and me and noted the direction of my gaze.

"Your sister is bold," she said.

I nodded slightly then focused on my friends.

"Henick, this is my friend, Ila."

Henick smiled and bowed over her hand. Within moments, they were fully engaged in conversation. It gave me time to observe Lord Ruhall and Blye.

He swirled her around the room at an aggressive pace. His gaze wasn't on her but was searching the dancers around them. She didn't seem to notice his distraction for she tilted her head back, laughed, and moved closer to him. Everyone turned to watch them. Her skirts flared out prettily, and I had never disliked my sister so much as in that moment. She only wanted him for his wealth and would ruin all the hard work Alec, Father, and I, along with the rest of the old staff, had put into this affair and the estate.

I wished he would announce his intent to wed. Blye certainly wasn't an option for him.

As soon as the song ended, I excused myself and approached the pair, planning to pull Blye aside to speak to her.

"Lord Ruhall, might I have a moment with—"

"Of course. We can speak as we dance," he said, releasing Blye abruptly and pulling me into his arms. He twirled me onto the floor before I could protest. We moved together as we had to the sweet bird song that day long ago. I couldn't deny I felt a thrill being in his arms. I tilted my head back to study him. His deep blue gaze remained locked on me, and I struggled to keep my wits about me.

"I meant to speak with my sister."

"Whatever for," he said, pulling me closer.

His body brushed against mine as we moved. I tried to gain distance but his hard hold wouldn't yield. So, I gripped his shoulder, fighting to remain upright during the dizzying pace he set.

He leaned in and breathed in near my neck, sending a shiver racing through me.

"That scent..."

"My hair," I said. I hadn't oiled my hair since the enchantment had broken.

Knowing it was dangerous, I allowed myself to relax. Just for a few moments, I wanted to pretend he truly loved and cherished me above all else. That he and I were together and happy like we'd been before the baker.

"I need you," he whispered. "More than the air I breathe. More than my freedom."

My heart thumped painfully at his words, which were so close to what I'd just been thinking. I pulled back again, searching his gaze for answers I so desperately needed.

"Don't forget that in the next few moments," he said with a wild look.

We stopped twirling and before my world righted itself, I was alone in the center of the room.

"Your attention, please," Alec called from near the drink table. "Everyone take up your drink for I would like to toast this feast."

While I wondered how he'd crossed the room so quickly, those on the floor left to obtain drinks; and those crowding the edges of the room, moved closer, filling in the empty dance floor around me.

"Raise your cups," Alec said, raising his own.

My pulse leapt. Would he announce his intention to wed now? My stomach gave a sickening twist.

Alec's gaze met mine, and my heart shattered all over again.

"To a merry harvest feast," he said loudly and clearly. "The first the North has seen in too many years. And I owe the success to Miss Hovtel, the beautiful, kind, and intelligent woman who has just consented to marry me."

My mouth dropped open as cheers erupted throughout the room. Alec's serious and slightly angry gaze held mine as he drank deeply. It was almost as if he were daring me to refute his claim. Suddenly, his words made his plan clear. He had just said that he needed me more than his freedom. He had warned me he would ruin the feast if I acted out against him in any way. If I rejected him here, now, he would do as he'd promised. He would ruin the feast and force Rose's hand.

My first reaction was anger. He'd planned to snare me all

along. Then, I began to wonder what he had to gain by doing that. Me. Just me. Could he truly care for me so much? Hope spread like wildfire, worrying me. I needed a moment to think.

Well-wishers pressed close, blocking Alec from my sight. I nodded, smiled, and thanked those who congratulated me. The music struck up once more, and most of those around me moved away to clear the floor.

Purposefully, I made my way to the open garden doors. The sun had begun its descent, casting long shadows in the garden. Overgrown as it had been, there wasn't much to see as my gaze swept the area. A movement to my right caught my eye but before I could focus, someone stepped out of the ballroom behind me.

I turned and saw Alec by the door. Behind him, dancers moved in time with the music, a bustle of motion compared to his still watchfulness. We eyed each other for several long moments.

"Why?" I said. "You lied to everyone and, through your threats, forced my silence. What kind of Lord does that make you?"

"A desperate one, I should think."

"Desperate?"

He let out a frustrated sigh.

"I've asked you to be my wife countless times to which you always answer no."

"With reason," I said in exasperation.

"Reasons that can be overcome. You care for me. You admitted it. Yet, you stubbornly refuse to believe I care for you. You have fears about being a wife but won't trust that I can be patient, though I've spent the last fifty years practicing patience."

"I would hardly call that patience."

He ran his hand through his hair. I watched him struggle to control his temper.

"Your unwillingness to see reason forced this lie. Have no

doubt I will carry through with my threat. Whether as the man you loathe or the beast you once loved, I will have you."

Again, pretty words. Could I trust them?

He turned and strode once more into the ballroom, and suddenly, Aryana's words rang in my mind. "Lies are necessary when truth fails." What truth had failed? My heart wanted to swell at the answer I found there. His love for me, because of my shattered trust in him and in men.

I turned away from the door and watched the sky change from blue to azure. High above, the first star sparkled in the darkening sky.

"Do you think this will change anything?"

I whirled at the sound of Tennen's voice. He stood just outside the door, partially hidden by the growing shadows. Surely, he wouldn't be so foolish as to try something with so many nearby to come to my aid.

"Yes, I do," I said, answering his question. "It will make you hate me more. A hate I do not deserve."

He snorted in disbelief and walked back into the ballroom.

Inside, the lit pillars and fire gave the large room a soft light. Near the food tables opposite the door, Alec watched me. His gaze followed Tennen briefly before returning to me. His observation made me feel safe, and I considered our engagement once more. If I were honest, it relieved me that he'd taken the decision from me. My heart hadn't forgotten his affection, though I'd desperately wanted it to. Could I dare allow myself to love him once more?

"You will make a fine Lady," Otta said softly, "if you can stop seeing innocence in everyone." The unexpected sound from behind startled me, as did the familiar words. I spun to face her.

Her small face began to transform, and I gasped as I recognized Aryana. I grabbed her wrist and quickly pulled her into the shadows.

"Speak your mind then leave," I said once I knew we were out of Alec's sight.

"You invited me."

"As yourself. I tire of your games. When will you leave the north and Lord Ruhall in peace?"

"When he is wed and settled. I'm not so certain you will be his wife, as he so clearly desires."

"And I'm not so certain you will leave us in peace when we are finally wed."

"Despite the trap he's laid for you, I could help you leave if that is what you wish."

I stared at her for a moment.

"I think that is what you wish. As Otta, you have watched for any excuse to return the curse. Speak true now. Why do you hate him so?" Then a thought occurred to me. "Did he hurt you like he did Egrit?" Compassion warred with distaste. "If he did, I must remind you that you allowed, no, encouraged his abuse of you. You forced it by purposely setting his freedom on a task he would misinterpret. Yet, I would understand if you did harbor hatred."

"No, he never hurt me. Egrit needed to learn a lesson as much as he did," she said with a sigh and a shake of her head. "Such a high price to pay."

"Was that why you allowed Tennen to take me? Was I to learn a lesson? If so, I believe I failed."

Her expression softened.

"Rape is never a tool to teach."

"But Egrit..."

"She was willing through it all, Benella. I thought she told you as much. She could have solidified at any time. She wanted him to use her, to find favor in her. She wanted to please him over her own self-preservation. That was the lesson she needed to learn. To put herself, her safety, before his desires. To value herself, she needed to learn to say no."

Aryana glanced over my shoulder, and her form began to recede into Otta once more.

"I will be watching," she said before ducking into the bushes.

"Miss Hovtel, Lord Ruhall requests that you come back into the light. He is concerned," Tam said from the doorway.

"I'll come inside," I said, moving toward him. "Will you dance with me?"

"Me?" He looked surprised. "I shouldn't think it suitable."

"I'm still the same. And, this is the harvest feast. If you dance with me, it will let the others know it's all right to do so as well."

"I would be honored," he said with a bow.

For the next hour, I twirled about the dance floor with various partners, carefully avoiding Bryn and Blye, who both seemed intent on speaking to me. When my feet grew tired, I begged my partner for a small break. Ila found me on the side of the room and offered me a glass of cider.

"I saw you dancing with Henick," I said. The Kinlyn boys were availing themselves to any willing partner and were truly making the feast a merry event.

"He's kind."

"And handsome, too," I said with a small, knowing smile. "I believe he and his brother are looking for wives."

She looked off in his direction.

"Do you think he will care?"

I knew she meant about her past.

"As you said, he is kind. I don't think he will mind at all."

She turned to study me then changed the subject.

"Lady Ruhall," she said. "That will be a change."

"Yes. Quite a change."

"You don't sound certain."

"I'm certain there will be a change. I'm not certain if it will be a positive one."

She leaned closer with a concerned frown.

"You've no wish to marry him?" she asked in a hushed tone.

I chose my words with care.

"The suddenness of the announcement and the reactions of a few have me doubting my wishes."

She straightened with a sigh and patted my arm.

"Follow your heart. It will lead you true."

I thought of Bryn and her infatuation with Tennen.

"Sometimes, I think the heart isn't a good leader," I said softly.

Before my cider had time to warm, Alec found me from across the room. His serious gaze held mine as he wove through people to reach my side. My heart gave an erratic beat.

"Will you dance with me?" he asked.

The reality of the announcement gripped me. He was mine. Should he be? Was this what I wanted? I thought so because the idea of him marrying someone else truly upset me. Yet, I still doubted his affection for me. I believed he cared for me, but did he care for me more than he did the estate?

He held out his hand, waiting for my answer.

"Yes. I'll dance with you."

He took the cup from my hand and set it on the table. My pulse leapt as he captured my fingers and led me to the floor.

He placed a sure hand at my waist, and we joined with the swirling dancers. He held me close, and I struggled to remain indifferent to his touch, my heart and my mind conflicted. What would a life with Alec, Lord Ruhall, mean for me? Bryn and Blye thought it meant luxury, but I knew better. There was little money; but even if it was plentiful, I wouldn't be interested in it. I wanted a marriage of love and consideration. Would I find that?

His gaze never left me, and the longer we danced, the more he frowned.

"What are you looking for when you study me so intently?" I said to distract myself.

"A hint, a sign of what you're thinking, what you're feeling. Before, I could read you so well. Not now."

"Before I knew what I thought and felt. Now, I don't," I said honestly.

He looked away for a long moment, and his hand on my waist gripped me tighter. When he viewed me once more, he seemed tormented.

"Do you still intend to leave, then?"

"No, Alec," I said softly. "I plan to stay and marry you."

"Why?"

"Because you said I would."

My words hurt him. I saw it in his expression and felt it in his arms but didn't understand why. Worried what he might do, I stepped close and briefly laid my head on his chest. A sigh heaved from him as he eased away. We swirled around the room in silence for the remainder of the dance, then he brought me back to my drink.

For the rest of the feast, I set aside the concerns over our future together and danced, ate, and drank until the guests began to leave.

The candle maker sat patiently in the chair he'd occupied all night, waiting for his wax. With the dwindling crowd, the chair beside him opened. I sat with a sigh.

"A feast well done, Benella," he said. "Much like the ones I remember."

"Thank you. Would you like me to help gather the wax?"

He shook his head and nodded toward Edmund. He already had a bucket and a thin, flat piece of metal for scraping. He blew out the pillar near the fire and started to scrape the candle and puddled wax away from the surface.

"The young baker already offered his assistance and a ride home. He's a good man. Too bad he married your sister."

"Sir," I said with censure.

He only chuckled.

"I said what we both thought. And it's the truth. I saw the way your sisters sought you out tonight, and how you avoided them. It's odd they're both missing now, hmm? I wonder what troubles they will cause you next."

"I dearly hope none," I said with a sigh.

He laughed again.

"I better help clear away the remaining food," I said, standing. "May I send any home with you?"

"I wouldn't be opposed to a pastry or two if there are any left."

I nodded and went to the table where Kara was combining everything onto trays and stacking the empty ones. I sent Retta over with two pastries for the candle maker, then picked up a stack of trays.

"You shouldn't be doing that," Kara said when she saw.

"Nonsense. If not this, then what?"

"Lord Ruhall is saying good-bye to guests. Perhaps you should join him?"

"I'd prefer to do this so I can seek my bed sooner." Alec's announcement had changed my desire to say farewell. Many, like my sisters and the smiths, would only speak to me because of my upcoming social elevation, when in reality they resented me for it. Those who would see me no differently were few.

Kara didn't argue further, and I made my way to the kitchen without interruption. As the rest of the staff set the ballroom to rights, I remained in the kitchen to wash the trays once I put on an apron. Edmund came in carrying his trays.

When I saw him, I paused washing to thank him.

"I had several people ask who made the pastries. I hope this helps business."

"I'm sure it will. Do you want Bryn to come help?" he asked, eyeing the trays Tam had just carried in and set on the table before leaving again.

"No. I'm sure once the ballroom is clean, Kara and Egrit will ban me from the kitchen."

"Oh, yes. Congratulations, Benella. You did look the picture of a Lady tonight."

"Thank you, Edmund."

He left, and after a few minutes, I heard the wagon rumble away from the door. No doubt to go to the front for his wife and the candle maker.

As I'd predicted, Egrit and Kara came to shoo me from the kitchen. Exhausted, I headed for my old room. After all, there no longer seemed any point to sleeping on the floor. And the bed in the Lady's room was so very comfortable.

I carefully hung my dress and buttoned myself into one of Alec's shirts that I'd collected. Then, I blew out my candle and settled into bed.

In the dark, I heard a faint rhythmic sound. Footsteps. They continued for a long while. Pacing. Eventually, the hushed noise stopped. I waited, thinking Alec would join me, but the door didn't open. I sat up and saw the faint light from under his door.

Curious, I left the warmth of my bed and approached his room. Pressing my ear to the door, I heard a slight rustling that let me know he wasn't yet sleeping. I nibbled my bottom lip and debated what to do. Then I heard him sigh. The hitch in it had me gently easing the door open.

He sat on the edge of his bed with his elbows on his knees and his head in his hands. He still wore his shirt and pants, but the jacket lay draped over his chair. His defeated pose struck a tender chord, and I approached him in silence.

He didn't move when I stood before him. I reached out to gently smooth his hair. His head jerked up, startling me. His tormented gaze held me. Then he reached out, gently gripped my waist, and pulled me to stand between his parted knees. He sighed shakily and set his forehead to my chest.

I stood there with my hands at my sides, looking down at his dark head. Finally, I gave into my impulse and reached up. My fingers brushed through his hair slowly as I tried to soothe whatever plagued him.

His hands tightened around my waist a moment before he lay back, pulling me with him. Sprawled on top of him, I stared down at him with wide eyes and a rising sense of panic. Did the announcement of our intent to wed mean...

He gently eased me to his side, his hand tenderly smoothing back the stray strands of hair from my face.

"Sleep, Benella."

Realizing I wasn't in danger, I sighed and curled beside him, content to stay as I was.

THE NEXT MORNING, I woke in my own bed and quickly dressed. The sun already lit the sky. Though I had no care to see Blye off, I wanted to thank Ila once more. However, when I knocked on Ila's door, her room was already empty. I hurried downstairs and met Mr. Crow coming from the kitchen.

"Did Ila leave?"

"Yes, Miss. Swiftly is driving her and the other Miss Hovtel back to the Water with the carriage."

A swell of relief and regret washed over me. That Blye had left without a word did not bother me.

"Your sister, Bryn, is waiting to speak with you in the kitchen," he said.

I had no desire to speak to her, yet curiosity won. She should be with Edmund; she'd seemed so delighted with his company last night.

"Very well," I said and went off to the kitchen. The warm room welcomed me as did Kara's smile.

"I have a plate waiting for you," she said, glancing at the table where Bryn sat.

"Thank you, Kara. Are you managing comfortably this morning?"

"Yes. The men are working in the second apple orchard instead of hunting this week."

"Good," I said with a nod. With only cooking duties, Kara could handle the kitchen duties well without Bryn. I turned to address my sister.

"Bryn. I thought you and Edmund meant to spend some time together," I said, moving toward the table to claim my breakfast.

"I thought we could take a walk," she said, standing.

I paused and eyed my plate for a moment. That she wanted to speak with me made me more curious than hungry. That she wanted to do so where no one could hear worried me.

"Of course," I said, moving toward the kitchen door.

Kara stared after us as we left.

Bryn set a moderate pace down the drive and remained quiet until we'd progressed a good distance from the manor.

"Congratulations on your engagement," she said. "When do you plan to wed?"

"By winter solstice."

"So quickly. Is there a reason to hurry?" She glanced at my stomach. "Perhaps the baker was successful?"

I shuddered at the unwanted memory.

"No. He was not." In the distance, I saw the gate.

"Lord Ruhall, then?"

"No. Why are you asking these questions?" I said, studying her.

"I'd only thought it would be nice to have a sister likewise with child. Someone to share the aches and fears of pregnancy." She sounded sincere.

"I'm sure I won't be long behind you once I'm wed." I tried not to think what that meant. My mind wasn't ready to grasp what would occur in less than two months.

She set her hand on her stomach.

"The babe moves now. Flutters that make me smile. Thank you for allowing me a week with Edmund. Waking early to walk to the estate and departing after dinner leaves us little time together. I've missed him."

"I'm sure Edmund misses you just as much. I hope business improves so you won't need to work at the estate."

She nodded as we neared the gates.

"And if it doesn't?" she asked.

I remained quiet, certain she would reveal the point of this walk soon.

"The people here are more tightfisted than before," she said. "Soon, we won't have the coin we need to buy flour because customers insist on bartering for bread. Yet Edmund continues to trade."

My lips thinned as I recalled how many times she had sent me to the baker to try to trade.

"His solution is that I keep toiling in your kitchen. He knows that won't work once the babe comes. What happens when we run out of coin? His father plans to remarry so we can't go back," she said as we walked through the gates.

I had a moment's unease leaving the safety of the estate, but remained silent.

"Edmund keeps telling me we need to give it time and refuses to discuss other options. When I press him, he only becomes upset with me."

Empathizing with Edmund's strained patience, I continued to walk and wait for her to arrive at her point. We cleared the dense trees that surrounded the estate and moved through the outer woods along the road.

"You can imagine my relief when Lord Ruhall announced your engagement last night."

My insides chilled. She meant to use me again. But how?

"Blye had hoped it would be her; but as long as he chose one of my sisters, I don't mind."

"How does our marriage ease your mind?"

"As you've said, you'll be with child soon enough, and with our mother gone, you will need my help with the birth. Certainly, you'll want me closer once your time comes. And, Edmund's talents are wasted in the village. I've heard many estates in the South pay handsomely for a private baker. Working for Lord Ruhall would be his dream come true."

Edmund's dream? I doubted that.

"With such a large, vacant manor, we could even have our own suite of rooms. I don't expect you to pay Edmund the annual forty gold he would earn in the South. Thirty-five would do well."

She meant to live at the manor and have Lord Ruhall pay Edmund an exorbitant amount of money the estate couldn't afford. And why? Because she was worried the business at the bakery wouldn't pick up. I could understand her concern to a point and might have been moved to grant a reasonable request. But not this.

"No."

She stopped walking and turned toward me. We stood just on the edge of the tree line. In the distance, I could see the village.

"What do you mean no? It's a fair wage."

"Does Edmund know you are discussing this with me?"

She grimaced and a flush colored her cheeks.

"I thought not. Go home, Bryn. Spend time with Edmund. Show him you love him, and stop scheming."

"I should stop scheming? You had better look at yourself. According to what Mrs. Wimbly said, you've been playing the Lady since you arrived there. Your plan to ingratiate yourself may seem to have worked for now, but Lord Ruhall will see through you eventually and know you're no better than the rest of us. I wish it would have been Blye. She's not nearly as selfish."

My mouth popped open as she whirled and stomped away from me.

"Selfish," I said, following her. "I went to the very baker who tried to rape me because you asked it. I've walked the estate and set traps for meat, so you could hoard the coin that Father gave you to purchase food. I've been called a whore, though we both know it's not me who deserves the title." Her face flushed scarlet. "And still, I spoke up on your behalf when you needed employment. I've done much and more for you, Bryn. What have you ever done for me?"

I stopped following and stared after her as she hurried away from me. We'd almost reached the village. From the shadow of the smithy, I saw movement. Bryn didn't notice it as she passed but then Bryn didn't notice much unless it benefited her.

Splane stepped further into the light and watched Bryn walk by. I backed into the shadows of the trees, then pivoted on my heel. Where was Tennen?

CHAPTER
ELEVEN

A HEALTHY DOSE OF SELF-PRESERVATION HAD ME PICKING UP MY skirts and running. Tennen's words from the night before rang in my ears, and I cursed myself for a fool. I should have asked Tam to follow me. Better yet, I should have stopped at the gate and told Bryn I wouldn't walk further.

Busy with my self-recrimination, I wasn't prepared for Tennen when he stepped from behind a tree. I ran right into his extended arm, and the impact sent me flying backward. I landed so hard, it knocked the breath from me; and my lungs refused to inhale.

My mouth opened and closed like a fish out of water as he dragged me by the arm further into the trees. My vision danced from lack of air, and my heart pounded fiercely in my chest. I finally managed a weak inhale just as he dropped my arm.

Tennen fell upon me, his expression twisted with hate. The impact robbed me of my hard won breath, and I weakly struggled to get out from under him. He caught my hands and held them tight within one of his.

"I heard what you said to Bryn. I think it will be my babe that grows in your belly. Just like with your sister's."

His other hand started pulling at my skirt. As it hitched higher, baring my legs to the air, I mouthed my denial. I had no air to speak it. Thrashing beneath him caused his grip to tighten painfully on my wrists. Heedlessly, I tugged harder, trying to free them.

He leaned on me to pin me with his weight, then set his mouth near my ear.

"I'm not like the baker. I won't fail. You'll bleed on my shaft." He laughed. "If you haven't already bled on someone else's."

I panted with fear.

His grasping hand found my bared thigh and gripped it tight. He pulled it to the side to settle his hips firmly between my legs. His coarse pants abraded my tender skin. When he let go of my thigh, he pulled back just enough to fumble with his pants. His harsh breaths filled my ear as I continued to buck and tried to free my hands. Twice our hips connected, and I felt the bulge of his desire. Nausea and terror filled me.

Desperate, I turned my head, looking for something, anything, to help me. No branch lay nearby. No beast, either. I wailed, a keening sound thick with my despair, before the sight of his ear cut the sound short. I opened my mouth, bared my teeth, and darted forward. Clamping down on his ear, I held tight as he grunted then yelled.

He stopped fumbling with his pants and forgot my hands in his desperation to pull me from his ear. The moment my hands were free, I released my hold and shoved at him with all my might.

He flew from me, drifting up and away. I blinked, confused by my strength and disoriented in my fear and desperation. But, I wasn't the cause of his removal.

Alec stood behind Tennen, lifting him from me by the back of his shirt. Tam hurried to my side and said something I didn't hear. I stared as Tennen flailed for a moment then found his feet. A disconnected part of me registered Tam discreetly lowering my skirt. Mostly, Alec's rage-twisted face held my attention.

Before Tennen could stand, Alec changed his hold to the front of Tennen's shirt and drove his fist into Tennen's stomach. Tennen's drawn moan of pain didn't stop Alec, though. His next punch broke Tennen's nose.

Tam gently assisted me to a sitting position, which helped clear my head.

"Lord Ruhall," Tam said. "You'll kill the boy."

Alec didn't seem to hear as he drew back once more.

"Alec."

I didn't know why I spoke his name, but he stopped and turned his head to look at me.

"I want to go home."

It wasn't until I said it that I realized just how desperately I wanted not to return to the manor, but to Alec. The one who'd always made me feel safe whether beast or man. Tears welled in my eyes, and a soft sob escaped me.

Alec thrust Tennen to the ground and came to my side. He squatted beside me and gently smoothed my hair from my face. In his gaze, I saw the love and worry he held for me.

He carefully lifted me into his arms then set out toward the estate. I didn't look over his shoulder at Tam, who had Tennen by the arm. Instead, I rested my cheek against Alec's chest and closed my eyes.

When we neared the estate, he started issuing commands.

"Take Tennen to the Head. Get Egrit. Benella needs her help to wash and change."

He mounted the stairs as he spoke, and I was certain he left Tam and Mr. Crow scurrying in his wake.

We'd barely entered my room when Egrit arrived. Alec

carefully set me on my feet. I trembled but stood on my own. My mind was blank as I watched him walk out the door.

Egrit didn't speak as she helped me from my dress. I shook too badly to do it on my own. When I stood in my underthings, she wet a cloth and washed my face, arms, and hands. Then she knelt and wiped the backs of my calves. It was the part of me that had touched the ground when Tennen had yanked up my skirt. I trembled harder.

"Did he...?"

I shook my head and closed my eyes. He hadn't, but I could still feel the press of his hips against mine. Tears started anew.

When no dirt remained, Egret pulled a nightgown from my wardrobe and helped me into it.

Once she got me in bed and under my thick covers, she left. The door remained closed for no more than a moment before it opened again. Alec strode across the room and sat on the bed beside me. He pulled me into his arms and just held me as I continued to cry.

I was so angry. At Bryn. At Blye. At Tennen. At the whole Coalre family, really. And, at Rose. How was the North any better than it had been before the enchantment?

Alec's hand ran over my hair again and again. I knew he meant to soothe me. And, he did. Eventually, the tears stopped, and my hitched breathing slowed.

Safe, I slept.

Dreams plagued me. In them, I ran through the trees from a monster toward the beast, neither one gaining or receding. My heart raced until gentle hands and words pulled me from my terror-filled world.

"You're safe. I'm here with you." Alec stroked my hair and held me close. The dream faded, and I fell into a peaceful sleep.

I woke sweat-dampened and alone. Frowning, I looked around

the room for Alec. The sun had passed its zenith, and a tray waited beside the bed. Sitting up slowly, I winced at my sore wrists and aching legs. I swallowed hard and refused to think about why I was sore. Instead, I eased from the bed, ignored the tray, and put on the remaining clean dress that waited in my wardrobe. The one I'd worn was gone.

With a steadying breath, I left the room and walked the familiar hall. Each step anchored me. I belonged here, with Alec. Not because I thought myself better than anyone else, but because I wanted to make the North a better place. A safer place. My home.

When I reached the stairs, I heard raised voices.

"—harmless prank."

"Prank?" Alec's shout echoed through the halls. I hurried toward the sound. It came from the entry. "He attacked her, and this wasn't the first time."

Alec was speaking of Tennen.

"He's always liked the girl."

I recognized the smith's voice and started to descend the steps.

"He only went too far trying to get her attention. I'll sit him down and speak to him," Tennen's father said.

"It's too late for paternal talks," Alec said just before Mr. Coalre came into view.

When Mr. Coalre saw me, he flushed. Alec turned and met me at the bottom of the steps. Behind him, Mr. Coalre took two steps toward us.

"Benella, Tennen isn't a criminal. Do the right thing."

His words struck me like a blow, and my steps slowed. The right thing? What did he think was right? To let Tennen go? Of course Mr. Coalre would think that. After all, he had gotten away with so much. My thoughts collided as Alec scowled over his shoulder at the man.

"Yes," I said half to myself, "I will do the right thing." I focused on Mr. Coalre.

"Go, get Sara."

Alec's shocked gaze flew to meet mine.

"Alec, we need to go to the Water and speak with the Head."

Mr. Coalre didn't even thank me before he rushed out the door.

Alec held out a hand as I reached the third step. I wrapped my fingers around his.

"Why, Benella? He deserves to be punished for what he did."

Alec looked angry and concerned. It was only right. He'd saved me from Tennen so many times.

"He does," I agreed. "But there are truths you do not know."

"Then tell me."

"Patience," I said softly, alighting from the last step. I wrapped my arms around his waist and held him close. He embraced me in return. Behind me, I heard footfalls on the stairs.

"She is well, Mr. Hovtel," Alec said without releasing me. "She wants to go to the Water and speak to the Head on Tennen's behalf."

I didn't disagree.

"Eat," Alec said, handing me a meat pie before we cleared the gate.

My stomach twisted with nerves, but I took the food and nibbled on it. We continued a distance in silence while Alec watched me closely.

"What are you thinking?" he said softly.

"That I'd rather not go to the Water."

"We can turn around."

"No," I said with a shake of my head. "We must go." I needed to make the North safer in order to have a future here.

Too soon, we stopped before the home of the Head. Alec opened the door, stepped out, and turned to offer me a hand. As I descended, the door behind Alec opened. I recognized Mr. Pactel, the Head, immediately. Alec kept my hand on his arm as he turned to greet the man.

"Welcome, Lord Ruhall. It's good to finally meet you in person. A pity it's under such poor circumstances." He turned to me.

"Miss Hovtel," he said. Nothing more.

But really, what could one say to a woman twice almost raped? Any attempt at condolence would sound inane. However, I found it interesting that he came to greet Alec personally.

"Sir," I said in acknowledgement of his greeting.

We followed Mr. Pactel inside where he led the way to his study.

Sara and her husband already waited within. Pale Sara sat in a chair, her hands demurely folded in her lap. She didn't look up when we entered but kept her gaze on her hands.

"I admit to skepticism when Mr. Coalre told me you meant to speak on his son's behalf," Mr. Pactel said as we took our seats.

"I would prefer to continue this conversation without Mr. Coalre or Lord Ruhall," I said. Mr. Coalre objected loudly; and Alec frowned at me, not in anger but speculation.

"Please," I said softly, meeting Alec's gaze. He nodded and stood. Mr. Coalre had no choice but to follow Alec out the door. Mr. Pactel eyed me expectantly but I didn't address him. I turned to Sara.

"Silence brought me unfounded hatred from the men in your family. Silence brought me abuse at the hands of Tennen and then Mr. Medunge. I only kept silent because I thought I protected you.

Now, I fear what silence will bring me next if I continue to keep company with it."

She lifted her gaze and met mine. Tears ran down her cheeks.

"I won't speak for Tennen," I said to her. "I have much to say against him. He is malicious and views women with contempt, much like his father.

"I asked you here to give you a choice, Sara. A choice to save yourself and your other son. Splane hasn't yet fully adopted his father's or Tennen's attitude."

Pain reflected in her gaze as she understood what I meant to do.

"I won't keep silent any longer."

I turned to Mr. Pactel and started at the beginning of my tale. I spared no detail of what I'd witnessed so many months ago or of the torment Tennen unleashed upon me with Splane's help. Mr. Pactel listened to each encounter with a stoic expression that cracked only once. He frowned as I recalled Edmund's mention of Mr. Coalre's visit to establish the same deal with the new baker as he'd had with the old.

When I finished, Sara turned to me.

"I didn't know. I am so sorry."

Mr. Pactel made a sound of disbelief and leaned forward in his chair.

"Miss Hovtel said you were there when the prior baker attempted to rape her. Were your eyes closed?" he asked sharply. "For if they were open, how could you not know?"

She paled further at his words but didn't take her gaze from me.

"I didn't know Tennen and Splane chased you and hurt you. I didn't know Tennen waited in the house for you." She faced Mr. Pactel. "I didn't know why we needed to go to the baker that morning. I thought it was for me. For more bread. It broke my heart that my son meant to send me. When I saw Benella, I was first so relieved it wasn't me." She turned to me, her expression full of remorse and apology. "Then you started to fight. I wanted to step forward but...Patrick stopped me. I was so afraid."

"I believe you," I said. Fear of her husband had stolen her courage to stand up for herself. How could she ever stand up for me? I didn't blame her for her inaction; I pitied her.

"You would have me see her as innocent?" Mr. Pactel asked me.

His words brought back what Rose had once told me...that I would call the guilty innocent. I'd thought she'd meant Alec, but now I understood. My silence had protected Mr. Medunge, Mr. Coalre, and Tennen.

"Coerced and controlled by her husband, she kept her silence, just as I kept mine. I believe we are both innocent of any crime. Our guilt lies in our fear and compassion. Consider that as you judge those who are guilty of much greater crimes."

Mr. Pactel sat silent for a long while, studying Sara.

"Your husband will be sentenced to work in the mines for one year for his crimes against you. With my ruling, he forfeits his rights to any material wealth. Your son, Tennen, will work five years and also forfeit any material wealth. What is theirs is yours as recompense.

"You can choose to remain in this room as I sentence your husband or you can leave."

She stood. Trembling, she straightened her shoulders.

"Before the Head, I sever my marriage to Patrick Coalre." Then, she turned and walked out the door.

Through the open door, Mr. Pactel asked that the guard fetch Mr. Coalre and Lord Ruhall.

I stood.

"I would prefer to leave for the sentencing."

He nodded and led me through a side door into a very small sitting room.

"I will have Lord Ruhall join you as soon as I've spoken with him."

Minutes after he closed the door, I heard the murmur of low voices. Then, the smith began to yell and curse. The sounds of a struggle reached me before the room went very quiet. It remained so for a long while. The abruptness of the door opening to my left brought me to my feet. Alec paused in the doorway as he caught the fear and panic in my eyes. After a moment, he stepped in and continued toward me.

"We can leave now," he said softly.

I studied his face. The slight downturn of his mouth and the thin line of his lips held me in place.

"You're angry."

He sighed and gently took my hand in his.

"You should have told me."

"It wasn't my truth to tell."

"It was. Because you were the one to suffer the most. I would have protected you and brought the smith and his son to the Head's attention sooner. Instead, I paid the pair to pick apples." He didn't mask his disgust.

"I needed to give them a chance to choose to reform like Rose did for you."

"You are not Rose. You are fragile, easily hurt."

The bruises on my wrist told the truth of his words. Why had I suffered through the abuse I had? Was my lesson to learn not to trust or give second chances? I thought not and held firm to my belief that we were meant to make mistakes and learn from them. Perhaps I only needed to learn to be more wary of who to trust and who might deserve second chances.

With his hand warming my back, he guided me from the room.

Tam hopped into the driver's seat as soon as we emerged into the late afternoon light. Alec helped me into the carriage. Once we settled into our seats, he called to Tam. The carriage lurched forward.

"When Kara told me you went for a walk, I became worried. Rightfully so, it seems. Why did you leave without someone?" Alec asked gently once we crossed the bridge.

A half snort escaped me, and I looked out the window.

"I did leave with someone. I left with Bryn. She had asked me to walk with her." I shook my head. "I was foolish to go. We upset each other, and she left me near where you found me."

"What upset you?"

"Her selfishness," I said, meeting his gaze. "She told me she was glad we were marrying. Then proceeded to outline how you could hire Edmund, pay him an enormous annual wage, and allow them a suite of rooms at the manor. When I said no, she accused me of being selfish and that Blye would have been better suited as your wife."

He remained silent, studying my face, then looked out the window for a time. The tense clench of his jaw showed his emotion.

"Tam," he called.

"Sir."

"Take us to the bakery in Konrall."

A jolt of concern struck me.

"Edmund had no knowledge of our conversation."

"I guessed as much," he said.

"What do you plan to do?"

"Tell Edmund what his wife has caused."

I sighed and nodded. Keeping silent served no purpose.

When the carriage stopped before the bakery, I took a steadying breath. Alec disembarked first, then reached to help me descend. Down the road, Splane carried items from the smithy to the wagon, filling it with all manner of tools and metal.

"What will they do?" I asked quietly.

"Sell what they can and start anew elsewhere," he said, glancing in the direction of the smithy.

Tam hopped down from the driver's seat and took the horses by the lead.

"I'm going to see if there's something we can use."

Alec nodded and led me inside. He kept my hand on his arm, and I was glad for the support. I didn't want to face Bryn.

"Welcome, Lord Ruhall," Bryn said with an eager smile. She didn't glance at me.

"Bryn, Tennen attacked your sister after you left her this morning," Alec said without preamble.

Her gaze flicked to me before returning to Alec. She remained silent, watching him expectantly. Edmund appeared from the kitchen.

"Good afternoon," he said pleasantly. His welcoming smile faltered when he saw Alec's displeased expression. "Can I help you?"

Alec repeated his statement, and Edmund's eyes flew to me.

"Were you injured? Would you like to sit?"

"Thank you, Edmund. I'm fine, now. Alec came upon us before I suffered anything serious." Alec's fingers twitched over mine, and I gave his arm a gentle squeeze.

"We came because I hold your wife responsible," Alec said with a good deal of anger.

Bryn's mouth dropped open, and her face paled.

"After Benella told Bryn that she would not hire you and allow her sister and you to live at the manor, Bryn grew angry and left Benella alone on the road."

"I've walked that road twice a day for weeks without incident," Bryn said in quick defense.

"But Tennen didn't hold a grudge against you," Alec said, lowering his eyes to her belly. A small gasp escaped her, and her eyes began to water. "You knew he disliked Benella, and I suspect you also knew he'd attacked her before. Long before your family moved to the Water."

Alec turned to Edmund.

"My feelings toward your wife do not extend to you. I believe Bryn has manipulated you as much as she has Benella. No man should suffer a manipulative wife who carries another man's child."

Bryn flinched and paled as she understood what Alec was suggesting. With panic, she looked toward Edmund. Edmund's cheeks flushed, and he wouldn't look at her.

"But that choice is yours alone," Alec said.

"No," Bryn said wretchedly, finally finding her voice. She rushed the few steps to Edmund's side and clung to his arm. "Don't sever our marriage. I only spoke to her for you. You work so hard. You deserve so much more than this."

I looked away from the display.

"This?" Edmund said. "I'm proud to be a baker. I am a damn good one. If you're not proud of that, if you don't want to build a future with me, here, in this bakery, if you don't want to work beside me and share the success earned by our own labors, you should marry another."

His footsteps marked his retreat. I looked up and saw Bryn standing there, shaken. She stared at the door to the kitchen, not even noting us.

"Decide, Bryn," I said quietly. "Who do you want to be? A loved wife or a lonely woman always wanting more than she has?"

Her gaze turned to me, and I saw the flash of anger there. Then her shoulders slumped, and the emotion disappeared. Like Edmund, she turned away from us and fled into the dreaded sitting room off the store.

I SAT IN THE LIBRARY, pretending to read the book I held. Neither Father nor Alec disturbed my contemplations under this pretext. Today's events needed consideration. Not Tennen's attack or the Coalre family's departure or even Bryn's numerous hurtful rejections. No, the events that held my mind revolved around Alec, who currently paced quietly in his study.

How he'd reacted when he'd found Tennen on me, the enraged expression on his face, the way he'd struck Tennen...that was the beastly way he would have acted while enchanted, the way I'd wanted him to act when he'd found the baker atop me. He'd never changed. Not really. And I had refused to see that for so long. He had held my heart as the beast; and though I'd tried to deny it, he held my heart still. He wasn't perfect, but I'd never wanted perfect like my sisters had. I'd wanted real. I wanted someone who could love me as I was and who I could love as he was.

The crackle of the fire almost drowned out the distant sound of Alec's footfalls as he paced.

How many times had I hurt him with my denial? The lonely beast, punished for fifty years, was still there despite the clothes and title. And he hadn't lied when he'd said he needed me. I'd thought he just meant my body or perhaps even my assistance. But it wasn't any one thing he needed from me; he needed all of me. My love. My company. My compassion. My cool head. Living with Alec wouldn't be easy, but I already knew that. It would be an adventure filled with love and consideration. I had been a fool to wait so long to accept what he offered me. I wouldn't wait a moment longer. Our life together would start now.

I softly closed the book and stood. Father looked up at me, and I gave him a reassuring smile as I started toward the study. Alec caught sight of me and stopped his pacing. He waited patiently with worry furrowing his brow until I stood before him.

I reached up and gently ran my finger along the crease.

"Why are you worried?"

His gaze searched mine, then he took my hand in both of his. He traced the mottled bruise circling my wrist. The gentle touch and the anguish in his gaze made my stomach twist. He closed his eyes and pressed his lips to my palm. I rested my other hand against his cheek, trying to comfort him. He held me like that for so long, I thought he wouldn't speak of his concern.

"I worry that I've done you a greater wrong than those sentenced today," he said, opening his eyes. "Last night, when we danced and I saw your conflict, I wanted to grant you your wish to go your own way, but I couldn't. I'm too selfish to let you go. I want you as my wife; yet, you fear what that entails. A selfless man might offer to give you time, might promise not to touch you after we speak our vows. I'm not a selfless man. My need for you might be what finally drives you away. And I can't stand the thought of losing you."

My heart constricted then grew for the man before me. The hold on my hand loosened with his admission. He worried he'd trapped me into a marriage I didn't want. I thought of Bryn and Edmund and soothed my fingers along his cheek.

"I have fears," I agreed softly, "but I do not fear you."

He exhaled, warming my palm.

"I need you to need me as badly as I need you," he said.

I had no words to soothe or reassure him; I wanted reassurance myself. He'd made his plans clear. As soon as we spoke the vows, he would make me his wife. The thought made my stomach clench and my pulse leap as my hands fell to my sides. The experience with the baker and Tennen had been rough and disgusting. Yet, before either had hurt me, Alec had shown me there might be another side to the act. Fear warred with remembered passion. I wanted to trust him, but the idea of what he wanted to do to me was terrifying.

He seemed to sense my uncertainty because he closed his eyes with a grimace.

Seeing him so upset broke through some of my fear. Alec held my heart. He had since the first day he'd held me while I slept. I needed him, and he needed me just as much.

I struggled to calm my breathing and rose up on my toes to lean into him.

"I have fears," I said softly, repeating my words, "but I do not fear you."

He opened his eyes and studied me. With deliberate slowness, he lifted his hand to my cheek, stroking my skin with a gentle finger.

"I can feel you shaking," he said softly.

His pained gaze held mine.

"I don't know how to ease your mind, Benella."

I didn't know if he could.

"Every time I see you, I want to..."

He released my hand and ever so slowly lowered his head. My breath caught, and I grew hot and cold in waves.

"One kiss. Say yes."

My heart stammered, and I trembled as he hovered inches from my lips. His breath fanned my face.

"Yes."

His hands rose, capturing my head and delving in my hair. I

licked my lips. His gaze dropped to my mouth and the pained expression he wore became more strained.

"So beautiful," he said softly.

He pressed his lips to the corner of my mouth, a chaste kiss. Then he slowly nibbled his way along my jaw. My skin heated, and I exhaled on a sigh. I tilted my head to give him access to my neck. A shiver ran through me when his lips found the tender place just below my ear.

"When we are husband and wife, I won't attack you. I'll love you," he whispered.

I shivered again. He pulled back to study me. Lifting his hand, he ran a thumb along my bottom lip. Then, he leaned in once more.

Warm and firm, his mouth brushed against mine; and his hands drifted to my arms. He held me for a moment then pulled me to his chest. The angle of the kiss changed, and his tongue stroked my bottom lip. I shivered and lifted my hands to set them upon his jacket.

His mouth left mine; and only then, did I realize I'd closed my eyes. When I opened them, I found him studying me with concern. Had he thought I meant to push him away? I smiled slightly and leaned forward, lifting my lips.

He groaned faintly and met me. His tongue traced the curve of my lower lip before his mouth opened and nibbled at my lip. I made a small noise. He took advantage of my parted lips and dipped his tongue inside, touching mine. My heart leapt at the sensation, and I opened further. His hands tightened on my arms before one slid down to the base of my spine. He pressed me firmly against him. I felt the evidence of his desire, and a sliver of fear shivered through me. But, I pushed it aside and focused on the kiss and the memories of the things we'd done before. His mouth on my breast. His tongue between my legs. A heat grew within me, and I pressed myself against him.

He broke away from the kiss and stared at me.

Dazedly, I returned his regard. My lips tingled. My pulse raced. Kissing Alec was more thrilling than I had imagined possible. I hoped the rest would be as well.

"I think I'll retire for the evening," I said softly.

He nodded jerkily.

Father was already gone from the library when I stepped from the office. As I walked to my room, I wondered what the night would bring. My stomach tightened with coiled nerves as I undressed. After I lay in bed, it took a long while for sleep to claim me.

The feel of his lips on the back of my neck and his arm around my waist roused me from a dream.

However, when he only settled behind me, I drifted back to sleep.

I woke the next morning with no recollection of Alec coming to me. I glanced at the empty place beside me, but it looked untouched. Puzzled, I dressed for the day and went to his room. The bed lay undisturbed. Perhaps only remade?

After a long search, I found Alec near the barn. He and Tam were loading baskets into the wagon. I watched the fabric of Alec's shirt stretch over his well-muscled back with each move. The kiss from the night before rose to my mind, and I blushed. He caught sight of me while my face was still red and paused in his labor.

"Good morning," I said.

His gaze swept over me. Concern deeply etched his face.

"Good morning."

"If you wait a moment, I'll fetch a wrap and join you."

Alec set the basket he held into the wagon then approached me.

"It would be better," he said softly, "if you stayed here." He gently brushed a loose strand of hair from my face. "We'll return before dinner."

He turned away and climbed into the wagon with Tam. Tam clucked to the horses, and they rumbled off. Frowning, I watched them disappear around the manor. Why did he think staying here better for me than picking apples?

Still puzzled, I went inside to see what I could do to assist Egrit and Mrs. Palant. Both assured me they didn't require help and suggested I read in the library. Withholding a sigh, I went to the kitchen. Since Bryn was with Edmund, surely Kara would need assistance. However, she gave the same answer and sent me off with a biscuit and egg for breakfast.

My disappointment only lasted a moment. I didn't much care for cleaning and cooking, anyway. Hurrying to my room, I changed into my long forgotten pants and shirt and grabbed my bag from the bottom of the wardrobe. It felt odd, yet pleasant, to fit the strap across my shoulder and feel the bag rest at my hip. Recalling the last time I'd gone without word, I went to the library to find my father.

"I'm off to explore the east side of the estate," I said from the door, already turning to walk away.

"Wouldn't you rather read in here?"

His words, so similar to everyone else's, stopped me.

"No. I've too much energy for that. I'll see you at dinner." I waved and left before he could say more.

I walked toward the grove of picked apple trees, then beyond. The vegetation between the trees grew thick and slowed my progress. I found several berry bushes, long shed of their fruits, and noted their location for next year. Walking through the trees didn't distract me as I'd hoped it would. My mind kept turning toward Alec.

The remembered feel of his lips on my neck warmed me. Preoccupied with my idle thoughts, I jumped badly when Rose stepped out in front of me.

Thinking for a brief moment she was Tennen, alarm widened my eyes and robbed me of breath, and my hand flew to my chest.

"Benella," Rose said quickly, "it's only me." Worry filled her gaze as she wrapped her arms about me. "What have we done to you?" she said softly, holding me tight.

Her tone and comforting touch reminded me too much of Aryana. Angry, I pulled away.

"Why are you here?"

She released me and stepped back to study me.

"To check on you." Her gaze flicked over me, settling briefly on my wrists. "Two are gone and two remain. I worry for you."

"What two remain?" I asked, a cold terror filling my stomach.

I heard my name and turned toward the distant call to cock my head and listen. It sounded like Alec. I glanced at Rose but found myself alone.

With her last words echoing in my ears, I quickly started toward the direction of the call.

CHAPTER
TWELVE

I CALLED BACK TO ALEC, AND A FEW MINUTES LATER, HEARD THE snapping of twigs as he forced his way through the bramble. When he finally appeared, he was red-faced and disheveled. Twigs and leaves decorated his hair, and his sleeve had a tear. I'd never been so glad to see him. However, the way he rushed to my side concerned me.

"What happened?" I asked.

"Why aren't you reading?" His angry, demanding tone surprised me.

"I wasn't in the mood to read." I waved at the woods around us. "It's too beautiful a day to spend indoors. Soon the leaves will fall and the snow will come. I'll spend enough time indoors then."

"Benella, you need to rest."

"Is that why you came rushing through the woods? You think I need rest?"

He ran his hand through his hair, seemingly frustrated; and it touched me that he worried so about me. I stepped close. He stilled and looked down at me as I laid my hands on his chest.

"Go pick your apples. I will keep myself busy."

"I'd prefer you return to the estate."

His surly expression made me smile.

"Why? I'm perfectly safe out here." Doubt made the words bitter. Who were the two that remained?

"Benella, yesterday..."

And, with that, I understood why no one needed my help.

"Yesterday was yesterday," I said. "I refuse to dwell on it. Learn from it, yes, but not dwell. Tennen and the baker are gone, and I'm safe enough within the estate. Stop worrying so much and go pick your apples."

He reached up to gently run his knuckles along my jaw.

"Do you know how many times I've thought I lost you?" He didn't wait for my answer. "As a beast, each time you came to me and left again, I thought it would be the last I saw you. Then, you agreed to stay. But only on the condition I allow you to leave the estate once every seven days. Again, I thought each time would be the last. Then, when Rose gave you that dress," he said the word with anger, "I thought some man would woo you to him.

"But you returned. You always returned. Yet, I couldn't trust your devotion was real. Was it for me, or only to spare your father? Then you gave me the answer to free myself, to become a man who might win your heart. But instead of finding you in your bed that morning after the curse was broken, you were gone. And when I finally found you, abused and fighting for your freedom, you wanted nothing to do with me. You left."

I understood then that leaving the manor so soon after Tennen's last attack had scared him. I stepped closer.

"Shh. It's done. They're gone, and I returned then and will not leave now. Instead of the past, let's focus on the future. When do we want to wed?" I asked, hoping to distract him from his worry.

His gaze searched mine.

"Do you wish to wed me, Benella?"

His uncertainty tugged at my heart.

"Yes. I do." I took his hand in mine and gently tugged him toward the path he'd made. "So, how soon would you like to wed?"

"How much time do you need to plan the wedding feast?" he asked.

Looking over my shoulder, I made a quick face at him then turned back to the path.

"We've already welcomed those closest to the estate, so I see no need to do so again by winter solstice. And I would rather not invite your peers—much too expensive. The idea of a private wedding followed by a dinner with the staff is more appealing. If you agree."

He remained quiet for a long while.

"Are you certain that is what you wish?"

I stopped to face him.

"Only if you wish it as well."

"Someone once told me a woman's wedding should be a pageant of beauty and extravagance."

"Displays of extravagance for the sake of extravagance are wasteful. And a wedding can be beautiful without a crowd."

He stepped close to me and cupped my face.

"I want whatever will make you happy." His lips brushed mine in a gentle, brief kiss before he stepped back once more.

In the distance, I heard another voice calling both our names. Alec looked off in that direction.

"Swiftly was searching near the apple grove. Come."

He led the way to the grove, let Swiftly know I was fine, then escorted me to the house. When he tried to steer me toward the library, I groaned.

"Why do you keep insisting that I read?"

"I thought you liked reading."

"I do. But if you recall, I'm not fond of being ordered about. Why does everyone want me to read so badly?"

He stopped walking and turned toward me. Worry etched his features, but his appearance distracted me from it. His hair and clothes were still a mess.

"You should go change and clean up. I'll find something to occupy myself."

He hesitated.

"Have you eaten yet today?" he asked.

"Yes. An egg and a biscuit."

"I believe Kara is making pheasant soup and bread. The bread was in the oven when we left to find you."

My mouth watered at the idea of fresh bread.

"I'll check to see if it's done," I said, already turning.

"I'll join you. There's no point in changing when I plan to pick more apples yet today."

We walked to the kitchen together. I suspected his reluctance to change had more to do with keeping an eye on me than concern over dirtying another shirt.

When I stepped into the kitchen, I saw everyone already at the table. My steps faltered when I met Otta's gaze.

I'd thought when Otta had exposed herself as Rose the night of the feast that Otta wouldn't return. Her presence as Rose in the woods had firmed the belief that I wouldn't see Otta again. Yet, there she was.

"Are you all right?" Alec asked, reaching around to steady me.

I plastered a smile on my face and met his gaze. Determination and worry kept me from glancing in Otta's direction again as I nodded.

"I have a tray ready," Kara said from the butcher's block, pulling Alec's attention from me.

"Thank you," he said. "I'll carry it."

I turned and left the kitchen without waiting for him. My heart was pounding. Should I tell him? I'd kept Sara's secret and learned my lesson. Yet, Rose wasn't doing anything to hurt me. Nor had she caused any problems since the announcement. Telling Alec she was here would anger him; and undoubtedly, his temper would cause trouble.

Worrying my bottom lip, I hurried my steps to the library. Father sat behind his desk, reading yet another book. He looked up when I entered.

"Benella," he said, standing. He came and hugged me. "I'd hoped you and I might speak privately. You ran out too quickly this morning."

"I'm sorry about that, Father. Yes, we should speak," I said, thinking of Rose, "but Alec is just behind me with our meal."

"Afterward then?"

I agreed. Alec entered a moment later and set the tray on the table before the fire. Father sat in his chair and Alec next to me on the lounge.

"Without needing a celebratory feast, how soon can we wed?" I asked as he passed our plates to us.

He glanced at me, then Father, then cleared his throat.

"I will write Mr. Pactel today and inquire when he might be available. Would you prefer the ceremony in his home or here?"

"Here, please," I said before testing the soup. Hot and delicious, I took another quick bite.

"Is there a reason to rush?" my father asked, sounding nervous and strained at the same time.

"No," I said quickly with a glance at Alec. "There is no reason to wait either."

Father nodded and considered his soup. Something weighed his mind, but he remained silent. Alec picked up his soup and began to eat as Bryn's words came back to me.

"Father, I'm not pregnant."

Alec choked and sputtered on his soup. I patted his back absently while meeting my father's pained gaze.

"I swear. That is not the reason for a quick wedding. I don't care if others think that, but I don't want you to think it. I've settled my mind, so there is no reason to wait. I'll wed Alec but I want nothing to do with the pomp of Bryn's wedding. I want a simple dinner with those who mean the most to me. It takes little to plan for that."

I realized I still patted Alec, though he'd stopped making noise. Turning to him, I found his face flushed.

"Are you all right? I should have warned you, the soup is hot."

He shook his head, cleared his throat, and addressed my father.

"If you would prefer we wait—"

"No. Benella is right. She has never been the type of girl to fawn over a dress," here he smiled at me, "or waste time. A quick wedding suits her, and I have no objections."

"I will write the letter and send Swiftly with it today," Alec said.

Once we finished our soup, he went to his study to pen the letter, and I took the tray to the kitchen after a promise to return.

Kara was washing the bowls when I set the tray on the block.

"Would you like some help?" I asked.

"No. There's not much to do besides this. I already have a stew for dinner on the fire."

"Kara, Lord Ruhall and I were just discussing the wedding."

She immediately stopped washing and turned to me.

"Have you already decided how many guests?" Nervous excitement laced her words, and I smiled.

"Yes. Only those who live in this house. As I'm sure you've noticed, most people here have shunned me because of—"

"It shouldn't matter. You're marrying a lord. No one would say no."

"Exactly. They would only attend to be seen, to find favor or elevate their standing in the community. I've been used enough. I don't want that for my wedding day."

Understanding lit her gaze.

"Of course not. What did you have in mind?"

"The ceremony will be here with a dinner afterward. Everyone here can attend. I'm fond of roast if you think it manageable."

"A wedding roast," she said, nodding. I could see she was already planning. "When?"

"I'm not certain, yet. Lord Ruhall is sending a note to the Head as we speak. Soon though, I hope. I would prefer not to wait."

"I will let Mr. Crow know," she said. "Please tell me as soon as you've set the date."

I left her in the kitchen to plan and returned to the study. Alec was already gone and Father was waiting.

"I admit I was surprised when Lord Ruhall announced your engagement at the feast," Father said, as I sat beside him. "You'd given me the impression you were still opposed to the idea."

"At the time of his announcement, I was." His brows rose. "However, since then, I've realized several things. He truly does care for me. He doesn't always show it well, but it's there. I trust him completely, and I can't see myself with anyone else."

"Do you love him?"

"Yes, I do. It's frightening and makes me feel sick with worry at times; but it also warms me. When he's near, I feel safe and loved."

Father smiled and hugged me.

"Good," he said close to my ear. "I'm glad something pleasant is coming from everything that's happened."

"Something very pleasant," I said, pulling away. "But there is a reason to hurry this wedding."

"Oh?"

"Otta is Rose, Aryana, whoever. She's here, and she's watching."

His mouth dropped open.

"My hope is the sooner we're wed, the sooner she will leave."

"Have you told Alec?"

I shook my head.

"Can you imagine his temper and what he might do? I think it best to keep this to myself or he'll find himself re-enchanted."

Father nodded slowly.

"Then, we will see what the Head has to say."

Swiftly returned by dinner with the Head's answer. Alec and I would marry in seven days. Alec called the staff together to make the announcement and to invite them to join us in celebrating our union. A few displayed shock. I wasn't sure what reaction Otta gave as I kept my gaze purposefully averted from hers.

Egrit's reaction, however, was hard to avoid. She rushed to me, her arms spread wide to wrap me in a breath defying hug. The excited squeal she let loose while she was pressed to my ear nearly deafened me.

"I'm so happy for you," she breathed before she let me go. She beamed at me, a wide and almost crazed smile, before Tam gently pulled her away.

Mr. Crow hushed the gathering and turned to me.

"Do you have any special instructions?"

I thought for a moment then shook my head.

He gave a slight nod and motioned for everyone to return to their duties. Alec wrapped his hand around mine and led me back to the library. Father was already gone for the evening.

"Will you read to me?" Alec asked, already moving to select a book.

I smiled and sat on the lounge, pretending that a swarm of

butterflies hadn't invaded my insides. Alec brought me a book then moved to close the library door.

"Why are you closing the door?" I asked warily. He'd never closed it before.

He chuckled.

"Look at the book."

I glanced at it and found no title on the leather cover. Opening it, I discovered why. A fiery blush claimed my face as I stared at the sketched image of a naked woman in the arms of a man. My eyes devoured the caption, "The many ways to please a woman."

"I can't read this." I turned a few pages and found the amount of descriptive instruction equal to the images.

Alec sat beside me, and I jumped.

"And that is why you should read it," he said. "Your only experience with this has been unpleasant."

I opened my mouth to argue, and he silenced me with a finger over my lips.

"Because of your experiences, you're afraid of something that can be quite pleasant. I don't trust Bryn to instruct you as your mother might have, and I surmise your father would prefer to ignore the subject completely. I thought if you read this, you might not be so nervous on our wedding night."

He lowered his hand, and I glanced at the book once more with a frown.

"Not aloud, though," I said, looking up to silently plead with him.

He sighed and nodded.

"To yourself might be wise. But promise you'll come to me with questions."

"Yes. I swear."

I couldn't relax and read until he went to his study. Then, for the next hour, I found the answers to questions I hadn't known to ask and a few that Aryana had refused to answer. Before long, the room—and my face—grew too warm to continue. Closing the book gently, I stared into the flames and considered what I'd learned.

Alec thought I feared our wedding night. I didn't fear it because I knew he wasn't the baker or Tennen. Yet, I hadn't looked forward to it, either. The book had me reconsidering. The author expounded on the need to tease a woman's body before introducing one's manhood. The ridiculous term, even in my head, made me wince.

"Are you finished?"

Alec's voice startled me, and I squeaked and turned. He stood just behind me, looking down at me. I quickly stood, clutching the book.

"For tonight. I'd like to keep it, if that's all right."

He nodded and offered his arm.

"Shall we retire?"

I set my hand upon his arm and let him lead me from the room.

That night, he only waited until I slid beneath the covers to join me. He pulled me back against his chest and set his arm about my waist as he usually did.

"Thank you," he said softly.

"For what?"

"For staying. For agreeing to be my wife. For saving me from a life of depravity, deceit, and devastation."

But had I saved him? I couldn't be sure until we wed and Rose left us in peace.

I woke with my head on Alec's chest and my leg over his thighs. He wore a nightshirt and linen shorts. Regardless of his proper sleep attire, embarrassment would have flooded me, had it not been for the hand currently kneading my breast.

His touch was light yet, I still felt a thread of concern. Was he preparing me for more as the book had suggested?

I lifted my head to meet his gaze.

"Good morning," he whispered, continuing his gentle massage.

"Good morning. Shouldn't you be gone already?"

"There's too much to keep me here," he said.

Suddenly, he rolled so I was under him. Before I could panic, he ducked his head and closed his mouth over my nipple. I gasped in shock then pleasure as he suckled gently, sending waves of need rolling over me. Threading my fingers through his hair, I held him and tried to remember to breathe.

He lifted his head and grinned down at me.

"May I do that again tomorrow morning?"

That was all he wanted to do? I eagerly nodded.

"You can do it again now, if you'd like."

He chuckled.

"I think not. We'll be missed if we linger too long."

With disappointment, I watched him flip back the covers and leave the bed. He didn't turn back to look at me as he strode across the room and left me alone with my racing pulse.

I washed and dressed; and, by the time I finished, my pulse had returned to normal.

I opened the door to my room and found Alec waiting for me in the hall just as he had so long ago. His attendance touched something inside me and banished the remaining threads of doubt regarding our future together. I smiled at him and accepted his arm.

We spent the day together playing games in the library. Father joined us for a few of the games but mostly left us to our own amusement. Once Father retired after dinner, I again picked up the book and read until the room grew too warm. Alec escorted me to bed without comment.

Though he joined me and snuggled me predictably, my pulse still leapt at the memory of what had transpired that morning and what he'd promised would occur again. With a smile of anticipation, I closed my eyes.

He woke me with insistent kisses on my cheek, jaw, and neck. As soon as my eyes fluttered open, he kissed his way lower. My shirt already lay open for him, and I arched, reveling at the sensation of his exploring lips. His mouth closed over the same breast as the day before. The pleasant heat spread to my stomach and lower.

When he lifted his head, I gave him a sleepy smile.

"Good morning," he whispered.

"It is," I agreed.

He placed a kiss on the valley between my breasts then sat up. I wanted to pull him back down and beg him to continue for just a while longer. I considered doing just that, until he lifted a tray from beside the bed and turned to me.

"Please tell me Egrit did not bring that," I said with worry.

He laughed, his amused grin making him impossibly handsome.

"I went to the kitchen and brought this myself."

"In your nightshirt?"

He laughed loudly, and I clapped a hand over his mouth to muffle the sound. He licked my palm, pulled my hand away, and kissed my knuckles.

"Don't worry. I put on pants." He leaned back and picked up a piece of dried apple from the tray and fed it to me.

"Phillip mentioned we have a fair store of meat and lard but are low on everything else. Mrs. Wimbly did the purchasing when she was here, traveling to Konrall for flour and occasionally visiting the Water for produce. However, Mr. Crow wasn't sure if you wanted Kara to attempt it or if you wanted to make the purchases yourself during your next trip to the Water."

"I can make the purchases. Do we have apples to trade?"

"We do. Will you take Swiftly with you?"

"Of course."

SWIFTLY PULLED the wagon to a stop in the market district and hopped down from his seat. As he came around to help me from my perch, I took a fortifying breath and eyed the different merchant stores that offered produce. The last time I'd tried to trade hadn't gone well.

"Thank you," I said. "If you want to stay with the apples, I'll see if I can find someone willing to trade."

The first merchant greeted me with an air of indifference and said he would take a basket from me but only offered a few coppers.

"There are apples everywhere," he said. "It's harvest season. You won't find a better price."

I thanked him and tried several more merchants only to receive similar answers. With a frown, I returned to the wagon.

"They're not worth the trade. We would be better served to press the majority into tart cider as my father suggested." That meant I would need to part with some gold to buy the supplies I needed. Supplies we couldn't bring back with a wagon full of apples.

"Let's move the wagon to the trade street, Swiftly."

Doors opened before we even parked. Homes with children

received the milk and cheese Kara had sent; however, the apples were so plentiful, we gave some to every house. Retta's mother didn't ask about her children, but she did thank us for the apples.

Back on the market street, I went to the merchants who had advertised the lowest prices and purchased sacks of vegetables and a small bag of sugar. While I waited by the wagon for Swiftly to carry the sacks, a familiar voice called my name.

I turned and saw Blye briskly walking my way. Her bright smile confused me, as did her exuberant hug.

"You look well," she said, her volume hurting my ear. She pulled back and smiled at me as she gave my arms a sisterly squeeze. Her gaze slid to the side then returned.

"How are the wedding plans? Have you and Lord Ruhall set a date?"

Movement around us slowed, and I realized her game. I averted my gaze to hide my anger and spotted Ila not far away. Her gaze met mine, and I found understanding there.

"Excuse me, Blye," I said, pulling from her false embrace. "I don't have much time here and need to speak with someone." I turned toward Ila.

Behind me, Blye twittered.

"I understand. I'll see you soon," she called.

Ila smiled in greeting as I joined her. Her hug felt true and welcoming.

"How are things with you?" I asked, withdrawing from her embrace. We started a slow walk toward the house of the Sisters.

"Well," she said with an excited grin. "Henick came to take me for a ride yesterday." Her eyes sparkled with excitement. It was the most animated I'd ever seen her.

"Ila, I'm so happy for you. He knows everything, then?"

She nodded. "Just as you said, he didn't care. Have you started to make plans for your wedding? Is your sister making your dress now that you'll be Lady Ruhall?"

I snorted in a very unlady like way.

"No, Blye will not make my dress, though I'm sure she'd like to. I'll wear the one you made me. Alec contacted the Head, and we'll marry in a week. I would like you to attend, Ila. It will be a very quiet ceremony," I said quickly, "so please don't mention it."

"I won't say a word. And I would be delighted to attend."

When we reached her house, she turned around and started the walk back to the wagon with me. Swiftly had everything loaded when she and I parted with a final hug.

"I will see you soon," she said with a wave. Her words made me smile.

THE TIME until the wedding whittled away. Alec entertained me with walks, games, and fishing during the day. At night, I continued reading the book. The author's descriptions, and Alec's attentions when I woke, convinced me there could be more to the experience than I'd been exposed to. Though it reduced my hesitancy and my fears, nervous anticipation remained.

The day before my wedding dawned bright. I found myself on my back, my shirt spread open, and Alec's fingers tracing an idle path between my sternum and bellybutton.

"Good morning," he said with a secret smile that made my toes curl.

"Good morning."

Though he hadn't touched them, my breasts already ached because I knew what was to come. He didn't disappoint. He leaned over and set his mouth on me. I closed my eyes with a contented sigh. His fingers continued to trail my stomach, then down my legs.

I knew what he was about and didn't mind. I trusted him and relaxed my legs.

Instead of trailing closer to where I ached, he pulled away from me altogether and stared down at me.

His face was flushed and full of want.

"One more day," he said, his voice husky, "then you're mine. Forever."

I nodded. "One more day." Saying it made my nerves jump but I didn't let it show.

"What would you like to do today?"

"If Kara doesn't mind, let's do something in the kitchen. We can do better than coddled eggs and egg tartlets."

He grinned and nodded.

"Dress," he said. "I'll meet you there."

I quickly obeyed and hurried to the kitchen, excited to spend another day with him. To my surprise, Bryn was at the block, kneading dough. When Alec had confronted her at the bakery, I hadn't given any thought to her returning to work in his kitchen.

She looked up at me, hurt painting her face.

"Were you going to tell me?" she asked.

I knew she meant the wedding.

"You've made it quite clear you want nothing to do with me as your sister, and I want nothing to do with you as Lady Ruhall."

Her gaze turned sad, and she nodded.

"I have. And I'm sorry for it. I hope one day that changes."

I inclined my head, neither agreeing nor disagreeing and left the kitchen. As much as I didn't want her there, I didn't have it in me to turn her away for Edmund's sake and her babe.

Alec met me in the hallway.

"Do you no longer wish to cook?"

"No. I was thinking we might talk to Father about fermenting apples."

Thus, we spent the day before our wedding pressing apples.

EGRIT WOKE me with a chipper good morning and a laugh when I sat up in a panic.

"Don't worry. I warned him I would wake you this morning."

I blushed crimson as she took my gown from the wardrobe and laid it out on the bed.

"Would you like a bath?"

I shook my head no. Sticky with the juice from far too many apples, I'd had no choice but to bathe the night before. My hair was oiled and dry.

"To relax?"

"Not now, but I might need one after dinner."

"Then, if you're ready, there is someone here to see you. She thought you might like company and offered to do your hair."

A smile lit my face.

"Ila?"

Egrit nodded.

I spent a pleasant morning closed in my room with Ila. She took her time braiding and weaving my hair and helped me into my dress.

"Do you have any questions about tonight?" she asked. "Are you nervous? Frightened? It would be understandable if you were."

"I am nervous but not afraid."

"Good," she said, stepping back to eye her work. "You are a beauty."

I laughed lightly.

"Thanks to your efforts. Thank you for staying with me, Ila."

She hugged me tightly. "I'm glad I'm here." When she pulled back, she wrapped my hand around her arm and led me from the room. My heart fluttered at the reality of what would soon take place. I would marry Alec.

Neither of us spoke as we walked down the hall toward the library. My nerves prevented it, and she seemed to understand.

All my trepidation evaporated when we turned the corner, and I spotted Alec pacing outside the library doors. He froze when he saw me. Beside me, Ila excused herself and went in.

Alec and I stared at each other for a moment before he exhaled slowly and strode toward me. He was dressed in dark pants and a matching jacket. A red bloom was tucked into the lapel, matching the threads in my gown.

When he reached me, his blue gaze swept over me.

"You are beautiful," he breathed. He reached for me, gently running his knuckles along my cheek.

"Will you stay? Will you be my wife?"

I turned my head to kiss his hand.

"I will stay. I will be your wife."

He pulled me close and set his lips on mine. The passion behind his kiss robbed me of thought.

A throat cleared and reluctantly Alec pulled back. I blinked at him and then glanced toward the doors. My father stood there, his amused smile causing me to grin in return.

"I wanted to hug you one last time as my daughter before you become Lady Ruhall," he said, approaching me.

Eagerly, I hugged him.

"I love you, Father."

"And I you." He held me tightly for a moment more before surrendering me to Alec.

Alec offered his arm as Father went inside. Holding him tightly, I let Alec walk me in.

The Head waited for us along with a small audience. I barely saw them or heard what the Head said. Time moved too quickly and soon Alec was speaking his vows to love and honor me in this life and the next. Nerves danced in my stomach as I realized my turn had come. Taking a calming breath, I spoke my vows to do the same.

Cheers erupted around us, and Alec pulled me in for another kiss. Another throat clearing and good-natured laughter forced us apart so he could lead me to the dining room.

Someone had set the length of the table. Alec took the seat at the head with me at his right and Father at his left. Everyone joined us and that was when I noticed my sisters. Bryn quietly sat beside Father. She didn't look at me. Instead, she struck up a quiet conversation with Father.

Blye almost sat beside me, but Egrit stopped her.

"One seat over, Miss Hovtel."

Ila took the seat beside me, and I sighed in relief.

Mr. Crow, Kara, and Egrit brought the food out. As I'd asked, they had kept it simple. We served ourselves and passed the portions to the next person. Conversation flowed around the table, and it was a relaxing meal...until Ila excused herself for a moment.

Blye took that as an opportunity to speak to me.

"Now that you're Lady Ruhall, you'll need new dresses. I could stay here and work on them."

The horror of the idea certainly had to have shown on my face because the conversation around the table quieted. I looked away and caught Otta glaring at Blye. I wanted to smile at her.

"No," Alec said. "You will not make her dresses, and you aren't welcome to stay here any longer than it takes for you to visit with your father."

Blye's face flushed scarlet, but she said nothing further. Ila returned and eyed the quiet table as she resumed her seat.

She leaned toward me and softly asked if everything was all right.

"Yes," I said, taking a bite of roast.

"It's been brought to my attention," Alec said to Ila, "that Benella is in need of a few more dresses in her role as a Lady. The dress she wears now is beautiful, and I would like to see her have a few more of that quality."

I frowned at Alec, not for his snub of my sister, but for asking for additional extravagant dresses.

"This might be a bit more formal than I will need for every day," I said diplomatically.

Ila laughed and patted my hand.

"Have no worry. I know what kind of dress you like."

She did. I smiled at her and turned to Alec.

"I still prefer my pants," I whispered.

He choked a bit on his food and shook his head at me. As we finished, Bryn and Kara collected the empty plates and asked us to remain seated as they excused themselves. When they returned, they carried a large cake.

"Edmund and I made it for you. A gift to celebrate how sweet life can be. If you let it," she said quietly.

My eyes watered. I wasn't ready to trust her to be my sister, but her gift, her words, and her new consideration of Father gave me hope.

A TUB of water waited in my room when I finally excused myself from the table. I sent a silent word of thanks to Egrit and stripped off my gown.

The manor was settling in for a quiet evening, and I knew what that meant for me. Nerves coiled in my stomach. By giving me the book, Alec had hoped to ease my fear of the unknown. Though I appreciated his thoughtfulness, the author's side notes about easing the pain of the first time hadn't reassured me. I would have preferred to remain ignorant of that part.

With a shaking hand, I hung the dress in the wardrobe then padded to the water. Steam curled from the surface. I'd no sooner slipped into the water when the connecting doors opened. I jumped slightly and turned to watch Alec enter. His gaze locked onto mine as he slowly closed the door behind him.

"Will you douse me with water if I watch you?" Though the words were playfully said, his expression remained serious.

"No, husband, I won't." I attempted a smile while trying to calm my stomach.

He didn't linger by the door but came to the tub and knelt beside it, watching me as he rolled his sleeves from his corded forearms.

"Are you afraid?" he asked.

"Are you?"

"Very. I'm afraid you'll run or worse, stay and hate me afterward."

Hearing his fears helped ease a few of mine.

"I won't hate you, Alec."

He looked down and dipped a finger in the water. My pulse leapt because I knew he could see me clearly. Yet, he didn't reach for me. Instead, he exhaled slowly.

"You didn't answer. Are you afraid?"

"No, not afraid. Very nervous." I lifted my hand from the water and held it out so he could see my tremble.

He glanced at my hand, and his expression took on a pained appearance. I reached for his hand and held it.

"Nerves have never stopped me before," I said softly.

He met my gaze, and his lips curved in the barest of smiles.

"And for that, I am grateful."

He stood, keeping hold of my hand. When he gave a gentle tug,

I knew he wanted me to rise. My heart beat harder as I rose. His gaze drifted down my torso then back up again.

"Wife. A lifetime will not be long enough."

The warm bath water lapped at my calves as his fingers remained locked around mine. He swallowed hard several times and released my hand. His heated gaze lifted to meet mine as he reached out to trace a finger along the underside of my breast. It took a large amount of effort to keep my breathing steady.

"Will you promise to tell me if you become frightened?"

His thumb brushed over my nipple, and I shivered.

"Yes. I promise."

He dipped his head and kissed my shoulder.

"Do you promise not to run?"

His lips skimmed my skin from collarbone to the top of my breast. I brought my hands up and dug my fingers in his hair. A small noise escaped me as his breath washed over my nipple.

"Benella. Do you swear?"

"I swear."

His mouth closed over me. The strong pull sent a tingle to my stomach and further still to the point between my legs. Too quickly, the insistent tug stopped. His lips moved from my nipple, nuzzling me and spreading kisses from one breast to the next before he lifted his head. My hands fell loosely to my sides. His eyes glinted with fervor as he studied me closely, a hungry beast once more.

He wrapped his hand around mine and helped me step from the tub.

"Sit on the bed, Benella."

My pulse thundered, and my knees felt weak as I turned to do as he asked.

Sitting, I looked up at him as he unbuttoned his shirt. The bare expanse of his chest claimed my attention as he shrugged the garment off. I exhaled slowly. He knelt before me, and I clenched my hands in my lap to hide the shaking. He reached for them and smoothed a thumb over my knuckles. Our gazes remained locked as he leaned forward and placed a kiss on my knee.

My breath hitched as I recalled the last time he'd kissed me there. He lifted his head again.

"Will you give me everything?"

"Yes."

His hold on my hands shifted to my legs. His fingers traced my skin from knee to ankle as he kissed higher up my leg.

"Lay back."

With a blush, I lay back on the bed and opened myself to him. He made a low sound and fitted his torso between my legs.

The first touch of his tongue made me gasp. My fingers fisted in the covers, and I arched, trying to press myself against him. He set a hand on my stomach to hold me in place as his tongue circled my sensitive nub. A small noise escaped me.

"My beauty," he said as he teased me. "My heart."

His free hand stroked the inside of my leg, knee to thigh, then teased the hair between my legs. His tongue distracted me from his intention until his finger probed my opening. I tensed, expecting a painful thrust, but none came. He continued to tease me with his tongue while he idly explored with his fingers.

After a few moments, I relaxed and lost myself to the sensations of his mouth on me. A familiar need began to build, and I groaned with want. He closed his mouth over my nub and began to suckle. I gasped and twisted my fingers in his hair. He sucked hard and flicked his tongue at the same time he slowly slid a finger into me. The invasion didn't take away from the tension coiling tighter and tighter inside me. He eased his finger out then back in, and my legs began to tense. My release was close.

His mouth and hand left me. Dazedly, I opened my eyes. He

stood between my legs as he stripped away his pants. Before I had time to worry, he leaned over me and bent his head to my breast. His hot mouth tugged on my nipple as he ran a hand between my legs.

Something pressed insistently against my opening. He switched to torment my other breast, distracting me from thought, then kissed a trail up to my collarbone. He claimed my lips for a searing kiss before pulling away to look down on me. With both hands braced on the bed, one on each side of me, his heated gaze met mine.

It took a moment to realize the pressure had remained between my legs.

"I love you," he said as he slowly pressed forward.

A sudden sharp pain had me bracing my hands against his bare chest. He stopped moving and began raining kisses upon my brow.

"Wait," he said. "Please, wait. It is a moment of pain for a lifetime of pleasure. I swear."

I heard the fear in his voice and held myself still. After a moment, the pain faded.

Tilting my head back, I found his face so close to mine. His jaw was tense and sweat dotted his skin.

"It's better now," I said.

He kissed me hard.

"No, but it soon will be."

He reached between us and set his thumb on my sensitive spot. He circled it twice then started to move his hips. I drifted in the pleasure of his touch, reveling in the coiling tension, while I gasped and reached for the release I knew would come.

With a cry, I found it. He thrust into me several more times before he groaned and stilled. His sweaty chest pressed against me. Between us, he twitched within me.

"Tell me you don't hate me."

"I don't hate you. I love you."

He kissed me soundly.

A NOISE WOKE me in the middle of the night. When I opened my eyes, I found Rose beside the bed and sat up with a gasp. Panic flooded me while Alec remained undisturbed in his slumber.

"What are you doing here?" I asked.

"I'm here to thank you, Benella," she said, surprising and confusing me. "And to say good-bye. What I set out to do has been done. Alec has found purpose and love. I only hope that someday you'll forgive me for the lies and manipulations I used to bring you two together."

"You're leaving?" I didn't trust that I'd understood her correctly.

She smiled at me.

"Yes. As I promised. I was only waiting for you to see the truth. A truth I saw within you so long ago when your family first came to this area. The possibility of love—for him."

"What do you mean when we first came here? I didn't meet you until we moved to the Water."

She studied me for a moment before answering.

"I've watched over the North for a long time. I knew of you as soon as you entered its boundaries. I've watched you since you were young, observed how you overcame each trial life gave you. You are intelligent, determined, courageous, and kind. And I knew once I sent you to the beast, you would find a way to free him. Yet, I worried for you. Your strength was also your weakness. You were too kind. Too willing to sacrifice yourself for those you cared for. I helped you as much as I could while still keeping both of you unaware. Alec had so much to learn; you had so much to teach him.

"Hold fast to your love for one another, and this life will not disappoint you. You will balance each other well."

She turned to go.

"Wait," I said, believing she really meant it. Though I still resented the way I'd been used, I also realized, without her manipulations, I wouldn't have met Alec.

She stopped and looked back at me.

I slipped from the bed, unconcerned with my nakedness and crossed the room.

"I already forgive you. Thank you for sending me here, for bringing me him."

Rose surprised me by sniffling.

"I wanted to spare you but not as much as I wanted you to truly find happiness." She hugged me tightly.

"You don't need to leave."

"I do," she whispered in my ear, "but I will return for the birth of your babes."

She pulled away and left the room. I returned to bed, and Alec pulled me close.

"She's gone?" he asked, his hand settling over my stomach.

"For now," I said.

A BREEZE PLAYED WITH MY HAIR AS I SAT ON THE BENCH IN THE orchard. Tam glanced at me and gave a nervous smile. I smiled back, trying to reassure him. From somewhere behind us, a sweet soprano rang out in a song about union and love.

Alec offered his arm and helped me stand. I absently rubbed a hand over the bump of the babe's foot, currently lodged just below my ribs, while turning to face the back with the rest of those assembled. Egrit walked the path between the apple trees. She wore a green dress Ila had made for her. Delicately embroidered leaves adorned the skirt, and a wreath of real leaves adorned Egrit's hair. I glanced at Tam wondering if he saw the wood nymph I remembered. Based on the love in his gaze, I decided he saw the nymph and the woman as well.

Egrit gave me a radiant smile as she passed us on her way to Tam. As soon as the two clasped hands, the short ceremony began. After the Head announced the union between them, I heard Tam breathe "finally" right before pulling Egrit into his arms for a passionate kiss.

Alec wrapped his arm around me and pulled me tight to his side.

"I know just how he feels," he whispered in my ear. "I remember well the moment I realized you were finally mine."

I smiled and turned toward him. He was ready with a kiss.

"None of that now," Father said from beside me. "This is about Egrit and Tam."

I laughed and pulled back to see Tam reluctantly doing the same. The pair waved to the well-wishers and invited everyone to join them inside for dancing and a feast. Most of Konrall was there, and hosting the wedding was our gift to the bride and groom.

The children on the bench behind us cheered. I turned to grin at Retta, Lettie, Mrs. Palant and her little ones, and the new children who'd joined us over the passing months. Like before, Mrs. Palant kept the young ones busy with light chores in the evening, but mostly they were with us for their education and care. My smile grew bigger as I thought how Father had even started teaching with Mr. Roost, dividing the class to make it more manageable.

As soon as Tam and Egrit passed us, we stood and followed the newly wedded couple. As we passed by the Kinlyn clan, who were all seated on a bench near the back, I grinned at Ila who sat next to her husband, Henick. He'd found his rainbow in her.

The walk inside took longer than it should have because of my waddle. My back started to ache, but I kept any sign of discomfort from my face. Regardless, Alec glanced at me continually. He knew.

"Don't even consider it," I warned him.

"If I carried you—"

"You'd draw attention to us. This is about Egrit and Tam."

He made a slight growling noise, which made me grin.

"Beast," I whispered.

"Beauty," he said, bending to kiss my cheek.

I snorted.

"Only you would think an apple with legs beautiful."

He threw his head back and laughed. Then, despite my warning, he scooped me up in his arms.

"You are hardly an apple, madam." He stepped aside so the guests could pass us.

There were no censuring looks, only knowing grins. When Bryn spotted me, she moved to the side to stand with us.

"Is everything well?" she asked.

Since our wedding, Bryn had changed considerably. She'd started visiting Father regularly and stopped worrying about her social standing. Instead, she'd focused on her marriage. It was easy to see she and Edmund were truly happy now as Edmund carried little Benard, who babbled and watched the leaves above us.

"Everything is well. The walk taxes my back," I said, assuring her.

Once her selfish nature had disappeared, I'd welcomed her visits as well. Alec hadn't been as quick to forgive. It was only her genuine concern for the babe and me that had brought him around.

"And she was too slow," Alec said with a teasing smile.

"She'll slow down more," Edmund said. "Like a loaf of bread. When the rising slows, it's done."

Bryn made a sound between a laugh and a groan.

"You would compare pregnancy to a loaf of bread?" She shook her head and laughed when he grinned at her.

The last of the guests filed past us, and Edmund moved to follow.

"I'll take little Benard in and see if we can't give Kara a hand in the kitchen."

While Bryn gave her son and husband a quick kiss, I nudged Alec.

"Put me down."

"Not until we're inside. You wouldn't want to tire yourself before we even have a chance to dance, would you?"

I shook my head and looped my arm around his shoulders as he started to walk behind Edmund. Bryn kept us company.

"I received a letter from Blye yesterday," she said.

"Oh? Has she found a suitable shop, yet?"

"Yes, she'd found one since her last letter, but I don't think she'll be there long. Her mistress doesn't care for the extravagance of Blye's creations," she said with a smile. Recalling Blye's gown for the feast, I had no doubt Blye's mistress had valid concerns.

"She mentioned she wrote Father, too," Bryn said.

I nodded, having read the letter as well.

"Nothing as detailed as you received. Just that she was doing well and sends her love to all of us. How far south is she now?"

"Almost to Towdown."

"I'm sure that's been her destination all along," Alec said.

We broke through the trees to the breathtaking view of the manor. The vines and vegetation were gone, replaced by a fine lawn under Tam's care. People milled about the front entrance, congratulating Egrit and Tam.

"I agree," I said to Alec's observation. Blye wouldn't be happy until she was making gowns for the rich and elite of Towdown, the center of trade. No, she wouldn't even be happy then. She'd want to become one of them.

For a moment, I felt pity for Blye. Her search for material wealth and social standing wouldn't bring her happiness. Happiness wasn't so easily obtained. It took kindness and some true sacrifice, neither concept truly understood by my sister.

I sighed and ran my fingers through the hair at the nape of

Alec's neck. He glanced at me, a look so full of longing and love that my pulse fluttered. His expression turned knowing as I flushed and gave him a small, secret smile.

"Bryn, I think Benella is feeling a bit worn. I'll take her to her room to rest for a few minutes before we join the feast."

Bryn laughed and waved us ahead as Alec's stride lengthened.

"I'll make excuses for both of you. Don't take too long."

"No, not too long," he said, pressing a kiss to my cheek. "Just a lifetime."

This series is the result of my huge love for Beauty and the Beast. The original version, the Disney adaptation, the TV series from the 1980s...I loved them all. Yet, I had one teeny, tiny problem some of the retellings. The reason behind the beast's curse never matched the severity of his "punishment." I mean, being a shallow snob? We've all had moments where we tried on those traits. I wanted his curse to be for a more significant reason. To be a necessity.

I didn't want to modernize my version of the retelling but keep the feel of the original. Just bigger. Boy, did I go bigger! I also made the beast truly beastly.

To give you an idea of just how depraved he was in his thinking and selfishness, I've included a few scenes from his point of view. Be sure to keep reading!

As for the main tale, I hope you enjoyed reading it as much as I enjoyed reimagining their story! While Alec and Benella have found their happily-ever-after, their's isn't the only story to take place in this world. Be sure to check out the Tales of Cinder for a glimpse of what happens to Blye! Or, better yet, find out why the Hovtel family moved to the north in the first place in Disowned, a prequel to the Tales of Cinder that ties into the Beastly Tales.

Happy reading!

Melissa

SCENE EXTRAS

First Trespass

The splintering of wood did little to ease my temper. That the bed immediately started to repair itself only enraged me further.

Another night wasted. Instead of the reward I'd sought, I'd received mockery for my efforts.

I hefted the wardrobe and threw it onto the splintered remains of the bed. Letting loose a roar, I searched for something else to destroy. Before I could find a target, the crow flew in through the open window. I growled at the intrusion but listened to its report with a cocked ear.

Intruders at the gate. Two boys and a girl.

Damn village children and their curiosity. Come to stare at the beast. My skin tingled as my hackles rose. Storming from the room, I left my cursed prison and took off toward the front of the estate, pulling on the magic to darken the area near the gate. With a thought, I opened paths before me and raced through the trees. The many years of my enchantment had taught me much. Stealth had been the second lesson.

"This is what you get, Benella," a voice said in the distance.

I slowed and hid myself in mist and darkness, creeping forward until I saw the gate.

The crow was a blind idiot. Two boys were racing away from the gate, free from my estate. The third, a lad in breeches and a threadbare shirt, remained locked inside. He clutched the bars tightly. My gaze fell onto the long, dark braid that lay just over the strap of the lad's shoulder bag.

Not a lad. A girl. Females used to represent a bright

entertainment. No longer. All they did was weep and beg. Except for the hag, who cackled with twisted humor.

The girl looked up at the top of the gates, giving me a glimpse of a soft profile. Her pale skin contrasted with her dark hair, and her small, pert nose only drew more attention to her generous lips. I hardened at the sight, and my fury increased as she continued to study the gate. Females were good for one thing. Fucking. Having been robbed of that option, I had no use for her.

I resented her beauty and her freedom.

My lips curled back as I stood on my back legs and left my hiding place. The birds quieted as I came to stand behind the girl. She stiffened, noting the change around us. She knew. I waited for her hysterics. None came.

She dropped her head so it touched the gate. I leaned in and inhaled deeply, smelling soap and a light sweat. How long had it been since I'd smelled something so sweet? My exhale moved her hair.

In the distance, her companions still laughed. She, however, only loosened her grip on the bars and let her hands drop to her sides, remaining unexpectedly calm for one caught trespassing.

Odd creature.

Gripping her firmly, I tossed her over my protective wall while commanding the vines on the other side to catch her.

I hoped, for her sake, she never returned.

Second Trespass

The crow warned me she was back. Yet, when I prowled the border, it wasn't just her that I heard. Had she thought since I spared her once that she might bring a companion to take from me that which was mine? The girl would feel my anger this time.

Outside the wall, the pair made a goodly amount of noise as

they raced through the trees toward the gate. I kept pace with them, willing the gate to open, a dare for them to enter. Pulling the mist around me, I waited and watched the gate. The girl dashed through, and I slammed the gate closed.

She spun to face her partner. He didn't speak, only stared at her with a growing smile. Did he think her safe? Did he think I would fall for her pretty face?

I stepped from the bramble and approached her. The boy's eyes widened when he saw my mist. He backed away and then ran. The girl didn't move other than to let her head fall forward.

"I'm sorry," she said softly.

I studied the back of her torn shirt and the blood seeping from a ragged scrape. The scent of it teased me. I stepped closer, inhaling. How long had I been a beast? Longer than I'd been a man. Yet, the scent of her blood wasn't making my stomach rumble as it did with a fresh kill. No, the scent of her blood brought a small measure of seldom-felt pity.

Without thinking of the consequences, I licked her wound. She hissed in pain and made to move away. A growl from me stopped her. Continuing, I licked the wound several times, letting my enchanted saliva heal her.

As soon as new skin covered the wound, I used the magic of the estate to create a soft pile of hay just over the wall. Then I tossed her.

Turning away from the gates, I wandered the estate. The taste of her clung to my tongue, and I could think of little else but her soft skin. My cock remained uncomfortably hard, and I took a moment to stand on my back legs to rub it. I imagined her hand on me and growled in frustration. Her hand would never willingly touch me. Only one hand touched me now. The thought of Rose's wrinkled hands withered my shaft.

With a grunt, I fell to all fours and began walking once again. Perhaps, if I were lucky, the girl would be back.

Third Trespass

Need gnawed at my gut and hardened my cock as I stalked through the moonlit trees. A faint wisp of the nymph's scent led me east, away from the manor. I paused to scratch my back against the bark of an old tree, pretending I had no care or purpose, before continuing in the general direction of the female's scent.

My patience was rewarded when I spotted the pair of nymphs through the foliage. The female was not the flesh and blood beauty I'd encountered the day before but a wooden replica with twin, trim trunks for legs, lithe branches for arms, and burls for breasts. Had those mounds on her chest been soft flesh, they would have been swaying ripely in her current position.

Knowing better than to pay too much attention to the pair, I pretended to lean down and sniff a spring flower while I studied them from the corner of my eye. The male had her bent at the waist and pounded into her from behind. His grunts and her light gasps filled my ears, and my shaft, already hard, dripped with my need to take his place.

All I needed to do was quietly pace closer before the damned enchantress noticed me. Her fog had already ruined far too many attempts to relieve my lust on something other than her dry, gaping old cave.

I took a step closer.

"CAW!"

The pair froze, their heads turning toward the sound and gazes searching the bramble where I hid. Seething at the crow's ill-timed arrival, I charged forward. But it was too late. A thick mist rushed in, swallowing me and my rage-filled roar.

"I will rip your wings from your twitching carcass, you wretched—"

"The girl is at the gate," the crow clacked at me.

Swinging my head in its direction, I snarled. The sound changed to a low rumble as I realized the interruption wasn't a hardship but fate's fortune finally shining down on me. The girl was the reason I'd been stalking the woods in the first place.

My thin lips pulled back in a parody of a smile. Rose might be able to keep me from the nymphs, but it was my right as the liege lord to deal with all who trespass on my lands.

The crow took flight, and I followed, racing silently through my domain, increasing my speed as I left the mist. The faint groan and creak of metal against wood slowed my steps. Wary of the familiar sound, I approached the gate and watched from the cover of shadows and brush. The old wagon rolling into my domain belonged to the nearby village and was only used when the villagers wanted to offer up one of their own to appease *The Beast of the North*. My lips pulled back in a silent snarl, and I eased my way forward, silent and slow. Every offer had been a trap in one form or another.

"I hope the beast catches you!"

Hearing the familiar, female voice enraged me. It had been years since the villagers attempted to sacrifice one of their own to me. Why now? Why her?

I slipped through the last bit of underbrush and saw the girl writhing against the vines that bound to the pole that was affixed to the wagon. Behind her, two boys laughed as they jogged outside the wall then dared lay their hands on my gate to close it. The scent of her blood filled my nose, killing my lust and kindling my rage.

"We're not afraid of that thing," the bigger of the two boys said, adding to my fury.

"Bold words for little men standing outside the gate," the girl taunted. "Come inside and see if you fare so well. Do your own dirty work instead of waiting for someone else to do it for you!"

"Someone? You mean something. This is the third time for you, isn't it, Benella? You won't bother us again."

Hearing them speak, seeing her struggle and the resulting blood on her wrists...I seethed. Did they—men barely old enough to shave—think to use me as their executioner? I was no man's lackey.

Laughter rang out from the pair as if mocking that thought. My fur bristled, standing on end at the depth of my hate for these creatures who walked around on their two legs like they owned the world.

Eyes reflecting my wrath, I prowled forward. The sight of me killed their merriment and robbed their faces of color. The fear in their eyes wasn't enough though. Their trespass demanded retaliation.

A low growl escaped me as I stood on my back legs and placed my bestial hands on the cart. With a heave, I sent the cart crashing into the gate and had the satisfaction of seeing the pair scurry away, a piss stain on the younger one's trousers.

The girl barked out a harsh laugh, reclaiming my attention.

"Two little girls, that's what they are. They should be wearing a dress," she mumbled.

Strung up as she was, I could clearly see the swell of her breasts and the lean, trimness of her waist. Her scent filled my nose as I inhaled deeply. What trap did the villagers lay for me this time? Or was her mere presence to torment me as well?

"Why have you returned?" I demanded.

She closed her eyes with a sigh.

"That should be apparent, I'd think. To die."

I considered the girl. The long, dark strands of her tangled hair hung over her face, hiding me from her view, based on the way her eyes shifted behind the curtain. Despite her disheveled and bloody appearance, her beauty wasn't lost on me.

"Why do you wish for death so badly?" I asked, less angry.

"Does it look to you like I came here by choice?" She laughed humorlessly. "It's not my wish, but theirs, that I die." She canted her head in my direction. "Recent events having left me in a poor mood, I'd rather not waste any more time on idle conversation. I hurt everywhere and think I may vomit soon, so please, just be done with it."

The way she spoke to me, irreverent and unafraid, eroded my tolerance. Yet, for a willing fuck who wasn't the enchantress, I could tolerate a bit of impudence. The vines holding the girl's wrists gave way under one of my claws, and the girl tumbled forward against my chest.

My cock surged at the contact, and I breathed in her fresh, sweet scent. An image filled my head. The girl stripped bare before me, bent at the waist, ready to receive my cock. Craving her sweet surrender, I heaved her over my shoulder, intent to find a place away from the gate where we could—

She made an odd burping noise a moment before a wash of vomit ran down my back. I shuddered at the feeling and, with a snarl, tossed her to the ground.

"You will pay for that," I growled.

She didn't apologize or scramble away in fear. She lay before me, sprawled out.

The exposed portion of her slim ankle and shapely calf distracted me from my anger. Focused on the display and wanting to see more, I curled my hand around her leg and tugged her closer. Her complete lack of resistance as her skirt rose higher penetrated the lust fogging my mind, and I looked at her sleep relaxed face.

An angry growl rumbled from my chest as I understood the situation. I had a hard cock, aching for release, and a woman—young and firm and real—lay within my reach. But she'd passed out.

It wouldn't be a proper fuck while she was unconscious. Could it? I shook my head. I've never had to force my seed on an unwilling woman. They came to me. Begged me for it. This one would too. Once she woke.

Reaching out, I tapped her cheek with my furred digits. Her head lolled to the side, and she groaned but didn't wake.

Growling and cursing, I paced around her and debated what to do. She bled from her wrists; however, I doubted that was the reason for her current, unresponsive state. I had no knowledge of healing, but I knew someone who did. An agitated snort escaped me the moment I thought of Rose. Her price would be high even if she would be willing.

The thought of having to fuck the old crone again sent another shudder through me, and my gaze shifted to the creamy expanse of the maid's inner thigh. If only it had been someone as young and beautiful as the maid to curse me. I would have easily pleasured her in a night's time and won my freedom years ago.

Sitting back on my haunches, I stroked myself. How long had it been since a hand other than my own touched my cock? Longer than I could remember. Long enough that I couldn't endure the thought of more nights spent with the crone.

I wanted this girl.

Angrily, I grabbed the girl and tossed her over my shoulder before running toward the old cottage the enchantress occupied when the mood struck.

The telltale curl of smoke from the chimney should have given me hope, but I'd lived in this state for too long to let such a foolish notion take root. With the meaty side of my fist, I pounded on the crone's door.

It swung open almost immediately. The old woman, stooped and weathered like a shriveled potato, scowled at me from within the dim interior.

"I'm not in the mood tonight."

"For which I am grateful. I'm not here for a taste of the dry cavern you call a cunt. The villagers tied this girl to the wagon, and she passed out after I untied her."

Rose howled with laughter.

"One look at you would do that to any sane woman."

Hate filled me at the truth of her statement. Yet, she stepped aside and motioned to the bed. I spoke, angry, bitten words, as I deposited the maid.

"She didn't see me. Her hair was in her face. She said she hurt everywhere before she vomited on me."

"Oh? I can't tell. You smell the same to me."

My thin lips pulled back into a brief snarl before I composed myself. Rose watched me knowingly, waiting for me to lose control so she could find some new way to punish me.

"Will you fix her? Please."

"You've never brought anyone to me before. People enter, and you toss them out. It's been the same for decades. Why do you care about this one?"

Her gaze pinned me, one corner of her mouth lifting in a cruel smirk. She knew why. This was her game. She toyed with my needs. Laughed at me. Taunted me like the villager's had.

My hackles slowly rose.

"Fix her," I growled.

"Why should I?"

I growled, and a second later, the young woman roused enough to gag.

"Leave us," Rose commanded.

Unable to stop myself, I silently snarled at the source of all my misery, Rose. She smiled maliciously before an invisible force yanked me from the cottage and the door slammed in my face.

I roared and slashed my claws against the surface. However, like the wood in the manor, it repaired itself before I could do any damage. Vines curled around my back legs and pulled me several yards away. My rage boiled, yet I forced myself to calm and reminded myself that this was her game. The worse I behaved, the worse she behaved.

Minutes later, the door opened again. The maid, barely standing on her own feet, vomited on the crone's floor as she exited the cottage. Rose laughed from within, and the door closed behind the girl.

It took everything in me to hold still and wait for the vines to release me on their own.

The girl stumbled forward several staggering steps and heaved again. While she did, the vines loosened slowly. I cared not about the girl's sickness, only that she was awake. I growled, desperate to reclaim my prize before Rose changed her mind. The vines slithered away, and I stormed forward.

"Vomit on me again, and you will suffer," I promised before swinging her over my shoulder.

I ran from the cottage, heading to a clearing I knew, but the girl began to slacken against me. Unwilling to lose her to unconsciousness again, I stopped and set her down.

She swayed on her feet in the moonlight and her eyes listlessly searched the shadows as if she couldn't focus. Had Rose done nothing for her?

"What did she say?" I demanded.

The girl collapsed heavily onto the ground. Her face paled further as she set her hands on the ground.

"Don't sleep or eat until my stomach stops twisting," she mumbled. "Drink lightly, and get out." She struggled to her knees and heaved again. "Running upside down made it worse."

I bristled at the accusation in her voice and circled her.

"You blame this on me?"

"Well, it was your fault that I hit the back of my head against the pole. Before that, only my wrists bled."

I roared in frustration. She was on her hands and knees, but sick and complaining, not begging for my cock in her—

She lay down on the lush grass, and the moonlight flickered through the leaves, washing her face of color as she closed her eyes.

"What are you doing?"

"Going to sleep."

"The witch said not to."

"And you just roared at me. So what? If I die, I die. I'm tired of being bullied by you and the idiots in the village. If I live, so be it. At least, I'll have had a few moments of peace."

Her words extinguished my anger. How often had I had similar thoughts? Something I hadn't felt in a very long time twinged in my chest.

I stopped pacing and approached her. The moonlight danced over the back of her head, showcasing a bloody patch there and the swollen lump that rose from her scalp. Huffing out a breath to part her hair, I exposed the wound and bathed it with my tongue.

The girl sighed, a sound that went straight to my cock.

"Thank you," she whispered.

I grunted and kept licking the wound. Her scent wrapped around me as I worked, and the size of the lump slowly shrank. She made another small sound and let out a gusty breath, sleeping peacefully in my presence.

Sitting back, I studied her. I didn't know what she'd done to warrant her delivery to the gates, but I was glad for it. She was young, beautiful, and, despite her disrespect earlier, not a shrew. Rose had never once thanked me for anything.

My gaze swept over the girl's lithe form, and I reconsidered what I wanted from her. I still wanted to fuck her, but now, I also considered keeping her afterward. I wanted to hear that sigh escape her lips every time I touched her. Need hit me with an intensity that hardened my shaft to the point that not even thoughts of rutting Rose could wither it. I froze and stared, watching the slight rise and fall of her chest.

The answer to my freedom lay before me. But Rose was right. The girl would run screaming at the first sight of me. While I could trap her here, I refused to force myself on her. I wanted her willing. How, though?

I needed to know more about this girl. Why was she here, and what could entice her to remain within the estate?

"Crow, I have a task for you."

Did you know that I write under another name? I do! Check out these books by Melissa Haag (also me).

Hope(less)
(perfect for readers who love shifters and swoon worthy heroes)

Being a human, Gabby didn't count on meeting a silent, ruggedly-handsome werewolf with a single-minded determination to make her his mate. When she tries to run, he's not the only one to follow. Something truly dangerous is after her, and Gabby must turn to Clay for help if she ever hopes to discover who is hunting her for the secrets she's spent her whole life protecting.

Fury Frayed
(perfect for readers who love mythology, a multitude of shifters, and heroine badassery)

Abandoned in a town of mythological creatures, Megan must discover why she's part of a world she never knew existed and who is killing humans before she becomes the next victim. Her only consolation is the shy guy hot enough to melt the pants off a popsicle. Bring it.